Sacrifice

A Tale from Angel Mountain

Brian John

Greencroft Books

2009

First Impression 2009
Reprinted 2010

Published by
Greencroft Books
Trefelin, Cilgwyn, Newport,
Pembrokeshire SA42 0QN
Tel 01239-820470. Fax 01239-821245
Email: greencroft4@mac.com

All characters in this story other than those clearly in the public domain are fictitious and any resemblance to real persons, living or dead, is purely coincidental

ISBN 978-0-905559-90-2

Typeset and designed by the author in Palatino 10 pt on Apple iMac computer with Pages

Printed and bound by Antony Rowe Ltd, Chippenham, SN14 6LH

CONTENTS

Map of the Plas Ingli area 4
Key Characters in the Story 7
Glossary of Welsh Terms 10

The Brilliance of Edward Billings 11
Editor's Note 40

Martha Morgan's Story

1. Brief Encounter 41
2. Matters of no Consequence 60
3. The Beginning of Things 71
4. Innocence and Guilt 88
5. Web of Intrigue 101
6. Light in Dark Places 129
7. Spring Gleaning 164
8. Harvest of Fear 197
9. The Hunters and the Hunted 223
10. The Visit to Eastwood 252
11. Aftermath 281
12. Redemption 298
13. Morfran 334

Acknowledgements 349
About the Author 352

North
Pen Dinas
Newport Bay
Pwllgwaelod
Sea Quarries
Dinas
Turnpike Road
Werndew
To Fishguard and Pen Caer
The Common
Mountain Track
Bedd Morris
Dinas Mountain
Roads
Tracks
Cliffs
Crags
Cwm Gwaun
One Mile
Pontfaen

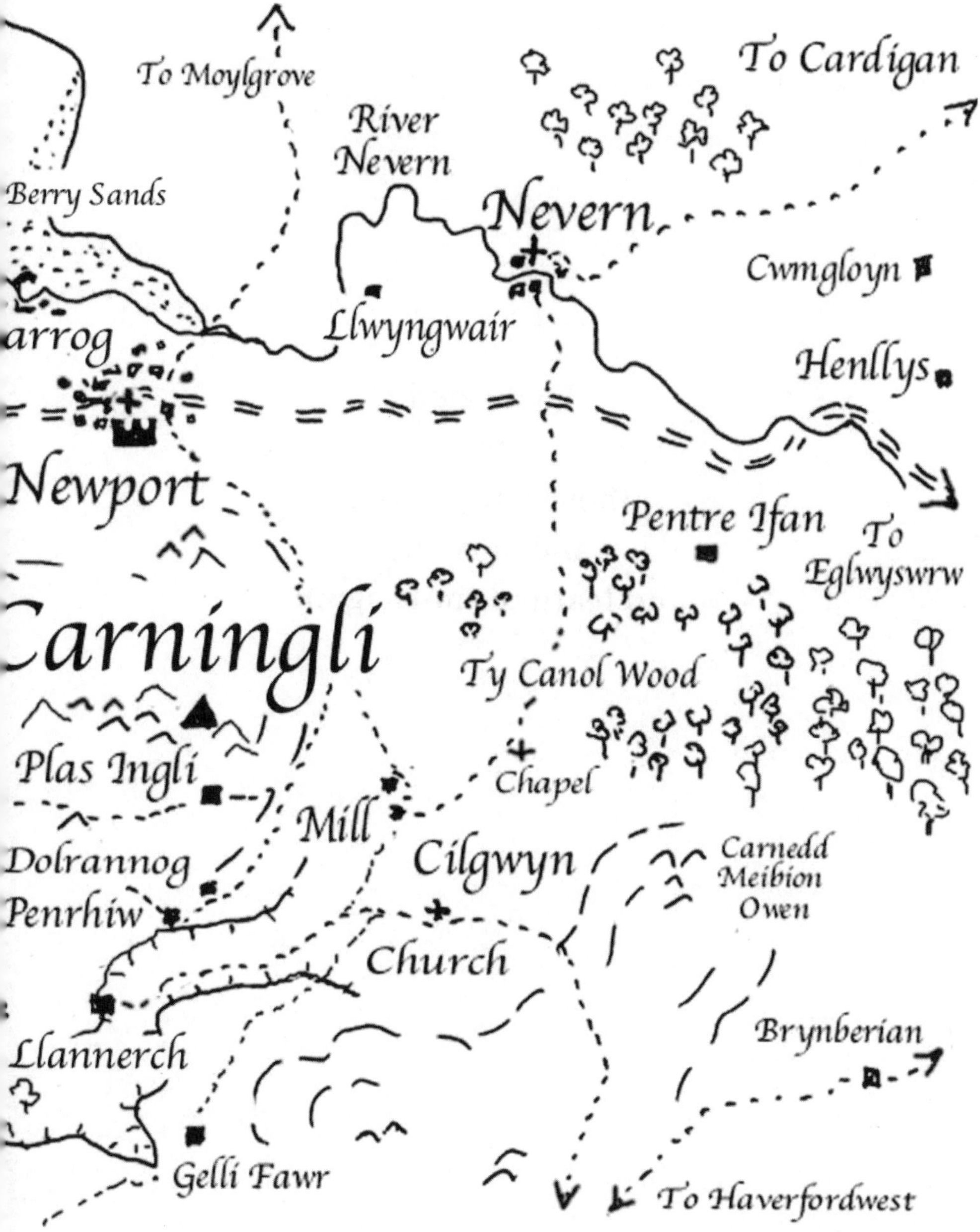

To Moylgrove

River Nevern

To Cardigan

Berry Sands

Nevern

Cwmgloyn

Llwyngwair

arrog

Henllys

Newport

Pentre Ifan

To Eglwyswrw

Carningli

Ty Canol Wood

Plas Ingli

Chapel

Mill

Dolrannog

Cilgwyn

Carnedd Meibion Owen

Penrhiw

Church

Llannerch

Brynberian

Gelli Fawr

To Haverfordwest

Dedicated
to
those who suffer,
and survive,
and learn to smile again

KEY CHARACTERS IN THE STORY

The Morgan family of Plas Ingli

Isaac Morgan (David's grandfather), b 1740, m 1758.

Jane (David's grandmother), b 1742, m 1758.

David, b June 1777, the second son of William and Bethan Morgan, who died 1794. Married to Martha on 21 August 1796, d 12 Feb 1806.

Martha, b as Martha Howell on 12 May 1778 at Brawdy. Married to David on 21 August 1796. Recorded death 27 Feb 1855, aged 76.

The children of David and Martha

Betsi, b 22 March, 1798.

Daisy, b 10 April, 1801.

Dewi, b 4 Feb, 1803.

Sara, b 19 March, 1805.

Brynach (adopted), b 7 April 1807.

The Howell family of Brawdy

George Howell (Martha's father) b 1745, m 1765, d 1817.

Betsi (Martha's mother), b 1748, m 1765.

Morys (older brother), b 1770, Baptist minister in Haverfordwest, married Nansi 1797. Three children, Edward, Jane and Robert.

Elen (oldest sister), b 1773, emigrated to USA 1807. Married Tom Bradshaw 1810.

Catrin (sister), b 1776, m James Bowen 1800. Children, John and Mark.

Plas Ingli staff

Billy Ifans, b 1763. Carter and senior man. Started at the Plas aged 14.

Shemi Jenkins, b 1782. Gardener and farm labourer. Started work 1797, aged 15. From Blaenwaun. Married Sian Williams 1810.

Hettie Jones, b 1770. Worked at the Plas from 1795-1801. Lodging house keeper on Parrog. Part-time dairymaid.

Blodwen Owen, b 1750. Housekeeper/cook (widowed, four children: Bethan, Sian, Dafydd, Will). Started at the Plas 1765, died 1814.

Will Owen, Mrs Owen's son, b 1780, shepherd and cow-man from 1806.
Bessie Walter, b 1776. Maid. Worked at the Plas in 1795-1799. Moved back after death of husband and son. Housekeeper from 1812.
Sian Williams, b 1779, daughter of Caradoc and Bethan Williams of Gelli, taken on as nursemaid in 1798. Married Shemi 1810.

Other Key Characters

Skiff Abraham, b 1782, small-time criminal and friend of Will Owen. His accomplices are Abby, Faggot, Halfpint and Daffy.
William Abbs (Abby), b 1784, labourer living on Parrog.
John Bateman, Martha's tutor and steward of Pontfaen estate.
Eleanor (Ellie) Bowen, b 1776, oldest daughter of John Bowen, Squire of Llwyngwair. Martha's friend. Married Walter Phillips 1808.
Dominic Cunningham from Limerick, b 1779.
Will Daniels, Clerk to the Justices.
Edwin Dashwood, b 1774, West Wycombe, grandson of Sir Francis.
David Davies (Davy Death), carpenter / undertaker / chandler.
John Devonald, Rector of Newport, mostly absentee.
Jenkin Edwards, Squire of Llwyngoras, friend of Grandpa Isaac.
Patty Ellis, once a prostitute living on the Parrog. Married Jake Nicholas 1807. Martha's friend. Daughter b 1808.
Richard Fenton, Squire of Glynymel, and a good friend of Martha. Scholar and antiquarian. Died 1821.
Reynard Foley, b 1776, son of Herbert Foley of Ridgeway. Installed as Squire of Great Canaston.
Will Gittins, wife Annie and two daughters, labourers, living at Trefelin.
Gethin Griffiths and wife Liza. Tenant farmers at Dolrannog Isaf. Good contacts in smuggling world. Three children.
Joseph Harries of Werndew, known as "the wizard", born 1761, died in 1826. Doctor, herbalist, sleuth, and Martha's friend and mentor.
Charles Hassall of Eastwood, b 1754, d 1814. Land surveyor and agriculturalist. Wife Harriet. Daughter Oriana.
William Havard Medical -- the only qualified doctor in Newport.
Mark Higgon, magistrate and Squire of Tredafydd.
Morton Hitchings, b 1764, and wife Janet, farmers on Skomar Island.

Morris Hughes, Steward of the Barony of Cemaes.
Nancy Humphrey, prostitute from Parrog
Harry Hurry, old man from Newport, used by Joseph Harries as a spy.
Tomos Huws, labourer from Plain Dealings.
Abel Jenkins, Brynaeron, and wife Mari. Labourer.
Abraham Jenkins, Brithdir Bach, farmer and supporter of Morgan family.
Daniel Jenkins, Blaenwaun, cottager, father of Shemi.
Mary Jane Laugharne, b 1775, oldest daughter of John and Olwen Laugharne of Pontfaen.. Married Dafydd Stokes of Trecwn 1800. Children William and Samuel. Martha's best friend.
Owain Laugharne, b 28 Dec 1780, youngest child of John and Olwen Laugharne. Took over Llannerch in 1802. Lost at sea May 1806.
George Lewis Legal, family lawyer from Fishguard, b 1740, d 1828.
Meredith Lloyd, b 1770, wife Jane, two small children, took over as Squire of Cwmgloyn on death of old squire in 1805.
Geordan McCleod, b 1771. From Scotland, and involved in the Carlton House Set in London.
Fancy Miles, prostitute from the Parrog.
Iolo Morgannwg (Edward Williams), b 1747, d 1826. Antiquarian, stonemason, farmer, forger and founder of the Gorsedd of Bards. One of the architects of Welsh nationhood.
Jake Nicholas, sailor and fisherman, married Patty Ellis in 1807.
Joshua Palmer, b 1766, from a London merchant family. Father made his fortune in the slave trade. A member of the Carlton House Set, and friend of the Prince of Wales.
Jeb Phipps, tenant at Brithdir Mawr after purchase in 1804.
William Potts, Parrog, temporary and reluctant constable.
Owen Pritchard and wife Sally, new tenants at Dolrannog Uchaf.
William Probert (Will Final Testament), family lawyer from Newport, b 1755, d 1833.
Gwynfor Rees, b 1781, wife Emily and 3 children. Local thug, taken on as carpenter at the Plas in1809.
John Small (Halfpint), b 1768, accomplice of Skiff Abraham.
Lizzie Tasker, lodging house keeper in Newport.
Daniel Thomas, new Mayor of Newport (also Coroner).

Thomas Tucker, wife Mary and three children, tenants at Penrhiw.
Caradoc Williams, b 1771, and wife Bethan. Tenant farmer at Gelli; also manager of the Sea Quarry at Aberrhigian.
John Wilson, cooper, from Newport, most experienced constable.
Judge Wynford Wynn-Evans, assize judge from Plas Dinefwr, Llandeilo.

GLOSSARY OF WELSH TERMS

Bach: "little one" (a term of endearment)
Bara brith: literally "speckled bread" or traditional currant cake
Calan Gaeaf: All Saint's Day, 1st November
Cariad: darling
Carn: heap of stones, rocky hill summit
Ceffyl Pren: wooden horse (used in mock "folk trials")
Cnapan: old ball game, thought to be the forerunner of rugby football
Coed: wood or trees
Crachach: snobs, gentry (used abusively)
Cwm: valley or hollow in the hillside
Duw: God
Dyn hysbys: literally "knowing man", wise man or wizard
Ffynnon: spring or water source
Foel: bare hill or summit
Gambo: a flat two-wheeled cart with no sides
Gwylnos: wake night or vigil, before the funeral
Hen Galan: the Old New Year, January 12th
Hiraeth: longing or belonging. Refers to a region or a special place
Ingli: probably an old Welsh word meaning "angels"
Parrog: flat land along a shore or estuary (Newport's seaside community)
Plas: big house or mansion
Plygain: candle-lit Christmas service ending at dawn
Sul y Blodau: Flower or Blossom Sunday, the Sunday before Easter
Toili: phantom funeral, interpreted as an omen of a death to come
Traeth Mawr: Big Beach (Newport's sandy beach)
Wrach: witch or hag (used for the last tuft of harvested corn)

The Brilliance of Edward Billings

"The gaps just don't make sense." That was the title of an Email message received one day in August last year from a forensic psychiatrist called Edward Billings. In the text, he wrote that he had just read the autobiography of Mistress Martha Morgan of Plas Ingli, based upon her diaries and published in the six volumes of the Angel Mountain series. He could not for the life of him understand the gaps in the narratives. He wrote that he would like to meet me, if it would be convenient, and reported that he was on holiday in St Davids. He would happily drive over to Newport.

We met in the cafe on the Parrog for a cup of tea and a slice of cake. He turned out to be a short man in his mid-fifties with thinning hair and too much weight around his middle. He had intense blue eyes and a small untidy moustache. He had immense self-confidence, and others might have found him irritating, but I liked him immediately. After chatting for a while about insignificant things, he said: "Now then -- down to work. It's obvious that your Mistress Martha was an obsessive diary writer. She maintained her diary writing activities through the most appalling and difficult of times, even following a miscarriage and the death of her husband in her early years, and during all manner of disasters later in life. OK? And she also recorded many intimate things including descriptions of love-making with her husband David and with her betrothed and beloved Owain, and -- very late in life -- with the Prophet Jones. Most diary writers do NOT include the sort of detail which Martha gives on page after page of her manuscript. The whole community would have been scandalised if her diaries had been discovered and read during her lifetime or in the lifetimes of her children or grandchildren....."

"Of course," I said. "That's why she wrote the diaries in her own private language, and then hid them away, here, there and everywhere."

"Not uncommon at the time. Many thousands of educated people kept detailed diaries in Regency and Victorian Britain. Many were written in code, and many of the writers used cross-writing, to save paper. Very few of these diaries ever saw the light of day -- and of those that did, the majority were turgid and uninteresting, except to academics."

"I'm aware of that. But Martha went to the most extraordinary lengths to protect her little books from prying eyes, thereby leading me on one wild goose chase after another. Wretched woman!"

"Come off it!" laughed Edward. "You pretend to be irritated with her. You are not irritated now, and you never were. You were fascinated and stimulated by the excitement of the chase, just as your old friend Abraham Jenkins loved every minute of his time as official translator of the first five diaries written in that strange Dimetian dialect. And as you got to know your exotic and eccentric Martha, your fascination and excitement turned into a sort of love affair, didn't it?"

"Excuse me! You are talking to a happily married man, with wonderful children and grand-children........"

He nodded and held up his hand. "Of course. I don't doubt your devotion to your wife and family. But it's perfectly possible for well-balanced and mature individuals to experience something akin to love for a film star, or a sporting hero, or even for somebody seen from a distance and maybe never communicated with directly. The ultimate form of this sort of obsession is stalking, which may be innocent enough initially, but which can become a nightmare for stalkers' victims when they discover that they are being followed or subjected to close surveillance. If a stalker is rejected, or becomes jealous because the object of his or her devotion is clearly and ostentatiously in love with somebody else, things can become very dangerous indeed. I know of scores of murders committed in just such a set of circumstances."

"You mean that the stalker will kill the very person to whom he or she is devoted?"

"Precisely," he said. "Disturbed individuals kill the people they love all the time, sometimes out of jealousy. Just think of Othello, who was a man with rather interesting problems. Sometimes such people have an irrational desire to save loved ones from some terrible fate, and sometimes they want to prevent anybody else loving them, as in the case of a messy divorce."

"Sorry, Edward, but what's this got to do with Mistress Martha Morgan of Plas Ingli?"

"More than you might think. It's clear from the diaries that Martha knew a great deal about men..........."

"That's true enough," said I. "She enjoyed sex, and she enjoyed the company of men. She says several times in the diaries that she hates the very idea of being a celibate spinster, and she refers often to having "certain needs." Mind you, she could also be very mischievous and manipulative with men whom she did not respect, and she had to be taken to task several times in the pages of the diaries by Grandma Jane and by her maid Bessie for taking too much pleasure in engineering the downfall or humiliation of assorted pompous squires."

"Yes, I have noticed that in my reading of the stories. Very much the flawed heroine, which is one of the reasons why I'm a little in love with her myself."

He paused for a moment and gazed out to sea, where a dozen or so small sailing boats were racing along, driven by a stiff onshore breeze. Now it was my turn to laugh. "Aha!" I said. "Forensic scientist admits to personal involvement. Case dismissed! Seriously though, I think Martha knew that every man who met her in her life fell in love with her, and that those destined to encounter her more than a century after her death would also be besotted with her."

Edward took another sip of tea, followed by a mouthful of chocolate cake. "Don't I recall her saying, somewhere in the dairies, that this was the greatest cross she had to bear?"

"Maybe not the greatest, in my humble opinion as Editor" I replied. "She had other crosses too. One was her tendency to sink into the darkest sort of "melancholia" now and then, which may have been something inherited or which may have been triggered by her own traumas -- of which there were many. Another cross, which was so heavy as to almost break her back on more than one occasion, was her tendency to be vindictive."

"True, true. And at times, from my reading of the texts, she was pretty paranoid too. Just look at her obsession with the Nightwalker in *Dark Angel*. Believe me, I have had some very interesting discussions about Martha's character; a couple of months ago, I led a course at the Police College, and as a project I asked the students to read the six published diaries and to give me a psychological profile of Mistress Martha. Have you heard of psychological profiling? Both fascinating and rewarding. I must tell you about it some time."

"We were talking about obsessions and stalking..........."

"Ah yes, so we were. The point I was going to make is that Martha knew men so well that she knew somebody like you would find the first diary and then move heaven and earth to discover the others."

I had to agree. "Yes indeed. She treated it as a sort of sport, dreaming up ever more elaborate means of secreting the diaries away in the most unexpected of places."

"Classic scenario. The female of the species playing hard to get, and the male of the species stimulated by the chase!"

"That makes it all sound very biological, if I may say so."

Edward grinned again. "Of course. And so it was, and is. This is not simply a matter of psychology."

"But what if a woman had found the first diary and had decided to pursue the matter?"

"Martha knew that it would not be a woman. A woman would not have shown the same persistence as you have shown, and no woman would have been driven by the same urge to read the diaries and to publish them. It's a sex thing."

I began to feel uneasy. "This begins to sound very politically incorrect."

"Quite so. Sex is responsible for a great deal of misery, but it also drives the greatest creativity in music, art, the theatre, and literature. Moving swiftly on, I also have to say that in your single-minded pursuit of the diaries, and in your determination to understand every facet of Martha's character, you have shown the same sort of devotion and obsession as a typical stalker."

"I hope I have not become unbalanced or dangerous in the process."

"You look sane enough to me, and from the manner in which the preludes to the books are written, I would judge you to be relatively harmless."

"That's a relief," I said. "But can I ask you one question? Why would Martha have gone to the trouble of writing her diaries in Dimetian Welsh, which nobody else could understand, if she really wanted them to be read after her death? Did she or did she not want the diaries to be read by the rest of the world?"

"That's three questions for the price of one. Of course she wanted them to be read by following generations. Doesn't she say that on several occasions? Writing in a private language is a common trick. Obsessive diary writers do it all the time, for reasons that are very complex. I think it adds excitement to the writing process, as well as avoiding the obvious risk of the immediate family discovering the manuscript and seeking to read what is written about them. In Martha's case, she may also have felt a sense of mission to keep the Dimetian dialect alive by forcing the finder of the diaries and the translator to get to grips with its grammar and its vocabulary."

"Sadly, there is now nobody left with a knowledge of the language. My old friend Abraham Jenkins passed away almost immediately after finishing the translation of the diary reproduced in *Flying with Angels*."

Edward nodded. "I was aware of that. Bad business........"

"But I think he died happy," I said, "with a job well done."

"I can understand that. From what you have written about the translation of five diaries, and Abraham's obvious pleasure in the work, a painless death at the conclusion of a long journey was perhaps appropriate for an old man with not much more to look forward to."

"So Dimetian Welsh is dead and buried -- gone, like the dodo and the woolly mammoth, with no fanfares."

"More's the pity, since there's clearly more translating work to be done."

I gasped, and my heart missed a beat. "Whatever do you mean?"

"Surely you can't be so naive as to believe that there are no more diaries? It's absolutely certain that there are -- or were -- others, written by Mistress Martha Morgan in that strange old dialect............."

"I refuse to believe that. Of course I have given that question an enormous amount of thought. I've searched high and low for clues, and analysed the manuscripts and the translations in minute detail. There is absolutely nothing to indicate that she wrote more diaries, as yet undiscovered."

"I think I might dispute that," said Edward, sounding like an argumentative witness in a court of law. "I need to look at the original manuscripts, in Martha's own hand. Are you in possession of them?"

"I have the first manuscript, used for the book called *On Angel Mountain*. The second one, used for *House of Angels*, is in the old library of Pontfaen House -- but I have a photocopy of every single page. The third, on which *Dark Angel* is based, is in the National Library in Aberystwyth. But again, I have a copy -- this time on microfilm. The fourth, used for *Rebecca and the Angels*, is in Melbourne, of all places, but I have a copy on a computer disc, scanned from the original. And the fifth, found right here in Newport and edited to create *Flying with Angels*, is my prized possession, since it is my favourite of all the stories."

"Excellent. Then we have something to work on."

"I've already told you that I have hunted for many hours for clues and have found precisely nothing."

"Let's go back to where we started with this conversation. I repeat -- Martha was an obsessive diary writer who continued to write even when faced with deaths in the family or when trying to cope with mayhem in the community or even in her own house. You've managed to find an extraordinary number of her diaries -- but when you look at the total narrative, there are some large gaps. Right?"

I confirmed that that was the case. "From memory, the first was a gap of two months in 1796, when Martha suffered from depression."

"That gap was too short. A young woman suffering from deep depression, and under close surveillance and medical care, would probably not have written entries in her diary during that time. And next?"

"Then came a gap of several years, when she was producing children. With a house full of babies, she would have been constantly tired, and very busy. Maybe it would have been difficult for her to find the time to write a diary every evening. Then she picked up her quill pen and started writing again. There were no obvious gaps in *House of Angels*,

I think, and the diary appears pretty complete over the course of almost one year."

"Fair enough. And next? What about the *Dark Angel* diary?"

"Much bigger gaps. There was one gap, as I recall, of around seven months over the winter of 1807-8. Then a very big gap from July 1808 to April 1817.........."

Edward patted the table with the palm of his hand. "Now we're getting somewhere. Almost nine years. You can take it from me, on the basis of thirty years of work in the fields of criminal profiling and forensic psychiatry, that Martha Morgan continued to write diaries during that time."

"I don't believe you."

Edward shrugged. "Well, that's your privilege. But trust me. I'm never wrong on this sort of thing. I'll stake my reputation on it. When you get home today, dig out that microfilm. You could examine it on the microfilm reader in the County Library. Or better still, ask the National Library for a scanned version on disk, so that you can examine it at home, on your computer screen. I wouldn't mind betting that they have already scanned and digitised it, as part of their ongoing programme of digitising everything of value."

That was the gist of our conversation. I paid the bill, and we got to our feet. Edward had to get back to St David's in time for supper. I thanked him for his interest and advice, and agreed that I would follow up on his suggestions and then contact him again. We shook hands and went our separate ways.

Ten minutes later I was on my way home with my mind racing. On impulse, I took a short detour and drove up to the little car parking area on the flank of Carningli. It was a gorgeous late afternoon, with the sun sinking down towards the craggy western end of the mountain. I walked towards the ruins of Plas Ingli, the house inhabited by Mistress Martha and a host of angels back in the days of young Victoria, before she was Queen. I'm not sure what I was expecting -- some sign maybe, from the ravens or from the old blue rocks of the mountain itself? I sat down on what was left of the house's eastern gable end, under a lattice of gnarled oak and ash branches which were in the process of bursting into leaf. A cuckoo called from a copse close to Dolrannog. Above my head, on the highest branch of the tallest ash tree, a blackbird gave the world his variations on a five-note musical theme. Over the common there were at least half a dozen skylarks combining (or were they competing?) in a virtuoso performance which could be nothing other than a celebration of spring. I could hear them, but they were so high up that I could not see them. There were sheep everywhere, newly turned out onto the common and accompanied by the lambs born in March and April. Some of them had fleeces smudged with black and grey, following forays into the areas of spring burning that had previously been impenetrable thickets of gorse and heather. Twenty or so longhorn cattle ambled by, heading for Ffynnon Brynach where they would slake their thirst after a long hot day. The gorse bushes on the walls of the old garden were in full bloom, so heavy with blossom that the spikes and the greens were obliterated behind a cascade of yellow, orange and gold in subtle combinations. The scent was almost overpowering, bringing into mind coconut and vanilla and tropical islands...........

Then I realized that the sounds of birds, sheep, distant dogs and murmuring traffic had all disappeared, and that I could not even hear the sound of the whispering breeze in the branches over my head. The new leaves and the old white grasses that had survived the winter stopped moving, and an eerie stillness descended on the landscape. I had experienced this sort of thing on Carningli before, but only in connection with a blanket of sea mist that had rolled inland from the coast a couple of miles away. Now there was no mist; the sun still shone brightly out of a cloudless evening sky. I held my breath, not sure whether the silence was ominous or benign. Gradually I became attuned to the fact that there was indeed a sound in the air -- almost imperceptible at first, but gradually getting louder. I could not work out what it was, until it dawned on me that I had heard this sound many times before. It was the low rippling and rustling sound that you hear from the vibrating wing-tip feathers of ravens when they are cavorting in a high wind. You have to be quite close to the ravens to hear it, but if you cuddle down on the rocks near the summit of the mountain, and if the resident ravens do not know you are there, they may well fly very close to where you are sitting. Then you may see them at close quarters, and when they see you they will wheel away, leaving that sound of pulsing wing-beats engraved on your memory. It is something subtle yet powerful, for they are big birds.

Now I was puzzled, for there was no wind, and yet the sound of wing-beats was all around me, very close indeed. I could see nothing in any direction. Others might have felt apprehensive or even scared in such circumstances, but I now know Mistress Martha well enough to know that she plays tricks when it suits her. But always in the past, when she had wanted to communicate through her incarnation as a raven and as the guardian angel of the mountain, she had appeared to me (and others) in the physical form of a large and powerful -- and even intimidating -- black bird. But now she chose to remain invisible. Was this just another good-humoured game, a sign of approval, or a demonstration of displeasure? Was she aware that I was on the trail of another diary? But how could she be attuned to my state of mind to an extent that I was unaware of myself? After all, I was highly sceptical about the existence of another diary -- and had said so to Edward Billings over our tea and chocolate and walnut cake. I thought that on balance she was saying something to me. But what was her message? I was pondering deeply on that point when -- suddenly -- there she was.

I recall looking towards the mountain on the skyline, and when I glanced back towards my immediate environment there was a large black raven, in her prime, preening her feathers while perched on the iron gate between the old house and the common. Her plumage, supposedly as black as coal dust, shimmered like anthracite with unimaginable colours. She was about ten yards away from me, as nonchalant and unafraid as ever. Then she looked at me and made a sound I had never heard before from a raven -- a gentle purring sound, interspersed with soft clucks. I imagined that these might be the sounds made in the nest by a female raven communicating with her chicks. They certainly appeared to indicate pleasure, and I took those subtle sounds as a sign that she was perfectly at ease with me, and that she was happy with whatever I decided to do. Lazily she launched herself into the air. This time there was no sound from her wing-beats. She flew purposefully straight towards the mountain summit and perched on the highest of the old blue crags. I could see her quite clearly from where I sat. Then she disappeared, and I became aware of the fact that her departure was accompanied by a return of all the commonplace sounds of the mountain -- birds and sheep, the rustling of wind in the branches over my head, and the modern sounds of tractors, distant traffic and transatlantic jets still climbing westwards as they approached the navigation beacon of Green One near Strumble Head.

As I walked back to the car I mulled over some of the things that Edward had said to me in the cafe, and decided that it was time for another phase of detective work. I also recalled that I had had a very similar encounter with the raven in the ruins of Plas Ingli a few years back, just before the publication of *Dark Angel*. I took that as a pointer towards that particular diary, and decided that clues to any missing segments must be found within its pages. When I got home I took the volume down from the shelf and looked for gaps in the narrative. The first gap, of about nine months, in the winter of 1807-8, was not particularly promising. When Martha finished her 1807 entries, on 27th September, she was attempting to escape from her obsession with hunting for a mysterious figure called the Nightwalker, who had been sighted many times on the mountain and near Plas Ingli. She was also seeking forgiveness from her nearest and dearest for her petulance and her inability to trust others. When she took up her diary again, on 7th April 1808, she reported on various winter and spring events in a quite natural and unhurried fashion, and in her words I could see no clues at all as to secret or embarrassing episodes that might have been "edited out" or glossed over.

Then I turned to the longest gap in the sequence of diaries -- the gap of almost nine years. I rediscovered my note written at the time I had edited the diary, and published on page 312 of the book's first edition:

Editor's Note:** **There are only occasional diary entries for the period between 17 July 1808 and 6th April 1817. Most of these relate to estate and family matters, childrens' illnesses and education, and the weather. Since they do nothing to advance this story, they are omitted from this text. There are some long gaps between entries, and it seems that these gaps coincided with intermittent periods of depression. In

1810, 1814 and 1815 Martha also made long visits to the Lake District and to Yorkshire to visit distant relatives, and there are records of a number of shorter social visits to London and Oxford. There are also many references to "lessons" with the wizard Joseph Harries.

There were some short and inconsequential diary entries, which I had chosen not to reproduce. But they had been included on the microfilm copy of the manuscript and then translated faithfully by Abraham Jenkins, and I had a photocopy of his full hand-written version in a box-file in my office. I dug out the pile of paper, cleared my desk, and settled into a close examination of the diary entries. I had made a mess of Abraham's manuscript during the editing process, but I was reminded now just how meticulous he had been in his translation work, with many crossings-out and revisions of wording, and little footnotes and comments added in both English and Welsh. It was clear that in many places he had made use of Meredith Morris's *Glossary of the Dimetian Dialect,* and it was also clear that he had remained remarkably faithful to Martha's phraseology and figures of speech -- a difficult thing for any translator to do. I noticed two things. First, that his pages were prominently numbered; and second, that some of his pages had not been filled with his hand-writing. I was intrigued by these blank spaces, and wondered whether he might have made adjustments during the translating process in order to keep his page numbering sequence in step with the page numbers in Martha's own hand-written diary. I decided that I would have to check this.

Then I turned to the diary entries themselves, for the nine problematical years. There were fifteen entries altogether. I had not noticed it before, but -- if Abraham's translation was to be believed -- they were very brief and matter-of-fact, and staccato in style. Verbs were missing from sentences, and there was a total lack of colour and emotion in the writing. They covered events which were mundane and even banal. The only clues to serious happenings were four entries following gaps of more than a year, in a very abbreviated form: "Bout of melancholia"; "Very miserable time"; "Most unwell -- several weeks"; "Feeling better at last -- Joseph is a hero." Then there were the entries relating to travels: "To the Lakes"; "Away in Yorkshire"; "London three weeks and Oxford ten days"; "Tour of the nephews and nieces." There were a few references to carriage and coach journeys, places and people, and the weather. I wondered whether those entries had been written on the dates given to them, or whether they had been put in retrospectively. What might have brought on those bouts of depression? With whom had she travelled to these various places in distant parts of the country? Why had she not been more expansive in her entries? After all, hundreds of her published diary entries had been written as honest records of events which would have appeared to her to be quite innocuous at the time and which only acquired significance later on as part of an unfolding narrative. Why had she written expansively of these apparently innocuous events before July 1808 and after April 1817, but not between those dates? I felt uneasy about something during this period of nine years, but I could not put my finger on it. I began to appreciate why Edward Billings had raised the possibility of "something missing."

Next day I travelled to the County Library in Haverfordwest, having booked myself a session on the microfilm reader. I carried with me my copy of the microfilm of Martha's diary which had been made at Aberystwyth, hoping that it would give up some of its secrets. I settled down in front of the machine and started to work through from page to page, seeking to match what was on the screen with the manuscript translation provided for me by my old friend Abraham Jenkins. The experience was deeply unsatisfactory. For a start, I could not decipher Martha's steeply sloping and strong handwriting -- and even if I had been able to read particular words, I would not have understood them. The only things I could make out properly were dates, numbers, place-names and personal names; and they tallied neatly with what Abraham had written. But I could see no page numbers on the microfilmed version of the diary. Had they been written too faintly for the camera to pick them up, or had they been missing from the beginning? After two hours of intensely frustrating and unproductive work, I gave up in disgust, having convinced myself that if there were clues to be found, they would have to be found in the three volumes of the original diary, now housed in the archives of the National Library in Aberystwyth.

When I got home I rang the Library and asked for the Curator of

Records -- namely Catrin Mathias, who had originally discovered and catalogued the diary in 1983. It had been in a box among the Price family papers taken from Cwrt in the Gwaun Valley. In 1983 Catrin had been a very junior research assistant, but quite recently she had been promoted to the post of Curator after a distinguished career.

"Hello? Catrin speaking."

I had not met her for several years, and the first thing I had to do was congratulate her on her elevation. Then I said: "Catrin, I need your help. Do you remember those Martha Morgan diaries written in the Dimetian dialect and translated by Abraham Jenkins?"

"Of course I do. They are still here, in the vault, counted among our most prized possessions."

"Something has arisen which gives me cause for concern. I've had a long chat with a forensic psychiatrist called Dr Edward Billings. He's quite convinced that there are major gaps in the diary sequence, and I'm beginning to think that he is right. No time for a full explanation, but the focus of attention is the three-volume diary that you hold in Aberystwyth. That's the one I published as *Dark Angel*."

"I'll help if I can. What do you want me to do?"

"Well, I've looked at the microfilm, but it's difficult to pick things up on that -- the fact that I don't read or speak Dimetian Welsh is just part of the problem. I'd like to have full sight of the diary volumes and all the other papers -- receipts, envelopes, deeds and so forth -- which you found in that box from Cwrt. Is the collection of items still intact?"

"I'm pretty certain that it is. It may not be in the same box, but we try not to disperse the items we find in old collections like these. Sometimes the things that are apparently insignificant turn out to be immensely valuable to researchers. They will all have been catalogued and examined, but you can take it as read that nothing will have been thrown away."

I felt a surge of enthusiasm and optimism. "Fantastic! Can I come up to Aberystwyth, and will you help me to look through the material?"

"It will be a pleasure. Would you like your friend Dr Billings to come as well? I've worked with forensic psychiatrists before, and they sometimes bring an extraordinary light to bear on things that appear very murky. Dr Billings is very well known -- didn't he help to track down the murderer in that terrible case in Tregaron?"

So it was that a fortnight later the three of us met up in the library, with a collection of volumes, bundles of paper, envelopes and legal documents laid out on the table before us. Catrin, a striking woman in her mid-fifties, provided us with some coffee and assured us that we, and the material before us, would have her undivided attention for the whole of the afternoon. Edward made an immediate impact on the proceedings. Without saying a word he picked up the volumes of the diary, one after another, and subjected them to minute scrutiny. First, he checked that no pages had been pulled out or cut out. Having satisfied himself that the books had not been tampered with, he then looked at me and said: "Right. As you suspected, there are no numbers on the pages."

"I've thought about that," I replied. "Maybe it's not such a big deal. If these were manuscript volumes, bought from a printer or a stationer, they would not necessarily have numbered pages. Martha's first diary, for example, was written in a book acquired from her husband David's grandfather Isaac, and it had unnumbered pages."

"These three are different. The volumes were bound after the diary was written."

I raised my eyebrows. "How do you know that?"

"Just look at the volumes carefully," he said, as if addressing a small child. "The binding is good, and the pages are well trimmed, but if you look carefully you will see that several different types of paper have been used. Some sections of the volumes are made of thinnish paper with little ink spreading; other parts are made of paper which is heavy and bulky, and if you look through a magnifying glass at the inscribed letters on the page you will see that the ink has spread, so that the edges are slightly blurred."

I looked through his magnifying glass and confirmed that he was quite correct. Catrin smiled. "Edward knows what he is talking about," she said. "These volumes were bound at the same time, around 1825. The bookbinder was Thomas Evans of Cardigan. We know that because he always placed a small gold-blocked insignia -- an elaborate representation of the letters T and E -- at the base of the spine when he worked for private clients. Also, the heavy marbled paper used on the insides of the covers was not produced before 1823."

I was impressed. "So what do we deduce when we consider these un-numbered pages?"

Edward now looked like a hunter closing in on his prey. "That Martha composed this whole diary on loose pages of paper, of which there are over a thousand sheets across the three volumes. I suspect that at one time there were many more pages. Let's just check this out............"

For a few minutes Edward looked at the dates of the diary entries in all three volumes, and then subjected the third volume to intense scrutiny. He slammed it shut. Then he decided to play a little trick on Catrin and me. With a gleam in his eye, he asked: "What was the date of the first diary entry after that nine-year break?"

I consulted my notes and replied: "6th of April 1817."

"Would you like me, with my eyes closed, to open the diary at precisely that date?"

"Oh all right. Your favourite party trick? If you insist."

So with a flourish he closed his eyes tightly, took the volume in his hands, and ran his fingers over the edges of the pages, occasionally opening the book slightly so that he could assess page thickness and the texture of the paper. Then, with his eyes still closed, he opened the book with a flourish and announced: "Hey presto! This page was written on 6th April 1817. Tell me I'm correct!"

Catrin and I gazed at the open book and she giggled: "Very sorry, Edward, but you are wrong. This page says 15th September 1812. You are way out!"

Edward opened his eyes and grinned. "I am never wrong. Well, not very often, anyway. When I was a young man, more interested in forensic science than the mysteries of the criminal mind, I learned to trust my sense of touch." He examined the pages preceding and following the one at which he had opened the book, and nodded sagely. "Look here," he said. "This is definitely the point at which there is a paper change. After this point, the paper is whiter and more heavily compressed. And there are differences in the handwriting too. I'm not a handwriting expert, but an individual's handwriting changes a lot over the course of a decade. Look here at the letter "T" as Martha has written it at the beginning of a sentence. More elaborate on the pages up to this point, and simpler and straighter on the pages after this point." He then proceeded to show us other differences as well, and convinced us that the group of diary entries from this enigmatic period of almost nine years, contained on just eight pages of the manuscript, were not written on the cited dates at all, but in the year 1817, probably in the month of March or at the beginning of April.

"Martha's little April Fool's joke!" he exclaimed. "Now for confirmation. Let's look for page numbers. You cannot play around with a thousand loose pages of paper and hope to keep them in the right order, especially in a house full of small children. Martha was pretty organized, and she must have numbered the pages somehow."

"Invisible ink?" asked Catrin.

"That's one possibility. I've seen that -- or not seen it, as the case may be -- in a number of diaries before. There are other simpler techniques, and Martha must have used one of them."

Five minutes later, and after a good deal of shuffling back and forth through the pages of the three volumes, Edward had cracked the code. He invited Catrin and me to do the same, but try as we might we could get nowhere. He was of course delighted, and chortled as if he were Just William relishing the success of his latest prank. So he shared the secret with us. "Look at the fifth, tenth and fifteenth lines of every page," he said. "Let's try page 123." He went to volume one and thumbed through the pages until he had the right one. "See here. Right in the middle of line five there is a number one, tagged onto the end of a word I don't understand. Well, it's in a very strange language, isn't it? Then, running down to line ten, look at the number at the end of the line. Number two. And again, when we run down another five lines, at the beginning of the line we have the number three. Page 123. The same technique is used everywhere, but Martha was smart enough to vary the positions of the numbers on the line between one page and the next. She was also smart enough to use Roman numerals in some places and our modern method of representation elsewhere."

"Amazing!" exclaimed Catrin. "But why go to such extraordinary lengths to hide page numbers? If you assume that somebody, in the distant future, will want to read your diary, why make it so difficult for them?"

"Maybe because it gave Martha the option of editing the text, or extracting great chunks of it, without it being immediately apparent to the reader from some later generation. She probably expected from the beginning that parts of her text might have to be expurgated, maybe because of the frankness of the revelations or because certain famous persons might be compromised."

"But why didn't Abraham pick up on this? He must have been immensely irritated by these apparently random numbers scattered across the pages."

"He didn't need to worry about them. The pages he was asked to translate were on microfilm, all in the correct order. He saw the numbers, wondered about them, and probably concluded that they were simply inserted as footnotes or as *aides memoires* for the writer. After a while he probably just read through them and paid them no attention at all."

After all of this mental exercise we all needed more coffee, and a break in the fresh air drifting in off Cardigan Bay. As we strolled, we talked of families, and the weather, and other things. But Edward found it hard to relax, and his brow remained as furrowed as a February field. As we headed back into the depths of the Library, he said quietly: "Moment of truth, folks. Now we will discover just how many pages have gone missing."

Back at the table, he dived straight back into volume three of the diary. He perused the pages around the diary entry for 27 September 1814. He wrote down some numbers. Then he leafed forward for maybe twenty pages, writing down more numbers. Then he did some sums. Then like a Las Vegas jackpot winner he punched the air and ran round the table, shouting "Yes! Yes! Yes!" at the top of his voice. I was considerably embarrassed by this display of emotion, and thought he might be forcibly evicted for disturbing the silence of a hallowed place, but Catrin roared with laughter.

"Calm down, Edward!" she said at last. "Tell us everything."

"Six hundred and fifty-three pages missing," said Edward

triumphantly. "Just look here. In the early part of this volume the numbers go up to 613, 614 and 615. That's the last number. Turn the page, and what do we see? On the page that should be 616, there are four lines that have digits on them. Line twenty has been brought into play. The number of this page, using Martha's code, is 1269. Turn over, and what's the page number? Naturally enough, 1270. Then 1271, 1272 and so on. The page number for the entry dated 6th April 1817 is 1277 -- as it should be. So the preceding eight pages were not written and inserted over a period of many years, but very shortly before that next dated entry was completed."

I must have looked like a goldfish out of a pond, and Edward slapped me on the back. "Don't look so gob-smacked," he said. "You should be delighted. This means that somewhere out there, in the great wide world, there is a missing story of eight or nine years of Mistress Martha's life, contained within 653 pages of hand-written manuscript. My hunch was right -- and people always act in character. She was indeed an obsessive diary writer, who would have kept on writing even if she had been witness to the end of the world."

When I had recovered my equilibrium, I shook Edward warmly by the hand. "Thank you Edward -- your deductive skills leave me far in your wake. I am lost in admiration. So where do we go now? How do we start on the hunt for all, or some, of these missing pages?"

Catrin had already given me the answer, for she was already examining the other items on the table. These were the things that had been placed in the original box at the old mansion of Cwrt. There were bills, receipts, notes, little sketches, and even bits and pieces of newspapers and magazines. Some of the items were written in Martha's hand, in English and Welsh. Others were written in hands we did not recognize. Places and names popped out at us, and we discussed some things at length, but we could find no common themes and nothing of real significance. Then Catrin said: "Wait a moment! What have we here?" and continued feverishly to thumb through assorted bits of paper, organizing them in a way that must, to her, have been revealing. Edward and I stood back with bated breath.

At last she said: "Who is this fellow Dominic?"

Edward shrugged and looked at me. "I have not the faintest idea," I said. "Nobody of that name has ever appeared in the diaries, so far as I am aware. Isn't that an Irish name?"

"Quite possibly," said Catrin. "But here is the name, popping up off the page five or six times in assorted notes, and even hand-written in a few places on the margins of newspaper cuttings. No surname. So he must have been well known to Martha -- a friend or relative, maybe? But there are no letters to him or from him -- and indeed, correspondence is conspicuously absent from this collection of papers. Maybe that in itself is significant..........."

"Wait a moment," said Edward. "Where did I see that name? I'm sure I saw it somewhere just now." And he went rummaging back into a pile of documents which he had already examined in minute detail. At last he waved something in front of us. "A bill of sale from somewhere called Wiston. For the milling of one sack of corn. Made to Mistress Morgan, Plas Ingli. Here on the margin the name Dominic is written in what appears to be Martha's hand." He rummaged again, and produced three more bills, each one from Wiston Mill and each one for the milling of one bag of corn. The signature on the bottom of each one is "Benjamin Skyrme, Miller." All duly paid. What do we know about Wiston and its corn mill?"

"Not a lot," I replied. "There was a castle and a manor there once. It's a good place for a corn mill, with a reliable stream, and easy access to fertile farmland in the area around Robeston Wathen and Narberth. Wheat would succeed in that area -- hence a demand for a mill. But why would Martha go all that way to get her barley and her wheat milled? It must be at least a dozen miles from Plas Ingli. There was a perfectly good corn mill in Newport, and another on one of her own tenanted farms, at Gelli. And yet another over the river from Trefelin, sometimes operating and sometimes destroyed by floods. And why would she take just one sack to be milled, when we know from other diary records that she had a cart capable of carrying at least ten sacks at a time? Very strange indeed."

While I spoke Catrin was consulting a computer in the corner of the room. Within a couple of minutes she said: "Wiston Mill. Thomas Skyrme, died 13th August 1814, aged five. Record number 11 in the burial index. So there was a young family there at the time. There were lots of people named Skyrme in South Pembrokeshire -- but we can find out more, I'm sure, if we give a little time to it."

By now it was well after five o'clock, and we had to go our separate ways. Edward had a train to catch, and I had a long drive home to Newport. But before we parted we congratulated ourselves on a job well done, and promised to consult further in our common pursuit of the missing chunk of Martha's *Dark Angel* manuscript.

On the way home my mind was so preoccupied with the latest diary hunt that I probably wildly exceeded the speed limit in half a dozen villages and hamlets along the A478. However, the speed cameras appear, in retrospect, to have been switched off, and my expected summonses never appeared. Who was Dominic, and what was the link with Wiston? Those questions went round and round in my head, but I had no way of finding answers. I did not sleep well, and next morning I prowled around on the internet for a while in the hope of turning something up. Then the phone rang. It was Catrin. "Good morning!" she said brightly. "What an exciting afternoon we had yesterday. I must say that I am full of admiration for your friend Edward. I have some good news. A colleague has looked at the 1811 census. It took place on May 27th, and at Wiston Mill on that date we find two adult males, both classified as millers, one adult female, and three male children and two female children. There were no names recorded in that census, but names were recorded in 1831 and in later census returns, and Skyrme is always shown as the name of the miller. So the trade was probably maintained by several generations of the family. The second miller shown in 1811 might well have been an apprentice or an assistant, who appears to have been living in the mill with the family. Could this have been a young man called Dominic? It's a reasonable hypothesis, anyway........"

This might well have helped us with one minor problem, related to the *dramatis personae* of the missing chunk of Martha's diary, but it did nothing to help in the discovery of its whereabouts. I did not dare to get too excited at the prospect of finding it. After all, I had had extraordinary luck in discovering no fewer than six diaries thus far, each one worthy of conversion into a published book. The chances of survival of **all** of the scattered diaries of a person who lived and died more than 150 years ago were vanishingly small. And yet I dared to hope, and dared to think that fate might have decreed that the whole of Martha's life story would be preserved and protected, and would -- in small fragments maybe -- see the light of day.

I needed some inspiration, and decided that the only place to find it was the top of Carningli. It was a breezy day with heavy black clouds rolling in from the west, and with the threat of rain in the air. But I packed my waterproofs into my rucksack, together with some sandwiches and a thermos of hot chocolate, and off I went. Thirty-five minutes later I was on the summit, with the whole world spread out beneath my feet. Well, not the whole world, but that part of it upon which I was trying to concentrate. The wind was too strong to stand upright on the topmost crag, so I cuddled down beneath one of the overhangs and tried to work my way into the mind of Mistress Martha. I was not blessed -- or afflicted -- by anything supernatural, but four ravens were enjoying the blustery conditions above the mountain summit. They gave me a display of aerobatics that would have done justice to their smaller relative the chough, wheeling and diving and very occasionally flying upside down. I had to laugh at such exuberance, and I reminded myself that I had been taking this business of the missing chunk of diary far too seriously. It was not actually a matter of life and death, and nobody would suffer if those 653 pages of hand-written manuscript turned out to have been lost or destroyed. But if they were still in existence somewhere, it would, I thought, be quite a pleasant thing to find them.........

Suddenly the image of a portly red-faced man with extravagant whiskers came into my mind. Wilmot Gwynne! The successor to Squire Price at the Llanychaer estate, the owner of Plas Ingli towards the end of Martha's life, and one of her greatest friends -- surely he must hold the key to this mystery? He was a rough diamond who made his fortune in the Swansea Valley as an industrialist and who moved to Pembrokeshire with the intention of becoming a respectable member of the local gentry. There had been a very close bond between him and Martha, based upon mutual respect and real affection. And he had proved himself, particularly in the course of the *Guardian Angel* narrative, to be both a true gentleman and a man of sharp intellect. With mounting excitement I recalled that the box of Price family papers and volumes which included Martha's three-volume diary had been one of several boxes passed to the National Library of Wales around 1970, when the Gwynne estate went into administration. Wilmot Gwynne and his expansive wife Delilah had taken over the estate in 1845 and had enlarged it considerably by the time of Martha's death. When the family became bankrupt several generations later, the Price papers (which were probably of no great interest to the Gwynnes) were passed to the National Library. But what about the Gwynne family papers? What had happened to them? I realized that if there was one man in the whole world that an elderly Martha Morgan would trust with her life, it was her old friend Wilmot, since all her other closest friends -- including the wizard Joseph Harries, the preacher Amos Jones and her beloved maid Bessie Walter -- were long gone.

I gobbled down my sandwiches and consumed my hot chocolate, with my mind racing. It had to be Wilmot. No doubt about it. Everything pointed towards it. Off I went down the scree slope, doing my best to imitate a mountain goat and setting off minor landslides now and then. Such haste is not very sensible on an unstable mountainside, and in retrospect, I was lucky to survive. But twenty minutes later I puffed and panted into the house and headed straight for the telephone.

"Catrin? Is that you? Splendid. Can I ask you something?"

"If you are quick. I'm in the middle of a meeting."

"Those boxes relating to the Price estate. You said there were several of them. Have you examined the others?"

"Yes. I have. The others made no reference to Martha at all. They just contained tenancy agreements, legal documents, bills of sale and so forth. Typical estate papers. Somebody -- maybe old Squire Price himself -- had put all Martha's material carefully into one box. I have even double-checked -- there is nothing else that is relevant."

"Very well. That accounts for the Price papers. And what happened to the Gwynne family papers?"

"I'm pretty sure we have never seen them at the National Library. I did all the original indexing of the estate records from the 1800's, and if anybody would know about them, it would be me. All I can assume is that they went with the family when they left the Plas."

"Excellent! Thanks a million! That's all I wanted to know. I'll be in touch."

Now I was on the trail again, experiencing what Edward Billings had referred to as "the excitement of the chase." I had assumed that the collapse of the estate around 1970 had involved the last of the Gwynnes. But when I checked with the solicitor Elwyn George, who had handled the disposal of the estate assets, he said: "No no, I assume that the Gwynnes are alive and kicking. In 1972, when I last heard of them and when we finally sorted out the last details of the estate transfer, they were living in Cardiff, and were not terribly well off. Wilmot Gwynne -- presumably named after his illustrious ancestor -- was quite a young man, maybe in his mid-thirties. He had a wife and four children, I think. So now, if he is still alive, he will be in his sixties. That's all I can tell you."

From that point on, it was a simple matter to track the family down. I managed to find Wilmot's son James on Facebook, and discovered that he lived in Reading. He told me that his father had died of cancer a few years ago, after a successful career in banking. He was now the oldest of the Gwynnes. I told him that I was hunting for something in the Gwynne family papers and asked him if there was any chance he might be able to help. "Maybe," he said, sounding suspicious.

"May I ask whether the old papers relating to the estate where your father was brought up are still in the family?"

"Oh yes," he replied. "But I don't have them. When my father died, we split everything up, and my sister was the only one interested in family history and all that sort of stuff. The rest of us were quite happy for her to have them."

"Might I have your permission to contact her and ask her a few questions?"

"It's a free world."

We talked more, and I got the impression that James was not the easiest person in the world to get on with, and that he was not on the best of terms with his sister. It was like getting blood out of a dusty skeleton, but at last I managed to extract her name and her telephone number. Her name was now Mrs Delly Jenkins, and I assumed that her real Christian name was Delilah, incorporated as a family favourite in remembrance of Wilmot's exotic wife. Delly lived -- much to my surprise -- in the village of Puncheston, less than thirty minutes' drive from my home.

So it was that I arrived, by arrangement, on the front doorstep of a pleasant modern bungalow in Puncheston. All that I had told Delly on the phone was that I was investigating certain matters of family history. She turned out to be a very attractive young woman in her late twenties, who appeared capable of maintaining an easy serenity in spite of the fact that three boisterous toddlers were apparently intent upon discovering which of them could shout loudest. Before I had a chance to say a word, she said: "I take it you have come for the manuscript?"

I spluttered, and she laughed. "You look as if you have just seen a ghost!" she said. "You'd better come inside and sit down. The kettle has boiled. I'll make a pot of tea. Don't worry about the children. They are having a noise competition, which is more creative than fighting."

Five minutes later, as we sipped our tea, she continued to amaze me. "We -- by which I mean my family -- have been waiting for you for about a hundred and thirty years. That's five generations. Among the Gwynne family papers there are two handsome bound volumes which contain a manuscript that is gobbledeygook to me and to everybody else who has looked at it. One generation after another has wondered what the volumes are all about, since there is no title page, and the papers are not signed by anybody. All they have known is that they came from somebody called Martha. But I know that this has to be part of the lifetime journal of Mistress Martha Morgan of Plas Ingli. I know because I have read the six books based on her other diaries, and I love them. I wish that I had been Mistress Martha myself -- my God, hers was a life lived to the full, wasn't it?"

"I'm so glad that you have enjoyed the narrative thus far. But can I ask why, if you knew you were in possession of some missing fragments of Martha's story, you didn't get in touch with me? You must have been fully aware of my hunt for other diaries, from all the press coverage and so forth."

Her blue eyes sparkled. "That would have been to break a family code of honour. Here -- I have something to show you." She got up and went to the sideboard, and returned carrying a bulky parcel tied up with ribbon. She opened the parcel to reveal two volumes beautifully bound in red leather. Embossed on the spine of each one were the words: *For my Angels. From Ceridwen.* She then took out an envelope from inside the cover of the first book, and handed it to me without a word. I have to admit that my hands trembled as I took it from her. I opened it and found within two sheets of heavy paper. They were battered and frayed at the edges, for the letter had clearly been read by many people down through the generations. The writing was faded but still legible, and there was a florid signature at the bottom of the page -- that of Wilmot Gwynne. At the top of the page were the words: "To my children, and their children, and however many generations may follow."

I looked up and asked Delly with my eyes whether I should read on. She nodded.

This is what the letter said:

My Dearly Beloved

On this day, the twelfth of May in the year 1869, I have to ask your indulgence and I have to crave your trust. I also enjoin you, as honourable members of an old and worthy family, to show me your love by doing exactly what I ask.

It is ten years to the day since a most wonderful friend left us to be with the angels. Some time before she died, she entrusted to me and my dear wife Delilah for safekeeping a pile of paper with a densely written text upon it, explaining that it constituted a diary written many years since, at a time of life when she was young and very foolish. She appeared to be somewhat ashamed of the contents, and she asked that it should not be examined and translated by others until long after her death. She urged me -- and whichever generations of Gwynnes that might follow -- never to voluntarily give it away, or sell it, or otherwise place it in the public domain. I say to you now that it must be guarded as a matter of family honour. But one day, she said, a man would come to the door in search of it. Then it was to be passed over to him without question and without condition.

It is my wish that the request should be honoured in every detail. It has been my privilege to bind these papers into two stout volumes, as a mark of love and respect for my dear departed friend. So here these volumes are, and here, in the loving arms of my family, they must stay -- until such time as a gentleman calls who has shown sufficient understanding of my dear friend that he will know where to look for her words. He will have shown most admirable persistence in working out that the narrative exists; and he will have shown even greater persistence in tracking it down. In placing it before the world, he will honour the name of my beloved Martha and show to the world that my family truly deserves its reputation for gentility and sensibility.

May God bless you all.

Wilmot Gwynne

When I had finished reading, I was stunned, and I have to admit to a tear in my eye. Wilmot, and his family, had kept the faith. He had appreciated that to pass on the manuscript, or to sell it on the open market, would have constituted a betrayal of Martha's trust. The old man (for he would have been 74 years old when he wrote the letter) always had been desperate to show that a rough industrial diamond like himself could become an honourable -- and honoured -- member of the gentry; now, indeed, the members of his family, down through the generations, had shown that Martha's trust had not been misplaced. And this was in spite of the fact that the family had clearly fallen upon hard times, and now saw itself as solidly embedded in the British middle class. As I mulled over such matters as friendship and trust, Delly picked up the two volumes of the diary and placed them into my hands.

"There!" she said. "Duty discharged. Don't thank me or my family -- but I can see in your face what this means to you."

"But I do have to thank you, from the bottom of my heart. I'm very moved and privileged to be a part of such a contract between honourable people. Now, do you mind if I just check something?"

I opened the first volume at its first page. There was no title page or preamble -- just a diary entry dated 5th October 1808. I looked at the fifth, tenth and fifteenth lines of the text, and found that this was page 616. Then I went to the last page of the second volume. There were digits written into the text on lines five, ten, fifteen and twenty. Page 1268. The diary was complete. I thumbed quickly through some of the pages, and saw that the text was written -- as ever -- in the Dimetian dialect. Then I looked again at the last page, which was a sort of Postscript to the rest of the text, and saw that the name Dominic was mentioned twice. So this was the man called Dominic whose name had been written onto those scraps of paper examined at the National Library. Who was he, and what was the nature of the relationship between him and Martha? Then there was another name -- that of somebody called Morfran. From a quick scan, I saw that his name was mentioned several times in the last few pages of text. Then, on the very last page, there was a dedication in English: *For you, my beloved Morfran. I will always love you.*

Another man? Another lover? I immediately wanted to find out who on earth these men were, and I assumed that the world would share my sense of anticipation. But then I groaned as I recalled that I did not have a translator for the diary. Abraham Jenkins -- my friend, Dimetian-speaking scholar and devoted translator, was dead, and he had been the last person with any command of the language. As far as I knew there was nobody else capable of undertaking the work. I explained this to Delly.

"Don't you worry," she said. "You will find a translator quite easily -- I know it."

When I arrived home bearing the precious volumes my wife immediately picked up on my strange mood -- a mixture of elation and gloom. She also felt confident. "Something will come up," she prophesied. "There is such an interest in old languages these days that you will certainly find somebody out there who will understand Dimetian Welsh and might even be able to speak it. The six published narratives have created a huge amount of interest in academic circles. Ask Catrin if she can help. You must ring her anyway, to tell her about the new discovery."

I did not even have to ask Catrin. As soon as I had told her about the Puncheston diary and the strange contract between the Gwynnes and Mistress Martha, she said: "Fantastic news! And I have a translator for you!"

"What? Abraham was certain that he was the last in the line of

Dimetian Welsh scholars and speakers........"

"So he was. The last scholar, certainly. But there was another old lady, aged 94, who lived in Solva, who knew the dialect. Her name was Nancy Howell. That's interesting in itself, since that was Martha's maiden name, and her family of course came from Brawdy, not a stone's throw from Solva. She was blind, but in the years before her death last year she insisted on having all six of the Angel Mountain narratives read to her. Most of that task -- or pleasure -- fell to her great grand-daughter Delyth. So Delyth also fell in love with the narrative. She was of course brought up with Welsh as her first language. Three years ago she obtained a brilliant first in Celtic Studies at Aberystwyth University, and was offered a grant to work for her doctorate. With my encouragement, and that of her great-grandmother, she decided to extend and improve Meredith Morris's *Glossary of the Dimetian Dialect* and to dig deeply into its origins. As the work proceeded, she talked endlessly with the old lady, and she systematically worked through the Abraham Jenkins translation of *Dark Angel* alongside Martha's Dimetian Welsh original which was held at the National Library. So she can even read Martha's somewhat difficult and heavily slanted handwriting! She now reads and speaks the dialect fluently, and there are even a few others in the Welsh Department at Aberystwyth with whom she can converse. The dialect appears to be all set for a renaissance!"

"Good Lord! That's amazing.........."

"She has just been through her doctoral *viva*. She is now Dr Delyth Howell, Lecturer in Celtic Studies at Jesus College in Oxford University. I can give you her mobile number."

That was all twelve months ago. When I showed Delyth the two volumes, and invited her to do the translation work, she leapt at the chance to renew her acquaintance with Mistress Martha. First of all I worked through the manuscript, just to make sure all the pages were there, in the correct order. I explained to her what the strange numbers on every fifth line meant, and she was greatly impressed when I explained how Edward had cracked the numbering code. She worked efficiently and quickly, fitting her translating time into the spaces in her lecturing and tutorial commitments. She also had the benefit of translating software and modern computing power. That made my task as editor easier too -- compared with the previous nightmares of reading Abraham Jenkins's handwriting, transposing it onto a word processor, and correcting some of his mistakes. In truth, Delyth did much of the editing for me, since trained academics abhor scruffiness on the printed page.

When the task was complete, and the text was ready for publication, we had a small celebration at my house. Edward Billings was there with his wife, as proud as ever over his role in the affair, and the life and soul of the party. Catrin was there with her husband John; and then there was Delyth down for the day from Oxford, Delly Jenkins and her husband and three small children, my publisher and a few people from the book trade, and finally my wife and family. We all had a splendid time, and drank a toast to Mistress Martha and her misdemeanours.

I will say nothing more of the Puncheston diary held in trust by the Gwynne family for all those years. All is revealed in the pages that follow. But there is just one further small matter to report. When we were all chatting over our champagne I could not resist asking Delly how it was that when I knocked on her front door all those months ago, she knew that I had come in search for those two old red leather-bound volumes. She laughed. "I did not have to be a genius to work that out," she said. "During the twenty-four hours that elapsed between your phone call and your arrival on the doorstep a fully-grown raven took up residence in the apple tree at the top of our garden. Occasionally it just sat in the tree, preening its feathers, and occasionally it took off and circled above the house. It never made a sound. I had never seen a raven that close before, and I have not seen it since."

Editor's Note

Martha Morgan is the Mistress of the small and struggling estate of Plas Ingli in North Pembrokeshire, located high on the flanks of the mountain of Carningli and about two miles from Newport. She is already a widow, following the death of her husband David at the hands of four murderous conspirators during the annual *Cnapan* contest on Newport's Traeth Mawr (Big Beach) in the year 1805. She has four children of her own -- Betsi (10 years old), Daisy (7), Dewi (5) and Sara (3). Then there is Brynach, a foundling discovered on the doorstep of Plas Ingli and adopted by Martha in 1807. In that year Martha was engaged to be married to Owain Laugharne, the younger son of the Squire of Pontfaen, but he disappeared in the month of May whilst on a fishing trip out in Newport Bay, and no trace of him has been found since. Martha thinks that Owain's disappearance may have something to do with a mysterious figure called the Nightwalker, who appears infrequently on the mountain and elsewhere in the neighbourhood, and who is believed by Martha to be either a ghost or the Grim Reaper. Martha's friend and mentor, Joseph Harries, disagrees, and considers that the Nightwalker is harmless. He is convinced that Owain's boat was sabotaged, and that his murder was committed at the behest of Squire Price of Llanychaer, one of Martha's enemies. For more than a year after Owain's disappearance Martha has held to the hope that he is still alive, but now she has to be realistic, and has to get on with her life. She has a responsibility to manage the estate, to look after the household and her servants and labourers, and to provide for her young family........

1. Brief Encounter

5th October 1808

We are into October, a month sometimes wild and wet and sometimes blessed with autumnal sunshine and peace. This year, so I am assured by Grandpa Isaac, the signs are that we will have calm and sunny weather and that the leaves will stay on the trees until Hallowe'en is come and gone. As I look out across the gentle acres of the bottom meadow, the daylight is fading fast, and here and there I can see the specks of light from moving lanterns as the people of the *cwm* shut up their animals and check that all is well before the foxes and the owls begin their nocturnal predations. The smoke from the cottages and farms is settling in a thin veil across the landscape. That means we will have frost before midnight. No matter. This evening my spirit is glowing like a golden sunset, and I feel free as a birch leaf dancing in the eddies of an autumn bonfire.

It has been a joyful, wonderful day. In spite of my continuing uncertainty about the fate of my beloved Owain, and my consequent erratic moods, I decided some weeks ago that the three older children and I needed a treat. At the age of 30, widowed and with no new man at my side, I was beginning to feel like an old maid. I wrote to my brother Morys in Haverfordwest to say that he should expect us for Portfield Fair, and I promised Betsi, Daisy and Dewi that we should have a thrilling day out. We were up well before dawn, and I had to deal with a furious Sara, who was not at all amused at the prospect of being left behind with her great-grandparents and baby brother. While she embarked upon a considerable tantrum, the rest of us ate an early breakfast, and Mrs Owen made us a picnic of cooked meats and hard cheese, crusty bread straight from yesterday's oven, fresh butter, spicy pickles, apples and spring water. We packed everything into a wicker basket. Then I managed to settle Sara and little Brynach down with Grandma Jane, and we were off at seven o'clock in the best trap with Freckle-face between the shafts.

Soon we were making our jovial way across the mountain. I enjoyed driving the trap, and thought that I must do it more often. The sun was climbing above Foel Drygarn now, and poor Freckle-face was sweating as he dragged us from the inn at Tafarn Bwlch up to the the summit at Bwlch Gwynt. Then we were on the other side and on the way down, with the smoky early-morning haze of Haverfordwest visible on the far horizon. The children were in high spirits, since they had never been to a big fair before, and there was wild speculation as to what fantastical things they might find there.

"Have you all got your pennies safe and sound" I asked.

"Yes, Mam!" came the chorus in reply.

"Don't call me Mam," I scolded. "You must remember your station in life. Only common children call their mothers Mam. You must call me Mother, and show me the respect I deserve."

"Yes, Mam."

"So what are you going to do with your money?" I inquired, thinking it best to change the subject.

"Buy one of those huge gob-stoppers made of peppermint and sugar," cried Daisy. "Jenny Plain Dealings had one last year at the fair. She showed it to me when she came home, and it was **amazing**."

"Huh!" said Betsi, wise in the ways of the world. "And when she stuck it in her gob it almost killed her. Willy told me her dad had to take her by the ankles and swing her round his head for ten minutes before it popped out, and then she was sick all over the scullery floor."

"That story might be slightly exaggerated," I advised. "But in any case Doctor Havard tells me that peppermint and sugar rots away your teeth, and that you'd be better off sticking to nice green apples if you are hungry."

The children moaned and groaned and writhed about on the floor of the trap in mock agony. Betsi, as the oldest, appointed herself as their official representative and said: "Mam, we've been eating horrible green apples from the orchard for weeks and weeks. Fed up with them, we are! The little red ones from the top tree aren't too bad, but as for me, I'm giving up apples as from now." The little ones cheered and giggled, and then Dewi piped up.

"When I get to the fair I'm defn'ly going to buy a girl-friend," he announced, having reckoned that at the age of five he was now ready for anything. "The other day I heard Billy Bollocks talking to Hettie Half-pint in the dairy, and he said he'd had Moll Liberal Affections for tuppence at Fishguard Fair, and thought that was very good value. Mam, why are you going all red in the face?"

I must admit to not being a very good parent, for I burst out in a fit of giggles that did not subside for several hundred yards, and the children had to stop the pony near Waunfach and give me a sedative drink of water from the picnic basket. Freckle-face munched some fresh grass from the hedge bank for a minute or two, and while we were there Shoni Transportation went past with his four-horse wagon from Newport, full to overflowing with friends and neighbours on their way to the fair. They stopped to ask if we needed help, and then went on their way, shouting and laughing and waving their scarves and neckerchiefs.

When I had composed myself and got the expedition back onto the road I gave Dewi a good scolding. "Dewi," I said in my best motherly voice, "you must never, never refer to Billy Ifans as Billy Bollocks. That is extremely rude, and you should leave rude language to rude people."

"But Mam," complained Dewi, "everybody calls him Billy Bollocks, and nobody will know who I'm talking about if I call him Billy Ifans."

"Well, it's best, in that case, if you don't talk about him at all. You can take it from me that the sort of girl-friend you can buy for tuppence is not worth buying, and in any case you've only got a penny."

Dewi and the two girls thought about this long and hard as we trotted on past Tafarn Newydd, up towards Tufton and then down through the foothills of Mynydd Preseli towards Ambleston. Soon we were over the invisible line that separates the Welsh from the English, and I pointed out to the children how the landscape was getting gentler and the trees taller and fuller. Some of them were still thick with russet and ochre leaves which had been turned and painted by a few nights of late September frost.

Suddenly Dewi said: "If I can't buy a girl-friend I'm going to spend my farthing seeing the Man from Borneo with Three Heads." There were hoots of derision from Betsi, but Daisy shouted "Yes, yes! I'll come too!" Seeing that he had an ally, Dewi persisted. "Davy Jenkins Brithdir went to visit him last year, very cheap, and he says he's a very simple sort of person who doesn't speak Welsh."

"Well, he wouldn't, would he, if he comes from Borneo?" asked Betsi, not expecting an answer.

"Davy says he lives in a cage because he is very hairy and dangerous, and he lives on black pudding, and his name is Boolaboola, and he has a sign round his neck saying that he and his tribe have three heads so that they can see all the panthers and crocodiles and elephants and dragons and pythons that are prowling about on all sides in the jungle trying to eat them up."

"I think that if he's got three heads he's not very primitive at all," mused Daisy, "since three heads is better than one, and he must be three times more clever than ordinary people."

"Huh!" said Betsy, acting the big sister and trying to protect the little ones from the stuff and nonsense that might have come from Davy Brithdir. "Forget about the three heads. I bet he's only got one, and that's the one in the middle. The other two are probably made of bits of paper and hair and marbles and things, and stuck on with glue."

"No, no. Davy says the three heads are definitely real."

"I bet when he makes his roaring noises, and speaks in Borneo language, the noise only comes from the mouth in the middle. That's how you can tell if the heads are real or not."

"Well then, we'll all go and see," cried Daisy. "Davy and his mam and dad are going to the fair today, and if we see them we'll all go and see the Man with Three Heads together. And if you are right and Davy is wrong, he'll have to give you a kiss at Michaelmas."

Dewi, who had been sitting silent for a while, somewhat overwhelmed with all this scientific talk, suddenly perked up and said, with a flash of God-given inspiration: "If he really has three mouths and speaks with three voices, he can probably sing like a sort of male-voice choir all on his own!"

At this the girls screamed and giggled, and I was myself much taken with the thought of the Wild Man of Borneo giving a close-harmony rendition of *Love Divine*. After that, it was downhill all the way. Betsi said: "What if the voice in the middle is a gentleman's voice, and the other two are lady's voices?" "Don't be silly," said Daisy. "He can't be a woman and a man at the same time, for all his private parts would be mixed up." And Dewi added: "He could come and perform for us like the three gentlemen who came and sang boring songs at Grandpa's birthday party! But it would be just him, so probably Grandpa wouldn't have to pay so much."

Then we all remembered at the same moment that dear old Mr Collins, the oldest of the trio, had farted loudly every time he almost hit his top C, and the thought of the three-headed Wild Man of Borneo singing in harmony and farting in the drawing room at Plas Ingli was too much for all of us. The giggles degenerated into total hysterics, and my memories of the last part of our journey into Haverfordwest are vague to say the least. I recall some very frightened pedestrians who retreated into the hedge as we passed through Crundale. I have a picture in my mind of Mr and Mrs Tomos Fachongle Uchaf going past in their trap, he smiling cheerfully and she looking as if the Devil had just broken his chains. She said nothing, but her face said it was disgraceful the way those people from Plas Ingli behaved, making fools of themselves so early in the day when most honest people still haven't cleared up after the morning milking. And I have some recollections of the good folks of Prendergast giving us some strange looks as we passed them, staring up from their sun-lit doorstep-washing operations and no doubt commenting to each other on the strange and disreputable mountain people attracted nowadays to the fair. No doubt it was not like this in the old days. I was nominally in charge of our vehicle, but as we proceeded in a haze of tears and gales of laughter and acheing ribs, it was dear old Freckle-face who guided us serenely to our destination. To his eternal credit, he kept his dignity throughout this shameful episode, and he delivered us on schedule to my brother's house at the top end of town. As we arrived, I recovered my composure and said: "Oh my God, you children will be the death of me!" And I loved them from the depths of my soul, and gave them each an extra tuppence to spend at Portfield Fair.

Morys and Nansi and their three children (Edward, Jane and Robert) welcomed us with open arms, while their man took Freckle-face and his trap round to the back with a promise that he would be wiped down, watered and fed. Then we went indoors for a wash and a refreshing drink of blackberry cordial. The journey had taken us three hours, and we should have been tired, but we were all in a state of high excitement, and the six children could not sit still whilst we adults were making polite conversation. Edward and Jane had permission from their parents to join us at the fair, but little Robert was deemed to be too small for all the noise and bustle. So, although it was still only mid-morning, I said to Morys and Nansi: "We'd best get up to the fair before these children explode. We'll go and have fun, and see you when we get back." So off we went, up through the gay streets of the town, joining a merry throng of farmers and servants, farm-hands and merchants, street urchins and families from the country, all intent on a day of fun before the unremitting darkness and drudgery of winter set in.

Up at the top of Portfield, on the wide green area they call The Racecourse, the fair was in full swing, having no doubt started at dawn. At the town end of the fair there were market traders selling fruit and vegetables, salt butter and lard, pickles and preserves, smoked hams and barrels of herring, Lawrenny oysters and Llangwm cockles, barley bread and oatmeal flour. Somebody was baking wheat bread in a portable charcoal oven, and the fresh crusty loaves smelt like heaven. The spinners and weavers from Narberth were there, and a man selling packets and sacks from Prendergast Paper Mill, and someone else from Llanelli selling tin boxes, and a fat lady selling silks and velvets off the roll and ribbons by the yard, and so much else that we could not take it all in. There were dancing bears and pathetic little chained monkeys doing tricks and begging for coins, waving upturned felt hats in front of the people who passed within striking range and chattering angrily at them if they failed to respond. Ale and cider were in plentiful supply, and some of the young men in from the farms were looking tipsy already. The air was fragrant with the scents of charcoal smoke, baked potatoes, Irish stew and Welsh cawl, spilt beer and smuggled rum. There were jugglers and stilt-walkers, fiddlers and drummers, and a group of gypsies danced provocatively around a pompous young man with a smooth chin who stood on a wooden box and thundered on about the need for salvation. Most of the people at the fair were speaking English (this being the language of South Pembrokeshire), but there were many who chatted in Welsh and Irish too, bartering and trading in whatever language suited them best. There were swings and slides for the children, and clowns and puppeteers competed for the attention of those who looked as if they might have a few spare coppers.

As we walked through to the top end of the Racecourse we came to the place where servants are hired, some of them mere children, fresh-faced and keen to make their own ways in the world, and others who had been here, and changed masters and mistresses, many times before. The old hands were seeking new employment either because they were dissatisfied with their lot, or wished for a change of location, or sought advancement or a change of trade. There were great crowds of them, male and female, chatting and laughing. No doubt they were passing on all of the latest gossip about the goings-on in the farms and mansions of the county, and advising one another about those locations to be greatly desired, and those to be avoided like the Black Death. Each of the servants for hire carried the sign of his or her trade. Cooks carried big wooden spoons, which came in handy as weapons in case of unwelcome advances from inebriated and amorous young men. Men who worked with horses carried whips, and hedgers bore gleaming metal bill-hooks. Gardeners carried spades, cowmen carried bright tin pails, and roofers carried long-handled slate cutters. Thatchers had bundles of straw or reeds thrown over their shoulders. Blacksmiths wore horseshoes in their hats, and masons carried trowels and hammers. Shepherds showed off their long crooks topped off with elaborately carved horn. Weavers carried hanks of dyed wool, and tailors sported large pairs of scissors which would have put the fear of God into Napoleon's army.

And wandering through the throng there were the squires and gentlemen, dressed to impress, and the agents and stewards from the larger estates who were old hands at sorting out the wastrels from the workers. They examined posture and assessed strength, and looked at hands as a horse dealer might examine hooves. They also had an eye for the prettiest girls who might enhance the beauty of the kitchen or the bedroom. The stewards employed by the big families were all there -- the Philippses, Bowens, Lloyds and Owens. I recognized them, and there was much curtseying on my part and bowing and doffing of hats on theirs.

Brief Encounter

Although it was still before eleven o'clock in the morning, there were already many young people in high spirits, clasping their silver shillings given to them as pledges by their new employers. With the business of selling their services out of the way, they formed into little groups of friends, with the gaggles of girls wandering round the fair in a clockwise direction and the swaggering boys anticlockwise. There was much flirting, cheerful banter and horseplay when these groups passed each other, for these encounters were the precursors of more serious attempts to find boy-friends or girl-friends later in the day. Some of the stalls selling china fairings and other little gifts were doing brisk business, as young men purchased tokens of their affection which were formally presented to their favoured young ladies, usually through intermediaries. For their part, the girls competed with one another to accumulate the greatest number of fairings -- and their role in this elaborate pre-courtship ritual was far from passive, for one of their favourite sports was to try to grab a spray of artificial flowers from the lapel of any young man that took their fancy. I knew (for I had done all of this myself, at St David's Fair when I was young and innocent) that by late afternoon there would be a deal of fetching and chasing and pairing off, not to mention drinking and kissing and fondling, and I thought it just as well that by then the children and I would be well away from it all.

We came to the livestock area, with noisy, restless, stinking multitudes of horses and cattle, sheep, pigs and goats, chickens and geese, all freshly arrived in town from all points of the compass. The smaller animals were in pens, but most of the others were tethered or simply controlled by eager sheepdogs and corgis. Serious business was being done here, by men wearing big boots and muddy gaiters, and with frowns on their weatherbeaten faces. Whether buying or selling, they knew their animals. They talked about new breeds, blood-lines and animal ailments, fatstock prices and the relative abundance of oats and hay. Haunches, teeth and hooves were inspected, flanks were smoothed and patted, hands were shaken and silver coins passed from purse to purse.

Then we bumped into little Davy Brithdir, and his sister and his mam and dad, and we were given the essential information that the Wild Man of Borneo was in a red and white striped tent near the back of the

Horse and Jockey Inn. So it was that a few minutes later I found myself sitting in the sun beside the tent, having seen the five children off safely into its darkened interior. The grassy verge was soft, the midday sun was warm on my face, and I felt happy and drowsy. I munched on a sweet apple, put our picnic basket down beside me, and leaned back against the side wall of the inn. I might have nodded off for a moment or two or three, but when I opened my eyes I became aware at once that I was being watched. For a flickering instant my eyes met those of a fresh-faced young man, who was standing perhaps twenty feet away. I let my eyes drop, as was proper in the circumstances, but noticed anyway that he was of medium height, tidily but simply dressed in a grey flannel shirt and tweed waistcoat, with brown corduroy breeches held up by a leather belt with a brass buckle. His boots were well blacked and polished. He held in his hands a well-worn and shiny felt hat. I thought that he was about my age, or perhaps a little younger.

I became aware that he was walking towards me. "There are few things in the world more beautiful than the sight of a pretty lady asleep," he said. "I'm sorry if I sound familiar, but I was much taken with your black hair, for most of the people in these parts are fair-haired, and I wondered what colour your eyes might be."

"Young man!" I remonstrated. "You are being very familiar with me, for I have no chaperone and I don't believe that we have been introduced." At once I bit my lip, for I liked the look of him, and I must have sounded like a brittle old spinster chiding an unruly child. So I added: "I thank you for your compliment, but before you say anything more, I think I have every right to know what your name is, and where you come from."

His hands had tightened around his poor crumpled hat at the sound of hostility in my voice, but now he relaxed and pushed the hat into the deep pocket of his breeches. "I'm sorry if I upset you," he said. "My old mother said to me the day I left home that I would need to learn some manners if I was to get on in the world, but I'm not a very fast learner. My name is Dominic Cunningham. I have been living at Wiston Manor for a little while, but I have just hired myself to Mr Skyrme at Wiston Mill and I'll be starting there immediately. Ten sovereigns a year, a little hut of my own, and all food found."

"I'm pleased to meet you. I am Martha Morgan, and I'm just here for the day, waiting for my brother who is doing some business about horses up at the top end of the fair." God forgive me, but lies are necessary on certain occasions.

Dominic fixed me with his eyes again, which had the colour and sparkle of cut emerald. "Dark, very dark," he said, no doubt referring to my eyes. "In fact, as dark as polished oak. And fancy that, I'd guessed they were the colour of hazel nut shells."

He laughed, and I laughed, and for a few minutes we talked about the fair, and the weather, and the terrible price of flour following a miserable summer. He reckoned that flour shortages would be good for trade at the mill, and that his master would soon be a wealthy man. In turn, this would be good for him in his efforts to make his way in the world of commerce. As he spoke I noticed that his skin was fair and freckled, and that his voice had a touch of Irish in it. Then he said: "May I sit on the grass beside you?"and I said: "It is probably public grass," so he sat down. He looked at me intently and said: "You've been crying, haven't you? You are all red around the eyes."

"No, I haven't," I replied. "As a matter of fact I've been laughing a great deal this morning at something too complicated to explain, so the tears have been tears of happiness. And I still have a stomach-ache and battered ribs from all the hilarity."

"Thank the Lord for somebody with a sense of humour," he said. "Since the Revival came to the village my friends say that everybody's been going round talking about sin and repentence and salvation, and I can't stand it any longer, which is why I decided it was time for a move to somewhere out in the country." And without stopping for breath he asked "Where are you from, then? You forgot to tell me just now. You look as if you might be from outside town, although your dress and bonnet are very well made, if I may make so bold."

I had to smile at his effrontery. "I'm not from this area," I said. "I have a small estate near Newport, on the other side of the mountain."

"And your husband?"

"His name was David. I'm afraid he died three years since..........."

"Oh dear. I am very sorry to hear that. He must have been a very happy man, to have had such a beautiful lady for a wife."

"You are very kind. Nowadays I manage the estate alone, with the help of my late husband's grandparents, as best I can. And I must not complain. Life is truly very good to me, and I have five beautiful children."

"Good, good," said Dominic.

There was an awkward silence, and then he realized that I had no particular wish to be miserable, or to talk about the past. He continued: "So you live up among the mountain men! I hear there are some seriously rough people up there who don't even speak English."

"Not as rough as you might think," I countered, rising to the bait. "In fact, I live in the most beautiful place on earth, and most of my friends can speak two languages. I'll wager sixpence to a kiss that that's one more than you can speak."

I had no time to regret the hastiness of my wager, for Dominic bellowed with laughter and shouted: "Hooray! I win! I come from County Wicklow, and I have spoken Irish ever since I was knee-high to a leprechaun."

He fixed his green eyes upon me and launched out upon some romantic verse in his mother tongue, just to prove that he was telling the truth. He spoke in a charming soft lilt, and I was pondering on the fact that I recognized some of the words he used when the verse suddenly came to an end.

Then he said, very softly: "I claim my prize!" And with that he tipped up my chin with the back of his hand and planted his lips upon mine. The kiss seemed to go on for an eternity, but I didn't have the heart to object, since he had won his wager fair and square. His lips were soft and tasted of sweet cider. Instinctively I closed my eyes and opened my lips, and then to my amazement I found his tongue inside my mouth, playing little games with my emotions. This fellow called Dominic seemed to have a special technique that didn't require breathing either, and at last I was forced to come up for air. I struggled with as little enthusiasm as decorum would allow, kicking my feet in the air, and I yelled at the bottom of my voice: "Help! Help! I'm being attacked!"

It came out as a strangled whisper, and Dominic whispered back: "Oh no you're not. You are being given a little loving kindness, which is only right and proper for a young lady with jet-black hair and gypsy eyes and lips like gentle thistledown."

And all of this in broad daylight, in a public place! In fact a little crowd of people had stopped to watch the entertainment, and they now burst into laughter and spontaneous applause. One who didn't was Mrs Dilys Tomos Fachongle, the wife of one of the Caersalem deacons, who stood a little way off with a countenance like the darkness of a winter ice house. Dominic shouted: "Clear off!" to the audience with a grin as wide as a six-barred gate on his face, and I realized that the time had come to draw this encounter to a close. I was terrified that the children might come out of the tent at any moment, following their detailed study of the Wild Man of Borneo.

"I think it's best if you go now," I said quietly to Dominic. "My brother will be here any minute to collect me, and in any case it's not seemly for me, a young widow, to be sitting here on the grass with a total stranger at my side."

"Quite right you are," he replied. "I hope I haven't embarrassed you or harmed your reputation. I have some things to buy before I walk back to Wiston. I'll be off then." And with that he gave a funny little bow, pulled out his crumpled felt hat from his pocket and put it on his head, and disappeared into the crowd.

The whole episode had taken maybe ten minutes, but it felt to me that a century's worth of revolutions and military campaigns had marched through my emotional defences, and I leaned back against the wall and closed my eyes again as I tried to compose myself. Then the heathen hordes came roaring out of the red and white tent, and they were all over me with ever more outrageous tales of the eating habits, anatomy, language and lifestyle of their three-headed friend within.

I remember very little of what happened as the afternoon went on. We ate our picnic on the grass, spent all our money on entertainments and sweetmeats and items from my shopping list, and returned to Morys and Nansi for a quick chat before we headed north over the mountain. The little ones were already exhausted, and Dewi and Jane could hardly keep their eyes open. I was keen that we should get home before it was too dark, so at four o'clock we packed ourselves and our purchases into the trap, said our fond farewells, and I took the reins and pointed Freckle-face towards Prendergast and the road north. Little Dewi cuddled up to Betsi, and Daisy found a space between a roll of flannel and a brown paper parcel full of dried fruits. Before we had travelled half a mile all three of them were fast asleep. I stopped for a moment to cover them with blankets, then we trotted northwards as the shadows spread and the chill of the evening began to settle.

They slept like angels all the way home, and we arrived just as the lights of Cilgwyn were beginning to twinkle down in the *cwm*. I am ashamed to admit that for most of the journey I thought of this interesting young fellow called Dominic, and that some of my thoughts were anything but pure.

7th October 1808

In spite of the priorities that I have to deal with, on a daily basis, as a mother and owner of a good little estate, for the last couple of days I have tried to reassess my priorities; and in that process I have found it almost impossible to concentrate on mundane things. In short, I cannot get Dominic out of my head. That is quite absurd, since I have only met the fellow, in the most bizarre of circumstances, for ten minutes; and yet I feel like a fourteen-year-old girl who has tumbled into mad passionate love with the big boy next door. Why? Simply because I have been kissed again, for the first time in eighteen months? Is kissing that important to all women, or is this something that is unique to me? Probably, like a little girl, I will realize that my silly obsession is not love at all, and I will tumble out of it just as quickly as I tumbled into it. And to make matters more complicated, I feel guilty too, since I am still betrothed to Owain, my gentle and courageous hero and poet, who went out onto a calm sea in May last year and never returned. Is he alive or dead? If only I knew one way or the other! When he had been missing for twelve months, I resolved to accept the fact of his death, and vowed to move on. Does that mean living without a good man at my side and in my bed, or should I accept my needs as normal and acceptable in a society such as ours, and find a new partner? I know full well that there are good men -- some of them very desirable indeed -- seeking introductions and arranging chance encounters, and I have received hints from my family and friends that maybe the time is now right for a new master to move into the Plas and to provide the father that the children need.

I have to admit, as well, that while I enjoy managing the estate and dealing with tenants and servants, I am involved in something that is truly a man's work, and I sometimes think that I lack the application and the discipline to continue with it month after month, year after year. My mind strays too often to children and domestic matters, and sometimes, when I am discussing ploughing and planting schedules with Billy or arguing the merits of buying a new ram with Will, I wish that I could simply sit in the sun with a sampler on my knee, surrounded by happy children. But now I am being petty. Life is truly not that unkind to me, and if I am honest with myself I am very happy with my lot. I am privileged to live in a house high on a sacred mountain and inhabited by angels. The angels have their little quirks and weaknesses, but they are nonetheless angelic.

I am also privileged -- unlike most of the mistresses of the surrounding estates -- to be both protector and employer. I do my best to let that responsibility lie lightly on my shoulders, but it is not always easy. Just now there are fourteen human beings beneath the roof of the Plas, eight of us upstairs and six servants downstairs -- in a house that is not as large as many of the other gentry houses and mansions of North Pembrokeshire. Somehow or other, we all get on, even if none of us has the privacy that we might desire. We find private space for ourselves when and where we can. Grandpa takes his favourite dog and goes for long walks in the woods, claiming that he does not like the mountain. Grandma loses herself in the music of her harp, and many are the times on which I have seen her in a private reverie, with her fingers gliding and rippling over the strings, quite oblivious to the small children causing mayhem around her. My shepherd Will finds his peace on the mountain with a starry sky for his ceiling, and at tupping time, and in the lambing season, he may be on the rocky slopes almost continuously for days at a time, returning to the Plas only occasionally to be scolded by his mother for not eating enough, and to be given vast nourishing meals quite out of phase with the rest of us. As for me, Carningli is my temple, and that is where I go to commune with the ravens and the spirits of the mountain when occasion demands. And when I really crave peace and solitude, there is my cave, known only to me, accessible only by a tortuous scramble among crags which are not even reached by the mountain sheep.

What would life be like if I had a husband who could take over many of the tasks that currently fall into my lap? Easier, certainly. But if I am honest, I have to say that it would be less interesting and probably less convivial. For a start, I would miss the regular business contacts with our tenants. Assorted commercial transactions occur weekly, monthly and annually according to ancient tradition. In lieu of cash, my tenants pay parts of their rent in eggs, plucked chickens, ducks and geese, hams, cheese and other surplus produce at times specified in their agreements. Just a fortnight since, I greatly enjoyed making a new agreement with Gethin Griffiths of Dolrannog Isaf to replace a part of his rent previously paid in ploughing time with sacks of black wool, on the basis that I want black wool and he has more than enough of it. Anyway, he is not a very good ploughman. The stewards of the large estates of England (who measure wealth only in terms of acres, pounds, shillings and pence) would probably be appalled by such arrangements, but they suit us remarkably well, since we live in an area where there is little cash in circulation, and the frequent traffic between tenants and landlord (namely me) tends to maintain a tight bond of friendship and mutual dependence. In fact, I doubt that I gain very much from all of these prescribed visits from the Dolrannog Isaf, Dolrannog Uchaf, Penrhiw, Brithdir and Gelli tenants, for whenever they call with their "payments" they stop a while and seldom depart until my working day has been disrupted, and until many mugs of tea and slices of *bara brith* have been consumed.

Now it is late. I must stop reminiscing and speculating, and put down my quill pen. I shall blow out my candle and gaze for a while over the silver-washed *cwm* which is lit by a waning moon. I shall count the stars, to make sure that they are all present and correct. Then I shall go to bed content, and hope for sweet dreams of handsome men and close encounters.

8th October 1808

"I hear that you kissed a fellow at Portfield Fair," said Bessie nonchalantly, as she combed my hair.

"So? What if I did?" I replied sharply, observing from the image in the mirror that my cheeks were on fire.

"And in full view of Mrs Tomos Fachongle and a thousand others. She says you apparently enjoyed it."

"Bessie! How dare you? It is none of Mrs Tomos's business, and none of yours either!"

In that infuriating way of hers, Bessie continued to comb my hair for what seemed like an age, without further comment. Then she said: "I just thought you might like to know, Mistress, that the word is all around the town, and the *cwm* as well."

With my cheeks still blazing, I replied: "Well, so be it. Let idle people gossip, if they have nothing better to do. And if the thought of me kissing a stranger in public sends them into paroxysms of righteous anger, I can only feel sorry for them."

"So you don't deny it, Mistress?"

"Why should I? The kiss was the price I had to pay for a foolish and harmless wager. I bet an Irish fellow who was wandering around that he could only speak one language, and it turned out that he was fluent in two. That's all there was to it."

Bessie gave the slightest of smiles, which I observed in the mirror, and carried on with the combing. "Was it a good kiss?" she asked.

"As it happens, it was. He tasted of sweet cider. But then I sent him packing, and I shall probably never see him again."

Bessie tried to contain herself, but then our eyes met in the mirror, and the pair of us collapsed into hysterical giggles, like silly little girls. That was the end of the combing, and we had to embrace in order to stop ourselves from falling over. We made so much noise that Betsi was woken up in her room next door, and came in carrying her favourite doll and rubbing her eyes. "Mam!" she scolded. "You woke me up, and it's still far too early. Why are you making all this noise?"

I recovered my composure, and took her in my arms. "Just a little joke between us, *cariad*. Bessie and I sometimes laugh about the silliest things, just as you and Daisy do. Come now -- let's get you dressed, and you can tiptoe downstairs and have breakfast with us before your brothers and sisters are awake. They will probably be very jealous......"

Later on, with breakfast over and done with, and with Sian embarked upon morning lessons with the children, Bessie found me in my room and returned to the subject of the kiss. "What is done is done, Mistress," she said. "But perhaps it would have been wiser not to have made that silly wager in the first place with this Irishman. The Irish always win their wagers. And if I may say so, it might be as well to remember what happened before and after your betrothal to Owain."

I bristled at that. "Nothing happened, Bessie, that might have given cause for tongues to wag."

"I will accept that, Mistress," she replied, with her voice perfectly calm. "But people hereabouts are very strict about chaperones and such like, and they also have vivid imaginations. Don't you remember the gossip when you rode out with Owain at the Beating of the Bounds a couple of years since, and don't you remember how he was accused of coveting the Plas Ingli estate just because the two of you had been seen together, and obviously in love?"

"Yes, Bessie, I remember all too well. But what are you suggesting? That I am a fickle and flirtatious widow, ready to jump into bed with any gentleman that might take my fancy?"

"Of course not, Mistress," she said. "It's not what I see or suggest that matters. What matters is your reputation, and that of the Plas. We all love you too much to allow you to be diminished in the estimation of your peers. As Grandma Jane has said over and again, you must ensure that you maintain your value as a widow and a future wife. Wagging tongues do not matter if you, like me, have nothing to start with. But you have a fine estate and a tidy fortune, and loose talk can and will damage you. It will not take much, Mistress, for those suitors who might now be setting their sights upon you to lose interest and look the other way."

"Huh!" I exclaimed. "If they are so sensitive and so fickle, good riddance to them. Those whom I respect know that I have been a model wife and mother, and indeed an exemplary widow as well."

"Not everybody shares that view, Mistress. Remember that only nine months after David's death you were out of your widow's weeds and trembling with excitement at the mere mention of Owain's name."

"Please, Bessie! Now you are becoming insufferable! Can you, or I, predict when love will come and how we will react? Let those who are obsessed with ancient traditions and etiquette freeze in a miserable winter of their own making! As for me, I hope to go to my grave with the words "A life well lived" inscribed upon my headstone!"

Bessie did not pursue the matter any further, but I have to say that tonight, when I blow out my candle, I will place my head upon my pillow in a state of some irritation.

9th October 1808

I have had a thoroughly miserable day, caught up in my own imaginings while the rest of the world has, by all accounts, gone on as usual.

Last night I took an age to go to sleep, with Bessie's cruel words going round and round inside my head. Then, when the eastern sky was already beginning to presage the arrival of the sun, I fell into a fitful sleep, and I wish in retrospect that I had stayed awake. My nightmare was a dreadful one, in which I was a lost soul wandering through a fearsome desert in which there was no water, no shade and nothing green. The sand was red and the sky was made of flames, and the sun was the colour of blood. As I roamed and stumbled about, the heat was so terrible that I had to cast off my clothes one by one, until I was as naked as a newborn babe. Then the heat became even worse, and my skin began to burn and blister. Suddenly there was a respite as a huge shadow came and shielded me from the sun. I looked up and saw that the shadow was cast by a magnificent angel with spreading wings, gliding through the air towards me. Blessed relief! I waited for him to descend to earth beside me, and I though that he was the handsomest man I had ever seen. Then he came closer, and I saw that he was not an angel, or even a man, but a demon, with red eyes and pointed ears, and goat's horns on his head. He landed beside me, a towering figure with outspread wings. I cowered in his presence, not knowing what might happen next. "I am Lucifer,"he said. "And you are mine!" He moved towards me, but before he could reach me I became aware of other shadows falling onto the burning sand of the red desert. I looked up, and the air was suddenly full of angels, circling like vultures, gliding round and round in a vortex. They started to descend, and I thought for a moment that they had come to rescue me. My spirits were lifted. Then I saw that they were, like Lucifer, not angels but devils, and I was gripped again by terror. As they came closer I could see their faces, illuminated in a brilliant red light. They all had red eyes, and I could see their horns and their fangs. Then the noise started, softly at first but rising in a crescendo, until I could hear each one of them shouting and screaming "No Lucifer! She is mine! She is mine!" The noise became louder and louder and at last the air was filled with mighty wingbeats just over my head. They fell upon me, and everything turned from red to black, black, black, as I realized I was not in a desert at all, but in the deepest part of Hell.

Then I woke with a start, perspiring profusely, with my heart beating wildly, to find that I had kicked all my blankets onto the floor, and that the world was perfectly still, and that the sun was flickering on the far eastern horizon.

For an age I lay there, almost frightened out of my wits. But at last I calmed down, and then Bessie tapped on the door and came in with the kindling for my bedroom fire. "Good morning, Mistress!" she said, as bright as a skylark. "The sun is up, and it's going to be a lovely day. Did you sleep well?"

2. Matters of No Consequence

10th October 1808

Today was one of Hettie's milking days, and when she had finished in the dairy she sat down with us for breakfast. "Small news from town, Mistress," she announced to all and sundry. "An Irishman has been seen in town several times in the last few days."

"That is extremely small news, Hettie," said I, rather too quickly. "Irishmen are seen in town all the time. Probably he is a ploughman, looking for work on the autumn ploughing."

"No no, Mistress! He was far too well dressed for that. I saw him myself. Rather handsome, he was. Asking questions, too."

"Oh indeed?" asked Grandma, all innocence. "And what was he asking questions about?"

"They do say he was enquiring after Mistress Martha and the Plas."

They all looked at me, and in trying not to blush I must have made a very funny face, for they all burst out laughing. I had to laugh as well, for it was obvious that they had all heard about the kiss at Portfield Fair. Bessie rescued me from any further difficulties by diverting the conversation onto the prices of cheese and butter, and the rest of the meal passed off uneventfully.

Later on, after lunch and with time to myself, I pondered on my own reaction to Hettie's news, and I decided that the fluttering in my heart was down to more than just embarrassment. That made me both thrilled and concerned, as I recalled Bessie's recent admonishment and tried to take some message from the fearsome dream of the night before last. I felt claustrophobic and needed time on my own, and so I informed the servants that I would take a walk on the mountain. I put on my sturdy walking boots, and wrapped up well against the chill wind, and off I went. I had to go to my cave. I followed the water pipe up to the little spring that we call Ffynnon Brynach, and there I anointed myself. I do that every time I go up onto the mountain, and I have almost forgotten the reason for my ritual -- maybe I need to be blessed by holy water, or maybe my gesture is a mark of respect for the spring, and for the mountain, and for the tradition that old St Brynach used to climb up onto the summit to commune with the angels.

Having caught my breath and gazed down for a minute or two into the sunlit *cwm*, I gathered up my skirts and continued upwards from the slopes of bracken and gorse and into the area where bilberry and heather hold sway. Then I was in amongst the boulders and the rubble of the mountaintop, with the summit in sight not far above me. Onwards and upwards I climbed, until I was surrounded by great slabs of old blue stone and steeply sloping rock faces. I looked for the crevice that led me to a narrow ledge between rock pillars, too tight for a sheep and too well disguised for most of the human beings who climbed the mountain to notice. Precariously, I inched my way along it, dreading, as on every previous visit, that I might lose my footing and go tumbling down into the depths, never to be seen again. But at last, with my heart beating furiously, I came to the narrow slit in the rock, hidden beneath two mighty boulders and behind a little rowan tree and a cluster of ferns. Then I was inside, in the warm twilight of my sanctuary. Once my eyes had adjusted, I could make out my little bed of moss at the inner end of the cave, faintly illuminated by the sunlight filtering in through a number of cracks in the roof and along the southern wall. My sheepskin was still there, and everything was exactly as I had left it on my last visit.

St Brynach had used this cave, and now it was mine. As I settled down on the sheepskin, with my back against the wall and my knees drawn up under my chin, I tried to ask St Brynach, and the angels of the mountain, what I should do about Owain and this fellow Dominic. I do not know how long I remained there, lost in contemplation, but at last I noticed that the little streaks of sunlight projected onto the floor of the cave were no longer there. I deduced that it was late afternoon, and that I had better get back to the Plas before my absence caused concern. I still did not know whether to follow my heart or my head. My head told me that Owain was dead, and that it was quite in order for me to be open to the possibility of a new man in my life. But my heart told me that he might still be alive, and that I should remain steadfast in the sure knowledge that I would never find another man more worthy of my love and more capable of giving me all that I desired in life. My head told me that I was no more sensible than a silly girl in reacting as I had done to a single kiss from Dominic. But my heart still fluttered as I thought of his charm and his intelligence, and as my thoughts turned to speculations about his body. Maybe the ravens would help me to decide what to do? I would ask them when I met them on the way back down the mountainside. But when I did emerge from the cave, and made my cautious way down the craggy slope the ravens were not there. Was that in itself an omen? When I got back to the Plas, I was none the wiser as to what to do, and I was in a black mood.

"Mistress," said Bessie, "we must decide what you will wear to that wedding tomorrow. Your cream-coloured muslin frock with the light stays, and your blue pelisse because it might be cold, and maybe your black shawl to indicate that you are still in quarter mourning for the loss of Owain?"

"Oh, no!" I moaned. "Do I really have to go? I had totally forgotten about it, Bessie!"

"I'm afraid you do, Mistress. You accepted long since. Anyway, you will enjoy it. Your parents will be there, and your sister Catrin and her husband, and it is a little while since you met them. Mistress Stokes and Mistress Phillips are also among the guests, as are many of your other friends. You will enjoy their company, and exchange essential news, and at the ball afterwards I guarantee that you will not miss a single dance!"

"Very well -- I give in! But, my dear Bessie, I detect a cunning plan lurking in the background. You want me to look as alluring as a mermaid on a rock, with a view to finding some eligible squire who is out fishing. Very well. But forget about the quarter mourning -- I do not hold with all that nonsense. But I will not wear the cream-coloured muslin dress -- it is inappropriate for an October wedding. I will wear my white satin dress with the medium sleeves, and my new silk gloves. The only concession I will make is that I will wear no diamonds -- with Owain still missing, that would be vulgar. Just a pearl necklace, and my pearl earrings. There. Are you happy with all of that?"

Bessie grinned. "Of course, Mistress. That is exactly what I assumed you would wear anyway. Shall I come with you? You will need three changes of clothes -- one for the journeys back and forth, one for the wedding, and the other for the ball. You do not want to be viewed as a country bumpkin just down from the mountains........."

"Yes, yes, Bessie. Please come with me. Do I recall that Grandpa and Grandma are not coming?" Bessie nodded. "In that case I need a chaperone. Will can come too, to drive the covered trap. He will enjoy the tomfoolery downstairs while the *crachach* are gorging themselves and prancing around on the dance floor."

So tomorrow I will celebrate the wedding of Miss Jane Raymond of Trefgarn Hall and Master Edward Roche of Llether. He is marrying up, and she is marrying down, but I am sure they will be blissfully happy somewhere in the middle. I am invited because the Roches of Llether have always been on good terms with my family, the Howells of Brawdy. I have known Edward since he was a little boy and I was a moody adolescent. And come to think of it, the occasion could prove to be very diverting because Squire Raymond is probably the most eccentric squire in Pembrokeshire, renowned for being incapable of organizing a card evening for elderly gentlemen, let alone a grand wedding.

12th October 1808

Well, that was fun! The wedding turned out to be a memorable one, and indeed it is a miracle that it happened at all. We arrived in our trap well in advance of the appointed time, so that I would have time to change in a reasonably leisurely fashion, but when we rolled up the grand driveway which leads to the mansion we encountered a scene of utter chaos. There were young men on horseback rushing about everywhere, galloping across the paddocks and fields adjacent to the track, some blowing their hunting horns and others yelling at the tops of their voices. "Oh my goodness," said Bessie excitedly. "It's a horse wedding! I thought such things went out of fashion twenty years ago!"

It had obviously not gone out of fashion at Trefgarn Hall, and I recognized that the hunting set (of which I was not a part, since the Plas is not located in good hunting territory) was intent on a good day out, even in the absence of fox and hounds. The noisy riding back and forth was not quite as chaotic as it seemed, for the young men, including the bridegroom, were frantically searching for the bride. We gathered from the servants at the front door of the mansion that the bride, after elaborate negotiations, had agreed to accompany one of the young men on his horse so as to avoid the terrible fate of becoming a member of the Roche family. It was all done in jest, of course, according to some ancient ritual. At any rate, we heard that the heroic rescuer, and the bride, and the rest of his little gang, had gone galloping off into the distance and up onto the moorlands of Great Trefgarn Mountain. The bridegroom and his pursuers had been sent off in the other direction, and had not known where to look for a while, but then somebody told them that the blushing bride and her protectors had gone north, so off galloped the posse of twenty or so young bloods on their sweating hunters, in hot pursuit.

For half an hour after that, peace reigned at the mansion, and I was able to meet the proud parents of the happy couple, together with my dear friends Ellie Phillips and Mary Jane Stokes and their husbands. Ellie, Mary Jane and I sat ourselves down on a bench at the edge of the lawn and chatted as only good old friends can. My sister Catrin and her husband James turned up later with my own dear parents, and they were all on excellent form. The big gentry of the county were all missing, since this was very much an occasion for the smaller landed families. But there were some surprises, including the presence of Judge Wynford Wynn-Evans of Llandeilo and his family. They were related to the Raymonds through marriage, and the Judge was the man whose task it was to preside over the trials of the men responsible for the death of my husband David in February 1805 and the later torture of my dear Owain Laugharne. He recognized me, and greeted me warmly, and we exchanged pleasantries. We guests chatted and reminisced in the warm sunshine in front of the house, and none of us ladies thought it worthwhile to get changed for the church ceremony until we were sure that there would indeed be a wedding. One never knows with horse weddings, since we all recalled that before the turn of the century one of the boys of the Gilbert family, due to be married to the oldest daughter of the Mortimers of Wolfsdale, had been killed outright as a result of a fall from his horse, leaving the poor bride to blame herself for the tragedy and to vow to remain a spinster for the rest of her life.

After an hour or so news came that after much racing over the moor and round the lanes of Trefgarn, peace had been restored between the two factions, thus enabling the bridegroom to recover his bride. Eventually the riders all returned. The most exuberant of them clattered in at the gallop, with the winner promised the first dance with the bride; but others, whose horses were all but spent, trotted into the yard at the back of the mansion very slowly indeed.

I can report that the happy pair did get to the altar, but with great difficulty, since young Edward had fallen off his horse and had broken his ankle, and since Miss Jane had fallen off the horse of her "rescuer" straight into a prickly furze bush, leaving her covered with cuts, bruises and nasty sharp prickles. At the altar she had been patched up and made presentable, but was not, quite understandably, in the best of spirits. But she was better off than her bridegroom, who was hobbling about on crutches, with a horribly swollen foot and heavy splints up to his knee after being attended to by one of the guests who happened to be a doctor. The poor fellow was in great pain, and just about managed to get out the right words at the right times during the ceremony. To make matters worse, the Vicar of Trefgarn was so drunk that he could hardly stand, having been kept waiting near the cupboard that held the altar wine for almost three hours. At the end of the ceremony the consensus was that the unhappy pair were probably now man and wife, although nobody could be quite certain of it. There was of course much speculation as to how they might manage on their wedding night.

Squire Raymond beamed happily throughout the proceedings in the church, although he had just lost his best hunter in a wager that the happy couple would get to the altar unscathed after all the horseplay. Mistress Raymond wept, as is appropriate, for the loss of her daughter and the loss of the horse.

After the church service we were all starving, and to her credit the housekeeper of the mansion produced a wonderful meal with seven courses which were still edible after all the delays. We all ate too much and drank too much, but the meal did not finish until midnight, and the ball did not get going until one o'clock in the morning. By that time the orchestra players were also more than a little inebriated, to the point where they could not remember which tunes had already been played, and which had not. As I recall, one of the tunes used for the quadrille was played five times before dawn. Not that anybody minded. As predicted by Bessie, I danced every dance, many of them with rather silly young men (some of whom were sporting injuries sustained in the horse chase) and some with very pleasant gentlemen whose company I enjoyed. I received many kind compliments about my dancing and about my dress, although with reference to the latter I was very over-dressed -- or maybe under-dressed, from the point of view of my dancing partners.

Bessie joked with me afterwards that if I had worn the cream-coloured muslin frock with its demure neck-line, as she had suggested in the first place, I would only have been called to the floor for half of the dances. I replied, having had far too many glasses of wine, that it was my purpose in life to bring a little simple pleasure into otherwise blighted lives, and that the white dress was designed and made by a happy genius who knew exactly how the women of this world must obtain power without the use of force.

"Balderdash!" said Bessie. "Without the use of force? Those are pretty deadly weapons you have there, Mistress, on either side of that cleavage. And you know how to use them. Those poor innocent gentlemen in tight breeches must have spent much of the night in total agony, and after each waltz I swear that the dance floor was littered with badly wounded males who had to be resuscitated with smelling salts!"

She was exaggerating mightily, of course, but I can forgive her because she had had too much to drink too, downstairs with all the other resident and travelling servants. In any case, my dear Bessie has a licence to insult me or poke fun at me when necessary, and to tell me uncomfortable truths when she deems it appropriate, just like the jester maintained in the old days by the Squire of Llanreithan.

By some miracle, since Will was fast asleep in the driving seat, we arrived home at the Plas just as everybody else was finishing breakfast. I fear that all three of us made ourselves very unpopular by spending the rest of the day in our various beds, dead to the world.

14th October 1808

Today I went down to town, as I often do on a Thursday, to visit my friend Patty. She is just a little older than I, and is so pretty that she turns every head in town when she passes by. In the bad old days she used to be a whore, but that miserable occupation was forced upon her by an evil monster named Joseph Rice, who is now in his grave, and now she is happily married to a fisherman named Jake Nicholas. They live in a small cottage on the Parrog, where the spring tide laps at their doorstep. I would find such proximity to the sea quite unnerving, but they love it there, and Jake claims that before he gets up in the morning he can tell from the smell of the sea what fish he will catch that day, and where. He is probably exaggerating, but like all tradesmen he likes to mystify and impress those who know nothing of his trade. He is a big, hard man, but he is so gentle and loving with Patty that every time I see them together I sense a tear in my eye. And just now he is especially gentle, because the pair of them have a new baby called Mary, born about six months ago.

"Mistress Martha!" she exclaimed as she opened the door. "How good it is to see you! Come inside, please. The kettle is on the hob, and in a minute we'll have a cup of tea. But first I must feed little Mary, if you don't mind. She has been grizzly all morning, and maybe an extra breakfast will settle her." Without further ado she opened her dress and put Mary to the breast, and with the little one thus silenced we were able to talk about horse weddings, and kisses at Portfield Fair, and children, and everything else. Then, with reference to nothing in particular, Patty said: "I gather, Mistress, that there are four strangers in town. They are definitely not local. They arrived yesterday."

"Well, Patty, that news is marginally less interesting than the news that an Irishman had been seen in town. Should I be excited?"

"I doubt it, unless one of them proves to be an eligible and good-looking squire."

"And how would I find that out? Are they likely to come and parade themselves in the back yard of the Plas?"

"Well, you never know your luck. The news is that they are four surveyors from London, working with that mad fellow called Charles Hassall from Narberth. The one who is in that endless dispute with the Knox family, and who is so hot-tempered that he would pick a quarrel with Jesus Christ if he could, and challenge him to a duel with pistols."

"So Master Hassall is with them?"

"Not as far as I know. They say that they are working under his direction, making an assessment of the local estates for the Board of Agriculture and the Government."

"Well, that makes them somewhat more interesting. Any other intelligence?"

"A couple of the fellows from the shipyard met them in the Llwyngwair Arms. The oldest one, who calls himself the Chief Surveyor, says his name is Tomos Griffith."

"That's not a very English name, Patty."

Patty shrugged and said: "He claims to come from a good family in the neighbourhood of Hereford."

"Very well. And where do they drink?"

"Nowhere, as far as I can gather," said Patty. "They have stabled their horses -- good horses, so they say -- at the Llwyngwair Arms, and seem to keep very much to themselves."

She reported that the four men were out all day making "observations" and that they returned each evening to their lodgings in town. They were apparently well spoken, and seemed to know what they were talking about. Then the conversation turned to babies and other things, and I thought no more about the surveyors for the rest of the day.

After supper, as I sat with Grandpa and Grandma in the parlour, we discussed the news. I told them about the surveyors working for the Board of Agriculture under Charles Hassall, and was a little surprised to see a frown appear on Grandpa's brow. "That is a very strange thing," he said. "I thought that Hassall's work was done, and that he completed his report for the Board of Agriculture long since?"

"Well, that may be true," I replied. "But things change, do they not? Maybe these new fellows are revising their maps, and making note of new enclosures, and the great changes in agriculture since the turn of the century?"

"Maybe, maybe," said Grandpa, with a shrug of the shoulders. "But it sounds as if somebody has misunderstood something, for Charles Hassall, who has many enemies, was relieved of his Government post seven or eight years ago, and has subsequently been acting as Secretary of the Pembrokeshire Agricultural Society. Isn't that right, Jane?"

Grandma nodded. "Quite correct, Isaac. And in that capacity, Master Hassall has his work cut out. There is no way that he could be directing the map-making activities of four officials from London. Are these four fellows telling the truth?"

15th October 1808

This afternoon Billy, Shemi and Will were out on the mountain with the dogs, gathering in the sheep. It is now time for them, in good condition after a summer of grazing on the common, to be shut into the top two fields with the four rams which we bought in August at Cardigan Market.

When they got back, with the ewes and the rams settled in together, Billy reported that he has seen four men in the distance, on the summit of the mountain. He said they had a spyglass with them, for he saw it glinting in the sunlight. He approached them, in the hope of striking up a conversation, but they appeared to be in a hurry, for they waved to him and then went off down the path back towards Newport. So he did not get close enough to speak to them.

"That would be the surveyors from the Agriculture Board," said Will, "going about their business of surveying things."

"What do they do?" I asked. "Has anybody asked them directly about their activities?"

"We don't need to ask them, Mistress," said Billy. "We know that already. They record which fields are fallow and which are in use, which crops are planted and where, where the limit of cultivation may be on the mountainside, and where there have been enclosures of the common. Then they make lots of coloured maps, they do, and write a report. Isn't that right, boys?"

Will and Shemi agreed, and Billy continued. "At least, that is what Charles Hassall did when he was hard at work a few years back. I remember it well, indeed. He was here at the Plas several times, and so was that strange fellow Iolo Morgannwg who was a sort of assistant. These new surveyors are obviously making a revision of their old maps and recordings of acreages. They will no doubt call and ask us for our cropping and animal records before long."

"Huh!" said Grandpa, who had been listening in on the conversation. "They are no better than enemy spies, interfering in our lives. When they are done, the Government will increase our tithes and our taxes, or invent some new tax designed to grind hard-working little estates into the ground. No good will come of it -- just you wait and see."

3. The Beginning of Things

16th October 1808

This has been a truly terrible day, for my dear friend Joseph Harries has been involved in an accident which leaves his life hanging by a thread. He will not welcome my prayers, because he does not believe in such things, but nonetheless I pray to God that he will not be taken from us. We do not see him every day at the Plas, and not even every week, but we know that he is always there, in that pretty cottage of his on the other side of the mountain, and that if he should ever be needed he will drop everything and rush to our assistance. Many other families across a swathe of north Pembrokeshire see him in exactly the same light, for he is a true *dyn hysbys*. He knows things. He heals people and animals, solves mysteries, acts as an intermediary in disputes, and dispenses advice which hardly ever proves to be unsound. Above all, he is a friend, and his friendship is a commodity too valuable to measure. Dear God, what will we all do if he were to die?

I must endeavour to keep my emotions under control, and to describe what happened, so far as I know it. News came, just before dusk, that Joseph had been almost killed in an accident in a narrow lane not far from his home. According to John Bateman, the steward of the Pontfaen estate, who passed that way shortly after it happened, he was trampled by a herd of bullocks after falling off his pony. He was going one way, and they were stampeding in the other direction. The lane was so narrow, with high hedges on both sides, that there was no escape for him, and he was knocked off his feet and rolled along as they rushed by. Nobody knows how much time passed before he was found in a crumpled heap in the middle of the road, but a neighbour called Philip Williams came by and discovered him, and first thought that he was dead. As one might imagine, he was hardly recognizable as a human being, covered as he was with mud, blood and cow dung.

Mr Williams heard Joseph moan, and tried to make him comfortable, but then saw that his right leg was badly broken. So he rushed home to fetch his wheel-barrow, which was the only means of transport that he, as a very poor labourer, had at his disposal. He came back with his wife Dot and his conveyance, and after putting Joseph's leg back to more or less where it should have been, the two good people contrived to fix some rough splints onto it, and then took him back to their cottage. There they had to strip him of his filthy clothes, and they managed to wash him from head to toe with hot water and carbolic soap. All this time Joseph was hardly conscious, and probably in a state of shock, for he did not complain of any pain. Then Master Bateman came along the road on his horse, having found a riderless pony a mile from the scene of the accident. Philip ran out and stopped him, explained what had happened, and urged him to gallop into town and fetch Doctor Havard as a matter of urgency. He left the pony and rushed off, and in due course returned with the doctor.

The doctor, who is a close friend of Joseph, confirmed that he had a very badly broken leg, and treated it as best he could before fixing it with new and better splints. Then he set to work with cleansing his many wounds and trying to stop the flow of blood. Joseph was by then in great pain, passing in and out of consciousness. We do not know much more at present, but the news is that the doctor did not want to move him from the cottage, for the daylight was already fading and he was afraid that there might be other injuries as yet undiscovered. He explained to Master Bateman that in cases such as this, involving heavy animals, there might be many injuries inside the body that are not manifested on the surface, and that a watch must now be maintained for signs of internal bleeding. He also thought that the patient might have been concussed from hoof blows to the head, and he was dreadfully worried that there might be some brain injury. Apparently he has left Joseph in the tender care of his neighbours for the night, and will return in the morning at first light, to continue his treatment.

When I heard all of this, I wanted to go rushing off to the cottage near Werndew in the dark, in order to provide assistance. But Grandma and Grandpa would not hear of it, saying (quite rightly, now that I come to think about it) that my presence would do more harm than good, even if I managed to get to the cottage safely in the pitch-blackness. "Let him be, Martha," said Grandma. "The doctor will probably have put him under sedation, so he may not even be conscious. What he needs is sleep, and he will not get it if you are there, clucking about him like an agitated mother hen. Mrs Williams is perfectly capable of keeping him warm and comfortable. She is a good woman who has seen many injuries and ailments in her time. She will probably sit at his bedside all night, watching for any signs of a change in his condition."

"I agree with Jane," said Grandpa. "I know that old couple, and I know their cottage. It is very small indeed, and is crowded enough with three people in it for the night, let alone four. Go to bed, Martha, and try not to worry too much."

So I took their advice, and am now sitting here at my desk, with my candles guttering as the wind rattles the shutters. It is not a night for rescue missions. I will go to bed, but I doubt that I will sleep.

17th October 1808

I spent the night sleeping fitfully, and I was wide awake when Bessie came into my room to stir me and to kindle the fire. I ate an early breakfast with Billy and then we took the trap to the cottage on the mountainside above Dinas, where we hoped to find Joseph still alive, but feared that we might find him dead. When we got there Dr Havard was already in attendance, and we found Joseph alive but not kicking. He was very drowsy and in a great deal of pain, and it appeared that his broken leg was swollen grotesquely. His face was covered in lacerations and bruises, and one eye was shut because of an ugly swelling on his left cheek. However, he was pleased to see Billy and me, and was capable of discussing the treatment of his injuries with Dr Havard, so we breathed a sigh of relief on the grounds that his brain was undamaged.

While Dr Havard got on with his work, with enough daylight to see what he was doing, Billy and I waited outside and chatted with Philip and Dot Williams. I had never spoken to them properly before, and they proved to be kindness personified. They said they were quite willing to look after Joseph -- and the pony -- for as long as necessary, and that they would keep an eye on him when he was well enough to move back into his own cottage. But I perceived that in looking after our dear friend for one night, their resources had been severely stretched. They only had one bed, and with Joseph ensconced in it, they had had to sleep on the floor, one at a time, with the other keeping watch over Joseph. It was clear that they had hardly any food in the house, and that -- like many other cottagers and labourers -- they lived right on the breadline. The standard of cleanliness in the house also left much to be desired, and I was afraid that if Joseph stayed there even for a few days and nights, he might pick up some infection that might finish him off more effectively than a herd of bullocks. Dr Havard was also worried on the same score, so I said that we would take Joseph back to the Plas in the trap, assuming that it would be safe to move him, and that we would put Mrs Owen onto the task of nursing and feeding him.

So it was agreed by all, and having given our profuse thanks to the Williamses we carried Joseph gingerly to the trap, settled him into it and transported him back to the Plas with as few rattles and bumps as possible. The pony came along too, on a long tether behind the trap. Dr Havard had already declared that Joseph's life was no longer in danger, and he said he would come to visit him at the Plas in the late afternoon.

When the fallen hero arrived at the Plas, he was given a far warmer welcome than Jesus Christ when he walked out of the tomb. Before we had carried him to his bed everybody insisted on embracing him or shaking his hand, and I saw the poor fellow grimace whenever he was touched. The older children were as delighted as everybody else to see him, and each of them insisted on giving him a kiss, but Brynach was frightened by his grotesque appearance, and ended up in tears.

At last, with Joseph settled into a bed in the spare room behind the kitchen, I managed to find the time and the space to talk to him properly about the accident. I sat at his bedside and held his hand. I wanted to know what was true and what was rumour in the version of the story circulating in the community, and I asked him what he could actually remember. His recollections were hazy, but he said he was riding home from Newport around noon, feeling perfectly at ease with the world, when his pony suddenly reared up and threw him. He thought he was knocked unconscious, but regained his senses momentarily to find a dozen cattle rushing towards him. Before he could even think of escaping by scrambling up the steep hedge at the roadside, they trampled him, and he thought he was lucky to escape with his life. The next thing he remembered was Philip Williams tending to him in the middle of the road, and then being taken in a wheelbarrow to his cottage.

"So the story we heard from John Bateman was accurate in most respects?" I asked.

"Dear Martha," he mumbled, as best he could with cut and swollen lips, "I have no idea what story you were given. As I said, my own memories are very hazy......"

"But Joseph, why would your pony, which is the most placid of creatures, throw you like that without warning? And why would a herd of bullocks be stampeding along that lane in the middle of the day?"

"I have no idea, Martha. These things happen. Most accidents occur because of chance coincidences of unfortunate events. For example, a lapse of concentration combined with a slippery floor, or a rotten plank combined with an unaccustomed heavy weight......."

"Joseph, you are playing games with me, and not for the first time. Come now -- was that really an accident? Do you have any enemies who might be prepared to go to the lengths of trying to kill you?"

"In reply to both your questions, I have not the faintest idea. When this pain eases off, and I have the time to contemplate the matter, maybe my memories will become clearer, and I will get to the business of analysis and deduction. But just now it is very difficult."

"Dear Joseph," I said reassuringly, "I quite understand. Your priority, and ours, is to get the process of healing under way as quickly as possible. Do you think your leg will be saved?"

"I am in no condition to assess that myself, Martha. But William Havard knows his business, and he is always honest with me. He is confident that there is no great damage to nerves or muscles, and that the break will heal in time."

I was not really satisfied with what Joseph told me, but this was no time for a cross-examination, and he was obviously in need of more sleep. So I kissed him on the forehead, and closed the shutters, and let him sleep for a few hours.

Later in the day, after Doctor Havard had been to change dressings and to confirm his diagnosis that there were no serious internal injuries, I delivered some supper to Joseph and sat with him again. Suddenly he said: "Martha, I will say this only to you. I thought my time had come. I work with cattle all the time, and have cured more than I care to count of assorted animal ailments, but I know that one day cattle will carry me to my grave."

"How on earth can you say that, Joseph?"

"Don't ask me, Martha. I know it. You know certain things, too, that you would prefer not to know. That is a burden for the likes of you and me, and it is a strange thing indeed that others might consider it a gift or a blessing. No matter. I am too tired just now for profound ponderings. Much to my surprise, I appear to have survived....... and I suppose that is something to be grateful for. Cats have nine lives, and wizards have ten. That's another of them used up."

18th October 1808

They say that disasters come in pairs, and there has been another lamentable event that causes me to ask questions about conspiracies and enemies. George Lewis, to whom we all refer as Lewis Legal, has had his house burned down in Fishguard. That would be bad enough for anybody to cope with, but for Master Lewis it is a special tragedy, since his house was newly built in a fine location at the edge of town, and since I know it to be a fact that he had sunk all of his savings into it after a lifetime working as a lawyer in North Pembrokeshire. It was one of the grandest houses in town, with all the most modern conveniences. Luckily the lawyer and his family escaped, and nobody was injured.

The Beginning of Things

I have a special fear of fire following the loss of the old Plas Ingli -- and five of its residents -- in a terrible conflagration in 1794, before I came into the Morgan family. I recall seeing the remains of the old house, with charred timbers jutting into the sky and tumbled piles of blackened stones just across the yard from where the new Plas was erected. The remains of that funeral pyre stayed there for years, since neither family nor servants could bring themselves to move it. The memory of the fire, and the loss of his parents and three siblings, haunted my dear husband David throughout his cruelly short life. For others, fires might be assumed to be accidents, but I am the only person who knows that the Plas Ingli fire was no accident, and for me big fires mean one thing -- arson -- until conclusive evidence is brought forth to indicate that my suspicions are misplaced.

This morning, when we heard the news of the fire from Dai Darjeeling on one of his periodic visits, I began to wonder about yesterday's gentle reminder from Joseph that I have special powers which might be more of a curse than a blessing, and I got to thinking about that nightmare of a week or so ago. It was all about Lucifer and fallen angels and devils, but it was also about unbearable heat, and flames, and scorched ground. Everything had been red -- the colour of Hell and the colour of the hottest fire. I had thought that the nightmare might have been a premonition of something due to happen to me, but was it instead a warning of fire, afflicting not me but somebody close to me?

I decided to investigate, while at the same time passing my condolences to Master Lewis. That good man is a special friend of Granpda, but I also count him as a friend who has given us the benefit of his wisdom and experience both inside and outside of the court rooms of the land. He has advised me and represented me on occasion, and in giving his services he has often gone well beyond the call of duty. When Dai came in mid-morning with the news of the fire, Joseph was fast asleep, so I asked Billy to prepare the trap, and off the two of us went along the track to town and thence along the coast road to Fishguard.

When we got to the place where Master Lewis's house used to stand, the scene we encountered was very distressing. The house had been reduced to a pile of rubble -- and it was still smouldering. As we arrived, a gust of wind sent a flurry of sparks and white smoke spiralling skywards, and a great blackened beam that had been perched precariously on what remained of one of the internal walls came crashing down, sending charred fragments flying in all directions and causing a number of nearby bystanders to scurry away for their own safety. The neighbours who had been prominent in trying to fight the fire were standing around in small groups, with grimy faces showing exhaustion and resignation. Eddies of acrid smoke drifted across the wasteland, and those who were caught up in them spluttered and coughed and rubbed their streaming eyes. We found Master Lewis and his family standing together in the front door of one of the neighbours, clearly still in a state of shock. I immediately embraced each of them, offered our condolences and asked if there was anything we might do to help. "No, thank you, Martha," said Master Lewis. "All our savings and belongings are gone, but the people of this town are truly wonderful in their generosity, and with the fire still not properly out there is talk of a charitable fund to help us. And luckily both my wife and myself have large families in the neighbourhood -- we will not go short of food and clothing, and we will always have a roof over our head. We will rebuild the house, never fear. It will be somewhat less grand that the one destroyed, but we will show whoever did this that we will not be defeated or driven off to some distant place."

I was amazed to hear this, and asked: "Do you mean, George, that the fire was started deliberately, by somebody who wanted to harm and maybe even kill you and your family?"

"No doubt about it, Martha," he replied, choking with emotion. "Somebody has been seen observing the house over the last few days, and a neighbour heard the hoofbeats of galloping horses -- maybe two horses -- at two o'clock in the morning. That was Mistress Ifans, who lives five doors away, at the top of the street. She thought that spurring a horse like that was unusual at dead of night, and also hazardous, given that there was hardly any moonlight. Being a good citizen, or a busybody, depending on your point of view, she went out to investigate, saw the fire just as it was getting a hold, and banged on the door and threw stones through the windows to wake us up. We all got out just in time, but by the time the neighbours had been alerted, and had tumbled out of their beds and grabbed buckets of water, it was too late to save the house. Arson, Martha -- no doubt about it."

"Oh, you poor things!" I moaned. "Have you entered a complaint? Are the constables and the magistrates making investigations? Have you been threatened? Have you any enemies?"

He held his hand up and smiled, which I thought was extraordinary in the circumstances. "Not so fast, Martha!" he said. "One question at a time, if you please. It is too early for investigations, but the justices and the constables certainly know about the fire, and I am sure they will rush about with great enthusiasm. I doubt that they will achieve anything, and I am minded to call in our friend Joseph -- he is the only one in West Wales with the skills to get to the bottom of this, and to bring the culprits to justice."

"You know, I suppose, that Joseph has almost been killed in an accident?"

Master Lewis staggered back as if he had been poleaxed. "Oh, my God! When? I had not heard. Is he all right?"

"Two days ago. He was trampled on by a stampeding herd of cattle. He has a broken leg and many other injuries, but Doctor Havard predicts that he will recover. Just now he is at the Plas, under the tender care of Mrs Owen."

"Ah! Thank God for that. Mrs Owen would not dream of letting anybody die under her roof -- that would leave an indelible stain on her reputation. Please send Joseph my felicitations and hopes for a speedy recovery.........."

"I shall do that. But his injury does mean that any opportunities that there might have been for sleuthing around the scene of your fire will now be missed."

"I agree. I have to admit that I had high expectations of Joseph's help. This is very bad news for honest people and very good news for the criminal classes. They will now have a license to cause mayhem everywhere between here and Cardigan."

"I think that is a somewhat dismal prognosis, George. Remember that not all of the criminal classes know that Joseph is out of action for a while. I doubt that civilization will collapse just because Joseph is in bed with a broken leg."

Master Lewis shrugged. "Yes, you are right. But you asked about threats and enemies. I have to say that I have not been directly threatened. But of course I have enemies, Martha. What attorney does not? Every time I am involved in a prosecution, or send somebody off to the Assizes, or am deemed to be responsible for a transportation to the colonies, I make enemies. But in general, I am protected from the vengeance of those who wish me ill-will by the goodwill of the community, who think of me as a sort of protector...."

"Is there some recent business which might have made you into a target for some wicked people?"

"Well, there was that thug called Josh Siggins, whom I sent to the gallows by representing the interests of the Jinks family of Puncheston. You will recall that he beat Mary Jinks to death with a hammer. But he had no friends, and was feared by the whole community. I cannot imagine anybody wanting retribution for his demise....."

We got no further in our discussion, and I was reluctant to take up any more of the poor man's time, given the fact that we were standing before the smouldering and crackling ruins of his home. So I renewed my offer of assistance, and Billy and I took our leave. I remained deep in thought for most of the journey home.

19th October 1808

Is there no end to this? Another night, another terrifying event. As I write, it is ten o'clock in the evening, and I have not slept a wink since one o'clock this morning. I was fast asleep, and awoke with a start when I heard the dogs barking furiously. I wondered what was going on, and then I heard a clattering of hooves and a crunching of wheels on gravel. Somebody was shouting "Open up! Open up, for God's sake!" and then I heard heavy footsteps and a frantic hammering on the back door. When I got downstairs in my dressing gown Mrs Owen had opened up, and Billy and Shemi had already rushed outside to see what the fuss was all about. One by one all the adults in the house appeared in the kitchen, rubbing their eyes. A minute later the men came back inside, carrying what looked like a corpse, with horror writ large on their faces. It was Will Owen, my shepherd and Mrs Owen's son, covered in blood. They placed him on the kitchen table, and they were followed into the kitchen by Tomos Huws Plain Dealings, one of my labourers. "I found him on the Cilgwyn road at midnight," he moaned, slurring his words. "I was coming home from town with the gambo. A bit of a night on the town. Oh God, I wish I hadn't drunk all that bloody cider. I saw it was Will. Managed to get him on board, I did, and then I came hell for leather up the road. Couldn't see nothing. It's a bloody miracle we got here in one piece........." Then the poor man collapsed into a chair, and Bessie had to take care of him.

Even before he had finished speaking Mrs Owen had taken control of the situation. If Will had been my son I should have been reduced to a snivelling heap on the floor in an instant; but with tears streaming down her face she issued orders like a general in the heat of battle. "He is alive. Billy, hot water from the fire place! Shemi, get clean rags from the cupboard under the stairs! Bessie, get the fire going properly! Mistress, don't just stand there -- help me get the clothes off him! Grandpa, go and get Joseph from his room -- he is in no state to attend to the injuries, but he will know what we must do. Grandma, fetch the ointments from the medical chest!" and so on.

So we frantically unbuttoned his jacket and his breeches and pulled off his waistcoat, which was already unbuttoned. His shirt and undergarment were so covered in blood that we had to cut them off, and as we worked blood continued to pour from a multitude of wounds. He moaned, and we took that as a good sign. Within a minute or two, Mrs Owen and myself were also covered in blood.

Then I realized that there were five small children standing at the kitchen door which leads to the back passage. They had all been awoken by the shouting and banging, and as soon as they saw the bloody scene centred on the kitchen table, and saw the fear on all of our faces, they all burst into tears. "Mam!" wailed Betsi. "What's happening?" I was covered in blood, and was in no state to gather them under my wings like a mother hen, but to her eternal credit Sian reacted immediately and made the children her priority. "Children, everything will be all right," she said calmly. "Now just you come with me, and your Mam will be with you shortly." And with that she ushered them from the room and back up the stairs, with puzzlement and fear still writ large on their faces. I had no time to worry about what damage might have been done to the poor mites, for our priority was the saving of Will's life.

No sooner had the children disappeared than Joseph made his entry to the kitchen, hopping and hobbling and supported by Grandpa. He came up to the table and immediately said: "Wonderful, Mrs Owen. You have done everything that should be done. Now wash those wounds with carbolic soap -- he may scream with the additional pain, but it may well save his life." So Mrs Owen did as she was bid, without any dramatic consequences, since Will was still hardly conscious. But when we started to dress his wounds and bandage him up, he started to moan, and his teeth started to chatter uncontrollably. "Shock," said Joseph. "That's a good sign. Now he needs to be kept warm. Nothing broken, I think, except maybe for a couple of ribs. Get a blanket under him, and let's get him over here on the floor, in front of the fire, with more blankets on top of him."

Gradually the mess was cleared away, and Mrs Owen started to scrub the kitchen table, like a woman possessed. She still had tears rolling down her cheeks. It was time for me to assert my authority. "Mrs Owen!" I scolded. "Stop that at once! Bessie will deal with the table, and the rest of the mess can be cleared up in the morning. Sit you down this minute. Will is safe now, and you can relax." And at last, she did stop, and lost her self-control. After an hour or so of frantic activity, the tear drops on her cheeks were washed away by a veritable flood of tears. Grandma embraced her, and the two old ladies stood there, both of them weeping, rocking gently back and forth, in the middle of the kitchen floor. "There now, Blodwen *bach*," whispered Grandma. "Will is going to recover. You need to weep, but he will be all right."

"Oh, Jane *bach*, I do hope so. That boy! He will truly be the death of me........." Then she stopped weeping, and blew her nose theatrically on a large purple kerchief which she conjured out of a deep pocket in her blood-covered dressing-gown. The tension was suddenly blown away, and everybody started to talk at once.

"Oh God, my head!" said Tomos Huws. "No more cider for me, that's for sure."

"What happened?" said Joseph.

"Would anybody like a cup of tea?" said Bessie, as she scrubbed the blood off the kitchen table with a bucketful of soapy water and a stiff brush.

"That was a close shave," said Grandpa. "It's a bitterly cold night. Thank God you came by when you did, Tomos, or it would have been too late."

"Which bastards did this?" asked Shemi, in recognition of the fact that Will's injuries had been sustained in a vicious and probably premeditated attack.

With Will fast asleep under his blankets in front of the blazing kitchen fire and under the watchful eye of the Wizard of Werndew, the rest of us sat round the kitchen table, sipping mugs of tea and trying to come to terms with what had happened. Mrs Owen's tearful grief was now replaced by fury. "I thought that Will had reformed his ways!" she stormed. "And here he is, too drunk to stand up, beaten up in some tavern brawl by a bunch of thugs....."

"There you are wrong, my dear Mrs Owen," said Joseph from his settle by the fire. "This was no tavern brawl. For a start, this happened nowhere near an inn. It happened on the Cilgwyn Road, more than a mile from town. Will could not have walked that far after being so terribly injured. No -- he may have been drunk, but he was not too drunk to walk most of the way home. Then he was ambushed, and his attackers left him in the road to die."

Like the others, I said that I was shaken by the brutality of the assault. His injuries had clearly been made not just by fists, but by boots, knives and maybe clubs. We all agreed on that. I knew that Will had been in many scrapes before, having had a somewhat chequered past. But most of his escapades had involved petty crimes, a spot of smuggling, and brushes with the revenue officers and the constables. The constables would not have beaten him up, since at midnight they were probably safely tucked up in their beds. I was not sure about the revenue officers, who had a reputation for brutality. So I asked: "Shemi, you know more than the rest of us about Will's nocturnal activities. Did the revenue officers do this? Will has made them look like idiots many times in the past, and they may have decided to teach him a lesson."

"Absolutely not, Mistress. I happen to know that there is a cargo coming in to Abereiddi this very night, and if the revenue spies are as good as they claim to be that is where the officers will be, with the excise cutter not far offshore. These fellows have not been seen in Newport in weeks..........."

"But that brute Griff Hickey has several scores to settle with Will, does he not?"

"That he does, Mistress. And so has Squire Price and his cousin Edwards of Wervil -- but the little episode concerning the silver spoons was eighteen months ago. If they were going to try to teach Will a lesson, they would have done it long since. And why would they do **this**, for God's sake?"

As gently as if he were dealing with a newborn babe, Shemi removed the blanket which covered Will, who was still fast asleep. He quietly peeled away assorted dressings to reveal his chest. On it there were injuries that had clearly been made with a sharp knife. Three long parallel cuts about an inch apart, starting above one nipple and ending below the other. In the panic of clearing away blood and ensuring that Will stayed alive, we had all -- apart from Shemi -- failed to notice that these were not random cuts made by a slashing knife in the heat of battle. They had been made calmly, by somebody who knew what he was doing. I, for one, was frozen with horror as I realized the importance of this.

That was not all. Mrs Owen then fished a piece of blood-soaked paper out of her pocket. "And there's this," she said. "You wondered why I was in such a state not long since. Just as the children came in, and grabbed everybody's attention for half a minute, I found this, pinned to his skin........."

"Pinned to his skin?" I whispered, hardly daring to believe my ears.

"Yes. Pinned to the skin above his left nipple. With this pin." And with that she burrowed into her pocket again, and produced an iron pin about three inches long. She placed both the pin and the piece of paper onto the table in front of her.

"Oh, dear God," moaned Shemi. "Did he feel anything, Joseph?"

"I hope not," said the Wizard. "This might have been done when he was already unconscious. Can I see the paper, Mrs Owen?"

She pushed it across to him. He examined it carefully, and frowned. Then he moved it along to me. It was difficult to read, but the words ***"For Rhiwallwn. From Gruddnei"*** could just about be made out. The words were written not with ink, but with blood.

At this point I almost passed out with terror, partly because of the realization that somewhere in our community there was a man -- or several men -- capable of unspeakable sadism, and partly because the image of John Fenton's face came flooding into my mind. The cuts on Will's chest were exactly the same as the cuts made on the chest of my dear man Owain when he was abducted and tortured a couple of years ago by a group of villains who were subsequently executed for various crimes. I am the only one who knows that John Fenton was the one who used the knife, because I heard it from his own lips. But I also knew that Fenton was dead. After a truly dreadful experience involving the abduction of little Sara, I saw him sinking into a quaking bog and going down to Hell. My recollection was perfectly clear. Or was it? Maybe my recollection was, after all, only partly based on observation, and partly on a wish to put that experience behind me? Surely that monster cannot have survived? Are we dealing here with a man, or a devil, or a ghost? And could it be that the culprit -- or one of the culprits -- is the strange creature whom we call the Nightwalker, and whom we have seen often in the vicinity. Is that creature now no longer content to stand and observe, but resolved to cause injury and mayhem?

20th October 1808

Another day has passed, and Cruel Fate has decided against any further visitation to the Plas. That is something to be grateful for. We must also be thankful that Will, who is as tough as an old gander, will survive his attack, and that Joseph continues his recovery. I am also happy to report in the pages of my diary that the children appear to come through the episode in the kitchen without any great harm. I suspect that they were all more asleep than awake when they stumbled downstairs, and that they did not fully understand what they saw. I have to hope that they are now reassured by the fact that Will is talking and smiling again, and I have explained to them that Will was involved in some silly business following a visit to the Black Lion, and will soon be back to his duties.

Last night, after making my entry in the pages of my book, I found it hard to sleep although I was utterly exhausted. That was not surprising, I suppose, given that I had two terribly injured men under my roof, in the care of Mrs Owen and Bessie. And I had a recurring image in my mind of John Fenton rising from a bog down in the *cwm* with a knife in his hand, dripping blood............

With the two invalids well looked after, I knew that I had to give the day to the children, and that is what I did, to the exclusion of all else. The morning was rainy, and we played silly games in the nursery, and in the afternoon, when the black clouds and rain had swept through on their way to England, we went for a walk in the dripping woods near Dolrannog and held a competition to see which of us could hear and see the greatest number of woodland birds. That was a shambles, of course, but none of us worried about that. Dewi fell into a stream and got very wet indeed, Brynach scratched his leg on some brambles, and Daisy cried because she got mud onto her dress -- but otherwise we returned home unscathed, tired and happy.

During the morning, while I was preoccupied with the children, Joseph was able to attend to Will's injuries, even though he was still struggling on his crutches, and was still in great pain himself. At lunchtime he declared that he was happy with his original conclusion that there were no broken bones. He also purported to be mystified by the cuts and the note written in blood, and I was not in a mood to pursue the matter. But this evening, with the children in bed and with Will safely packed off to to his bed by his fierce mother, we were all able to relax. As Grandpa and Grandma and the servants snoozed in the warm candle-light of the kitchen, Joseph asked if he might talk to me alone. We went to his room, and sat on his bed. We talked about the cuts. He also remembered that Owain had exactly the same cuts when he was almost killed on a date fixed in my memory -- 28 October 1806. He recalled that the damage had been done by Alban Watkins and his cronies Rice, Howell and Fenton. Almost everybody in Pembrokeshire knew about those cuts, said Joseph, since Owain had showed them as evidence in court, to the accompaniment of gasps of horror from the public gallery and from the jury. Then he informed me that Watkins also had the same cuts made on his chest by the Irishman Daniel O'Connell when he executed him on the Parrog. I was horrified when I heard this news. I had known that Watkins had cuts on his chest, but I had not realized that there was a pattern to them, since I had not seen them personally, and Joseph had not previously described them in detail. I had not made any connection between these three apparently unrelated crimes, but now it was obvious to both me and Joseph that these cuts cannot all have been made by the same man. Two or maybe three individuals had each chosen to punish their victims in the same unspeakably brutal way -- but why had these victims been chosen, and what did the cuts mean?

And why should Will, of all the servants under my roof, have been singled out in this fashion, a couple of years after the other crimes had been committed? What was it that linked him with Owain and the late enemies of the family, Alban Watkins and John Fenton? As we sat together in his room, Joseph spent most of the time deep in thought, and would not explain for me where his speculations were leading him. I had to conclude that he was holding something back, and that made me irritated, and very afraid.

4. Innocence and Guilt

22nd October 1808

Six days after his accident, Joseph has returned home to Werndew, clutching a pair of crutches which he will have to learn how to use. Shemi took him in the trap, with the pony trotting along behind. He thinks his broken leg is healing well, since the swelling has subsided, and the pain is reduced. Dr George Havard is pleased with progress, but insists that he must remain in the splints for several weeks. I have lent him the trap, which he can now use with his own pony in order to get about. Both riding and walking are out of the question, and it will be difficult for him to harness the pony and get in and out of the vehicle, but luckily it has a low step and an easy door, and he says he will manage. If he has major problems, he can always call on Philip Williams for assistance. That is what neighbours are for.

Today I have found it difficult to deal with matters relating to the estate and the family, and I have been very nervous. For a start, there are far too many unanswered questions stuck stubbornly in my mind. For example, in the events surrounding Joseph's accident, where did the cattle come from and where did they go to after Joseph had been trampled? And with respect to the fire in Fishguard, if the house had really been under observation, as claimed by Lewis Legal, somebody must have observed the observer. Has anybody asked what he -- or she -- looked like? I was sure that there was some sort of pattern to the events of last week, but could not quite work out what was going on. Then, in an instant, things became clearer and much more terrifying.

In mid-morning my latest edition of the *Cambrian News* was delivered, and its main story seized my attention. It reported that Justice Wynford Wynn-Evans, the Assize Judge who sentenced Rice, Howell, Beynon and Lloyd to death (and four other idiots to transportation) had had his mansion near Llandeilo burned down. Arson was suspected, stated the reporter. This had happened while the judge and his family were away, on the night of October 10th and 11th. I discussed this with Grandpa Isaac, and said it was a sad event and a dismal coincidence, coming hard on the heels of the fire in Fishguard. Grandpa furrowed his brow and said: "No, no, Martha, the **news** comes hard on the heels of that Fishguard event, but the fire was earlier. Was that date not three days prior to the arrival of those four fellows in Newport, who claim to be surveyors? Is that really a coincidence? I wonder........" Then I recalled that the judge and his family, with servants in tow, were away at the time of the fire, at the horse wedding in Trefgarn Hall. Whoever burned the mansion must have known that it would be virtually empty for several days, and that in turn implied that there must have been an informer passing on vital information to the arsonists.

Suddenly I made a link with the trial which followed the treasure hunt which occurred in one of the Plas Ingli fields almost two years ago. I mentioned this to Grandpa, pointing out that the three men who were responsible for the conviction of the villains at the trial in Haverfordwest were Joseph Harries, who presented incontrovertible evidence of their guilt, Lewis Legal, who took charge of the prosecution case, and Judge Wynn-Evans, who sentenced the guilty men with a black cap on his head. Grandpa was thoughtful, and said: "You may be right, Martha. But we must not jump to conclusions. Remember that Justice Wynn-Evans has a thousand enemies. Probably more serious enemies than Lewis Legal, whose enemies are for the most part small men with small grudges. The Judge sentences people to death every month, and transports many others to the colonies. There are families and criminals all over South Wales who have sworn revenge against him, and who would kill him if they thought they could get away with it. We must wait for more information to emerge."

23rd October 1808

I never was very good at waiting for information to emerge. After breakfast I had a sudden inspiration relating to the possible link between the recent spate of crimes here, there and everywhere and the four strangers who are supposedly working in Newport and the farming community. I decided to do some research. Without warning -- which I admit showed a lack of courtesy on my part -- I went to see that strange man called Charles Hassall, who lives in a solid and unpretentious house called Eastwood, not far from Narberth. He is the one for whom the four strange surveyors claim to be working, and I thought it was time to check this out face to face.

I have known of Master Hassall for some little time, since he was involved in that farcical business that is nowadays referred to as The French Invasion, over a decade ago. David met him once, and said that he was too impulsive to be a leader, and too arrogant to be a follower. I am also familiar with his long and acrimonious dispute with the Knox family of Llanstinan, and his tendency to get involved in things that are none of his business. He is easily offended, and insults others with gay abandon, and one day I suppose he will die in a duel.

I travelled over the mountain on horseback (since Joseph still has our covered trap) in the company of Shemi and Billy. They insisted on coming, and claimed that I needed protection. I could not agree with that, but they said that if I went alone they would follow me anyway, whatever the needs of the farm might be. So I had to concede. In the event I was glad to have company, for it was a rainy day with low cloud swirling over the mountain and with heavy squalls coming in from the West. We did not see the sun all day, and even at mid-day there was nothing better than a gloomy sort of twilight. As a result, by the time we got to Eastwood I was wet and filled with foreboding. I suppose I was apprehensive in part because of Master Hassall's fearsome reputation. When I saw the house I felt even more uncomfortable, for it was a dark sandstone building with small windows and little ornamentation. The front facade was hemmed in so closely with tall trees that I felt a sense of clammy claustrophobia as we approached the entrance porch.

I knocked on the door, and after a while it was opened by a maid. I introduced myself and wondered whether Master Hassall might be at home. The maid invited me inside and confirmed that her master was in his office, and went to check that he would see me. She returned to announce that he would be pleased to meet me in five minutes. She invited me to wait in the front parlour, which I did while Billy and Shemi walked round to the back of the house with the horses, hoping to enjoy a jar of ale with the servants belonging to the Hassall household. I entertained myself by examining the furnishings and paintings in the parlour, which had French windows opening onto a grassy and unkempt garden.

The master of the house, when he finally came downstairs, proved to be a man of medium build and medium age, with a mop of red hair and a smoothly shaved chin. He had small furtive eyes set close together, and ruddy cheeks. He had the big strong hands of a man used to hard work in the open air -- and indeed he must have spent a great deal of his life in the open, working as a farmer and as an estate steward and agricultural surveyor. His dress was discreet and even dull, with everything in brown, grey and black. He seemed to me to be a bundle of nervous energy. He was not still for a moment when he was in my company, and whenever he spoke his head moved with a strange and unnerving twitch while the rest of his body was used for grand gestures. He gave me a deep bow in response to my curtsey. "Ah yes, Mistress Morgan!" he said, in a voice more Irish than Welsh. "I know all about you, although it has not been my pleasure to meet you before. Daughter of the Squire of Brawdy, I believe? I know your father well, and have enjoyed many a fine glass of port in his company, over discussions of crop rotations and blood lines. I find him a very learned and convivial man, and next time I meet him I must congratulate him on producing a daughter who has grown into such a beautiful lady!"

"Thank you, sir. You are very kind. While you are about it, you might also congratulate my mother, for I believe she also had something to do with it."

Master Hassall spluttered and then roared with laughter. "Ha!

Quite right you are! I see that you are a lady of spirit. I like that in a lady. Next time I meet Betsi -- that is your mother's name, is it not? -- I will raise a glass to her as well. And you married into the Morgan family of Plas Ingli. Terrible business about that fire. I knew William Morgan well, and he was a great help to me when I was working around that little mountain of yours, and on the common. The whole county was shocked when he and his wife and little children lost their lives in the flames. My condolences -- and indeed for the loss of your husband David, who was a fine young man. I met him once."

"Thank you, Master Hassall. I am touched by your kind words, and indeed impressed by the depth of your knowledge."

"My sentiments are genuine, I assure you. But I must admit that I do not carry full information about every Pembrokeshire family in my head. It is all in my library upstairs -- and I flatter myself that there is not a better one in West Wales relating to the ancient families of the nation. I have also kept my notebooks from my surveying days -- and they are full of useful little titbits. When I know somebody is coming, I have to admit to doing a little research in the hour before they arrive. In your case, I only had five minutes! I always do that, so that my memory is fresh. And it never fails to impress my guests!" He chuckled and cackled again. "But will you please promise that you will not reveal that to anybody? Shall we have it as a little secret between ourselves?"

"Of course. My lips are sealed," I said, having very rapidly come to the conclusion that this particular gentleman was not only arrogant and desperate to impress, but also very pedantic indeed.

I asked him about the new Agricultural Survey being done in the Newport area for the Board of Agriculture and Internal Improvement. "No no," he said. "The Board has moved on to other counties. The work here in Pembrokeshire is done. My report was published fifteen years ago. There is no new survey, and there are no new surveyors working in the county."

"How interesting. Are you sure of that, sir, given that you are now involved with other matters?"

"Mistress Martha, I can assure you that I am fully abreast of developments. I make it my business."

"But there are four men in Newport who claim to be working under your direction, Master Hassall. Should we now assume that they are impostors?"

"It would appear so, Mistress Morgan."

"But why the pretence which was bound to attract local interest? Why did they not come in the guise of ordinary travellers? We have anonymous people passing through town all the time, and they attract no attention whatsoever."

"Ah, but perhaps these fellows wanted some justification for visiting certain locations that they are interested in, asking questions about certain estates and individuals, and even observing farming routines and methods. That is exactly what I did when I was conducting my survey in your area, with the full approval of the Board of Agriculture and the kind cooperation of the local landowners."

"In other words, they are being very clever......"

"I do not know what is going on here, but I would think so. And the pretext of being officers employed by the crown gives them a certain respect, and places some distance between them and ordinary folk. Very convenient if you are up to something nefarious. They are not hunting for your treasure, by any chance?"

"My treasure?" I gasped. "Whatever do you mean, sir?"

He laughed. "I know almost every inch of Pembrokeshire, and I know all the good families. I also follow the large and small events which provide us all with entertainment. I recall the great trial in the Assizes that followed that treasure hunt in the field that you call Parc Haidd. How many idiots were there, scrabbling about in the field and knocking merry hell out of one another? Ten? Twelve? You will not have seen me, but I attended the trial, in the public gallery. Thoroughly entertaining, and that fellow Harries from Werndew proved himself a very able advocate."

"I do not find it amusing, or even mildly entertaining, Master Hassall, to see six men sentenced to hang, and others transported to the colonies."

Master Hassall was not used to being told off by a lady, and I saw immediately that I had ruffled his feathers. For a moment he looked startled and even resentful, and I wondered if I was about to observe something of his famous Irish temper. But then he relaxed and smiled. "I am sorry," he said. "That was crass of me, and you are right to pull me up short. My point is that the trial, and the events that preceded it and followed it, were widely reported in the newspapers, and for weeks the talk in all the fine drawing rooms of the county was of nothing else. Everybody in Pembrokeshire, and many from further afield, knows about the Plas Ingli Treasure, and the fact that those villains did not find it does not indicate that it does not exist. It may be assumed to lie in the ground where it always was, somewhere else on the estate. You should not be too surprised, Mistress Martha, if some fellows come from far away and start to hunt for it."

"I must admit that I had not thought of that possibility, Master Hassall. And I thank you for pointing it out to me. It does give me cause for concern, and one has to wonder how far they might go in seeking to extract information about this fabulous and imaginary treasure. Three people who might be assumed to have knowledge of the whereabouts of a treasure have already been seriously injured, and the injuries were not accidental."

"Is that so?"he asked, raising his bushy eyebrows. "Very interesting. Do you know anything about these four fellows who purport to be surveyors? I know all the Pembrokeshire gentry, and most of the smaller squires, and might be able to assist in identifying them."

"Thank you, sir. I am grateful for that offer, and might well, in due time, take you up on it. But at the moment we know hardly anything about them. I have not met them myself, and I do not even have accurate descriptions of them. All I know thus far is that one of them -- who calls himself Chief Surveyor -- claims to come from Hereford."

"Hmmm. Not much to go on. But if you find out more, by all means call again, or send me a letter. I will be delighted to assist, if I can."

That was really all that transpired in our conversation about the four surveyors. My host offered me a cup of tea and some currant cake to reinforce me for the journey home, and I shared a convivial hour or so in the company of him and his wife Harriet. The lady of the house was a plain and homely woman with greying hair and only a little more fashion taste than her husband, but I liked her immediately, and we got on splendidly. I sensed that she was desperate for female company and female conversation. So with Master Hassall looking slightly disgruntled by not being the centre of attention or the master of ceremonies, we talked of our families, as women inevitably do. She told me that she and her husband had lost a son in childhood and that their daughter Oriana, now aged nineteen, was a very sickly girl who was confined for most of the time to her room upstairs. I said I was very sorry to hear it, and offered my good wishes for her speedy recovery.

So in truth my visit turned out not to be so terrible after all, and on the way home I counted it as a blessing that I had not only survived an interview with the fearsome Master Hassall but had also found a gentleman who might prove, in the future, to be a very useful ally. I also had another angle worthy of investigation. Could these fellows really be hunting for the Plas Ingli Treasure? Only I know that it does exist, and exactly where it is buried. I had thought that all this treasure hunting nonsense was over and done with -- but now I was less certain. And if the "four surveyors" were looking for it, would they be prepared to maim and kill, just to get their hands on it?

24th October 1808

It has been another day of fruitful research. Somebody has to do it, with Joseph effectively out of action. In the company of Billy I have travelled around to some of the local squires, drinking many cups of tea, consuming considerable quantities of *bara brith* and griddle cakes, and asking if any of the "land surveyors" have called on them or examined their land. Not surprisingly, I have discovered that not one of them has received a visit. Furthermore, nobody knows where these men might have been during the days when they have been away from their lodgings. There have been various sightings of them -- mostly around Carningli. They seem, from a number of reports, to be reluctant to stop and talk to others -- and once or twice they appear to have ridden away or walked away rather than have face-to-face meetings with the locals. As a consequence, some think they are very arrogant fellows, unwilling to talk to servants and common labourers. Others think that they are spies employed by the church, gathering information which will be used to increase the hated tithe payments to the Rector of Newport.

25th October 1808

Just as I thought that my investigations were leading towards some interesting conclusions, and just as I was beginning to enjoy my amateur sleuthing, horror has returned to our lives.

My tenant Thomas Tucker of Penrhiw went to town early, and returned with the news that during the night Skiff Abraham, the toughest fellow in town, was grabbed, taken off in a cart, and beaten up, again after dark, by three men with mufflers across their faces. By all accounts Skiff put up a furious fight, and managed to injure one of them, but he was no match for three strong and determined men, and he was left on the riverbank between Parrog and Master Havard's shipyard, in more or less the same place that the body of the villainous Alban Watkins was found a couple of years since. His hands and his feet had been tightly bound, and a gag had been stuffed into his mouth. When he was discovered by one of the locals he was hardly conscious, and the rising tide had almost covered him. He would have drowned if another ten minutes had elapsed before his discovery. A number of people rushed to help him, and he was dragged clear of the muddy swirling water and carried to the cottage belonging to Jake and Patty. They tidied him up, cleaned his wounds, and made him comfortable. Then somebody went to fetch Doctor Havard, only to find that he was away visiting relatives for a few days. So Patty and Jake had to do the doctoring, as best they could. According to Thomas, Skiff has no broken bones, and was conscious but in great pain.

Later on Mrs Owen and Bessie had to go to town to do some

shopping, and they came back in mid-afternoon with further details of what happened. I was with Grandpa in the office when they arrived. They had visited Patty and Jake and seen the patient, and when I asked about his condition Mrs Owen said: "That fellow is tougher than Will, and didn't come out of it too badly, all things considered. Maybe the assailants were in a bit more of a hurry, since there are more people about in town than there are up on the Cilgwyn Road -- and maybe, Mistress, the intention was that death should come by drowning. But he was cut, just like Will........"

"Oh no!" I moaned, burying my head in my hands.

"Three cuts, Mistress. Identical in every way. And there was this, to." She took a bloody and crumpled note from her bag, and gave it to me. "It was pinned to his skin. Patty thought you might like to see it."

With trembling fingers I opened the note. There were some words on it, this time written in black ink but almost obliterated with patches and streaks of blood. I could just about make out the words: ***For Tinwaed. From Edenawg.***

"We spoke to Skiff," said Bessie. "He says he was fully conscious when the cuts were made, and almost passed out from the pain. He says they didn't speak a word either to him or to each other -- they just seemed to know exactly what they were doing. They had dark coats on, and he didn't see their faces since they were well muffled up."

"These are the actions of torturers and sadists," said Grandpa. "Nobody locally would do this -- Skiff has too many contacts among the low life of Newport, and his spies and cronies would certainly extract revenge against anybody guilty of harming him. So this was done by the same men who attacked Will -- and the four surveyors have to be the prime suspects."

"I agree," said I. "Do Skiff, Patty and Jake know the details of the attack on Will?"

"Yes, Mistress, I believe so. Remember that Tomos Huws was here for the whole time when we were dealing with Will's injuries, about a week ago. I suppose we have to thank him for saving Will's life, even though he was drunk at the time. He sobered up pretty quickly, and saw everything that the rest of us saw, and heard all of the conversation. He has a loose tongue, and next day every detail of what happened to Will was all around town."

"And every detail of what happened to Skiff will also be around town by now," said Grandpa. "If I was one of the guilty men, I think I might start to worry. I might get out of Newport while the going is good, or I might become even more careful and devious."

At milking time Hettie came up from town to help us in the cowshed and the dairy. She had more news. "There will be trouble, mark my words," she said. "People are mad about what has happened to Will and Skiff. The talk in town is now all about those four strangers. They may be well spoken and come from good families, but they may be thugs nonetheless. There's no evidence of them being up to no good, but if I was you I would keep an eye open for the *Ceffyl Pren*.........."

After supper I spoke to Grandpa and Grandma about these developments. I wanted to know why the Mayor, the magistrates and the constables were not, so far as we could see, seeking to bring the perpetrators of these crimes to justice.

"They have nothing to go on," said Grandpa. "If somebody made a complaint, or took out an indictment, then I, or any of the other magistrates, could take action -- through the issuing of a search warrant or an arrest warrant. But what do we have? An unfortunate accident in Dinas involving our old friend Joseph, with no sign of criminal activity. Joseph has not complained or pointed a finger at anybody. A house burned down in Fishguard. Very unfortunate. Another house burned down in Llandeilo. None of our business. And two rather disreputable fellows beaten up in Newport. People get beaten up all the time, usually because of petty arguments and too much alcohol. Why would the constables want to get involved? They will assume that Will and Skiff will get their own back in due course, if revenge is justified. Nobody has actually been killed......."

"I would put that down to good fortune, Grandpa," I replied. "But what about the torture, and the cuts on people's chests, and the bloody notes? Will and Skiff have been targeted and punished for something -- there is something sinister going on here."

"I think I would accept that, Martha. But there is nothing to connect those two beatings with Joseph, Lewis Legal, or the Judge. Maybe this is all down to a thoroughly bizarre coincidence?"

26th October 1808

I have now convinced myself that these four strange men are responsible for not just two of these crimes but all of them. I include the apparent "accident" that almost killed Joseph, for I am increasingly of the view that what happened to my dear friend was premeditated and orchestrated in some way, although I am at a loss to explain the whys and the wherefores.

This morning I found a reason to go down to town with Bessie and to call at the lodging house on East Street where the four strange men were staying. Bessie was not sure that this was a wise move, and Grandpa had already warned me to keep my nose out of things that were none of my business, but my instinct tells me that this is indeed my business, and that somehow I am responsible for the terrible things that have happened to five innocent men. I do not actually feel guilt -- but there is a great unease in my breast. So I disregarded the pragmatic advice of Bessie and Grandpa, and decided to follow my intuition.

Nothing dramatic happened. It was a bright sunny day, and Bessie and I felt quite safe in the middle of town, since there were good crowds milling about on the streets. We knocked on the door of the lodging house, and found that the four men were not at home. The landlady, one Lizzie Tasker, said that they had collected their horses straight after an early breakfast and had gone out as usual, for the day. She invited us in, and she was perfectly open and chatty with us. She said they were the only guests in the house at present, and that they had paid her to take no other guests while they were there. They were very secretive, she said, and they spent some time every day looking at maps, as surveyors do. She added that they were perfectly respectable guests, if occasionally somewhat boisterous, and said that they were obviously very old friends, perfectly relaxed in each other's company. They came and went at all hours of the day and night, but she said her front door was always unlocked, and it was none of her business to wonder what they were up to. As she reminded us, it was not at all unusual for her lodgers to return to their rooms at two or three in the morning, after a hard drinking session in the Black Lion or the Royal Oak; and nor was it unusual for a guest to stay out for the whole night while enjoying the company of one or more of the local ladies of easy virtue. "I clean their rooms unless they ask me not to, Mistress Martha," she said with a shrug, "and............"

"Unless they ask you not to?" I asked sharply. "And why would they not want you to clean their rooms, Lizzie? Is that not unusual?"

"Not unusual, Mistress. Guests often ask for complete privacy, or leave things lying about that they do not want to be disturbed. I'm not bothered, since it means less work for me. These fellows keep the doors to their rooms locked quite often. I just feed them and take their money, and if they leave without any debts and without smashing the place up, I am happy."

I left my visiting card, and asked Mistress Tasker to give my compliments to her guests when they returned. "Please tell them," I said, "that I will be only too delighted to talk of agricultural matters with them should they wish to call at the Plas in the course of their studies."

5. Web of Intrigue

27th October 1808

This morning Patty came up to the Plas at breakfast time with her baby on the pretence of going for a nice walk, but in reality to pass on the latest news. She said that the four strange men had left town, having blessed the community with their presence for about a fortnight. They left at dawn, in a hurry, having paid their bill and having said that they had more work to do "down in the English parts of the county." When I heard this news I suppose I should have been elated, but I felt a sense of disappointment and even frustration, because after all the talk about these fellows I had not even set eyes on them.

Later in the morning I went back to town with Patty, since I had arranged a dress fitting with Mrs Price Very Nice, and when that was over and done with I called in at Mistress Tasker's lodging house again, in the hope of obtaining the names of the four men. I was angry that I had not done that before. Lizzie greeted me warmly enough, and said that I was the third person since breakfast to call, asking about her recent guests. "And may I ask who your other callers were?" said I.

"I am not able to reveal that, Mistress."

I was furious about her reticence, but thought it best to keep my feelings under wraps. However, I did elicit some useful intelligence. The men had informed Mistress Tasker that their names were Tomos Griffith, William Evans, John Hughes and Glyn Owens. "Very funny indeed," I laughed. "Names so false that even Constable Wilson might raise an eyebrow. There must be a thousand others with the same names, in Pembrokeshire alone."

"What was I to do?" said the landlady, shrugging her shoulders. "They tell me their names, and I have to believe them. Anyway, they were no trouble, and paid their bills, with a little added as a mark of appreciation for services rendered."

"Oh, and what might they have been?"

She winked and then shrugged her shoulders. "A visit or two or three from Fancy Miles and Nancy Humphrey. They are good girls, and have to earn a living like everybody else. Considerable goings-on upstairs, there were........"

"Drunken revels and such like?"

"You could say that, Mistress, but my mouth is sealed. Then there were a few loaves of my famous crusty bread, with salty butter and newly made blackberry jam. Very hungry they were, those fellows. And a lot of extra washing of muddy breeches and shirts and jackets, not to mention the bedclothes -- they did apologise, but explained that surveying out in the country at this time of year is a very muddy and filthy business."

"And which one of them seemed to be the leader?"

"Master Griffith, I would say. Chief Surveyor, he calls himself. A big tall man, almost as strong as your Shemi, I would guess. Maybe forty years old. Very piercing eyes, but a man of few words. I never saw him smile, let alone laugh. I never did see his face properly -- he wore a thick muffler whenever I was in the room. He had a shaved head. And when he spoke, you really had to listen most carefully, for the sound was not much more than a whisper. He spoke in a sort of flat monotone, with very little in the way of ups and downs, if you get my meaning. The other three seemed a little in awe of him, and to tell you the truth he gave me the creeps. The others were pleasant enough, by comparison with some of the so-called gentlemen who have used my lodgings in the past............"

I wondered out loud whether the men had taken off because I was asking after them -- or maybe because they had got wind of the *Ceffyl Pren*. "Who can tell, Mistress Martha? They said nothing about any of that to me."

"And was there anything else about them that was noteworthy? I ask that because there are many people in town who suspect them of various crimes, including the beatings given to Skiff Abraham and my servant Will Owen."

"Yes, I have heard those rumours. But I cannot think that those gentlemen were thugs -- they were all very educated, and had London newspapers in their rooms. They seemed quite normal to me, except for John Hughes, who was a very strange fellow."

"What do you mean by that, Lizzie?"

"Well, just strange. Dreamy and absent-minded. I would say.

"Maybe he was a poet. Poets are like that. Did he drink a lot?"

"Not as far as I could see -- not on my premises anyway. Maybe down in the Royal Oak or some such place. The others drank good wine, in great quantities. When they left there were thirty empty bottles in the room used by Master Griffith and Master Evans. The one called Hughes sometimes stayed in his room when the others went out. He seemed to know Pembrokeshire better then the others. I think he may be from a good family down below the Landsker. And another funny thing -- the one called Glyn Owens was talkative enough with his friends, but he never said a word to me, except to ask, in a strange sort of accent, if he could have haggis for breakfast."

I spluttered and could not help laughing. "Haggis?!! And did you oblige?"

"No, I did not! I told him we don't grow them in these parts. But I did him some oatmeal porridge, and that seemed to keep him happy."

"Do you think he was from Scotland?"

"I would say so, Mistress. But Glyn Owens is a funny name for a Scot, don't you think? And I never did see him in a kilt."

When my business in town was finished, I walked home, took a light lunch, and decided that I would go for a ride over the mountain. I enjoyed myself greatly, trotting along with the wind in my hair. And I have to admit to a sense of relief that the four surveyors were unlikely, in present circumstances, to leap out at me from behind a rock or a stone wall. As I rode along I was deep in thought, and after a while, purely by chance, I found myself at Joseph's little cottage called Werndew. I expected to find him in bed, reading a good book, with his broken leg on a cushion. But much to my surprise I found that he had just returned home from somewhere or other. He had been using the trap, and was now wiping down the pony with sweat on his brow and much grimacing from his aches and pains. "Joseph, you are supposed to be taking it easy," I scolded him. "If you are not careful you will disturb those splints and put the bone out -- and then you could end up a cripple. Anyway, where have you been?"

"Investigating certain matters."

"Have you called in at Lizzie Tasker's lodging house?"

"I am not at liberty to say."

"Really, Joseph! You are very irritating sometimes, keeping secret the smallest matters which have no importance. I will resist the temptation to be offended with you. You know, I suppose, that Skiff Abraham has been beaten up and that Judge Wynford Wynn-Evans has had his mansion burned down?"

Joseph looked up with a start. "What? When? I knew nothing of either thing. Ach! I find it very frustrating, stuck here in my cottage with a useless leg in splints, unable to keep a track of what is going on."

I was very delighted to know some things that Joseph did not know, so I made the most of it, and said we had better go inside and sit down. This we did, and I played him like a trout on a line until he had extracted all the information from me, bit by bit. When I had told him everything I knew, I could see that he was seriously worried. But before we could get down to analysing the situation somebody arrived, very slowly, on a donkey. It proved to be old Harry Hurry, reputed to be the slowest man in Pembrokeshire, whom Joseph uses as a spy. He and Joseph had a whispered conversation in the corner of the room. Then he gave Joseph a piece of paper with writing on it. The wizard read it and frowned. Then he handed the old man a shilling and off he went.

"New information, Joseph?"

"Indeed. And I don't like it."

"Will you share it?"

He thought for a while, and then said with resignation: "I think I must, although my instinct is to protect you, Martha."

Joseph said that the note detailed the movements of the four men who purported to be surveyors. Old Harry had apparently kept them under surveillance since last Thursday. This could be interesting, I thought, as Joseph scanned through Harry's note. At last he said: "Ah yes. Here we are. It's all very abbreviated, but understandable, I think. *Thurs 19 Oct. 8 o'clock. 3 men leaving Mistress Tasker lodgings, including the big tall one. One left behind? Can't see which is which. Pick up horses Llwyngwair. Ride off up Market Street. Seen by Sally Huws up Cilgwyn Road. Ride back in hurry 11.15. Horses put back in stable. Back to lodgings 11.35 --*

looking furtive -- coats and boots very muddy."

"So that would be the time of Will's assault?"

"Precisely."

"And other entries in the list?"

"Let me see.... I really must give that fellow more lessons in handwriting. Right. This is it. *Mon 23 Oct. 6 o'clock getting dark. 3 men leave Mistress T lodging. No horses this time. Walking quick along West Street and then down Parrog Road. Heading for Parrog? No sign of 4th fellow. 3 back again 10.30, walking fast. Very dirty. Tallest one limping. Bad foot?"*

"Exactly right for the assault on Skiff. So we have our culprits, Joseph. So they must have targeted Will and Skiff, and planned their attacks very carefully. But how can they have anticipated -- or known -- their movements? Will does not go to the Black Lion every night of the week, and Skiff does not walk along the estuary every night either."

"But Will does go to the Black Lion every Thursday," said Joseph thoughtfully, "and Skiff does walk over to the Llwyngwair cottages every Monday -- he is seriously courting that pretty girl Maria Morris, and likes a bite of supper with her and her parents in exchange for a bottle or two of Canary sack."

"So the four were well informed," I mused. "That means, does it not, that somebody has briefed them? They cannot have known these things from their own observations, over the space of just a few days."

Joseph became quiet, and remained in deep in thought for several minutes. I became increasingly irritated, but knew him well enough not to break into his contemplation.

"Right," he said at long last. "I will tell you what else I know. I am still in two minds as to whether I am wise to do it, but with Owain still missing, and with the Nightwalker lurking somewhere in the back of your mind, I think it is for the best. Are you ready for serious news?"

"Really, Joseph! Do you take me for a child? Or are you playing games with me?"

"My dear Martha, may I remind you that there have been times, and not so long ago, when you have been overtaken with the blackest melancholia, and have been unwilling -- or unable -- to face your own children or to venture into the fresh air?"

"I accept that, Joseph. That was then, and today is today. Just now I am strong. Please do not patronise me!"

My body was tense, and I suppose that my eyes were blazing even though there was frost in the air. At last Joseph struggled to his feet, limped to where I was sitting, and kissed me on the cheek. He sat down again next to me. "I am sorry, Martha," he said. "I never was very good at judging the moods of women. Please accept that -- not for the first time -- I am torn between giving you information that might distress you, and trying to protect you. Very well. I have spoken several times to Mistress Tasker. I have accumulated considerable information about those four fellows, and the note from Harry simply confirms my suspicions................"

Just when Joseph was about to reveal his accumulated secrets, we were overtaken by events. A young lad galloped up the track on a pony. "Message for the Wizard!" he yelled. "*Ceffyl Pren*, half past five, Parrog!" That was all. And off he rushed to tell somebody else the news. We had no option in the matter, and knew that we had to terminate our conversation and get to town as quickly as possible. I would find things out from Joseph in due course. So I left my horse tethered, and in a great fluster we got the pony from the paddock, hitched it to the trap, and went off as fast as we could down to the coast road and thence to the Parrog, with me in the driving seat.

We arrived at the sea front to see the *Ceffyl Pren* charade in full swing. A rough-looking man was strapped to a ladder, covered with the remains of rotten eggs and food scraps, with a sign around his neck saying "Enemy spy."

The Foreman of the Jury, whom I did not recognize because he was dressed in female garb and had his face blackened, was in the middle of a mock trial. "Who is this spy?" he yelled. "Is he a Frenchman?"

"No!" came the shout from somebody in the "jury" composed of maybe twenty other men, all dressed in women's clothes and all with blackened faces. "A bastard close to home!"

"Who is he then?"

"Gwynfor Rees, who is the scum of the earth!"

"And what has he done?"

"Spied for them bastards from away!"

"With what consequence?"

"William Owen and Skiff Abraham, good citizens of this town, damn near killed."

"Oh dear, oh dear. What a pity," wailed the Foreman. "On whose evidence is he brought before the court?"

"Mine!" "Mine!" "Mine" Shouted three of the most disreputable fellows in town, whom I recognized in spite of their disguises.

"Seen talking to that bloody Scot in the Royal Oak six times at least," shouted one.

"Seen taking his silver too!" shouted another.

"Blood money it was!" shouted the third. "And spending it!"

Then the Foreman turned to Rees, who looked like a frightened chicken, trussed up and unable to move. "Oh dear, oh dear," he said. "Can this be true? Gwynfor Rees, you miserable bastard, do you plead guilty or not guilty as accused?"

"Guilty! Guilty!" roared the crowd.

"Not guilty!" croaked Rees, hardly audible.

"Bad hearing I've got," said the Foreman. "What did he say?"

"Guilty! Guilty!" roared the crowd again.

"Well, guilty it is then. And the sentence?"

"A good wash and hang him up to dry!"

"Agreed then. A dip or two in the river it is, by unanimous verdict of the jury of good men and true. Hand him to the Master of the Mechanicals!"

Six other men then took over the ladder on which Rees was strapped, and the assembled company marched about three hundred yards up the river to where the slaughterhouse was located. Joseph could not follow because his broken leg was giving him great pain, but I went along with the crowd. It was almost high tide, and the appointed ducking place was stinking to high heaven, with blood and gore, and entrails and bones all over the place. In the hot summer months the smell is almost unbearable, and they say that the rats in the vicinity are bigger than beavers. The ducking stool was already in place -- a strange contraption like a see-saw, with a long wooden pole hinged on a trestle so that it could be moved up and down and also swung out over the river and back again. The pole had a stool on one end and a stout rope coiled around the other. "How many coolings?" shouted the Master of the Mechanicals, whom I recognized as John Phelps.

"However many is needed to make him admit his crimes and sing for mercy!" shouted somebody from the crowd.

"It shall be done!"

So the guilty man was strapped to the stool, swung out over the river, and ducked slowly up and down, completely submerging each time, with great cheers from the crowd. Once or twice he was under for so long that I feared for his life. But at last, as I watched with bated breath, he raised his arm and pleaded "Guilty! Guilty! Now let me go, I beg of you, Johnny *bach*!"

The long wooden pole holding the stool was swung round, and Gwynfor Rees was cut free on the shore. No matter what his crimes might have been, I felt desperately sorry for him, for he looked truly pathetic. He stayed there for several minutes, on his hands and knees, coughing up water and looking like a dog that had almost been drowned. Then the gang decided that he had recovered quite enough. They tied a rope around his chest and under his armpits, and he was strung up from the low branch of a convenient oak tree. Somebody conjured up a pot of paint and a brush, and new sign was put around his neck, reading *Guilty bastard, washed clean. If anybody wants him, you can have him.*

Within a few minutes the whole crowd was gone. There had been no involvement whatsoever on the part of the properly constituted forces of law and order. I walked back to the Parrog and assumed, correctly, that Joseph would be waiting in Jake and Patty's house. I told him all about the ducking, while Jake was in the back room changing out of his exotic costume and cleaning his face. I had not realized that he had been one of the jury, and when he emerged, grinning, I complimented him on his fashion taste and his hairstyle. "You should not be surprised, Mistress Martha," he said. "I pride myself, I do, on keeping up with the latest fashions from the Paris salons."

I said I was worried about Gwynfor Rees. "Who will cut him down?" I asked.

"Oh, one of his drinking cronies," said Jake. "He will be all right -- he is unharmed, except for a big dent in his pride and a reputation now sunk to rock bottom."

Later on, over a cup of tea, and with Patty and Jake listening in, Joseph and I resumed our discussion which had been so rudely interrupted at Werndew. "Now then," he said, "to return to what I know about those four fellows. I was not able to visit their rooms -- Mistress Tasker did not think that would be appropriate while they were still in residence, and my abilities in the matter of climbing stairs are somewhat restricted just now. But I observed certain things, and she told me other things. They are certainly from London. They left several London newspapers lying around, and I was able to examine a coat and a pair of boots which they left in the downstairs passage when they were out one pleasant warm day. The boots were made in Stepney, and the coat, of excellent quality, had a label inside which said *Thurrock of Kensington, tailors of distinction.* There was also a name label stitched inside the collar, with the letters JP beautifully embroidered."

"JP? That matches none of the names given to Mistress Tasker."

"Precisely. But we knew those names were false anyway. Then there was another newspaper which they left lying around in the dining room. It was the *Carmarthen Times* dated 9th October. That newspaper is widely read in our neighbouring county, but not in Pembrokeshire.........."

"So in your view, Joseph, it could have been obtained in Llandeilo, or some such place, by four travellers passing through one or two days after the date of publication?"

He nodded. "Indeed. I did not appreciate its significance at first, since I did not know about the Llandeilo fire. But it might now provide for us a link with the burning of Judge Wynn-Evans's mansion. It is circumstantial evidence, but useful nonetheless. As to who these fellows are, the lady of the lodging-house says they are all four very well-spoken and polite, with immaculate table manners and an appreciation of good things. They brought with them several bottles of excellent French wine and one bottle of vintage port, and insisted that for their dinners they had the best cuts of beef that Dafydd Butcher could supply. They also had a "learned book" which they appeared to consult frequently, and on several occasions she saw them reading -- and apparently discussing -- a long letter which the one called William Evans carried around with him all the time, in a large brown envelope. The envelope had a crest on it."

"The book, Joseph," said Jake. "Did Mistress Tasker note the title?"

"She saw it but couldn't remember it -- something complicated, she said." Then Joseph rubbed his hands with glee before continuing. "And the last thing to reveal was my little visit to the good lady's rubbish dump, at the bottom of her garden. I find that rubbish dumps are very absorbing and informative places. Would you not agree with me? I found these, this very morning." He took out of his pocket two small bottles which had contained liquids and passed them to us to examine. They had the same label on them, reading: *Sydenham's Tincture, prepared by Culpeper of Knightsbridge.*

"What on earth is Sydenham's Tincture?" asked Patty.

"My dear, you have led a very sheltered life," he grinned, knowing full well that she had not. "It is a concoction of opium or laudanum, used very sparingly for the relief of pain but also taken as a matter of course by certain unfortunate individuals who will probably be killed by it in the fullness of time, having first gone mad."

"So one or more of these fellows suffers from an addiction?"

"Most likely -- Mistress Tasker says one of them -- the one called Hughes -- behaved in a somewhat slow and dreamy fashion for much of the time. Maybe he was the one who stayed at home sipping laudaum when there was dirty work to be done."

"So what is your conclusion, Joseph?"

"That these fellows are not professional criminals, let alone professional killers. They are far too careless to be called professionals at all. Their false names are ludicrous -- and it was even more silly to give a Scot a false name like Glyn Owens. Maybe that was some sort of private joke. No -- they are wealthy men involved in a mission. But now they are gone, and we can all breathe a little easier in our beds..........."

"Mission accomplished?"

"Only time will tell, Martha. If they come back, we will soon know that there is unfinished business."

28th October 1808

After the happenings and discussions of yesterday, I went to bed more convinced than ever that we were all caught up in a revenge campaign against those who brought Watkins, Howell, Rice and others to justice. This was confirmed in my mind when I received the latest edition of the *Cambrian News*. On one of the inside pages I found this:

LLANDEILO ARSON ATTACK; JUDGE OFFERS REWARD

*It is reported that Assize Judge Wynn-Evans of Plas Dinefwr, near Llandeilo, is offering a grand reward of £100 for information resulting in the conviction of those responsible for the cowardly attack upon his mansion very early on the morning of 11th October 1808. The house was burnt to the ground during one of the most horrid conflagrations to be seen in the county for many years. Luckily the Judge and his family and entourage were away from the mansion at the time, and the two servants who were in residence were alerted by the smoke and fumes, and managed to escape without serious injury. At first the constables thought that the fire was an unhappy accident, but our reporter understands that several men on horseback were seen in the vicinity of the mansion on the evening before the fire took hold. Furthermore, in an unexpected twist, when our reporter visited the grounds of the mansion during the course of his investigation into the facts of the matter, a servant (who could not read) asked him to read the contents of a note which had been found not two minutes earlier nailed to the main gate on the driveway. The note read "**For Urien. From Afaon.**" It was written in elegant script, on good paper. When Justice Wynn-Evans returned to his burnt-out home two days later, our reporter passed this mysterious and sinister note over to him as a matter of courtesy. It is understood that certain investigations are now under way, and it is hoped that with the willing assistance of this newspaper, and with the aid of the reward so generously offered, the guilty parties in this dismal affair will be swiftly brought to justice.*

That was enough to set my heart racing and my brain into frantic activity, but then things got more disturbing, for in the afternoon I received a letter from Lewis Legal, delivered by a boy on a pony. It read:

"Manorowen, 28th day of October 1808

My Dear Martha,
I write to express my appreciation for your kind visit, your message of condolence and your generous offer of help, following the tragedy that has afflicted us. But we are alive and unharmed, and we trust that -- in due course -- all will be well. In the meantime, we have been given space in the extensive accommodation of my dear sister and her husband, near Manorowen. And I am pleased to say that my documents and books were safe in my office in town, and are quite unharmed.

I am moved to inform you of a certain matter. I know that you are an avid reader of the Cambrian News -- as am I -- and I assume that you will already have scanned the pages of the latest edition of that excellent publication. You may have noticed the report pertaining to the fire in the mansion of Judge Wynn-Evans. You may also have noticed the mention of that strange note which read ***"For Urien. From Afaon."*** *I have not the faintest idea what that might mean, but I can tell you that on the night following the destruction of my own home I found a similar note nailed to a post on the roadside nearby. It read thus:* ***"For Tinwaed. From Cai."*** *I was, and still am, mystified as to what those names mean. I have never heard of anybody called Tinwaed, Urien or Afaon, but when I was young I knew a fellow called Cai who was then killed some years since, in one of the battles against the French. So I assumed at the time (October the 17th) that this was a coded message from some local fellow (or maybe his family) who had a great grudge against me. I had thought of bringing this to the attention of our friend Joseph in the hope that he might bring some enlightenment, but as we both know, the poor fellow is in no fit state for solving mysteries, following his unfortunate accident.*

I am no sleuth, but even I can see that there must be a link between these two terrible fires, and that the same person or persons must be responsible. My instinct is that there is something unpleasant going on here, and I urge you and your loved ones to take care.

With my kind regards and greetings to your family,
George Lewis

When I read this I was stunned -- not only because of this confirmation of a link between the two fires, but because Lewis Legal has chosen to share this information with me and warn me to take care. Why me, rather than anybody else? After all, neither of the fires had anything to do with me or my family or servants. Or did they?

29th October 1808

I have had another sleepless night, during which my feverish brain told me that the four mysterious men will return, and that I will be hunted down by them. At breakfast time Grandma commented on my black mood and my sunken eyes, and asked if was feeling ill. "No no, Grandma," I replied. "Just thinking about developments." I tried to settle into the office with a view to dealing with estate matters and doing some book-keeping, but I just could not concentrate on anything. I had to go down to town, so I put on my walking boots, took a basket over my arm, and said I was minded to do some shopping. Bessie saw that something was afoot, and offered to go with me. But I would not hear of it.

When I arrived in town I embarked on my hunt for Gwynfor Rees, the local thug who was dealt with by the *Ceffyl Pren*. I peeped into several of the local drinking dens, and at last I found him in the dimly-lit back room of the Royal Oak, chatting with some of his cronies. "Gwynfor, would you be kind enough to step outside so that I can have a word with you?" I asked.

"Bugger off!" he replied with a scowl. "I don't want nothing to do with you, Mistress Morgan. Nothing personal, mind. But I have had enough trouble already. All I want is a peaceful life, a sovereign or two in my savings, and a quiet drink now and again with my mates."

"I assure you that I had nothing to do with the *Ceffyl Pren*."

"I dare say you didn't. Very unpleasant it was. I am still recovering........"

"I might be able to help you in that regard."

There was a long silence while he looked at me. At last he shrugged and said. "Nothing to lose. I will step outside for a word. But make it sharp, if you please. I shouldn't like to be seen in company such as yours. Bad for my reputation. Besides, I am a very busy fellow."

The two of us sat in the yard at the back of the inn, away from prying eyes. I asked him about the four surveyors, and his dealings with them. I discovered that he spoke several times to them -- especially the Scot -- and was paid for certain information. "What information?" I asked.

"Oh, relating to certain individuals."

"Which individuals?"

"I am sworn not to say."

"Very well. But are you sworn not to nod your head should circumstances require it?"

"Nodding can damage the neck, and doesn't come cheap."

"Well, I have half a crown in my purse, and can just as well spend it on some groceries as leave it here."

He gave me a hard and long look in the eyes. I did not flinch, and he said at last: "Hmmm. Try me."

"Did the individuals include Joseph Harries Wizard, Skiff Abraham and my servant Will Owen?" He nodded.

"And there were others too?" He nodded again.

"Including Lewis Legal, the attorney from Fishguard?" He nodded for the third time, and said: "This nodding is getting very tiring, Mistress............"

I interrupted him, not wanting to break the flow of information. "Let me think. You were asked for details of their whereabouts, comings and goings, ability to protect themselves, and so forth?" He paused, and then nodded yet again.

"And did you help them in the execution of their crimes? Were you present when they attacked these innocent victims?"

"Crimes? Innocent victims?" growled Rees, with bulging eyes. Then he continued, with venom in his voice. "They said, Mistress, that Master Harries, and Skiff and Will, had done great harm to them and their kind, and that retribution was their great and noble duty. Damn and blast! Now I mentioned their names instead of nodding, and will surely roast in Hell because of it. But maybe Hell is where I'm headed for, in any case." He thought for a moment, shrugged, and continued. "So I might as well carry on and earn my silver.......... They said all they want is justice, and that they can't depend on the magistrates and the constables to get it since they are all corrupt and lazy. As it happens, I agree with them on that. They never told me what those fellows were supposed to have done, so as to invite punishment."

"Did they have a list of names?"

"Yes, and a long letter in a big brown envelope. The Scot looked at the list, and the letter, quite often when he was talking to me. But he never showed them to me properly."

"And what were the other names on the list?"

"I cannot tell you." He challenged me with defiance in his eyes and a hard set on his mouth.

"You are being very difficult, Gwynfor."

"And why should I not be difficult?" he hissed. "Why should I not make life hell for the likes of you, after what you have done to me?"

"I beg your pardon?" said I, considerably taken aback. "And what, pray, have I done to you?"

"Not you, precisely, but your kind, with your grand houses and your carriages and your servants, and your fine clothes, and tea parties in the orchard! Them that are squires and magistrates are bastards, the lot of them!" His voice was suddenly thick with emotion. "And you, a fine lady, are just as bad, with your fancy clothes, and dark eyes, and colour on your cheeks........"

His voice faded away, and there was a long silence. I noticed that there were tears in his eyes. In truth, there were probably tears in my eyes too, as I sat beside this deeply troubled poor man. I wondered what had provoked this outburst, and before I could restrain myself I placed my hand on his arm, in a small gesture of reassurance. "Gwynfor," I said, "I have absolutely nothing against you, and would never wish you ill. Why would you think that?"

He swallowed. "I am sorry, Mistress. That was unkind of me. I know that you are not like the rest of them. I have heard only good things about you from those who work on your estate. And I know you have suffered your fair share of misfortunes too."

"Indeed I have, Gwynfor. This is neither the time nor the place to examine them. As for you, what is the reason for your bitterness?"

"You don't know? I thought everybody knew."

"I know a fair amount about the goings-on in town, but I have no wish to nose about in the affairs of others. And I am, after all, a resident of Cilgwyn, far enough away to miss at least some of the chattering that keeps the townspeople amused. I have to admit that I know nothing at all about you. I simply perceive that you are an intelligent and educated man who drinks too much and who has fallen upon hard times."

He gave an ironic laugh. "Ha! You perceive correctly. And you might also perceive that I am a bitter man, and a victim of circumstance...."

"Explain yourself, if you please."

"Let me just say that for one reason or another I found myself in our glorious army, fighting the French. Have you noticed my limp, and my useless left arm?"

"Oh -- I confess that I have not."

"I disguise my disabilities well. In a skirmish in Egypt, we put in British muskets against French cannon, as usual. The usual result, too. I was knocked over by pieces of flying metal on my left side, from an explosion which killed five of my colleagues. I was scraping bits of them off my uniform for days afterwards. It's a wonder that my head wasn't blown off, too. By some miracle I survived, in spite of the tender attentions of several army surgeons. I was sent home and discharged, with a pension of five pounds. I'm supposed to be grateful. And if you want the full story, Mistress, I have no work, and I have a wife whose eyesight has deteriorated to the point where she is all but blind. Three of my children are alive, but in poor health, and four others are dead. None of those poor mites saw their fifth birthday. So you need not wonder any further at the source of my bitterness........"

"Oh Gwynfor, I am so sorry to hear all of that. But why have I not come across this information before?"

"Why should you have heard of my misfortunes? I returned to the town only five months since, and have done my best to cope with the pain of my injuries and my life. I still have some bits of metal embedded in my flesh, and I find that alcohol has a numbing effect. So I spend too much time in the cosy back bar of the Royal Oak. I admit it." He looked at me not with anger or defiance on his face, but in a state of unutterable misery, before burying his face in his hands with a deep sigh. On impulse I took the half crown from my purse and pressed it into his hands.

"Take this,"I said. "Where one human being is in need, and another has the capacity to help, common humanity demands that the one must do something for the other. But I want you to promise me one thing."

"And what might that be, Mistress?" he asked, wiping tears from his eyes.

"That you will spend this not in the bar of the Royal Oak, but on food and clothing for your family. Do I have a promise?"

"You do, Mistress. And I thank you from the bottom of my heart........"

"It is my privilege. It is my instinct that you are a trustworthy man." Then I thought for a while, and continued. "If I trust you, Gwynfor, will you promise that you will not betray me?"

"To be trusted is not within my expectations just now, following that meeting with the *Ceffyl Pren*."

"Well, I will trust my own female intuition on that point, and not the mad rantings and ravings of a mob. Do you want to work?"

He looked up with amazement. "That I do, Mistress, given my limitations."

"What is your trade?"

"I was a carpenter before I joined the Army."

"Is your right arm still capable of sawing and hammering?"

"Indeed it is. I can do most things, short of chasing sheep and wrestling with bullocks."

"Leave things with me. I will give the matter some thought, and contact you directly. Where do you live at present?"

"In that little hovel near Gamallt, down by the Clydach river."

I froze, and tried to retain my composure. "The one by the bog,"I asked, "which is said to be haunted?"

"The very same. I moved the family there about a year since, on my last leave from the Army. There were signs of habitation by various vagrants over the years, but its reputation tends to keep people away, which suits us fine. And it's dangerous, with that bloody bog not far from the front door. Nobody knows who built it, or who owns it. So nobody charges me rent -- which is just as well, since I could not pay it anyway. But at least I'm off the streets, which means I haven't been chased as a vagrant or as a burden on the parish."

As he spoke, I hardly heard what he said, for I was reliving my nightmarish encounter with John Fenton following the abduction of little Sara. For a moment I had a flickering vision of the ghost -- or the body -- of John Fenton, rising from the bog which I assumed to be his grave.........

"Are you all right, Mistress?" asked Gwynfor, jolting me back to reality. "You look suddenly pale."

"Yes, I do feel a little unwell. I must take my leave. I will be in touch with you."

"Very well, Mistress. I thank you for your half crown and your sympathetic ear. Farewell. But I urge you to take great care."

"Oh, and why should I take care?"

"Because, Mistress, what with chatting about one thing and another, I never did give you the other names which that bloody Scot was asking about. Your name was there, on the top of the list."

30th October 1808

Today I called a Big Meeting at the Plas, involving all the adults who live beneath its roof. I have done this many times before, when there has been a crisis, and I judged that there was now a certain and imminent crisis to be faced. I invited Joseph to come for supper, and to stay the night. He duly turned up at five, and appeared to be a little more mobile than he had been on our last encounter. At eight o'clock, with the supper things cleared away, and the washing-up done, and the children safely tucked up for the night, we got down to business.

First, I shared the information culled from the *Cambrian News* and from Lewis Legal's letter. Joseph banged the table with his fist, and said he was furious that the idiotic newspaper has mentioned the strange note and -- in effect -- triggered off a manhunt. He thought that would put the four impostors even more on their guard than they were already, and would cause them to lie low for a while. It would also, he thought, have the effect of making them much more careful in future -- and make it much more difficult for the forces of law and order (in which he included himself) to bring them to justice.

We all tried to work out what was happening, and for a while we all talked at once, in a utterly chaotic fashion. But then Joseph held up his hand and revealed -- not before time -- that he knew more about the episode in which he was almost trampled to death by that herd of cattle. "The animals were driven by at least three men on horseback," he said. "When I regained consciousness I realized that I had broken my leg, and that I would do more harm than good if I tried to get up and struggle back to town. So I lay there in the mud and cattle shit, and undertook certain investigations........"

"Oh Joseph, you are incorrigible," I moaned.

He disregarded my remark, and carried on, speaking very quickly. "There were clear hoof-prints from at least three horses, on top of the prints of the cloven hooves of the cattle. No doubt about it. And the horses were not local ones."

"How on earth can you say that, Joseph?" asked Shemi.

"My dear boy, observation and background knowledge. I know the work of every blacksmith and farrier within ten miles of Newport. Take it from me that those horses had city shoes, made for work in the city, where they have cobbled streets and paving stones." Then he took out a crumpled piece of paper from his pocket, and continued. "When I regained consciousness I found this pinned to my skin. It reads: **For Henben. From Edenawg**. I managed to pull the pin out and stick the note and the pin into my pocket before my good neighbour came along and found me."

I buried my head in my hands. "Oh no, not again!" I moaned. "You poor dear man. Why did you not tell us this before? Did they -- did they cut you as well?"

"No, thank goodness. I am a stoical sort of fellow, but my stoicism does have limits. A broken leg, an attached label and a good trampling by a herd of bullocks is enough to be going on with. Remember that my accident -- if we can call it that -- happened in broad daylight, on a public highway. I think that the fellows responsible found some way of spooking my horse. They then drove Willy Carter's bullocks from the paddock at the side of the road, probably with the intention of getting me killed. They came afterwards on their horses to see if I was dead. I was unconscious at the time, and in a shocking mess. Maybe they thought I **was** dead -- and maybe they did intend to cut me. One day we might find this out. But I think they were in a great hurry, and maybe heard somebody coming along the road. All they had time to do was to pin this note to my chest, and then off they went at the gallop."

"And the note, Joseph?" asked Grandpa.

"I have various theories as to its meaning, but I must undertake further consultations with learned men before I can be certain about things. All will be revealed. But the note itself -- one of a growing number -- is no longer a matter of speculation. It was written by one of Mistress Tasker's guests in the upstairs room occupied by Master Evans and Master Griffith, before they set out on their evil expedition and tried to kill me."

"How on earth did you know that? Did Mistress Tasker watch them at work?"

"No no -- she is a very discreet lady, and a model of sensibility. But she did tell me that she saw several quill pens, and some paper, and a pot of ink in one of the rooms when she was cleaning one day. I have been on another visit to her rubbish pile at the bottom of the garden. This time I grovelled about more deeply beneath the ash and the food scraps, and what do you think I found?" And without further ado, and accompanied by a smile as radiant as a thousand suns, he conjured up an inkpot and three old quill pens from one of his deep pockets. "I was looking for these on my first visit -- and the finding of those bottles of laudanum tincture was an unexpected pleasure which diverted my attention. Unforgivable in a professional man. I must seek to show greater discipline in future -- would you not agree?"

He looked up with a mischievous grin, milking the moment. "Kindly get on with it, Joseph!" said Grandma.

"Yes indeed. To continue. I have examined the ink under my strongest magnifying glass, and have subjected it to certain chemical tests as well, and it is the same ink as that on the note. It is quite a sophisticated iron gall ink, with the particles too fine to have been made in Haverfordwest or Cardigan. I also happen to have in my possession the note that was pinned to Will's skin, and that which afflicted Skiff Abraham. All three notes were written on the same paper, but by different hands. The note on Will's chest was written in his own blood, and so that was a particularly gruesome matter; but the note pinned to Skiff's chest was written in ink. The same ink. I will bet my last silver sovereign that it was also used for the note left outside Dinefwr Mansion, and indeed I have written to Judge Wynn-Evans with a request for a sight of it, so that I can conduct tests. I am also awaiting the arrival of the note found near Lewis Legal's house."

"Joseph, you are a genius!" I exclaimed, expressing the view of all us around the table.

"Quite so. You might also be interested to know that I have followed up the business of the horses and the hooves. Everybody knows that the four horses belonging to those fellows were stabled behind the Llwyngwair Arms. I managed to examine the horses myself, one day when the villains were supposedly out surveying on foot. Two of the horses had London shoes on them. The other two had shoes I could not recognize, possibly because they were re-shod by some farrier somewhere between London and West Wales. I also have further information from one of the ostlers at the inn, one Glasnant Gruffydd. An intelligent boy, whom I rescued once from the Press Gang. He owes me a favour or two, so he showed me the saddles and harnesses of the four horses. Three of them are of modest quality, but one is magnificent, made with much black leather and with brass fittings where most saddlers use iron. It must have cost a fortune, and was made for a big man............."

"Tomos Griffith, whom Mistress Tasker describes as their leader?"

"Quite probably. But inscribed on it were the letters JRTP -- so maybe this is the same man who owned the coat with JP inside its collar. And on the underside of the saddle the following words are embossed: *John Curtain and Sons, Highgate, Saddlers to His Majesty the King*.

"So the villain is a member of the Royal Family, Joseph?" asked Bessie.

"I doubt that. But he certainly is a wealthy man who moves in elevated company. That saddle did not come cheap."

"That is all, Joseph?"

"For the moment. Ladies and gentlemen of the jury, it is therefore established -- beyond reasonable doubt -- that these four men, who go by the false names of William Evans, Tomos Griffith, John Hughes and Glyn Owens, are guilty of the burning down of the mansion of Dinefwr in Llandeilo and the town house called Ty Newydd in Fishguard. Furthermore, they are guilty of the attempted murder of Joseph Harries Esq, of Werndew in the parish of Dinas, and of unspeakable and barbaric acts perpetrated against two law-abiding citizens of the parish of Newport, namely Master Will Owen and Master Skiff Abraham, while they were going about their lawful business. It can be argued that the accused also intended to kill those two gentlemen. I have numerous exhibits to place before the court. I rest my case."

He settled down in his chair, insofar as settling was possible with one leg in splints, and smiled beatifically upon us all. I had to smile too, but then all of us around the table realized that we were not in a court of law, and that these murderous men were still on the loose.

"All credit to you, Joseph, for your masterful sleuthing," said Grandpa. "You have enough evidence to send these fellows to the colonies if not to the gallows, that's for sure. But they are still out there somewhere, maybe far away and maybe just over the summit of Preseli, lurking beneath some rocky crag or in a sheltered hollow. And we still do not have the faintest idea who they are, where they live, what their motives may be, and when next they may seek out a victim."

I responded: "That is quite enough to keep me awake at night, and shivering with fear whenever something moves in the bushes or behind a stone wall.........."

Joseph then wiped the smirk off his face and became serious. He said that he was now certain that others would be targeted -- including Grandpa Isaac, Will Final Testament, Billy, Shemi and Jake -- and that the prime target would be Mistress Morgan of Plas Ingli. I shivered, and could say nothing. "Five or six more potential victims?" said Bessie. "And where does that conclusion spring from?"

"Just give the matter a little thought," said Joseph. "I am convinced that this campaign of vengeance has something to do with the trial, convictions and executions of those evil fellows a couple of years ago. Another who would have been hanged, if he had not been put to death by one of his erstwhile friends, was the monster Joseph Rice. Watkins would have hanged too, if he had not been executed by that Irishman. Just think about it -- the gang was brought to justice by all of us in this room, with the able assistance of Skiff, Jake, Lewis Legal, Will Final Testament, and of course Judge Wynn-Evans who represented the long arm of the law. Well, three good men who acted in the cause of justice are now battered, broken and bruised, and two others have to rebuild their homes if not their lives."

I asked: "Is there nothing we can do to protect ourselves?"

"At the very least, we need an arrest warrant," said Grandma. "Isaac *bach*, you are a senior magistrate. Will you issue one?"

"No -- I am too close to all of this. But one of my colleagues will do it, on the basis that we do indisputably have evidence against these fellows that would stand up in a court of law. I will ask my old friend Jenkin Edwards of Llwyngoras. He owes me a little favour. He'll do it."

"A warrant would be no favour to you, Grandpa" says Martha. "I would say it is a necessity for the safety of the community, with so many people already harmed and others in extreme danger from these men."

Everybody agreed with that. But Shemi frowned. "Master Isaac, what you say is all very well, but we do not even know their names. How can you issue an arrest warrant for people who do not exist?"

"That is no problem, Shemi. I have seen many arrest warrants in my time for people who do not exist in the parish records. The criminal classes use false names all the time. We will simply put on the warrant *"the men who call themselves William Evans, Tomos Griffith, John Hughes and Glyn Owens"*, or some such thing."

"Very well," says Joseph. "I concur that we must have a warrant. But it will be a mixed blessing. I doubt that it will help us to apprehend these wretched fellows. But there will be a hue and cry, and that will cause them to lie low for a while. With a bit of luck, it may encourage them to stay in England, where life is possibly more peaceful. But if they really do have a mission, and if they are determined to see it through, they could now become even more devious."

That was exactly the conclusion that I had reached some days since, but I felt that nothing would be gained from saying so. Before we all went off to bed with our flickering candles, Joseph urged all of us -- and me in particular -- to be very careful in case the four men might return. And he also mentioned something I had not thought of before, by pointing out that there might be others in the community who were working with them. "Oh my God," I thought. "Is it really possible that there might be a spy or a traitor in our midst?"

31st October 1808

Will is very weak but we are all greatly relieved that he is recovering. Like most men he hates being in bed all by himself, but quite enjoys being pampered. Poor Skiff will take longer than Will to recover from his injuries, because in spite of the loving care given to him by Patty and Jake in the first instance, and then by his own family, he has lost a lot of blood, and some of his wounds have turned septic. Joseph has made several visits to his sick bed, and is working hard to heal him, but he says that weeping wounds are very dangerous and require special medication. Skiff is furious about being in bed and about coming off second best in a battle. This attack has diminished his status and damaged his self-esteem, since he has always looked upon himself as a hard man, well able to look after himself. But his friends are sworn to take their revenge. His confederates Abby, Halfpint and others, with whom he has survived many past escapades, are already on the case, and they are apparently disinclined to display any Christian charity towards his enemies.

With the aid of Will and Skiff, I have set up a network of informers in the community in case the four impostors, or any other strangers, should return. There was no shortage of volunteers, all reliable men and women who have proved their worth over and again in the various crises which have afflicted the Plas and its inhabitants in the ten years or so since I arrived. I am now as certain as I can be that if those four impostors appear anywhere within ten miles of the Plas, we will hear about it within hours rather than days. And if they, or any of their cronies, threaten any of us, we will be able to summon an army of vigilantes in no time at all to hunt them down. After all, we now have powerful evidence of their guilt, and an array of witnesses who will appear in a Petty Sessions or in the Assize Court if necessary.

Now that Joseph has deduced the names of those who might be on the list mentioned by Gwynfor Rees, he has warned all of those who are unharmed thus far to take extra care. That means Billy, Shemi, Grandpa and myself beneath the roof of Plas Ingli, Will Probert the attorney in Newport, and Jake down on the Parrog. Jake has seen for himself what these monsters are capable of, and so has his wife Patty. But she has had enough trauma to cope with in her short life, and has a very small baby, so we have decided to protect her from unnecessary worry. Billy will meet Jake in the Royal Oak very soon and put him in the picture. It is then down to him to decide how much, or how little, he will divulge to his wife, and how best to protect himself.

At supper time today I told the other servants that I am minded to give employment to Gwynfor Rees as a carpenter. Will was allowed out of his sick bed to be present at the supper table, and he was furious when he heard the news. "Dammo, Mistress," he grumbled. "That bastard was an informer who almost caused the deaths of me, Skiff and the Wizard. You heard how he admitted to his crimes, with the gentle encouragement of the *Ceffyl Pren.* He will do anything for a few shillings, and I would not trust him with my bread and cheese, let alone my life. Are you really serious about this?"

"I am, Will," I replied, unmoved. "I have spoken to him at length, and I am convinced that he is not a bad fellow, but one who has had misfortune piled upon him. You know his family circumstances?"

Will nodded reluctantly. "I suppose I do. We are all aware that life in that little hovel is not easy for him."

"And he has served his nation in the wars against the French, and almost lost his life while doing his duty. I think that his little deal with the four famous surveyors came about partly because he was gullible -- in that he knew nothing of the real events that led Howell, Watkins and the others to their graves -- and partly because he was desperate for even a few coppers that might help him to feed his family."

"Well, Mistress, if my opinion is worth anything, I still think he is a bastard, and if I get a chance I will give him a little nudge into the river, next time it is in flood."

"You will do nothing of the sort, Will, for that will drive a small family and a blind mother into the arms of the parish, for which we will all have to pay. In any case, he has promised to apologize for his foolishness, face to face, in front of you, Skiff and Joseph. That will be the action of a brave man........"

Will would not give up. "He drinks too much," he said. "No wonder his wife and children are starving."

"I know that too. But he has promised to reform himself. And let me remind you, Will, that before you started at the Plas three years ago you were not exactly the whitest sheep in your mother's family. You were lucky not to be transported to the colonies. Have you forgotten that?"

"Too true, Mistress," Will mumbled, looking just a little shamefaced. "I admit that my life has been less than perfect until now. But I have tried to stay out of trouble, have I not?"

"Indeed you have, Will. There are still certain of your activities that I would prefer not to know about -- but I commend you for your efforts, and I declare that I have never seen a better shepherd or cow-man. Since you have turned from wayward youth to model servant, will you not admit that it is also possible for Gwynfor to undergo a sort of transformation? I ask you to give him the chance. What say you all?"

"I will trust your judgement, Mistress," said Billy at last. "But I will keep a very close eye on him, and if I see anything untoward he will be out on his neck, and back to the snug in the Royal Oak, where he belongs."

"Will, how about you?"

"I will go along with that, Mistress, but I will make sure I never turn my back on him. Let us see how he gets on."

"Very well. I thank you for your opinions and your support. It is decided. We need a carpenter anyway. I'll ask him to start on Monday."

Then we chatted of other things. Just before we all went off to bed, Bessie said nonchalantly: "You know that Irishman? Not much sign of him lately. But he was in town again yesterday, so I gather, fetching some sacks of wheat from Llwyngwair."

"Oh?" I replied, pretending to be uninterested.

Now I am sitting at my dressing table, listening to the tawny owls far away in the woods near Cilgwyn Mill. The moon is almost full, and it appears intermittently from behind a procession of heavy clouds coming in from the West. There is a stiff breeze which rattles the dry leaves that are still on the trees around the Plas. All might seem to be well with the world, but for some reason I feel frightened and even lonely. Maybe I am doubting my judgement in employing Gwynfor Rees -- and I was not exactly given a ringing endorsement by the servants. I try to be firm and decisive, but it is not easy. If only I had a good man by my side to make decisions about employment and such like in my place! Why do I have to do these things? Have I not got more than my fair share of problems already?

And I have realized with some force that the targetting of victims by these four evil and mysterious men has been anything but random. It has all been planned with a cool cynicism. In the space of a few days they have ensured that they will be safe from the attentions of Joseph Harries, the only man capable of investigating crimes and making clever deductions; Lewis Legal, the most effective attorney in the region; and the most intelligent and experienced judge in West Wales. And Will and Skiff, the two toughest characters in town, who would protect me unto the end of the world, are now also out of the way.

Who is left to enforce law and order and to pursue criminals? I know the answer, and it does not encourage confidence. We are supposedly protected by John Wilson and Evan Evans, two ineffectual constables who would much rather be doing something else; by the town Mayor and Court Leet, used to dealing with minor offences relating to straying cattle and boundary disputes; and by assorted magistrates who do their best, or their worst, at the Petty Sessions and who have no training in the law. Then there is Will Daniels, the clerk to the justices, who works hard to avoid involvement in anything other than the collection of his fees. So much for official protection. So one after another, the worthy men whom I have counted as my guardian angels have been removed from the scene. Suddenly I feel totally vulnerable, and at the mercy of events.

Ch 6. Light in Dark Places

1st November 1808

At last an arrest warrant for the four impostors has been issued. It was signed, in five copies, by two magistrates, Jethro Gittins Tredrissi and Jenkin Edwards Llwyngoras, both of whom are old friends of Grandpa Isaac and men of integrity. It was issued by Will Daniels, the Clerk to the Justices, on the basis of written complaints from Will, Skiff, Joseph and Lewis Legal relating to assorted alleged crimes -- including arson, grievous bodily harm, assault and battery, attempted murder, and stabbing. Much to my surprise, and no doubt down to the meticulous research of Joseph, five other crimes have also been added to the list, including the theft of a cart used to carry Skiff, bound hand and foot, from Newport down to the estuary; grave cruelty to a herd of bullocks owned by Master William Carter; use of false names; and the use of an illegal substance, viz laudanum, for purposes other than medication. That last one amuses me, since I am not sure where medication ends and recreation begins, and in any case I did not know that laudanum was illegal. But Will Daniels says that according to his learned books it is indeed banned, in spite of being widely used by the medical profession, and I suppose he must be right. The warrants have been issued in the names of "*the men who call themselves Tomos Griffith, Glyn Owens, William Evans, and John Hughes, all late of England, and none of whom being Welsh-speaking. The man using the name Griffith being tall and speaking in a whisper, and late of London, with the initials JP, and the man using the name Owens being a Scot.* That all makes up a considerable mouthful, but Master Daniels assures us that the extra details are necessary if the men (who might well be using quite different names by now) are to be apprehended.

Three copies of the warrant are currently held by Master Daniels in his office for use at a moment's notice by the constables or by any other officers of the law, and the signing magistrates hold one copy each. The locations of the warrants are widely known, and they can be used without any of the normal delays if one or another (or maybe all) of the impostors should be found and apprehended anywhere in West Wales. And copies of the Reward Notice issued by Judge Wynn-Evans, offering £100 for information leading the arrest of the Llandeilo arsonists, have now also found their way into north Pembrokeshire. One is posted on the church door, and another on the public notice board outside the Mayor's office. That is unusual, since the fire was in a town more than fifty miles from Newport. The notice has also been published in all the local newspapers, indicating that the Judge is taking this matter very seriously, and is prepared to spend a considerable sum of money on advertising and printing costs. And finally the Town Crier, Billy Bellow, has been out and about in the streets on several occasions for the benefit of those who cannot read and who might otherwise depend upon idle gossip and untruths for their essential information. He has bellowed lustily, and swung his heavy hand-bell, and announced to all and sundry the contents of the arrest warrant and the Reward Notice. If any person in town does not now know that the four impostors who visited Newport were up to serious mischief, he or she must be blind, deaf or permanently drunk. I think all of that does make it a little easier for me to sleep well in my bed in the coming days and weeks.

Last night was Hallowe'en, and before the children went to bed their Great-Grandpa Isaac sat them in front of the blazing and crackling kitchen fire and told them several very spooky stories about ghosts and goblins and strange happenings in the neighbourhood. He held them entranced for over an hour, and indeed the rest of us were thoroughly entertained as well, although in truth we had heard all of the stories several times before. But Grandpa is a master story-teller, and would no doubt have been a travelling bard had he lived in another century and had he enjoyed the patronage of one of the Welsh princes. The subtle nuances of his voice, his choice of words, and his instinctive mastery of timing caused me, as ever, to become lost in admiration; and I noticed that the greater part of his story consisted of silences -- pregnant pauses, sharp intakes of breath, and long gaps in which the listener was invited to anticipate what was going to happen next. How I loved him! And how I loved the little ones, sat there in their dressing gowns, eyes wide and mouths agape, hanging on every word and filling every silence with words of their own, inside their heads! When he was done, and to ensure that Sara and Brynach in particular would not spend the night suffering from childish nightmares, Grandma exclaimed: "Stuff and nonsense! Don't you believe a word of all that, children! Your Great Grandpa makes it all up, and ghosts and goblins don't exist at all. He just likes inventing silly stories to frighten small children." At last, they said their goodnights, and Sian and I took them off to their rooms, where we gave them an extra ration of hugs and kisses, tucked them down beneath their soft woolly blankets, and left candles burning in case the darkness -- on this particular night -- should frighten them.

I can admit in the pages of my diary what I would not admit anywhere else -- that I have tried a divination. That is an appropriate thing for a single woman to do on Hallowe'en. Grandma says that *rhamanta* is nonsense, and that charmings and divinations may be of some use for primitive brutes who live in caves, but have no place in the modern world. But I pressed her once on this, and she admitted somewhat shamefacedly that she had used the divination involving the blade bone of a sheep when she was a girl, and had dreamed that her future husband would be a tall man called Jack. In the event she married a short man called Isaac, and proceeded to enjoy a very happy married life with him. She laughed and so did I, but she did admit that it is in the nature of things for women to wonder whom they might marry. And every year, around the Plas kitchen table, we hear the old Hallowee'n rhymes, particularly from the unmarried female servants. One of them is this:

He who would my partner be
Let him come and rake with me

and this is another, used partly in jest and partly in despair:

There's a crow for every crow
Perched in every tree.
Who the devil shot the crow
Intended just for me?

Yesterday afternoon -- maybe because it is the time of month when I become moody and irritable -- I needed fresh air, and took a short walk on the common. I felt desperately worried and lonely, and angry with Cruel

Fate who had left me to face the dangers associated with the four sinister surveyors -- and maybe the Nightwalker as well -- without a husband by my side. My mind drifted to Owain, and then to Dominic, and I found that my thoughts were in a tangle. What should I do -- wait passively for Owain, who might be dead, or take steps to build upon the chance meeting with Dominic and see where it might lead? A month had passed since my one fleeting encounter with him, and he should have disappeared from my thoughts by now, but he had not. I determined upon a divination, and assumed, perhaps arrogantly, that since I do have special powers that enable me to see things that others do not see, I would be blessed by a truthful outcome. Which divination should it be? Some I had learnt as a girl in Brawdy parish, and some seemed to be restricted to the Newport area. One or two, said Grandma, were quite unique to Cilgwyn. Should I go down to Cilgwyn Church at midnight and walk around it nine times and then peep through the keyhole in order to see my future beloved? I thought that was not a very good idea, because this house is full of light sleepers, some of whom were bound to hear me trotting off on tiptoes at eleven-thirty and returning at dead of night. Anyway, the churchyard would probably be crawling with local virgins trying to find answers to their prayers and confirmations for their dreams. Then I thought of the divination involving the shoulder blade of a sheep, and rued the fact that I had not secreted one away long since on the basis that it might come in handy. It was too late for the love cake solution, too, since that involved pullet's eggs, wheatmeal flour and salt, and a lot of banging about in the kitchen, which would bring Mrs Owen rushing out of her room like an Amazon warrior if I should dare to try it when everybody else was in bed.

So I decided on the ash leaf charm, which was much more discreet. On my walk I found an ash tree that had not yet been stripped of its leaves by the autumn gales, and after a considerable search I found a twig that had five pairs of leaves on it, and one extra leaf at the end. I broke it off with my left hand (as is proper), secreted it in the deepest pocket of my coat, and then smuggled it into my room and placed it under my pillow. At midnight, when I assumed that everybody else was fast asleep, I took it out again, blew out the candles, and took off all of my clothes. Then, shivering because of the cold and the excitement of it all, I sat in the window with a faint moonshine filtering in and addressed the leaves as I had been taught by an old woman in Solva when I was a girl. Holding the twig in my left hand, I spoke softly to the single leaf, pointing to it with the index finger of my right hand and using the words: "Talk to me, *union onnen*." Then I had to address each of the pairs of leaves in turn, again pointing to them with my right hand. To the first pair I said: "Talk to me, *dwbwl gangen*." Then the next, and the next, and the last two pairs, using the words "Talk to me, *gwas a morwyn, clochydd a pherson, gwr a gwraig*" and so forth, until all the leaves had been addressed. Then I held the whole twig to my bosom, taking care not to touch it with my right hand. I sat there in the moonlight for as long as I dared, until my teeth started to chatter, and then with due reverence placed it under my pillow, put on my nightgown, and cuddled down under the blankets. According to tradition I was then supposed to dream of my future husband. All that happened was that I dreamt of assorted happy children, some of whom I recognized and others that I did not. When I woke up and tried to recall my dreams I could not for the life of me find a man, and decided that the dream about children was so normal for me as to be of no significance. In disgust I threw the ash twig onto the fire, and went down to breakfast in a foul mood. To make matters worse, I had caught a chill from all that sitting about without any clothes on.

Bessie observed that I was blowing my nose and wrapping up warm even in the cosy kitchen, and gave me a knowing look. "A bit of a sniffle this morning, Mistress," she said nonchalantly. "Not up to any mischief last night, I hope?" Impudent girl! I must give her a good ticking off. And why is it that she always seems to know what I am doing, even when I take great care to protect my privacy? Are there no secrets left in this life?

2nd November 1808

I have forgiven Bessie for her insolence, as I always do. Anyway, my little chill has passed over quickly, and my mood has lightened. I have had a very busy day, and trust that life is returning to normal at the Plas.

Today has not just been frantic, but dirty and noisy as well. That is because after *Calan Gaeaf* or All Saints Day the farm animals are traditionally gathered in so that they can be sorted into various groups -- those to be kept over the winter, those to be sold, and those to be slaughtered for salting, drying and turning into sausages, mincemeat and so forth. Before breakfast, all the sheep and this year's lambs were brought down from the mountain by Shemi and herded into one of the top fields. Normally Will would do that, but he is still out of action so the task fell to our gentle giant instead. Will always uses three dogs for the roundup, but Shemi does not use shepherding dogs. I watched him at work. He just walked up onto the common, whistled between his teeth and called to the sheep using words and sounds that nobody else can understand or repeat. Within a few minutes they had congregated around him from far and wide across the mountain. He then led them quietly back to the Plas, took them into the field, and shut the gate. Will watched the performance too, standing with me by the wall at the back of the house. He just shook his head in wonderment and envy. But the sheepdogs were less than pleased, shut in their kennels and denied the opportunity to do the work for which they have been bred. The only other man I know who has this ability to communicate with animals is Squire Richard Fenton of Glynymel, but he does not use his skill very often, and then only as a party trick, being more interested in books and antiquities than in cows and sheep.

Once the sheep were contained within stone walls they gave vent to their frustration, and even before we began sorting them they started a chorus of bleating which is only rivalled on one other day of the year -- when the sheared ewes and their lambs are reunited in a June storm of confusion caused by the loss of their heavy fleeces. The cattle, calves and heifers also picked up on the fact that something was afoot, for they were soon making a fearsome racket as well. Then the horses started, and the pigs, and the geese. Grandpa says that the animals can smell death, even before the slaughtering starts. We checked all the animals in turn, moving from field to paddock and into the farmyard itself. When it came to selecting which of the sheep were to be slaughtered, we always let Will do the choosing, for he knows without examining them which ones are old and ailing, which ones have a tendency to foot-rot and blowfly infestations, and which ones are the inveterate escapers and trouble makers. We keep the ewes that produce twins and triplets since they make up the foundations of the flock, and of course the yearlings will have preference over the battered old ewes with missing teeth and scraggy fleeces, for those matrons of the flock will probably not survive the winter snowdrifts and driving rains anyway. When it comes to cattle, Billy and Grandpa do the choosing, basing their selections on the age of the animals, their weight and condition, and their milking record. At the end of it all, there were twelve sheep and six cattle to be slaughtered, two old horses to go to the market, and another thirty ewes and eleven cows to be sold at Cardigan Market in a week's time and also to the local butchers. Since the beginning of time the animals from the Plas have gone to Dafydd Digit, the butcher on West Street who lost his index finger one day when making sausages and never did recover it. Other farms tend traditionally to sell to other butchers. The animals sold locally will no doubt be slaughtered down on the estuary, in that stinking place where poor Gwynfor Rees was punished by the *Ceffyl Pren*. In the spring we will see which animals have survived, and assess our needs, and maybe purchase some promising ram lambs and other stock to bring us up to strength.

The slaughtering started this afternoon, with six of the sheep. They had their throats cut by Billy, and then they were bled, beheaded, skinned and cleaned, and hearts, livers, kidneys and so forth were taken to the scullery. Then what was left of the animals was hung up in the barn where it is always cool. The carcasses will stay there for three days and they will then be butchered and handed over to Mrs Owen, who has cunning plans for every edible mouthful and presumably every bone as well. The other sheep, and the cattle, will all be slaughtered and dealt with in the same way over the coming week, involving all my male servants and several of our tenants as well. We like to be clear of the task by the tenth day of November. Don't ask me why. Then, immediately following Martinmas, we slaughter the pigs that have been fattened up for Christmas and the geese and ganders which are also needed for the festive season.

In the past I have always tried to keep the children away from all the bloody sights and smells associated with the slaughtering season, and this year Daisy and Sara say they will go off for long walks every day until the killing has ceased. I am happy with that, and Sian will go with them. Betsi is a very different character, and today she insisted on watching everything. She is far less squeamish than I am, and would happily wield the knife if I would allow it. Dewi and little Brynach are also perfectly nonchalant about the life and death of farm animals, much to my amazement, given their tender age. I think I know already which of my children will be farmers, and which ones will not.

This evening, in a welcome escape from the blood and guts of the farmyard, I dressed up in my favourite silk dress, and put up my hair with Bessie's help, and went off in the carriage to the Glynymel Autumn Ball, with Billy at the reins. He was in a foul mood, since we had forced him to use camphor balls and carbolic soap in abundance, to get rid of the smells of entrails and death. Grandma and Grandpa came too. On the way, I tried not to think about the occasion, two years since, when I had too much to drink, and made a considerable fool of myself. But I could not help thinking about it, and the recollection brought a cold sweat to my brow which I hoped that my fellow passengers did not notice. At the culmination of that shameful episode John Fenton almost had his wicked way with me, and I have to thank his father Richard for a timely intervention which saved me and led to the banishment of the wayward son from the house. The journey from the Plas took about an hour, and with the two old people in the best of spirits, the time flew by.

The Ball was, as ever, a very grand affair, delicately hosted by Squire Fenton and his wife Anne, and attended by almost all the best families of north Pembrokeshire. The food was plentiful and beautifully prepared and presented, and I kept to my vow of drinking more cordial than wine. My friend Ellie and her husband Walter Phillips (a dark and surly man whom I cannot bring myself to like) were present, as were Owain's sister Mary Jane and her husband Dafydd Stokes. He is a fine man, and the sort of fellow I could well have married myself, if Mary Jane had not got in first. As ever on such occasions, we three old friends danced a great deal with elegant gentlemen, and found time to exchange news and put the world to rights. Eighteen months after the event, other guests speculated about Owain's disappearance in May 1807, but there was also much animated conversation about the four evil surveyors and the injuries to Will, Joseph and Skiff. I can record, with a little pride, if that is in order, that I was in great demand on the dance floor as ancient squires assessed my shape and tested my mettle, and as their sons sought to impress me with their dancing skills and their good looks. I was perfectly impervious to all of that, and told anybody who wanted to listen that I was far too busy ever to contemplate marrying again. Out of respect for the transport difficulties of many of the guests who had travelled great distances and had to get home by the light of the moon, the Ball ended at eleven o'clock. I was grateful for that since Grandpa and Grandma had already nodded off, sweetly cuddled together, on a pile of cushions in the conservatory. On the way home, I sat opposite them, contemplating the fact that as middle-aged people become old people, they need to be looked after like children by those of us who are currently not quite old and not quite young.

One other piece of news from Fishguard before I blow out my candles and collapse into bed. Lewis Legal has put up posters in town offering a reward of £10 for information leading to the arrest of the four impostors, who are accused in print of *"nefarious activities, including impersonation, assault and battery, attempted murder, and the burning of property."* According to Ellie, Master Lewis is so furious at the loss of his home, and so impatient with the incompetence of the constables and the justices that he has decided to encourage somebody who might know something to come forward. He has taken this action, by all accounts, following conversations with Joseph, but Joseph is not so sure that a manhunt is a good idea, and thinks that a more measured response would have been more appropriate.

3rd November 1808

Today Skiff's disreputable friend Abby ambled up to the Plas with some small news. He said that according to the spies who have reported back to the headquarters in the back room of the Black Lion, there is no sign at all of the sinister surveyors anywhere within twenty miles of Newport. He said that after leaving Newport in a hurry, they were seen on their horses in Narberth, and then three days ago in Carmarthen. They stayed there in a lodging house, using the same false names, and then headed towards Llanelli and Swansea. "Them fellows have gone, Mistress," said Abby. "But if they come back, we will know about it, and before they gets here, indeed. Then we will deal with the bastards -- never fear."

That news was very welcome, and since Abby arrived very conveniently just as we were sitting down to our midday meal, he joined us, and ate a great deal. The best spies must be well fed, in order to keep up their strength and their concentration.

In the afternoon, with an assurance that the coast was now clear for comings and goings without chaperones and bodyguards, I decided to drive the smaller trap over the mountain to Wiston Mill -- ostensibly with a bag of wheat which needed milling. The others raised their eyebrows when I told them where I was off to, and why. "Off you go then," said Grandma Jane, "but I am at a loss to know why all the other mills within ten miles of here, including the Gelli Mill on your own estate, are not up to the task." I replied that the miller at Wiston had installed some new millstones which ground especially fine, and that I was minded to try his flour for the Christmas baking this year. Mrs Owen, who was up to her elbows in dough at the time, grunted but said nothing.

I arrived at the mill after a most bracing drive, and of course hoped to meet Dominic again. He was not at home, and so I had to talk to the miller Benjamin Skyrme instead. He agreed to mill my bag of wheat on the spot, since his millpond was full, and while the great heavy machinery thumped and squealed and rumbled, we made small talk for a while. Then I said nonchalantly: "By the way, by a strange coincidence I met a young fellow at Portfield Fair a month ago who said that he works for you..............."

"Ah yes," said Master Skyrme. "That will be young Dominic. I like him -- he is a cheerful sort of fellow, except when he is in one of his moods. Intelligent, too. He doesn't really need to work, here or anywhere else. He says he is a member of a wealthy Irish family who has lived until recently in London. Then he was at the big house here for a while. He says he wants to learn five trades -- which is somewhat ambitious, since I have spent a lifetime learning one, and still make mistakes. At any rate, he helps out now and then -- and sometimes goes off for days on end. But when he is here at the mill, he works hard and earns his keep.

"Has he been to Newport lately?"

"Oh yes, several times. He seems to like it there. He fetches some wheat from Llwyngwair Manor when I need it -- and sometimes when I don't need it, too. But it's a good hard wheat, and I like to mix it with the wheat from these parts to make my special flour -- which I call Wiston Wonder. Good name, don't you think? Want to buy a sack of it?"

"I think I might. I shall try it in a comparison with the flour from my own wheat. Good wheat flour is a rarity these days."

So we talked, and spent a pleasant hour or so in each other's company. Then I set off for home with two sacks of flour in the trap. I was more than a little disappointed that the miller did not, apparently, know too much about the mysterious Irishman. But he did say that Dominic goes to Haverfordwest Market every Thursday to sell sacks of flour, and never comes back with anything unsold. "He has the gift of the Blarney, Mistress," said Master Skyrme. "He could sell fish heads to a fishwife and a sledge to a wheelwright. I dare say he could tell people almost anything, and they would believe every word of his cock and bull nonsense."

9th November 1808

Gwynfor has started work at the Plas. True to his word, he has already been to visit Skiff and Joseph, and has apologized for his misguided actions. They have accepted his apologies with good grace. And a few days ago, when he arrived, he apologized to Will, who grudgingly agreed to let byegones be byegones, and shook his hand. Billy set him to work in a small stable that no longer houses any horses, and this will become the carpentry shop. He will continue to live in the hovel near the river and will come up to the Plas every day to work. There is much for him to do -- new gates to make for some of the fields, doors and roofs to repair, timber to be cut and stored, and structural repairs to be done on the leaky cowshed roof.

Since today was a Thursday, I travelled to Haverfordwest, on the pretext of a social visit to Morys and Nansi. I also wanted Billy to look at some black cattle bred on the Orielton estate which Grandpa thinks might be tough enough for our climate at the Plas and also suitable for breeding some extra bulk into future generations of our herd. If they look good, I told Billy that I might buy two heifers. So we drove off early in the trap, and went straight to the market. Billy went off to look for black cattle, and I went in the other direction to look for Dominic. I found his stall without difficulty, and our eyes met. "Why, Dominic!" I said. "What a surprise! I had forgotten that you come here on a Thursday. Doing good business, I trust?"

He doffed his hat and gave a little bow. "Good day to you, Mistress Morgan," he said, without a smile. "Yes, business is good. Here to see your brother, I suppose?"

"As it happens, yes. And maybe to buy some heifers." He lowered his eyes, and there was an awkward silence. Then somebody wanted a 14 lb bag of wheat flour, and he passed it over and took the money. I did not really know what to say next, so I made the inane comment: "I do believe it must be a month or so since we last met. How time rushes by!"

"Yes indeed."

"Master Skyrme told me that you are more than competent in selling quality flour to the good people of the county town."

"Yes," he replied, with his eyes darting back and forth and not meeting mine. "He did mention that you had called, and that you had chatted about this and that. You and the children are well, I trust?"

"Very well, thank you." There was another silence. Another

customer came and bought two small bags of Wiston Wonder flour, and embarked on a long eulogy about its merits. Then two more customers came and completed their transactions, while I stood on one side not quite knowing what to do with myself. When they had gone I resumed my conversation, and asked Dominic if he had been to Newport several times. He looked startled. "Why yes, Mistress Martha," he said at last. "I cannot deny it. I fetch wheat for Master Skyrme when he needs it."

"And have you -- shall we say -- made certain enquiries?"

"I have -- I cannot deny that either," said he, with a slight flush upon his cheeks. "My goodness, you seem to know everything."

"Well, Newport is a very small place. When a stranger arrives in town, everybody knows about it."

Then more customers arrived, and it was clear that our conversation was going nowhere. So I said: "Well, I see you are very busy. I'd best not waste any more of your time. Goodbye, and give my kind regards to your Master." He doffed his hat again, nodded, and said: "Farewell, and my regards to the family."

I walked away from the stall in a black fury, feeling that I had been snubbed. Had I travelled all this way to Haverfordwest just to go through the motions of a stiff and contrived conversation which lasted for just five minutes and revealed absolutely nothing about his feelings towards me? I had felt like an obnoxious little girl, put in her place by a sarcastic parent after interfering in some adult conversation. Wretched fellow! Well, if that was the best he could do in the way of civility, let him stay where he is, selling bags of cheap flour to anybody stupid enough to want it! I could not care less, and I would not give him a moment's thought from this point on. There were other fish in the sea, and more worthy of the effort of netting them. Why, had I not just been to the Glynymel Autumn Ball, where all the eligible bachelors of North Pembrokeshire had struggled to sign me up for the best dances of the evening, with a view to staking some claim on my affections? Well, to Hell with millers and their apprentices; they don't need me and I don't need them, and in future I will not even give a moment's thought to anybody beneath my own station. If I am ever to fall in love and marry again, I will marry up, and find a wealthy squire who will give me the respect I deserve.........

"Have you been weeping, Mistress?" said Billy when we met up at the cattle market.

"No no, Billy,"I lied. "It was very windy at the other end where all the produce stalls are, and I got some dust into my eyes which caused great irritation." Then, thank the Lord, we got to talking about heifers. My head man said he was not impressed with the Orielton cattle and would not advise any purchases. "Too soft by half, Mistress," he said with a sigh. "They would not survive a November frost at the Plas, let alone a January blizzard. Let them stay where they are, in the balmy South."

With nothing more to be done at the market, we called in on Morys and Nansi. Since I had not given them any warning, Morys was out making pastoral calls on the sick and needy, but Nansi and the children were delighted to see us, and we shared a simple midday meal with them. I told Nansi something about the events in Newport and Fishguard, and about the arrest warrant and the reward notices. She had picked up just a little of the news from the local newspapers, but none of them had mentioned the Plas by name, and indeed there was no reason for anybody like her to assume that Mistress Martha Morgan was involved in any way in the activities of the four impostors. Nonetheless, Nansi knows me rather too well, and as we took our leave her last words were: "Martha dearest, I may not need to say this, but I trust that you will have nothing to do with all of that business involving the four strangers. Concentrate on the Plas and the children if you will, and just you take care."

13th November 1808

This afternoon I went for a bracing walk on the mountain with the older children, with a view to discovering where the best rushes may be found in the boggy areas, so that in a few days' time we can collect them efficiently in time to produce the winter stock of rushlights. We have already been building up our supplies of tallow, following the animal slaughter, and the menservants are still rendering down the poorer quality animal fat in a big cauldron on a fire behind the cowshed. Grandpa says that in the past this was done over the kitchen fire, but the smell is so disgusting that one of the first things that I did on my arrival at the Plas was to banish the November tallow cauldron from the house on the grounds that the smell was still there at Christmas. Even with the foul mixture bubbling away outside, the smell billowing around the yard was quite unbearable-- and therein lay the real reason for our walk.

Having condemned Dominic to the eternal fires of hell, and having dismissed him from my mind, I am now in a state of confusion. That young man has, in short, restored some of my faith in humanity. When we returned from our expedition, and the children had gone off with Sian for their supper, Mrs Owen handed me a letter. "This came while you were out, Mistress," she said. "Delivered by a fellow who sounded Irish. He did not give his name, but he was good looking and quite smart. Maybe he was the one who gave you that kiss?"

I gave her a look that would have killed a less substantial woman, but I found the good grace to thank her, and scuttled off to my room to read the contents of the envelope. I sat down on my bed, and with shaking fingers I opened it, and found the following short epistle, neatly folded:

Wiston Mill
12th day of November 1808

My Dear Mistress Martha,

May I write to you in such informal terms? I trust so, since I cannot think of you as "Mistress Morgan" or as someone far away, out of reach on some grand pedestal. If you will not forgive me for my impertinence, I dare say there is nothing lost, since I cannot possibly sink any lower in your estimation following my disgraceful behaviour when we met in Haverfordwest Market the other day.

I write to offer you my unreserved apologies. I behaved in a manner that was despicable, and I come out in a cold sweat whenever I think of the way in which my words and my demeanour must have appeared to you. In response to your friendly and genteel attempts to converse with me, as one adult to another, I fear that I must have appeared brutish and quite lacking in sensibility. My father, I am sure, would have sent me packing from the house if he had observed my behaviour, and I will fully understand it if you have already sent me packing out of your mind.

I cannot say anything in my defence other than that I was utterly surprised to see you, and quite unprepared for our conversation, and that I had recently (ie within the hour) been involved in an ugly confrontation with a gentleman whom you will not know. So my mood was foul, and my equilibrium greatly disturbed.

That, I know, is the feeble excuse of a crude fellow. I do not suppose you will ever want to set eyes on me again, but at least I have now done something honourable, in asking for your forgiveness.

Yours truly
Dominic Cunningham

After reading the letter two, or three, or four times, I found that I was shaking like a leaf. This was not supposed to happen. Had I not banished the wretched fellow from my mind and my heart, and consigned the memory of him and **that** kiss to the rubbish heap?

If I had been ten years younger I would have penned an instant reply to the effect that all was forgiven, but I knew that in this case circumspection was required. So I put the letter under my pillow and now I will sleep on it.

25th November 1808

On the matter of that letter from Dominic, I waited a few days, as was appropriate, and then I sent him a short note in which I stated that I had indeed been somewhat upset by his demeanour, but that I now felt that in offering his fullsome apology he had shown his worth as a true gentleman. So I accepted his apology, offered my forgiveness, and said that the unfortunate episode was now quite forgotten. I did not offer any openings for future meetings, as that would have been too forward of me -- and indeed my nerves were still jangling as a result of my attempts to fashion a passing encounter into a relationship of some sort. If there are to be any further moves, they have to be made by him, and not by me.

On other fronts, things have settled down. There have been no further sightings of the strangers, either here or far away. Joseph, Will and Skiff continue to recover from their injuries, and my servant is getting back to light duties on the farm. He is grateful for that, since he has long since tired of being under the same roof as his mother all day long, and is desperate to get back to good solid work in the open air. I think he misses his sheep as a mother might miss her children if she does not see them for several weeks.

Joseph has been to the Plas now and then, and since it is now six weeks since he broke his leg and stared the Grim Reaper in the face, Doctor Havard promises that he can be out of his splints next week. He knows that his leg will be wasted away, and knows that he will have to walk in future rather than trotting about on that pony of his, so as to build up his muscles and his stamina. I have a suspicion that Joseph and the menservants have had several meetings while I have been out of the house. They will tell me nothing, even when I press them. Will said today: "Don't you worry, Mistress. We will look after you." I asked him whether they and the other servants assumed, regarding the four sinister surveyors, that the arrest warrant and the Reward notices might have had the desired effect of driving the men into hiding in England. Much to my relief, he said that that was exactly their thinking, until such time as evidence arrived to the contrary.

28th December 1808

Christmas is over and done with for another year, and in writing briefly about it I have to record that it was a very happy one, with added surprises. As ever, we women thought of little else other than the feeding of the ten thousand for the fortnight before Christmas Day, and although Mrs Owen was reluctant to allow it, I insisted that the children should help too, since I think it is good for them to learn how great and little estates prepare for grand occasions. I also think it reasonable that quite small children should learn a little about household economy and even how to bake a loaf and cook a goose. I trust that they will spend the greater part of their lives above stairs rather than below stairs, but the masters and mistresses of the estates of the next generation will be more emancipated than those of today, and they need to understand what goes into the making of a good servant. Mrs Owen, Bessie and Sian are excellent servants, and they have much to teach those of us who are destined to spend our lives eating meals prepared by others. So Betsi, Daisy and Dewi became kitchen assistants, and even little Sara and Brynach helped with assorted tasks such as mixing dough, filling baking tins and stirring sauces and milky puddings. There were accidents, of course, as when Brynach spilled a quart of whipped cream all over himself, and ended up weeping as if the end of the world had come. But we laughed, and consoled him, and licked him clean, and then got on with our appointed tasks. Strange to relate, even the fierce Mrs Owen seemed to enjoy having the children around, and although her customary efficiency must have suffered considerably she said hardly an unkind word to them. Looking at our Christmas preparations now, after the event, I think that the jollification was a sort of cleansing for her, after the terrible events in which her dear son Will figured so prominently. Now that I come to think of it, I hardly saw her smile in the month of November, so shocked and frightened had she been.

As ever, the cooking was all done by us women, as was the brewing by the men, before breakfast time on Christmas Eve. At ten o'clock prompt, Billy and the other male servants (and a few of the labourers) knocked on the kitchen door and respectfully asked me if I might find room for the plough, until it was needed again. I played along in this little charade, and found space for it under the kitchen table, and with due ceremony the grubby old implement, cleaned and polished just for this occasion, was brought in, placed in its resting place, and anointed with ale. It has done its work on the autumn ploughing, and will now not be needed until February, when the spring ploughing starts. According to tradition, all the women of the house then had to leave the kitchen to the tender mercies of the men, who spent the rest of the morning sampling the Christmas ale and chatting about animals, weather, the price of cider and assorted other manly things. This was the official start of Christmas, which is by no means over simply because it is now the twenty-eighth day of the month. At the Plas and in all of the other mansions of north Pembrokeshire it goes on until *Hen Galan* is over and done with on 14th January. Not much work will be done between now and then. Nobody will have a holiday as such, but there will be a lull in the farming calendar, with only the most essential tasks being done.

At three-thirty on Christmas morning all of us, with the exception of Will, Sian and the children, set off on our walk to town, to attend the annual *Plygain* service. It is a thoroughly boring occasion, filled with Bible readings and prayers and strange old carols heard nowhere else in the world, and I always find it hard to stay awake until the first glimmerings of the dawn bring the proceedings to a close. This year the Rector did turn up for the occasion, so we were greatly blessed. Mrs Owen always brings a flask of rum in her deepest pocket, and manages to take a sip from it now and then without anybody else noticing. How she does it is a mystery to me, but it is an established fact that the flask is always full when she enters the church and empty when she leaves. The part of the ceremony which I love, and which encourages me to attend each year even more than the desire to celebrate the birth of our Lord, is the candle-lit procession by the greater part of the populace of the parish. Nobody rides or comes by carriage, and every year I am entranced by the magical sight of a multitude of little lights from all over the *cwm,* from the Nevern Valley and from the flanks of the mountain, carried by family groups all headed for St Mary's Church. The Plas is the highest farm on the mountain, and when we leave we have the rare privilege of looking down on this milky way of little lights, gleaming and blinking, moving with imperceptible slowness towards the town. Above is another Milky Way, normally visible but this year hidden by a blanket of cloud. Before we entered the Church, Shemi looked at the leaden sky and said to me "Wet Christmas coming this year, Mistress."

And it was very wet indeed. It started to rain shortly after we left the Church at dawn to make our weary way home, and although we managed to get to the shelter of the Plas without a soaking, the heavens then opened and poured forth a veritable deluge. We all went to bed, with no thought of breakfast, but we could not escape it, for the children were rushing about as usual by nine, and at ten-thirty the tenants and labourers and their families appeared out of the deluge for their Christmas breakfast. They expect it, and indeed need it, since the labouring families subsist right on the breadline. And I do not begrudge it, for wages are low in this part of the world, and Grandpa taught me long since to view our Christmas hospitality as a component of the wages bill. So in they trooped, soaking and steaming, leaving a mountain of soggy boots and clogs and sodden oilskins and hessian sacks in the porch and the scullery. It was just as well that Mrs Owen had a roaring fire going in the kitchen, for many of the poor dabs were soaking wet and shivering with the cold. Then, when they had all warmed up, and the windows were streaming with condensation, they all got stuck in to their oat cakes and hot milk, toast and cheese and cold meats and scones, butter and blackberry jam. I gave a special welcome to Gwynfor Rees and his family, since his wife and children had not been to the Plas before. Poor Emily's eyesight has deteriorated further, and she is now almost entirely blind, but she is very brave and manages to maintain a cheerful attitude to life in spite of all her problems. But the little ones are very thin, with pale faces and running noses and deep coughs that are, according to Gwynfor, always present. I was quite distressed when I saw them, but my concern was alleviated just a little when I saw how well they tucked into their breakfasts and when they gave me effusive thanks afterwards.

By noon they had all gone, heading back out into the deluge and promising to see us all again for Christmas Dinner at five o'clock. After clearing up the debris, we all settled into an afternoon of warm indolence, with family and servants snoozing on their beds or on whatever comfortable chairs they could find. This was another Plas Ingli tradition, although I understand from travellers that in Spain they do it all the time.

Even the children were forced to take it easy because of the rain, since it was out of the question for them to go off catching squirrels in the woods near Dolrannog as they normally do on Christmas afternoons.

At three o'clock we were just beginning to stir ourselves for the last major efforts of the day -- milking the cows, feeding all the animals in their pens, kennels, hutches and stables, and starting to prepare the Christmas feast. Mrs Owen was first off the mark, as she always is, since she has an inbuilt timing mechanism more accurate than the most expensive pocket watch. I was rubbing my eyes and trying to force myself into action when I heard a tentative knock on the door. "Now who can that be?" said Grandma sleepily. "Not one of the tenants or labourers, I trust, since they are invited for half past four. Be so kind as to open the door, Billy."

Billy obliged, and who should be standing there, with water pouring off him in a cascade of droplets, but Dominic Cunningham. I was amazed, but I was the only one who recognized him, so of course I invited him in and introduced him to everybody else. "Very pleased to meet you all," he said shyly. "And a very happy Christmas to every one of you!" We gave him reciprocal greetings, and before I could adjust to his presence Mrs Owen took charge and said: "Right, young man. Your teeth are chattering, and those shivers will bring the timbers down if we are not careful. Into the scullery with you, and off with all those clothes, and we will have a steaming hot bath for you in three minutes!" He was in no position to disobey, and so he was herded into the scullery. The men looked after him and his bath while the female servants got on with preparing the dinner, and I rummaged about until I found some dry clothes for him.

In due course he emerged, with his hair plastered down and with assorted old clothes hanging off him. I had forgotten how good looking he was, with his green eyes, fair hair and freckled skin. I had also overestimated his size, for he now turned out to be a young man of slight build, reminiscent of my dear missing Owain. He did look ridiculous, wearing Shemi's old breeches and Will's tatty flannel shirt and jacket, but he laughed with us and that broke the ice. We put his sodden clothes out to dry in front of the fire and I said: "You must be crazy, Dominic, to travel all this way from Wiston in the middle of a monsoon. You didn't walk, did you?"

"No, I am not that crazy," he replied in his soft Irish accent. "I borrowed the master's pony, as usual when I come up this way. I tethered him in the barn, out of the rain, if that's all right."

"Can I suggest, then," said Shemi, "that you wipe him down and give him some oats? Take that oilskin behind the door and come out with me -- I'm going out anyway, to deal with the other animals."

So the two of them went out, and the rest of us got on with the task of preparing for the feeding of the multitude. When Dominic returned, he was carrying a big leather saddle bag. "I was so cold and wet that I forgot the main purpose of my journey!" he said. "Where are the children?"

"In the nursery," I replied. "There is too much chaos here in the kitchen for them, just now."

"Would you call them, please?"

"Of course," said I. "Sian, will you fetch the little ones?

When they came in they stood in a little row, and the girls curtseyed and the boys bowed, as I have taught them to do when introduced to strangers. Dominic introduced himself to them, and there was an immediate rapport. No doubt about it -- he had a way with children. Then he said: "Now then. To business." He turned to Betsi and said: "You are the biggest one, so you must be Betsi. Correct?"

"Yes, sir," said Betsi.

"Good, good. This is for you, and my greetings for a very happy Christmas!" And he conjured out of his bag a miniature doll's house, exquisitely carved from some soft wood. She squealed with delight, and said: "Oh, thank you sir!" Then the process was repeated with all of the others. Daisy was given a very pretty doll with bright blue eyes and red lips; Dewi received with rapture a little book about sea monsters; Sara's present was a box of hand-made and brightly coloured building blocks; and finally little Brynach was given a big rubber ball attached to a string.

"Dominic, you really are very kind," I said. "You even know the children's names!"

"Ah yes," said he, with a wink. "I am renowned for the excellence of my research."

"Well, you must stay for dinner. One more mouth to feed will hardly be noticed. Can you stay?"

"I can indeed, and thank you for your kindness. But I must be away by eight o'clock, even if it is still raining. I have my lantern, and the pony knows the way home."

There was not much time to talk to him after that, since the preparations for the Christmas Dinner were now in full swing. And to his credit, Dominic got stuck in with everybody else, putting out dishes, cutting bread, moving chairs and trestles, and doing whatever else Mrs Owen told him to do. Then the hordes of tenants and labouring families arrived out of the rain and came in through the front door as they are only allowed to do at Christmas and for funerals. They all shook the water off their garments, warmed themselves by the fire, and settled down wherever they could find seats in the kitchen, dining room or parlour. At the last minute, Joseph arrived, and made a great show of walking about without his splints or his crutches, with everybody laughing and clapping. I made a little speech of welcome, as I always do, and then family, servants and guests tucked in. Sixty-five people this year, all fed on goose and roast beef, ham and poached salmon, cabbages, potatoes and turnips, cheese and white bread (a great luxury for most of our visitors), mincemeat, stewed fruits and custard, puddings and cakes. They drank prodigious quantities of cider, punch and ale, and by half past seven some were drunk, some were asleep, and all were replete.

I had no opportunity at all, in the midst of the pandemonium, to talk to Dominic, but every now and then we exchanged glances and smiles from opposite ends of the room, and I made certain observations. I saw him deeply in conversation with Bessie and the other servants, and with Grandpa and Grandma. Joseph and he chatted for a while, and I saw that he recognized and greeted several others in the room, including Gwynfor Rees. I assumed, correctly as it happens, that these were people he had met previously on his visits to Newport.

Suddenly somebody started to sing, and before I knew what was happening Caradoc Williams, my tenant from Gelli, was standing on the table conducting a somewhat shambolic choir of men, women and children in an assortment of Welsh hymns, folk songs and silly ditties.

Many of the songs were in the minor key, and doleful in the extreme, but that is the way with the Welsh. We love to celebrate, and rejoice, through the singing of sombre tunes which bring a tear to the eye.

And speaking of tears, I realized, in the midst of this musical performance, that Dominic was nowhere to be seen. I went to look for him, and found him sitting on the bottom of the stairs with his head in his hands.

"Why, Dominic," I said, "what's wrong? I noticed that you had disappeared........"

He raised his head, and I saw that tears were streaming down his cheeks. He had a strange look in his eyes which I could not interpret. But there seemed to be great sadness in it, and desperation, and pleading. I could not resist sitting next to him, and putting my arm around him. "Oh, Martha," he whispered. "What good people you have here! Good, kind people! This is Christmas as I remember it at home, but with even more love and generosity in it. Good, good people. This is truly a house of angels........."

He wiped his eyes, and nothing more happened between us. He stood up, bowed, shook my hand, and went back into the kitchen. Then he said farewell to Mrs Owen and a few others who happened to be near the door, gathered up his things, and took his leave. I watched him, and his eyes met mine as he went through the door into the blustering rain of the December night.

29th December 1808

I was too tired last night to continue my narrative. We have had a peaceful day at the Plas, and I am minded to relate what transpired after that strange and emotional departure by my new friend Dominic.

In his conversations with others at the feast we discovered much more about him. He says that he is the son of the wealthy Squire of Limerick, sent out into the world to prove himself -- and I have no cause to disbelieve that. He told Bessie that he has spent time in London, where he wasted a part of the family fortune, and became ill. He was then "encouraged" by his father to move across to Wales, where he could enjoy the fresh country air, meet assorted relatives, experience some of the trades connected with a large estate, and recover his strength through hard work. "So I have worked as a groom, as a gamekeeper, as a shepherd, and now as a miller's apprentice," he said to her. "My father is very impressed."

Later in the proceedings Billy, Shemi and the other servants quizzed him about these various trades, and Grandpa pressed him about his estate in Ireland. He came through this interrogation relatively unscathed, although there was, says Grandpa, hesitation on some points. But he certainly got on famously with the children. Unknown to me, he found time during the feast to tell them some long and convoluted Irish stories, and played some silly games with them in the gap between the puddings and the fruits. When I found this out I was delighted. Sian said that Brynach, who is after all just a toddler, latched onto him and followed him everywhere, and that he also had a great rapport with Dewi, who is five.

When nine o'clock came and all the guests had gone home, we had a mightier task than usual in clearing up the mess and washing the dishes, since it was still pouring with rain outside, and nothing could be put outside the kitchen door or carried to the dairy without the protection of waterproofs. "Oh dear," I sighed. "Our guests will get soaked before they are home again, and I feel particularly sorry for Dominic and Joseph, who have farthest to travel. I hope Dominic doesn't get totally lost in the low cloud on the mountain."

When the washing-up was done, I sat down with Hettie (who had been helping out with the kitchen duties) and with Bessie. "Mistress," said Hettie, "that nice young Irishman seems very keen on you -- fancy him coming all the way over the mountain from Wiston, just to wish us all a happy Christmas!"

"Yes, that was indeed a very civil thing to do."

"Too civil by half!" said Bessie. "I would say it was carefully planned weeks ago."

"I agree with that, Bessie. But is that the cause of some concern? I feel quite flattered.........."

"And presents for the children too!" said Hettie. "The little ones all said the things from Master Dominic were the nicest presents of all this Christmas -- and he must have taken a great age in the manufacture of them."

"Very true, Hettie. But he has time on his hands, and helps the miller as and when he is needed. There is money in the background, that's for sure...."

"And does that make him a desirable gentleman?"

"Hettie! That was an inappropriate question. I do not discuss my personal affairs in a setting such as this, after the consumption of too much food and alcohol."

Hettie grinned. "As you wish, Mistress. But after seven years spent under this roof in your company, I think I know you rather well. Just remember this old saying: *The way to a man's heart is through his stomach. The way to a rich widow's heart is through her children.*"

I felt the colour rising in my cheeks, and Bessie noticed my blushes. She laughed. "Mistress," she said sweetly, "I think you recognize the truth when you hear it. That kiss at Portfield Fair has had a miraculous effect. But where would we all be without miracles? This blessed house has seen its fair share of them, over the years. In truth, I cannot bring myself to resent a good-looking and pleasant gentleman who is intent upon wooing a very beautiful and desirable widow such as yourself. But I do urge a little caution, Mistress. Remember that only eighteen months have passed since Owain disappeared -- he may still be alive, and you are still betrothed to him........"

"Please, Bessie, do not distress me. I am too aware of all of that."

"I urge you, Mistress, not to let your heart rule your head in this matter. After all, you know very little about Master Dominic."

"He has told some of us a good deal, and I see no reason to disbelieve what he says about his family and so forth."

"Believe him if you will. But remember that the Irish are renowned for their tall stories. His life history, as he has related it, may be no more reliable than the tales of fairies, heroes and leprechauns with which he entranced the children."

"And why would he invent a life history, and lie to me, Bessie?"

"To impress you, Mistress. What gentleman does not enhance and elaborate his achievements and his status in the process of impressing a lady? Men have been doing precisely that ever since they lived in caves and caught mammoths for their supper."

"Quite right you are!" giggled Hettie. "And I know for a fact that men are quite likely to be so caught up in the relating of their great imaginary exploits that they eventually become convinced that they really did happen, and entirely lose sight of the truth of the matter."

"I cannot disagree. It has been my good fortune to love two of the most modest men who ever walked this earth, in my dear departed David and my poor lost Owain,. But even David was quite convinced that he was the best shot in Wales, and that he won the *Cnapan* contest of 1802 single-handed, while opposed by more than a thousand brutes from the parish of Nevern!"

Then it was time for Hettie to return home. But as she got up, she said: "Mistress, if Providence intends a romantic attachment between Master Dominic and yourself, nobody will be able to prevent it. But I will just pass this on to you. That particular Irishman has been to town on at least five or six occasions over the past three months. In my lodging-house, and in town, I hear almost everything about comings and goings, and I have it on the best authority that on every occasion he has been asking about you and your affairs."

"Do you see something sinister in that, Hettie? I think I am flattered."

Hettie shrugged, and took her leave. When she was gone, and the house was quiet again after all the celebrations, I settled into the parlour with Grandpa Isaac.

"Grandpa, can I ask you something?" I said.

"By all means, my dear. What is it that troubles you?"

"I did not say I was troubled."

"You may not have said it, but I know it anyway. Pray continue."

"What do you think of Dominic?"

He looked over his spectacles. "Charming and intelligent," he said.

"And blessed with good looks, as you and the other ladies have no doubt noticed. Good with the children too. He is well read, and he has had a modest education. I suspect that he is less erudite than he pretends to be, and I doubt that Eton and Oxford have benefitted from his presence. He is well travelled too, and has seen a lot of the civilized and uncivilised worlds in his short life......."

"Whatever do you mean, Grandpa?"

"It's just that he is equally at home with low life as with high life -- not many of the gentry are as comfortable with servants and labourers as he appears to be."

"But surely that is a virtue, Grandpa? Is it not a good thing for a young man from a good family to mix with those below his station? After all, that is something you do with remarkable facility yourself! And David had that ability too, and was greatly loved by the servants because of it. As Dominic says, he is seeking, as the younger son of a good family, to learn the ways of the world and to master various trades, so as to become a better and a wiser master when it falls to him to take on great responsibilities for the welfare of others. That is the lot of the gentry, is it not?"

"You refer to the gentry, Martha," said Granda evenly, looking at me over the rims of his spectacles. "Do you think that Dominic is a true gentleman?"

"I have no reason to doubt it. He seems to be both gentle and kind, and I would judge him as being incapable of doing serious harm to his fellow men. As for his breeding, he says he belongs to the family of the Squire of Limerick."

Grandpa roared with laughter. "Martha, you are so wise in the ways of the world, and at the same time so innocent! And I love you for it! The Squire of Limerick? I might just as well describe myself as the Squire of Wales. You may take it from me, my dear, that there is no such thing as the Squire of Limerick, and never was."

When at last I collapsed into bed, quite exhausted by lack of sleep and unceasing hard work and over-indulgence, my mind was in a turmoil. In truth, that turmoil has not subsided. What am I to make of Dominic? Is he a confidence trickster, with designs upon my fortune? Or is he just a pleasant young man with a desire to impress, and a tendency to over-elaborate? Is he in love with me, or is it simply his intention to get me into his bed? The trouble with men is that you just never know what they are up to -- and I suspect that sometimes they do not know themselves.

10th January 1809

The winter snow has come, and as I write it is swirling about outside my window in a rising wind and under a sky that was black, last time I saw it. Over the past few days we have had intermittent flurries, and at first it was beautiful and even magical, and the children were entranced. But now it has really set in, and I suspect that with the barometer low and the wind in the east, we are in for a prolonged spell when outside work on the farm will be difficult if not impossible. The children have already tired of dancing about in the snowflakes, throwing snowballs, building snowmen and sliding about on their sledges, and now prefer to stay inside where it is warm. We are as well prepared as can be for a blizzard, and will survive maybe with the loss of a few animals, so long as the water from the spring does not freeze and stay frozen for days and weeks. But I have grave concerns for the poor people who live in the *cwm*, for they are not well prepared, and have few resources to fall back on.

About a week ago I received a charming letter from Dominic, thanking me and the family for our warm welcome at Christmas, and apologising for just turning up out of the rainy afternoon without any prior warning. I was very pleased to receive it, but still unsure of what was going on inside his head and his heart. Before the snow started, I climbed up to my cave in the hope that I might give some thought to the things that continue to trouble me. Is Owain alive or dead? Where are the four men whose campaign of retribution left three good men close to death and two others homeless? Have they finished their campaign, or will they return? If so, when? And what warning of their intentions will they give? And what about Dominic -- is he an honest young man, or is he a villain? And then there was the Nightwalker, that strange creature that seemed to live upon the mountain, and which has now not been seen for around six months. Has he gone away for ever, or will he return to haunt me? I found the quietness at the Plas unnerving -- there was too much time for thinking and worrying, and in some ways I prefer things to be happening, even if they are unpleasant things that terrify me.................

My visit to the cave left me in a more serene state of mind than I had when I climbed up the mountain, but many matters were still unresolved. In spite of, or maybe because of, the reservations of my family and servants, I determined that I must undertake more investigations relating to Dominic, for I am very attracted by him, and still feel that I need a good man at my side. And I also want to find out more about the "four surveyors." My instinct tells me that they are still a threat. I want to be prepared, and I am resolved to protect those of my family and friends who might also be in danger.

30th January 1809

Winter still has its icy grip on the landscape, and since the beginning of the year all the precipitation that normally comes in the form of driving rain has fallen instead as snow. There have been one or two brief thaws, with the sun shining for a day or two, and then the greyness has returned, and with it has come more snow. In one of the brief respites, on the thirteenth day of January, we celebrated Hen Galan (the Old New Year) at Pontfaen mansion with the Laugharne family. Grandpa, Grandma and myself, accompanied by Shemi and a very large shovel, took the trap and struggled through the snow to join the party. We were glad that we made the effort, for the party was as warm and jovial as ever. Squire and Mistress Laugharne, who might by now have been my parents in law, if fate had not taken Owain away, were on good form as the attentive and generous hosts. My sister Catrin was there with her husband James

Bowen, from Castlebythe, and of course Mary Jane was there with her husband Dafydd Stokes. During the evening Catrin, Mary Jane and I extracted ourselves from the poetry readings and musical entertainments for a while, and sat with glasses of red wine in hand in the squire's office. We reminisced about old times, and exchanged information. I told them about Dominic, and they were intrigued, but warned me that I should never get too deeply involved with a gentleman whose pedigree, and fortune, were not well known to both my family and my attorney.

From the fifteenth day of the month we had more heavy snow, and very low temperatures, with a high wind swinging between north and east. The snowdrifts piled up, and the servants had to work harder and harder to maintain some sort of order in the affairs of the farm. Everything came to a stop on the roads and tracks, and the only vehicles we could use for getting about were the old sledges normally used for getting peat and rushes off the mountain. Managing the animals became a nightmare, since Ffynnon Brynach was completely frozen, and snow had to be melted continuously in the kitchen to provide water for the animals. Some cattle and two good horses died from the cold, and when we come to a final reckoning we will probably find a dozen sheep carcasses on the mountain too. A week ago we began to get reports of great hardship among the poor people in the *cwm*, although in truth there was not much we could do to help, since we could not get out of the Plas and they could not get in.

Gwynfor failed to turn up for work for ten days or more, but at last he fought his way through the drifts and arrived, exhausted, to report that his family had run out of fuel and that one of his children was desperately ill with what he thought was pneumonia. There was nothing for it -- we had to try to get the whole family up to the Plas on the best of our sledges. As luck would have it, it had been repaired by Gwynfor in November, as one of his first carpentry tasks. We dressed up in our warmest clothing, with heavy coats, thick socks inside our long boots, and mufflers and mittens. We wore whatever heavy hats we could find, and we cursed the fact that we had no furs such as those used by the people of the northern lands. We could not take the horses, because they were sinking up to their bellies in the thick snow, so the men (including Will, who insisted on going although he was still not fully fit) set about hauling the sledge themselves, hitched up to the reins like some intrepid explorers intent upon reaching the North Pole. Gwynfor had little strength left in his legs, and he really needed an hour or two to recover, but he refused to stay behind, and so he came as our native guide. Billy, Shemi and Will started off by pulling side by side in the knee-deep snow, but soon found that that involved huge wasted effort, and they then pulled in line, one behind another, taking it in turns to lead and with the followers using the footprints of the man ahead. On they plodded, leaning far forward and using all of their weight and leg power to pull the heavy sledge forward, inch by inch. I walked alongside, as did Sian, who is stronger than Bessie. We had assumed that we would simply be keeping the men company, but we had to do our fair share of pushing and pulling too, every time the sledge stopped sliding.

The deluge of snow did not ket up for a moment, from the time we left the Plas to the time of our return. In fact, the weather deteriorated, and the soft damp snow that was swirling gently down as we set off was soon transformed by a rising wind and a falling thermometer into small hard flakes that blasted into us like sand grains, making it almost impossible to see. None of us had goggles, and we cursed our lack of foresight in that regard. Within half an hour of our departure the wind was screaming about us, and we could only communicate by shouting to each other. And although our faces were well covered by our mufflers, as we gasped and panted our way forward, the wool became sodden with condensation, which then froze and turned to ice. We were transformed into grotesque snowmen, completely covered in whiteness, moving forward so slowly that every yard gained was a triumph. As I looked at my companions I could not tell which was which. At last communication between us all but ceased, and when we talked afterwards about our experience of the journey, we all agreed that our minds had become dull, with the same thoughts going round and round in our heads over and over again, as we concentrated on using every ounce of energy, one step at a time, without falling over. Right foot. Left foot. Right foot. Over and over, on and on and on........

Although the hovel in the woods is less than a mile from the Plas, it took us two hours to get there, heaving and pushing and extricating the sledge and the pullers from deep drifts at frequent intervals. We were almost collapsing from the effort when we got there, and I for one had no feeling left in my fingers and toesin spite of the fact that we were well dressed. We all stamped our feet and massaged each others' fingers as we tried to get some circulation going, for we all feared the effects of frostbite. We found the hovel completely without heat and light, and with Gwynfor's blind wife Emily and three children huddled together pathetically under a pile of blankets in a corner. We could hardly see them in the gloom, and we feared at first that they were dead. But then they moved, and one of them -- a little boy -- went into a spasm of coughing. I felt his forehead and discovered that he was running a high temperature. The children were so numb that they could not even cry. I had brought a flask of rum with me, and we forced both mother and children to swallow a mouthful or two. Then with poor Emily whimpering like a baby, we wrapped them all up as best we could, got them onto the sledge, and started on the uphill journey back to the Plas.

That was a nightmare I will never forget. For a start, the sledge now had four persons on it, and it sank even more deeply into the soft snow. Then it started to snow again, and we quite lost our orientation, since all the familiar landmarks -- trees, hedges, stone walls, bends in the lanes -- were buried and obliterated. We could not for the life of us find the tracks that we had made on the way down. We inched our way uphill, straining at the ropes and reins, gasping and fighting for breath. For two hours we struggled, moving gradually uphill, until at last we recognized through the swirling and driving snow a particular ash tree on the side of the mountain and only about half a mile from the Plas. It was the very one from which I had collected my divination twig at Hallowe'en. Reassured that we now knew the way home, we struggled on, sinking knee deep with every step, and I am ashamed to say that at last I collapsed through sheer exhaustion. My mind was also playing strange tricks, and Sian told me afterwards that I had asked to be left there in the snow, to die a quiet and peaceful death. Luckily, they would hear nothing of it, and got me going again somehow or other. After four hours of unremitting toil and not a few episodes of sheer panic and confusion, we heard the Plas bell tolling. Grandpa had intelligently assumed that we would be lost in the blizzard, and that the sound might guide us home. It saved us, and I am convinced that without that old bell we might all have perished in the snow. We worked out where the sound was coming from, struggled on, and just as dusk was turning into night we saw the lights of the Plas ahead of us. They had placed candles in every window facing the *cwm*. Shemi staggered on ahead, and returned a few minutes later to the sledge with Grandpa, Grandma, Bessie and Mrs Owen in attendance, wearing whatever thick garments they could find. Between us, we got the sledge along the driveway, into the yard, and up to the kitchen door. We could not see the four poor souls from the hovel, for they and their blankets were completely buried in snow between the raised sides of the sledge. Luckily they were still alive, and we think now that maybe that layer of snow protected them from the worst of the cold. We rushed them into the kitchen, got them into dry clothes, placed them in from of the fire, and gave them copious quantities of Mrs Owen's secret reviving mixture which she had kept simmering for the last four hours on the hob. I still do not know what was in it, but it tasted of milk and honey and rum, with added herbs. The magic mixture slowly revived Gwynfor and his family, and the rest of us, as we slumped onto benches and fought for breath. After a while, the numbness of fingers and toes was replaced by excruciating pain, and we feared for Shemi's fingers which were white and swollen since his mittens had been full of holes. But he plunged his hands into warm water and kept them there for a long time. Gradually the blood started to flow back into his fingers, and no permanent damage was done.

We treated Gwynfor's little boy as best we could, and got some food into him, and as the evening wore on we saw some colour return to his pallid cheeks. The rest of the Rees family joined us for supper, and ate ravenously. Gwynfor was in highly emotional state, and when the meal was over he grasped my hand in both of his and said: "God bless you, Mistress! What have I done to deserve such kindness? Without you and my other friends in this blessed place we would now all surely be dead........" And his voice cracked, and tears rolled down his cheeks.

After the meal we made a space for the family in the hayloft above the cowshed, and that is where they slept and remain to this day. That may sound callous to anybody who does not know the workings of a farm, but the cowshed hayloft is the warmest place to be found at Plas Ingli, and the heat of the animals below is to be experienced to be believed. In all of the rooms of the main house the temperature goes up and down violently on a diurnal rhythm, and I calculated that Gwynfor and his wife and children needed constant warmth and the privacy that every family deserves. Purely by chance, Gwynfor already had a little space cleared between the piles of hay, for he had recently been working on repairs to the roof timbers and fixing some loose slates.

Speaking for myself, it took three days before the sheer exhaustion of that sledge journey passed away, and I think that the others took almost as long to recover as I did. I am happy to report that the little boy has made a remarkable recovery, and that his siblings and parents are coping very well with life above the cows. They join us for all our meals, and we have been able to find some old clothes for them to replace the sodden rags that they wore when we rescued them from the blizzard. When the snow disappears they will return to their hovel. I cannot keep them here for ever, and indeed they are desperate to get back to the place they call home. But still there is no sign of a thaw, and still we are blasted by bitter winds from the East. Andrew Gruffydd, who is Bessie's uncle, fought his way up to the Plas a few days ago, and reported that six of the poor people in Cilgwyn have died from the cold. We try to help some of our labourers with food and extra fuel, so as to bring a little light into dark places, but the scale of this disaster is such that only God in His Heaven can do anything effective about it. And, much to my disgust, He seems reluctant to intervene.

7. Spring Gleaning

3rd February 1809

God in His Heaven has heard my complaint -- and I dare say the prayers of others -- and the thaw has come. On the last day of January we felt the wind shifting round to the West, and within a few hours the air felt almost balmy. The accumulated snow on the roofs of the Plas itself, and all the farm buildings, started to melt from above and below, and soon it was sliding and crashing down to the ground. The children invented a new game called "dodging the avalanche" which was quite dangerous, given the sheer weight of the soggy snow coming down. I told them to be very careful but did not have the heart to stop them, since they have been cooped up inside the house for weeks. On both the front and the back of the house, sections of guttering were pulled down by big slides, and it remains to be seen what other damage has been done to the fabric of the estate. Shortly after the change of wind direction the heavy skies lightened and the sun came out. How we celebrated! We had all but forgotten the pleasurable warmth of the sun on our faces. It will take several more days for the biggest snowdrifts to melt away, and in the meantime we have to put up with slush, filth and running water everywhere. After the silence of the snow-covered landscape, the air is now filled with the sounds of water -- rushing and gurgling, dripping and singing -- and the sound of brittle icicles breaking into fragments of clear ice as they hit the ground. Yesterday Hettie managed to get up to the Plas, for the first time in weeks, to help with the milking. We need her, for the men are flat out, clearing piles of manure from the stables and cowshed, shovelling the soggy snow from gateways and trackways, and searching for sheep in the top fields and on the mountain.

The snow melted very quickly down in Newport and on the Parrog, assisted by the warm vapours off the sea, and so I decided to take a walk down into town. I had to negotiate a few melting snowdrifts on the way, and a few sheets of ice, but I was glad of the exercise and the fresh air, and the experience of being all on my own for a change. Once I reached town, I visited some of the shops, and exchanged essential news with shopkeepers and some of the locals who were out and about, and then I was moved to continue down to the Parrog to see how Jake and Patty and their little baby were getting on. They were about to eat their midday meal, and asked me to join them, and since I had a ravenous appetite I accepted. After all, I was in no great hurry. Then Patty asked if she might have a word in private, so the two of us went for a stroll along the estuary, arm in arm. I sensed that she was troubled in some way, and asked her what was wrong.

"Mistress," she said, "do you recall, before the winter set in and we all had to concentrate on survival, that I promised to help you if I could, in finding out more about those four surveyors?"

My heart missed a beat. "Indeed I do, Patty. They had all but gone out of my mind, but with the weather on the mend, I suppose there is always a chance of them reappearing. We know quite a lot about them, but not enough. So you have more news?"

"Old information rather than news, I would say."

"If you know something of significance, why have you not shared it before now?"

"I was not sure of its significance. You had enough to cope with at the time, with those three good men terribly injured....."

"So what is it that you now want to share?"

"Those cuts made on Will and Skiff. I recall that after Owain had been tortured by Watkins, Howell and Fenton, some years back, he was laid out on the kitchen table, as naked as the day he was born, covered in mud and blood. I was there when Joseph washed him and tried to repair some of the damage. He had cuts all over his body, but the deepest ones were on his chest -- three parallel cuts diagonally, starting above one nipple and ending beneath the other........."

At that, I must have drawn breath quickly and tightened my grip on her arm, for she said: "I am sorry, Mistress. Am I distressing you?"

"I fear that you are. But I must hear you out. Pray continue."

"I recall that you were shut out of the room by Joseph at the time, and saw Owain later only after he had been bandaged up. Those cuts will have taken weeks and months to heal, and will have turned into violent scars. You have seen them yourself?"

"I have, Patty."

"I will not delve deeper into whys and wherefores. What has gone on between you and Owain in the past is your own private business. But I can tell you now that I have seen identical scars on the chests of other men."

I was amazed and petrified. I simply looked at Patty and sensed that the colour had drained from my face. She continued: "During the worst time of my life, some four or five years since, and before I was rescued by the love of my blessed man Jake, I was forced into a life of whoring by Joseph Rice, the blackest demon that ever trod this good earth. When he used me -- and that was often -- he was no better than an animal, quite devoid of tenderness or consideration. May he rot in Hell!"

I realized that tears were streaming down Patty's cheeks, and I gave her a long embrace while she composed herself again. "Do not distress yourself, Patty," I whispered. "Those days are gone, and now you are safe. We can continue with this conversation some other time, if you prefer it.........."

"No no, Martha, I must continue. If I am more than a little emotional just now, put it down to the time of the month." She wiped her tears away with her kerchief, and the two of us continued our walk, arm in arm. "I hope that I am safe, but I cannot be certain of it. And now that I am, like you, a mother, there is a band of fear clamped around my heart."

I stopped and turned to face her. "But you are safer than you have ever been, Patty, with Rice in his grave, and Jake to protect you, and with neighbourly goodwill on all sides!"

"If only that were true, Martha. But I must explain myself. Rice was very fond of somewhat unusual activities in the bedroom, the likes of which I had never encountered before or since. Shall we say that he had a penchant for things which would have caused my other clients -- farmers and seafarers, for the most part -- considerable difficulty and embarrassment. The only other men who ever indulged in such activities with me were Rice's two cronies -- John Howell and John Fenton. Sometimes one after another, on the same evening. Sometimes going on until dawn. Sometimes all together, in the same room. And they used each other, Martha, as well as using me. On some occasions I was so harmed that I could hardly walk for days afterwards. Barbarians! Bastards! Animals!"

Again Patty dissolved in tears, and I had to embrace her again until she had regained her composure. "I have not even told Jake about these things," she whispered. "Promise, Martha, that you will keep all of this to yourself?" I promised that I would never repeat what I had heard. "It is not much in the way of consolation, Martha, but I do feel a little better for having revealed the full extent of the evil that permeated the lives of those three creatures who liked to call themselves gentlemen. Well, two of them are down in Hell, and the third is missing......"

"All three of them are down in Hell, Patty," I said quietly.

Patty looked me straight in the eye. "You know it, Martha? You know for certain that Fenton is dead?"

"I know it."

"Thank God for it. I will not press you for the details. But to return to the matter of cuts. I saw every one of those men naked, and all of them had scars upon their chests -- three diagonal scars, with parallel lines starting above one nipple and ending beneath the other."

At this point I fear that I almost fainted, and had to sit down on an upturned rowing boat on the shore. "What on earth does this mean, Patty?" I asked in despair. "Were those men also victims, forced to suffer at the hands of some sadistic monster? I cannot make head or tail of it. And what should we do with this information?"

"I think we should tell Joseph. He will know where this leads, and what we should do next. I have not seen him of late, because of the snow and ice. But he will appear one of these days............"

But we agreed that rather than leave things to chance, we would invite him to meet us in Patty's cottage three days hence. We further agreed that we would tell him all about the scars, but that we would not go into the sexual excesses and proclivities of the evil men who are now dead. The matter is in hand, and I have already sent Joseph a message.

As I walked home from town, I realized that in the midst of her distress and her fears for the safety of her little family, Patty had made no mention of the fact that Jake's name is on the list of men upon whose heads "retribution" might be visited. I assumed therefore that she was still unaware of that fact, and wondered if I should have raised the matter. But then I thought that if Jake was seeking to protect her from unnecessary worry, that was his decision, and it was probably for the best.

4th February 1809

Today we have been celebrating Dewi's 6th birthday. The little boy who will one day be the master of this estate is growing taller by the minute, and seems to require new clothes every fortnight. With his fair hair and sunny temperament he causes everybody to fall in love with him, and in ten years' time he will have every young woman within ten miles of the Plas swooning at the mere sight of him. After all the hardships of the last month, I thought that we should have a little party for Dewi, to help us all to recover. I allowed him to invite ten other little boys of approximately his own age. Some came from the other farms in the *cwm*, and some came from town. Luckily it was a cool dry day, and since remnants of snowdrifts were still left in the yard and behind the stone walls, there was, for a while, a snowball war , until a little boy called Twm fell over and hurt himself, and wailed lustily. I had to give him a cuddle, and wipe away his tears, and rub his wounds better.

Then the boys came inside. They had some slices of Dewi's birthday cake, and something to drink, and then they were all off again on some wild adventures. Total mayhem reigned, and while Brynach toddled about after the big boys as best he could, Betsi and Daisy were disgusted, and retreated to their room with Sara where they could play with their dolls and clothes in peace and quiet. The boys shut themselves into their room with their friends, and there was much whispering and giggling. Then Dewi and his confederates emerged and rushed about in the yard, yelling and screaming, with their faces streaked and ornamented with soot obtained from the chimney and applied with grubby fingers.

They were apparently the members of a "Secret Red Indian Tribe." They all got into a terrible mess, but I was determined to be benign, and managed to put up with it, while pondering on the mystery of where small boys get all that energy from. Sian was angry with them, but I told her that "boys will be boys." And when the little visitors had gone, and Dewi and Brynach were fast asleep, the peace and quiet was truly wonderful.

6th February 1809

As planned, Joseph turned up at Patty and Jake's cottage for our meeting. Much to our surprise, he was riding on a donkey which he won in a wager with Shoni Transportation the other day. When he arrived he was in a jovial mood, but he quickly appreciated that we were minded to explore serious matters. Jake left us in possession of the cottage and took little Mary for a walk on the beach. Patty made us a cup of tea, and then she told Joseph about the scars on the chests of Rice, Howell and Fenton. He furrowed his brow and lapsed into silence. "Things become clearer, my dear ladies," he said at last. "There appears to have been so much blood spilt here, there and everywhere, in the carving of lines on chests, that we might fill a bath-tub with it. I think this is the most grotesque matter I have ever had to deal with. Just between ourselves, I can now add a further detail and reveal that there has been one further victim."

"And who might that be, Joseph?"

"Never fear. Not one of our nearest and dearest, and not one who still stalks the land, even if, long after his death, he casts a long shadow. I speak of Alban Watkins, late squire of Llannerch and late resident of the penal colonies, despatched with a knife by a mysterious Irishman on the shore of the estuary some three years since. He was of course the oldest member of the gang that contained Rice, Howell and Fenton, not to mention the Ifans brothers, the last two being petty thugs whom we can forget about."

"He had the same marks on his chest? How do you know that, Joseph?"

"You will recall that I examined a putrid corpse and identified it as that of Alban Watkins, when the rats and eels had finished with him. Havard Medical and I shared the task and agreed afterwards that it was the most unpleasant thing we had ever had to do. I will spare you the details. Suffice to say that I had more opportunity than Master Havard to examine the body -- or what was left of it -- on the slab of the mortuary. The three cuts made by the Irishman before he slit Watkins' throat were plain to see, and indicated some barbaric ritual or torture. But what Master Havard did not see, and what the Irishman also missed, were three earlier scars, in an almost identical position, from cuts made many years earlier. They were very well healed, but with the aid of my magnifying glass I was able to see parts of them when I had wiped away all the congealed blood. Scar tissue is quite easy to identify if you know what you are looking for. I have never before told anybody of this -- but now I think we need to get to the bottom of this strange and unsettling business.........."

Just then there was a confident knock on the door. Patty rose to her feet immediately, and said: "Ah yes, that will be Fancy and Nancy. I asked them to call, and trust that they will have recovered by now from the excesses of the last weekend, which was very busy on account of all the frustrated males suddenly released from the icy grip of winter in the hills. She grinned, and winked at Joseph, and much to my surprise and amusement, managed to make him look embarrassed.

The two girls came in out of the cold. They were not exactly dressed for the winter, and wore no coats over their gowns. Their ample bosoms were more or less contained within their dresses. They had not had to walk far, since they both live on the Parrog sea-front in cottages easy to locate from both land and sea. Fancy was the shorter of the two, with her blonde hair done in ringlets. She wore a simple cotton cap. Her blue eyes and little nose made her look like a cheeky child. I thought her very pretty indeed, with full red lips and large quantities of rouge on her cheeks. She was a good deal plumper than she should be, and I guessed that she was maybe 25 years old. Her bright red cotton gown was very full, with a square neckline, a high waist and full short sleeves, with colourful braided trims. Nancy was maybe a little older, and taller by several inches, with dark deep-set eyes and a Roman nose which made her look like a goddess, or some stately inhabitant of southern Spain. She had her black hair piled high, to make the most of her long and elegant neck. Her dress was quite simple -- a metallic blue cotton frock with a rounded neckline and short straight sleeves. She wore white gloves, and was by a long way the more elegant of the two. But again, I thought, she would benefit from losing some weight and doing some hard work in a hayfield.

"Patty asked us to call," said Fancy, "and we are happy to be here, since she makes the best *bara brith* this side of the River Severn."

"Oh, very well girls," smiled Patty, taking the hint. "But no butter for you, Fancy, since your ample proportions are probably getting too ample for the liking of your discerning clients."

"I have no discerning clients, Patty," snorted Fancy. "And those that I do have like a bit of flesh to grab hold of while they are hard at work. It makes a change from those skinny wives they have at home!"

"Shall we change the subject, girls?" said Joseph plaintively. "This is a female conversation, and as the only male in the neighbourhood I would prefer to hear as little about your noble calling as possible."

"What?" said Nancy. "That's what I thought we were here to talk about. Is that not right, Patty?"

"Yes and no," said Patty, spreading butter onto some thick slices of *bara brith* while keeping an eye on the kettle. "Without going into the details of the trade, would you care to tell Joseph and Mistress Martha what you told me yesterday?"

Fancy and Nancy proceeded to settle themselves down on the wooden bench which served as a sofa in Patty's simple parlour, one on either side of Joseph. They both put their arms around him and kissed him, Fancy on his left cheek and Nancy on his right. Joseph looked considerably discomfited, since he was flanked by two considerable cleavages which drew his eyes whether he looked right or left.

"This dear gentleman is like a father to us, is he not, Fancy?" grinned Nancy.

"He is! Father Joseph, we call him. Rescued us from assorted scrapes more times than I care to remember, he has," said Fancy. "We each owe him at least a fortnight of pleasant evenings, but he refuses to take payment. I for one would have been somewhere east of Eglwyswrw by now, if he hadn't sorted out that business of the Squire of Monington, his prize carrot and his pickled onions!"

Nancy screeched with laughter, and the pair of them gurgled and wobbled with delight. Joseph looked even more embarrassed, especially when the pair of them cuddled up close to him. Nancy patted his cheeks and Fancy smoothed his collar. "Father Joseph!" said Fancy. "Master Harries, with a name like that you should be a saint or a holy man, saving people from sin........"

"Ha! He would be no good at all as a holy man," grinned Nancy, suddenly placing her hand on the front of his breeches. "As I thought, a rod of iron, just from a little cuddle or two from a pair of innocent young ladies. He is too old, or maybe too young, for holiness. Is that not right, Joseph?"

"My dear young ladies," spluttered Joseph, trying to re-establish his dignity, "I am considerably outnumbered here, and greatly put upon. I thought we were here for a serious meeting? Patty, will you please feed these two young ladies on some *bara brith* while I seek to regain my composure? Sit them down at the table, if you will, for as long as I am flanked by all these bosoms I cannot think straight. I try to think about serious things, and all I can do is ponder on which laws of physics might be responsible for the containment of said bosoms within those somewhat scanty dresses which you ladies seem to wear these days. According to my best calculations, those bosoms should have escaped long since......."

And so it continued for a little while, with much grinning and giggling as Fancy, Nancy, Patty and myself teased poor Joseph mercilessly. We ate our *bara brith* and drank some tea, and at last things calmed down enough for serious conversation to resume. "Now then," said Patty. "To continue where we left off. Tell Joseph and Mistress Martha, if you please, what you know about those four surveyors."

"Huh!" said Nancy. "If they were surveyors I am a deacon of Caersalem. Surveyors thrive in the fresh air -- and those fellows are much happier in boudoirs than in barley fields, unless I am very much mistaken. They hired us three times during their fortnight in town."

"What, together?" I asked.

" Yes, together," replied Fancy. "They paid well, but they had special requests and indulged in somewhat unusual activities, which we put up with on the first night, out of sheer surprise, but put a stop to on the second and third times of asking. We are a broad-minded pair of young ladies, but there are limits in our trade as in all others. Isn't that right, Nancy?"

"Indeed it is, sister. We never drink when we are working, but those fellows used laudanum as others use raspberry juice in making a cordial. Some of the time they were on the moon, that's for sure, and the one called Hughes was on another distant planet for most of the time. Isn't that right, Fancy?"

"Indeed it is, sister. They used each other with greater enthusiasm than they used us, which was very bad for our self-esteem. Well, that's their privilege and our problem, I suppose. They paid well for our silence, and for Mistress Tasker's silence too, so we have no reason to complain."

Then Patty piped up. "Fancy, you have still not told Joseph and Martha what you told me. Tell them please."

"Ah yes. The strange thing about them was that each of them had scars upon their chests. Isn't that right, Nancy?"

"Indeed it is, sister. Old scars, I would say. Three parallel lines each time, made with some sharp knife, and running from above one nipple to beneath the other. Isn't that strange?"

When the two girls had departed, Joseph, Patty and I tried to assess the significance of the new revelations. Joseph was lost in thought, and would say only that he was now convinced that the four men were part of some cult or sect involved in ritual revenge attacks and maybe even ritual orgies. He had heard of such things before, in England, but in all his years in West Wales he had never encountered activities like those described by Fancy and Nancy.

"Witchcraft, Joseph?" I enquired.

"I doubt that. I know what the pagans and followers of Wicca get up to, and that strange things do go on behind closed doors, in the anonymity of town houses and in the depths of the countryside. Now and then clothes and inhibitions are cast aside, but the ritual element is obvious to participants and observers alike, and there is a degree of reverence. Fancy and Nancy have not, so far as I can judge, been involved in any rituals, or consultations of ancient texts, or in any invocations or spells. If they had been, I think that they would have told us. No -- I judge that these men are involved in some strange cult which has no moral boundaries. Sadism, debauchery and even masochism may be involved. That is what worries me. Witches act according to a strict code and use their liturgy as the Rector might use his Bible, his prayer book and his order of service. This is much more sinister. I came to the view some time ago that these men might be capable of murder. Now I am sure of it -- and I am sure that they will be back when they deem that the time is right for them to cut down their next appointed victim. They may or may not have finished with me, and Skiff and Will -- and they may still be set upon a course which will bring them to harming six or seven others. We must continue to be vigilant."

10th February 1809

Over the past few days I have been greatly troubled as a result of these recent revelations and speculations, and I am convinced that the Nightwalker, that dark and mysterious creature who has not been seen since last summer, was an omen of terrible things to come. Maybe he was -- and is -- really the Grim Reaper, beckoning with his bony finger?

I went up to my cave today, anointing myself on the way up, and found that the ravens, which are normally perfectly calm in my presence, were restless and even agitated. They fluttered from one rock to another, making raucous calls one to another, and even when I sat for a while and watched them, they did not return to their normal quiet ways. I tried to find a cause for this unusual behaviour, but I could find no signs of others on the mountain, and no traces of recent visits. I was mystified and concerned. I tried to clear the fog of confusion from my mind, and to concentrate on key matters which might help me to understand what is going on. I knew that Joseph was hard at work with his investigations, but I was afraid that his slow and systematic methods would not lead him to the unravelling of the mystery before it was too late. The fog did clear to some degree, and I recalled some small titbits of information that appeared worthy of further investigation. First, what was the book which Lizzie Tasker observed in the rooms of the four villains when they were in Newport? Second, there was the large envelope with a crest on it, which contained some manuscript which was frequently consulted. Did that manuscript contain a list of people who must be eliminated or harmed? And if so, who wrote it? Maybe the writer was the man behind this whole campaign? And the one called Hughes, who seemed to come from a Pembrokeshire family below the Landsker........ might there be some more information about him to be elicited from either Lizzie Tasker or Gwynfor Rees? And finally those names -- Urien, Afaon, Edenawg and so forth. Old Welsh names, for sure, but so archaic that nobody uses them any longer. Where did those names come from? I thought that they must surely be pseudonyms? Suddenly I realized that the first name on each note must be the name of somebody now dead, on whose behalf revenge must be extracted. And the second name on each note must surely be the pseudonym of one or other of the conspirators who see revenge as their sacred duty? I was excited by this realization, but could not for the life of me remember all of the names, in spite of being blessed with a memory capable of remembering conversations in great detail. So in a state of high expectation I hurried back down the mountain to the Plas, risking life and limb on the slippery rocks, in order to consult my notes and the diary entries already written.

So I rediscovered the names. The first names were Rhiwallwn, Tinwaed, Urien and Henben. Could they be the pseudonyms (not necessarily in this order) of Watkins, Rice, Howell and Fenton, all of whom were brought to justice for assorted appalling crimes, and all of whom are now dead? And could the second group of names (Gruddnei, Edenawg, Afaon and Cai) be the pseudonyms of the four conspirators who stayed in Newport? I was sure that these questions could be answered in the affirmative, and I determined that I would make further studies. I now think that if the sinister surveyors are to return and commit further crimes, I might be able to head them off, or at least ensure that if they do harm any others who might be on their secret list, they will be brought to justice as swiftly as possible.

18th February 1809

The spring sunshine has continued, and the land has now dried out sufficiently for us to start with the spring ploughing. The heavy horses are working almost every day, and Billy and Shemi return to the kitchen each evening at dusk, muddy and exhausted. They recuperate well enough, after a few pints of ale and a good supper, and spend their evenings talking of farming matters. The great debate just now concerns the relative merits of oxen and horses for ploughing. Billy, who was brought up to believe that there is nothing to compare with oxen for ploughing and harrowing, argues that it was a mistake ever to switch over to horses, but Shemi is a horse man through and through, and says that they are more obedient, more flexible, and do less damage to the ground, especially when the seeds are sown and rolling is needed. As for me, I have never walked behind a plough and tried to keep it in its furrow, so I am not really qualified to comment, but I think I prefer to see oxen on our dinner plates and horses in the fields.

Gwynfor and his family, who have all survived the worst of the winter and have now got some colour in their cheeks, have gone home from the Plas and are now back in the scruffy hovel which they call home. I went down a couple of days ago to examine it, and it was even worse than I remembered -- with one small-ill-fitted window, a door that did not close properly, and a thatched roof full of holes. The floor was made of damp hard-packed earth, which was more like mud in one corner where the thatch had been leaking. A smoky fire simmered in another corner, but there was no chimney, and I imagined that in bad weather, when the door had to be kept closed and the fire had to be stoked up, the atmosphere within must have been unbearable. No wonder, I thought, that very few children from labourer's cottages such as this survived beyond the age of three. Something had to be done to help them, and indeed I was minded to help because Gwynfor has been an exemplary servant at the Plas -- cheerful, honest and hard-working, and considerate to the others. He is a clever carpenter. He is occasionally in great pain from his wartime injuries, and I sometimes see him grimacing from painful spasms, but he never complains. In recognition of all of this, and since this is a quiet time on the farm, I have allowed Billy, Shemi and Will to help Gwynfor improve and extend his cottage on two afternoons a week. They are making good progress, and the renovated building will have one extra window and even a chimney.

A couple of days ago, it was so unseasonally calm and warm that I decided to sit in the orchard and work on a small tapestry which I plan to give to Grandma on her next birthday. Suddenly, who should arrive out of the blue but Dominic! I must have been snoozing in the sun while he crept up on me, but then from the other side of the wall he coughed discreetly to wake me up, and put me in a considerable fluster. "Good afternoon, Mistress Martha!" he said. "I trust that I did not wake you up.:

"You know full well that you woke me up, Master Cunningham," said I. "But never fear. I am not offended, and in fact I am happy to see you. What brings you to Newport on such a fine day?"

"Well, the hope of seeing you, and the task of delivering two bags of wheat flour to Llwyngwair Manor."

Dominic joined me in the orchard, and we chatted for a while about this and that, and then he suggested that we might take a walk on the mountain. "That would be a pleasure, on such a day," I said. "We can walk up to the spring, and maybe even higher, and I can show you, perhaps, why I have such affection for this little mountain. It is the most beautiful place in the world."

"I would dispute that," he laughed. "The most beautiful place in the world is indubitably the Burren, in County Clare. It is scientifically proved."

"Stuff and nonsense, Master Cunningham! Your science is clearly antiquated, and needs to take account of the latest discoveries."

Then I told him that I would ask Bessie and Grandma to follow us at a discreet distance, on the grounds that they would enjoy a walk in the sun, and that it would be inappropriate for us to walk without a chaperone, since we had not been properly introduced. A shadow passed momentarily across his face, but to his credit he then laughed, and said: "Ah, the aftermath of that kiss! I knew that my victory in that little wager would only lead to a host of problems."

So we walked on the mountain for half an hour, with Grandma and Bessie following along in our footsteps. We enjoyed a pleasant and even frivolous conversation, but I sensed that he wanted to talk to me about much more serious matters which, in the circumstances, he dared not broach. I still wonder what those matters might have been. But the time passed quickly, and he thanked me for my courtesy in showing him the mountain before taking his leave. He doffed his hat and bowed politely for all three of us ladies, and we watched him as he collected his horse and trotted off down the driveway, with two sacks of wheat flour slung over the horse's rump behind the saddle.

Today I have managed to have another brief conversation with Gwynfor about the sinister surveyors. I asked him if there was anything else which might bring light to bear on the problem of what they were up to. "I am not trying to be evasive, Mistress," he said, "but I think I have told you everything I know. My memories are getting hazy, since almost four months have passed since they were in town."--

I said I accepted that, but pressed him on the list, the letter and the envelope. Could he possibly remember anything not already passed on? A big crest or a little one? What symbols did it contain? Dragons, lions, shields, or whatever? He remembered that there might have been a shield with a cross on it, and some animals on either side........

"And the list?" I asked. "How many names, Gwynfor? Four names? Six names?"

"No no -- more."

"You have already confirmed for me that Skiff and Will were on the list, together with the Wizard, the attorney and the judge. Five men. And you said I was there as well, at the top of the list. Was I the only woman on the list?"

"I believe so, Mistress."

"I will not ask you to name the others, in view of your oath of secrecy. I still remember your reticence, from our earlier conversation. But will you nod if I give you the other names I think might be there?"

"I can do that for you, Mistress, since I think I now have an interest in protecting you and your nearest and dearest."

So through this little charade Gwynfor confirmed for me the other names on the list -- Grandpa Isaac, Shemi, Billy, Jake Nicholas, and Will Final Testament. "Ten altogether. That's all, Gwynfor?"

"I believe so, Mistress. At least, they were the only fellows that they asked me about."

"And did you give the villains enough information to ease the process of harming these good men?"

"I don't believe so, Mistress. I simply said that Grandpa, Shemi and Billy lived at the Plas, that Jake was down on the Parrog, and that Master Will Probert the attorney lived in that big house at the end of Mill Lane. They could have found all that out for nothing, by asking anybody on the street."

22nd February 1809

Encouraged by my conversation with Gwynfor, I walked to town today, and talked to Lizzie Tasker in her lodging house. I wanted to extract more information before she totally forgot everything. She had no other guests in residence, since it is quiet time of year, and I perceived that she was in no hurry to do anything other than to pass the time of day in my company. We sat together in the kitchen. "I know that we have talked of these things before, Lizzie," I said, "but can we explore a little more deeply the origins of those four surveyors who stayed with you back in the autumn?"

"Some months have passed, Mistress, and my memory is not as good as it was............"

I nodded. "I appreciate that it is difficult to remember small details, but sometimes they do stay in the mind and reappear quite unexpectedly. I venture to suggest that it is important for the good of this little community of ours that we discover as much as we can about those fellows. You know, of course, that they are widely held in the community as being responsible for the beatings given to my servant Will Owen, Skiff Abraham from the Parrog, and the Wizard?"

"I knew about the damage done to Skiff and Will, Mistress. But the Wizard? I thought he had just had an unfortunate accident with some cows?"

"Be assured, Lizzie, that that was no accident. Neither was the burning down of Lewis Legal's house in Fishguard. Do you remember that?"

"Oh yes indeed. There was much talk about it at the time."

"Well, you may take it from me that there is sound enough evidence to convict those four fellows who slept and cavorted beneath your roof of arson, attempted murder and assorted other felonies including assault and battery, and even torture. That is why there is an arrest warrant out for them, and an offer of £10 as a reward for information leading to their apprehension. Have you not been tempted to claim the reward by volunteering information to Will Daniels?"

"Indeed not, Mistress. Why should I help him? He is an idiot, and since he became Clerk to the Justices he has become pompous as well as being a fool. Anyway, I know nothing of interest. And besides, reporting vagrants and such like is one thing -- reporting gentlemen to officers of the law is not something one does lightly."

"Lizzie, they may have appeared civilized to you, but I happen to know that they were no better than barbarians. They will be brought to justice, of course, and it may be that you will be required to give evidence against them, on oath, in the Assizes."

Mistress Tasker looked startled, and so -- somewhat unfairly, now that I come to think of it -- I plunged in the knife. "I am not an expert in the law," I said, "but I do hope that in view of the assistance which you gave to them quite openly, you will not be counted as an accessory to their assorted crimes.........."

"Oh my goodness," moaned Lizzie. "That would not be at all good for my reputation, would it?"

"I fear not, Lizzie. But I think transportation is unlikely, since a court might well decide that although your actions were such as to assist them in their dastardly deeds, your intentions were not inherently evil."

Having thus encouraged Lizzie to remember things which she had not previously divulged, I pressed her again to remember any small details about the four men. She furrowed her brow and concentrated. At last she said: "Well, two were English, and one was a Scot, and then the one called Hughes was from Pembrokeshire. He was the strange one. I think you know all that already."

I nodded. "You mentioned to me before that this Hughes fellow was from below the Landsker. Can you be more precise? His clothes, his conversation, his references to his family, and so forth?"

"Hmm. Let me think. Did he mention Narberth at some stage? I think he might have done.............."

"That would make sense. Narberth is below the Landsker. Maybe he comes from one of the good families in that area. That may partly explain his reluctance to appear in the taverns of the town while they were lodging with you -- he thought that somebody might recognize him. I shall investigate that further. I have also given much thought to the book that those fellows consulted, and the letter in the big brown envelope. Do you remember any little details?"

"Oh dear. This is very difficult. The book...... it was big and heavy, and bound with red leather. Gold lettering, it had. And a long title with strange words in it. Something about archaeology? Several authors, I think."

"Was it a new book, in good condition? Or a battered old tome such as we might find in a dusty library?"

"Oh, quite new and shiny, it was. They had it wrapped up sometimes, as if they were looking after it carefully."

"Let's think about the letter. You know, I suppose, that it contained a list of people whom these fellows were out to harm?"

"That's news to me, Mistress. Who told you that?"

"Gwynfor Rees. He saw the list, and heard all the names. But he was not able to examine it or even get close to it. One letter looks much like another from the other side of a room. But the crest on the envelope -- Gwynfor thinks that it had a shield with a cross, flanked by two animals -- dragons or maybe lions. Would you agree with that?"

"I think so, from the glimpses I had. But they were stags, not lions or dragons. I'm sure of it. White stags."

"Thank you, Lizzie. I think that's probably enough to be going on with. That has all been very helpful, and will help us to get to the bottom of this matter. Now, I had better get back to those children, who are waiting for me to deliver them some little treats from town."

"I am suddenly worried, Mistress. If those fellows are as evil as you say they are, might they return and ask for rooms again? What should I do if that happens?"

I laughed. "I don't think you will ever see them again, Lizzie. Too many people are now alert to their activities, and if they do resume their sinister campaign they will certainly not operate from a comfortable base in the middle of town. Too many people will recognize them, and they can't go around covered up with cloaks and mufflers. In fact, I doubt that they will stay in this neighbourhood at all. My guess is that they will come in from a distance, do their worst, and then get away quickly. They might not even use their own horses. We have certain measures in place, and my hope is that they will be apprehended immediately if they appear."

As I walked home, I had a sudden inspiration relating to the crest described by Gwynfor and Lizzie Tasker. Once back in my office, I went through my correspondence, old files and so forth, and discovered the invitation to the last Glynymel Autumn Ball. It had a beautiful crest on it -- a shield with a black cross, flanked by two white stags, and a motto underneath in Latin. I was suddenly chilled by the thought that the letter -- and list of names -- in the possession of the four "surveyors" might have been written by Squire Richard Fenton himself. That idea was too outrageous to entertain for a moment, but two other possibilities remained -- namely that the letter and the envelope had been written by somebody else in the Fenton family, or by a staying guest. But the most likely conclusion was that the letter had been written by John Fenton some time before his death in December 1806. He had been flung out of the house by his father two months earlier, and told never to return. But there was now the chilling possibility that the campaign of vengeance involving the four surveyors had something to do with Fenton -- and might actually have been instigated by him.

11th March 1809

There have been developments concerning those strange old Welsh names. On St David's Day, in the midst of our celebrations of the life of our patron saint, Grandma had an inspiration. "Martha," she said. "Those old names. I suddenly recalled reading, many years ago, an old tome containing the *Four Ancient Books of Wales*. It contained a description of the Welsh Triads -- full of the names of ancient heroes and so forth. The book was lost in the burning down of the old Plas Ingli in 1794 -- but might it be worth your while to investigate further?"

On the next day I wrote to my dear father in Brawdy to ask if he knew anything about the Welsh Triads. I hoped that he might be familiar with them, since he is a very erudite man, with a great knowledge of Welsh literature and language. He speaks and writes fluently in Dimetian Welsh, too, but I have to admit that he has aged a lot, and has become forgetful and vague. So I was not sure at the time of writing that I would get anywhere. But a week ago a messenger brought a reply from Brawdy, inviting me and the children to come for a short visit. Father said that he longed to see his grand-children again, and said that by a most fortunate coincidence he was expecting a visit from one Edward Williams, otherwise known as Iolo Morgannwg. He wrote:

"He is a fascinating fellow. He knows all there is to know about the druids and the bards, and about the ancient books of Wales. What he does not know, he

simply invents. So he is a charlatan and a fraudster, and many of the learned men of Wales will have nothing to do with him. But he has the interests of Wales at heart, and seeks ultimately to re-establish the ancient cultural glories of our nation. I am intrigued by him, and I have to admit to quite liking him in spite of his very unpleasant personal habits. He will be here as my guest on the night of March 10th -- come with the children on that day, if you will, and stay as long as you like."

I was intrigued, and immediately wrote back to accept the invitation, knowing that Grandpa and Billy could easily run the estate for a few days without me. Indeed, in view of my present distracted mood, I thought that they might be pleased to see me disappear over the horizon.

So yesterday I travelled with the children in the Plas Ingli carriage to Brawdy, with Shemi driving and Bessie also in attendance. There was great excitement when we arrived. We all settled in, and had something to eat, and my dear parents and I started on the process of catching up with all the news. And there was a great deal of it. Then Master Iolo Morgannwg turned up on a skinny white horse, putting me in mind of Don Quixote. He was not wearing armour, but I thought him quite capable of tilting at windmills. He was a wild fellow indeed, with sharp features, unblinking eyes and thin, straggly hair. He wore a long frock coat with an elaborate collar, and a grubby shirt that might once have been white. His corduroy breeches and heavy woollen socks were splattered with mud, and he had on his feet a pair of delicate shoes with silver buckles, quite unsuitable for use when riding on a horse. He was clearly utterly unconcerned about his appearance, and about what others might think of him. But he gave my father and mother warm embraces, and gave me a theatrical bow. I liked him at once. He was unpretentious and wildly eccentric, and his conversation was staccato and undisciplined, and quite unlike that of ordinary men, who tend to talk about one thing at a time.

Iolo took a bath, and then we had supper together, and with the children and servants off to bed, we four talked far into the night. We talked about Dimetian Welsh, and he insisted that my father and I should converse in that ancient dialect. So we did that, as a sort of entertainment, while he took copious notes and stopped us now and then with questions about vocabulary and grammar. I was very moved by the experience, especially when I remembered that I had not actually conversed with Father in the Dimetian dialect since I left home to get married, in less than ideal circumstances, back in 1796. Then the conversation drifted (with a little guidance from me) onto the Welsh Triads. I took out a piece of paper on which I had written all the names used by the four sinister surveyors, and passed it to him. "Aha!" he chortled. "Excellent names, all of them! Where did you get this little list from, Mistress Martha?"

"If you do not mind, sir, I will not divulge that. But your advice will be appreciated on the matter of what the names might mean."

"Delighted to help. Quite delighted. Now then. The names are all from the ancient Welsh manuscripts which I am seeking to assemble, edit and bring before a wide public before they are lost for ever. Be in no doubt -- the future of Wales depends on it, for without a written history, and a great tradition in literature, we are as nothing. Our nationhood would not be worth a farthing! Oh dear, where was I? Ah yes, those names, before I give you my favourite sermon. First, they were in the stories of the great heroes and so forth.

Then along came the greatest of all the bards, Taliesin, in the fourteenth century, and he wrote a great work called *The Triads of the Island of Britain* which collected things, according to ancient tradition, into threes. There are more than eighty triads altogether. All of the names on your little list feature in them. For example, Urien son of Cynfarch was one of the Three Bulls of Battle; Afaon was a son of Taliesin, famous as one of the Three Bull-Princes; Tinwaed was, if I remember correctly, one of the Three Strong Crutched-ones; and Gruddnei was one of the Three Heroes. Whoever has used or given these names is clearly an erudite fellow, with a great respect for the ancient literature and traditions of Wales."

"And if the names are pseudonyms," I asked, "what might they mean?"

"Ah, if the names are pseudonyms, then maybe they are chosen very carefully. I would guess, for example, that the one given the name Gruddnei might be a man of great personal courage and daring, striding into battle careless of his own safety. Urien might be a person of dogged persistence and great strength, not necessarily a leader but striking fear into the hearts of all those who stand in his path. And the name Tinwaed might be given to a man of great sexual prowess and insatiable appetite. Do you get my meaning?"

"Indeed I do, Master Williams. And do you have any idea who this erudite fellow might be, moving about in the literary circles of London?"

"I have not the faintest idea, Mistress Martha. I try to keep away from London. It is a foul place, full of pretentious and arrogant men who seek to deny the cultural riches of Wales. Some of them have even sought to commandeer some parts of our culture for their own pathetic purposes. I am in dispute with them all the time, and trust none of them. If you are looking for an expert on the Triads, look no further. I am your man."

Then I changed subject entirely, and asked our cultural expert about his days as a land surveyor. "Master Morgannwg," I said, "somebody told me once that you worked, in your younger days, as a land surveyor for the Board of Agriculture. Is that true? That seems a strange occupation for an academic gentleman such as yourself........"

"Ha!" he replied, with his hands on his knees. "You are well informed. Farming family, you understand. I offered my services to the Board of Agriculture twelve or thirteen years since, when they were looking for somebody to write them a report on South Wales. Nobody knew the region better, and nobody had a better grasp of farming matters than I. But I think my politics were too radical for them, and so they invited a bland and timid fellow called Walter Davies to do the writing. But I help unofficially, and still feed information to him. I have the knowledge and do the work, and he will get all the credit. Such is life, in a world governed by clowns. It will be some time yet before the Report sees the light of day."

"And have you worked with Master Charles Hassall?"

"The idiot who is currently the secretary of the County Agricultural Society? Oh yes. I had to work with him. A mad Irishman, very knowledgeable on farming matters, but so obsessed with his feud with the Knox family -- also mad, and also Irish -- that he spent more time plotting the downfall of young Thomas Knox than on agriculture. He sent letters by the ton to the Government, to the point where he became even less popular than Master Guido Fawkes. I had to do the work, while he played with feuds and politics. Why do you ask about him, Mistress? Do you know him?"

"Just a little. I just wondered whether you find him trustworthy............"

"Oh, I think he is trustworthy enough," sighed Master Morgannwg, "so long as you do not upset him, and so long as you and he are on the same side. But I would judge that Master Charles Hassall's main interest in life is the protection and preservation of Master Charles Hassall."

15th March 1809

When we got back to the Plas after our pleasant little holiday, we found that the world was more or less unchanged. The first thing that greeted us on our arrival was a beautiful new kitchen door, manufactured by Gwynfor from some of our own oak planks. "Just for you, Mistress," he said with a grin. "I thought you deserved a little surprise."

That was the small news. Somewhat more substantial is the news that Squire Richard Fenton called in today during his tour around Pembrokeshire. By all accounts he is working on a new book that will bring up to date Squire George Owen's *Description of Pembrokeshire* written more than 200 years ago. Grandpa Isaac is a willing subscriber to the new project, and the squire called on his old friend out of courtesy and to bring him abreast with progress regarding his investigations and his writing. Also, I flatter myself because I think he is very fond of me and the children. We have enjoyed a convivial supper together, and the traveller is now fast asleep in his bed. Tomorrow he will proceed to Nevern and Eglwyswrw *en route* for Crymych. During our conversations he asked Grandpa about all sorts of things in Newport and the surrounding district, and made copious notes. "Ah, my dear friends," he said, easing himself back in his comfortable chair, "I am greatly in your debt, as to information gladly and freely provided, and only wish that I could reciprocate in some way."

"There is no need for that, Master Fenton," I laughed. "This household is already considerably in your debt, and I, for one, recall at least one episode beneath the roof of Plas Glynamel which might have led to disaster had it not been for your timely intervention. And of course we have all enjoyed the Glynamel Autumn Ball -- the most desirable event in the calendar of the north of the county -- on a number of occasions."

"You are very kind. That is an event which gives great pleasure to both my dear wife and myself, and we will continue with it, God willing, as long as we have the strength and the resources for it. In truth, without such events, where would we all be? Those of us who have the good fortune to belong to good families must have something to talk about over the dark and rainy winter months!"

"On the matter of good families, may I ask you something, Master Fenton?"

"Ask, and it shall be given."

"Your family crest. I have seen it on your own correspondence, and also on an envelope in another context, and have had occasion recently to wonder about it. Is it very ancient, and very different from all the other crests owned by all the other great families of this country?"

"It is quite unique. The black cross is not a simple one. It is the Maltese cross, incorporated into the crest following the Crusades, in which one of my ancestors distinguished himself in the presence of King Richard. The white stags relate to the fact that a later ancestor owned a part of the New Forest, and once hunted down two white stags on the same day -- something that was deemed auspicious. The smaller features on the shield or crest are also redolent with symbolism. The design dates from around 1400. One of my London friends who belongs to the College of Arms has examined it, and says that in its elegant simplicity it is very special."

"I see that you are very proud of it. Are you the only member of your family to use it?"

" Well, of course it is used by my wife and sons in their correspondence also. I always ensure that we have adequate supplies of writing paper, visiting cards, envelopes and such like in my office."

"So your son John might have used such writing materials prior to the time when you and he fell out, and parted company?"

"Naturally. He liked to use the family crest. He thought it gave him status when he moved about in his circle of reprobates in London, and indeed when he was in Pembrokeshire. But now I know not where he is, or indeed whether he is alive or dead......" His voice cracked, and he lowered his eyes. I immediately regretted my question, and placed my hand on his arm.

"I am sorry, Master Fenton, to have brought such things to the surface. It was insensitive of me......"

"No no -- such things come to the surface quite often. John has left this family, having brought disgrace upon it and having squandered a sizable part of my fortune. He is cut out of my will, and that is the end of it. But of course his disappearance causes distress. A prodigal child who is missing carries with him, or her, a part of a parent's soul -- and I hope and pray that you will never have to learn that for yourself."

"I think, Richard, that Martha does know something of the disappearance of a loved one," intervened Grandpa. "She is still very young, but she has already lost a husband in the most cruel of circumstances. She has also lost Owain, to whom she was betrothed, and still has not the faintest idea whether he is alive or dead."

"I apologize, Martha. Of course you do know all about desolation. How long is it now since Owain disappeared?"

"The last time I saw him was on the fifth day of May in the year 1807 -- almost two years since. We are still betrothed, but life is not easy without him......"

"And you still love him?"

That is not the sort of question an elderly squire asks of a young woman, unless maybe she is his own daughter. But this elderly squire is a special friend, and so I was not offended. "Of course I do, Master Fenton. I retain the hope -- albeit a faint hope -- that he is somewhere, maybe in some foreign land, still alive."

"And I see that you still wear that betrothal ring which was a little gift from Anne and myself."

"I do, and it will remain on my finger as long as I live as a sign of my love and my loyalty."

Then the conversation drifted to other things. Bessie served some more port, and at last, when Squire Fenton was feeling very mellow, I said: "Master Fenton -- in another context, which we need not explore at the moment, I have come across some initials which have made me somewhat perplexed. I am talking of a gentleman of some social standing, with London connections. Do the initials JRTP mean anything to you?"

"How interesting that you should ask that! I was asked the very same question by our mutual friend the Wizard of Werndew, some months back. I will tell you what I told Joseph -- namely that they might be the initials of a member of one of the great families of Pembrokeshire. I refer to the Parry family which spreads across parts of north-eastern Pembrokeshire, or the Perrots or the Perkinses, or the Prices, Pictons or Powells. Then there is the biggest family of all, the Philipps family of Picton Castle. That family has sons, daughters, nephews and nieces all over Pembrokeshire and further afield -- and many of them have that surname. Many of the male members of all of those families have of course spent time in London during the season; some of them have been very prominent in the social scene. Why do you ask?"

"Well, I do not wish to make untoward accusations, or draw premature conclusions, but I have a feeling that somebody with these initials might have been involved in certain criminal activities and in scenes of debauchery which might be acceptable in London but which might well cause the deacons of Bethlehem to succumb to apoplexy, were they to find out about them."

"My goodness, Martha, you make this fellow sound very interesting!"

"I think the word "dangerous" might be more appropriate, Master Fenton. This has something to do with those crimes committed some months back in Newport and Fishguard. You will recall from your newspaper and from your knowledge of local affairs that there was an arrest warrant and an offer of a substantial reward from Lewis Legal."

"I remember it well. A very strange affair indeed."

"Well, we can thank the Lord that things have subsequently calmed down, and that there has been no further sign of the four impostors with those improbable Welsh names. To return to the matter of the initials JRTP. It might be a long shot, but do you think that your son John might have known -- might know -- somebody with those initials?"

The squire frowned and thought for a while, and then his eyebrows lifted and he looked at me. "The first one J and the last one P? Yes, maybe....." he said at last. "Let me think. Yes, there was a fellow once, some years back, who came to visit John at Plas Glynymel. I think his name was Palmer. Joshua Palmer. No idea what his middle names might have been. Very tall and powerfully built. A strange fellow he was, and a man of few words. He did not stay long. I think he came from a wealthy family of shipowners in London, which made its money out of the slave trade. Yes -- I remember now that I had a number of very unpleasant conversations with him, for he had attitudes towards his fellow men which were anything but enlightened. One should not be too surprised maybe -- his family had money but no breeding, and pretensions but no gentility........"

Not wishing to explore further the Squire's own prejudices towards the merchant class, I said: "Thank you, sir. That information is most helpful, and I shall follow it up."

"This is all very mysterious, Martha. It sounds to me as if you are involved here in a little sleuthing. That fellow Joseph Harries had better look to his laurels!" And he slapped his knees and roared with laughter.

I did not feel it worthwhile to pursue this matter any further, for fear of having to reveal more of the background. I felt that there were quite enough people digging into the context of the Newport crimes already, and that any further gossip, carried further afield by Squire Fenton on his travels around Pembrokeshire, might alert the villains and make them even more devious in their campaign of retribution. So for the rest of the evening we talked of spring barley, the herring fishery and the small intrigues of the Pembrokeshire gentry.

22nd March 1809

The barley threshing is in full swing, and for the last week there has been so much going on in the barn and the farmyard that I have hardly had a moment to myself. Our tenants and labourers have all been helping, as they are required to do by their tenancy agreements, which is just as well since Shemi and Will are hard at work in the fields sowing and rolling. Inspired by the miller of Wiston and by the taste of wheat bread, I am planting more acres of spring wheat this year, as an experiment. Anyway, these two things -- the sowing of the new seed and the threshing of the old harvest -- signify for me the coming of spring, just as it is announced by shy primroses and glowing daffodils in the hedgerows.

And of course spring is also announced by the birthdays of little Sara, on March 19th, and Betsi, who is eleven years old today. Oh dear, I do not want her to grow up, since she has been such a lovely ten-year-old; but I suppose I must gird up my loins and accept that before long, as she grows into a young woman, the Plas will have to put up with the high dramas of adolescence.

I allowed Betsi to invite six of her special friends for a little party this afternoon. While assorted girly games were going on, Joseph called in, riding proudly on his new donkey. He is very fond of Betsi, and she of him , and much to my amusement they have very adult conversations about politics, the world of nature, and science. He brought her a book about flowers and herbs, and she was so delighted with her gift that she flung her arms around his neck and gave him a big kiss.

After the party, when the guests had gone home and my own children were all packed off to bed, I had the opportunity to compare notes with Joseph about the four sinister surveyors. I reported on my conversations with Lizzie Tasker and Richard Fenton. I also passed on my new information about the Fenton crest, and told him what I knew about a fellow called Joseph Palmer.

"He must be the one who uses the pseudonym Tomos Griffith," I said. "He does not sound like a very pleasant fellow, Joseph."

"I think we knew that already, Martha. But your new information is invaluable, and establishes a strong link between these fellows and John

Fenton in particular. If he is still alive he might be orchestrating this whole business......."

"You can take it from me that he is dead, Joseph. Don't ask me, please, how I know. But I know it."

"Very well. I will not press you further. So maybe he is orchestrating things from beyond the grave, in the sense that these men have a letter and a list of names which might have been written by Fenton before his demise. They may be friends who are still searching for him, or who are sworn to extract vengeance for his death."

"And for the deaths of others?" I speculated. "Those notes, with *For Rhiwallwn, For Tinwaed* and so forth written on them, must surely relate to others for whom vengeance is now sought? In my musings I have assumed that they might be pseudonyms for Alban Watkins, Joseph Rice, John Howell and John Fenton and maybe others who are now dead."

"Exactly my thinking, Martha. I think that we are dealing with a cult or brotherhood of some sort here, with men who are prepared to break the law, and risk death themselves, because of some oath of loyalty which they dare not break. Remember that we already have enough evidence to send them to the gallows, should we ever succeed in bringing them to court."

"Do they know what evidence we have accumulated?" I asked.

"They have no way of knowing that, unless they have another spy in the neighbourhood who is reporting back to them information about our enquiries."

"I doubt that anybody would dare," I said, "after what happened to Gwynfor Rees. Nobody else wants to be hunted down by the *Ceffyl Pren*, that's for sure."

"Agreed. Now then. I have made progress on other fronts. You knew, I suppose, that John Fenton was a heavy user of laudanum?"

"Good gracious, Joseph. Can that really be so? How did you discover it?"

"I have taken the opportunity, in recent days, of talking to some of the servants at Glynymel. Mistress Anne Fenton is away with relatives just now, and as we know, the Squire is out and about on his grand tour of

Pembrokeshire, collecting information for his book. Very convenient. Some of the servants are indebted to me in various ways. I find it very convenient to waive payment for services rendered whenever I can afford it, and to depend upon the remembrance of debts when I am in pursuit of information or require assistance........"

"You are truly a wily old fox, Joseph!"

"Please, Martha, I am not old. I am even younger than I look. At any rate, Claude Tournellec, a Frenchman who was left behind after that ill-fated invasion of theirs some years since, obtained certain assistance from me in evading arrest, and is eternally grateful that I found him employment at Glynymel as a gardener. He never wanted to be a soldier anyway. Mistress Anne enjoys having a compatriot to talk to. And she does talk, a great deal. To cut a long story down to a manageable size, Claude tells me that John, who always was the blackest sheep in the family, used laudanum all the time, much to the disgust of his parents. When he had friends to stay, they used to sit at the bottom of the garden in a little pagoda by the river, sometimes in a state of high euphoria and sometimes incapable of stringing six words together in a sensible order. And from the Glynymel rubbish dump in the old quarry, I now have in my possession five bottles which contained Sydenham's Tincture, prepared by Culpeper of Knightsbridge. Master Culpeper appears to have one or two very regular customers."

"So John was truly addicted to opium?"

"I fear so. According to the servants, he was apparently highly expert at assessing the quality of the laudanum on offer, and in assessing the doses required for specific effects."

Suddenly I recalled the episode when that monster abducted little Sara and took her to the hovel in the woods near Allt Clydach. He had known exactly how much "magic potion" to give her in order to put her to sleep but not to harm her too much -- and I had never before given consideration to what she had been given to keep her quiet. I think that the colour must have drained from my cheeks as the recollection of the episode flooded back into my mind, and Joseph immediately noticed my distress. "Martha, are you all right?" he asked, with concern in his voice. "You are shivering, and your shoulders are tense......"

"I am all right thank you, Joseph. It's just that this new information suddenly makes sense, and explains another episode in the past which I have promised never to divulge to another human being, no matter how trusted he or she might be."

"Very good. I will respect that. We all have our secrets. Now then, I have two other pieces of news from my conversations with the servants. The first is that a frequent visitor to Glynymel, in the days when John still enjoyed reasonable relations with his father, was a young man named Reynard Foley, who was addicted to laudanum and whose life was in shreds. He was from Great Canaston, not far from Narberth."

"I have never heard of him before. Could he be the one who now calls himself John Hughes, whom Lizzie Tasker considered to be lazy and dissolute? Or is that to stray into the realms of wild speculation?"

"No -- a reasonable guess, I think."

"And the other piece of information, Joseph?"

"Have a look at this, Martha." And Joseph pulled from his pocket a bulky small envelope with the Glynymel crest on it. He gave it to me, and I opened it. It contained crumpled and creased cuttings from newspapers -- mostly from *The Times* of London. For some minutes I thumbed through them, reading the headlines and scanning quickly through the text. All of the cuttings related to the bacchanalian excesses, gambling debts, outrages, scandals and insults to politicians and religious leaders involving the Hell-Fire Club. Some of the cuttings were very old, and related to Sir Francis Dashwood, who died in 1781. Other cuttings related to other prominent members like John Wilkes and Lord Sandwich, most of whom were now dead.

I could not contain myself. "The Hell-Fire Club! Good gracious, Joseph. Wherever did you get this package from?"

"One of the Glynymel maids. Her name is Mair, and I think she was the one who looked after you when you became ill at the Glynymel Autumn Ball some years since. When John was finally sent packing from his father's home he left behind all sorts of personal possessions, and the servants were told to empty his room. His clothes were given away to the poor people of the town. The servants were given strict instructions to burn all his papers and small personal effects. Most of his books went onto the bonfire, since it appears that his father strongly disapproved of their contents.........."

"They were erotic or obscene novels and such like?"

"Yes, and also illustrated tomes and books about libertarian or seditious politics, republicanism, witchcraft, and so forth. He was a man of hedonistic habits and catholic tastes, by all accounts. At any rate, young Mair, having been charged with disposing of this material into the flames, was appalled but also a little intrigued by it, and could not resist secreting away this little envelope of newspaper cuttings. She has kindly given it to me as a present. I have not yet had the opportunity to go through the contents in any detail."

"So where does this leave us, Joseph? Now I am getting confused, and cannot for the life of me work out whether we are dealing with a group of harmless eccentrics or with men who are really dangerous and possibly insane."

"Do not doubt for a moment, Martha, that these men are intent upon mayhem and possibly murder. You, and many of your nearest and dearest, are still in mortal danger, and we must not drop our guard for a moment."

Now Joseph has gone home on his donkey, and I am sitting at my dressing table at midnight, trying to make sense of the current situation. Before I go to sleep I will do one more thing. I will write to Master Charles Hassall with regard to Reynard Foley. His home is -- or was -- Great Canaston, which is not far from Narberth, and since Master Hassall prides himself on knowing everything about everybody in that district, I am sure that more information will be forthcoming.

8. Harvest of Fear

23rd March 1809

Today, in the early afternoon, I received a message from Master Benjamin Skyrme of Wiston Mill. It said that Dominic had been shot early in the morning, and that he was seriously injured. The letter concluded: "*........he does not have many friends in the locality, but you appear to be one of them. So I took it upon myself to inform you of this sad event.*"

I asked Shemi to come with me in the trap, and we rushed off over the mountain, arriving in Wiston at about 3 o'clock. I found Dominic in his sick bed, being tended by the miller's wife. The ball had been removed from her patient's shoulder by the local doctor during the morning, she said, and the prognosis was that his life was not in danger. I wanted to talk to him, but he was heavily sedated, and could hardly keep his eyes open. His speech was slurred. He was, I think, pleased to see me, but he was very morose, and refused to divulge how he was injured. It was surely not an accident, I thought, as he slipped into a deep sleep. Afterwards, when I had decided that there was nothing more to be done for the present, I prepared to take my leave. I asked the miller to let me know if there was any deterioration in his condition, and he promised to do that. Out in the yard, as I was about to step up into the trap, Master Skyrme said: "You might as well know, Mistress Martha, that the injury was sustained in a duel............"

"What?! Are you sure of that?"

"Of course, Mistress. He went off very early this morning, at dawn. I was awake, and saw him creep away on tip-toe from his little hut by the pond. He was brought back here in a cart, by another young fellow who must have been in attendance. Pistols were used, and the chosen place was the ruins of Llawhaden Castle. That's a favourite location for duels. Three fellows killed there in the last twenty years, so far as I know."

"And his opponent, Master Skyrme? Do you know who it was?"

"No idea, Mistress. He was in no fit state to tell me when he got back here, and the other young fellow was very secretive. Idiots, they are!

Like mad March hares! This is probably the result of some petty argument about a girl or a gambling debt which turned to insults and then into a duel..........."

28th March 1809

Five days have passed since Dominic risked his life in some silly dispute, and I have been contemplating the stupidity of men. I just cannot understand why a man can risk being maimed or killed in a confrontation with somebody else just because his pride is harmed in some way! Charles Hassall is just as bad as Dominic -- I gather that he has been involved in three duels, and it is a miracle he has never been injured. Maybe he carefully directs his insults at men who cannot shoot straight and who cannot handle a sword. We women are infinitely more sensible. We do quarrel, I suppose, and I have heard of women from the lower classes actually coming to fisticuffs in some furious dispute, especially if they are drunk at the time, but I just cannot imagine two ladies of good breeding behaving in this manner. In my experience, catty remarks and imaginary back-stabbing are at the limit of female behaviour, and nobody comes out of these disputes actually sporting physical injuries. And men (even those who have wives and children) use lethal weapons, for God's sake! I thank my lucky stars in the firmament that I am a woman. If I had been a man, I probably would have been fed to the worms, six feet under, long since.

Yesterday was Palm Sunday, known as *Sul y Blodau* or "Blossom Sunday" in Welsh, early this year for reasons best known to the Archbishop of Canterbury and the Government. It was, as it should be on such a day, warm and mild, and since the signs on Saturday evening were that the weather would be kind, the five children and I decided that we would get up before dawn in order to conduct the Easter Water Ceremony on the summit of Carningli. When we came down, bleary-eyed, at half past four, we found that Will was already up, feeding the heavy horses in readiness for a day's ploughing. Shemi had promised to carry the water on this occasion, and he was sitting in the candle-lit kitchen drinking a cup of tea, waiting for us. With very few words passing between us, we all dressed up warmly, put stout boots upon our feet, and slipped out of the house. We all carried lanterns. To start with, Shemi was also carrying a shiny new pail, but before we had gone very far he was carrying little Brynach, who complained that he was tired and that his legs were too short, and I was carrying the pail.

At Ffynnon Brynach we filled the pail with sacred spring water, and according to tradition Shemi had to carry it, without spilling a drop, from that point right up to the summit. As we climbed up through the tumbled old blue rocks, the light from our swaying lanterns cast long shadows, but gradually those shadows lessened in their intensity, and we noticed that the sky was lightening. "We must hurry!" exclaimed Betsi, who is now eleven years old and bosses us about whenever she can. "The dawn will soon be breaking!" So we hurried onwards and upwards, puffing and panting, and even Brynach found new strength in his short legs. We reached the grassy summit of the mountain just in time to position ourselves on assorted rocks with our backs to the East, so that we would not see the sun as it crept over the far horizon. Shemi placed the bucket of water in the centre of the grassy patch, and then by means of assorted contortions, we each in turn contrived to see the reflection of the rising sun on the surface of the water before observing it directly over the distant hills of Ceredigion. A cock crowed somewhere in the *cwm,* and a tawny owl bade farewell to the night in the woods near Dolrannog. We all laughed and cheered, and held hands, and danced around the bucket of water. Then we anointed each other with the holy water, initially with due reverence, dampened fingers and delicate gestures, but since children are not very good at being delicate the anointments quickly evolved into splashes and scooped handfuls of water, and before long the bucket was empty and we were all very wet.

Strangely, after that we all became quiet, and sat on the rocks with our arms around each other, and watched the giant red orb of the sun climb slowly, slowly over the still sleeping landscape, casting shadows that were so long that the children were amazed. The early morning mist melted away before our eyes, and the dawn symphony of birdsong, which had started with a few intermittent and almost hesitant phrases from far away, grew louder and louder until we thought we could probably hear every bird within a radius of five miles exulting in the joy of Blossom Sunday. I looked at the children, and how I loved them! They were all agog, with wide eyes and pricked ears, hardly daring to breathe. Such was the intensity of the quiet sunlit early morning. I wondered if they would remember this moment, and moments like it, when they are old and grey, and looking back with nostalgia at the magic of childhood? I hoped so, and images flashed through my mind of those occasions when I, as a child, had sat on the clifftops near Solva in the early morning sunshine and watched the glassy sea far below, and listened to the sounds of seabirds echoing amongst the caves, crevices and seaweed-draped sea stacks. How privileged we are, I thought, to be able to sit here on a serene mountain summit, surrounded by beauty, when others suffer from deprivation and misery, day after day, week after week, hardly aware of the rhythm of the seasons or the sights and sounds of the world around them.............

"Mam! I'm hungry!" said Brynach. So ended my reverie, and half an hour later we were back in the kitchen of the Plas, tucking into a large and very noisy breakfast.

This morning I received a letter from Dominic. It was quite brief, and in it he thanked me for my visit to his sick bed and assured me that he was recovering well after his unfortunate accident. Then he wrote that he was fit enough to travel, and that he would be leaving immediately on the next packet boat from Fishguard for Wexford, with a view to seeing his family and seeking the medical attention for his injury that he could not obtain locally. He concluded his letter thus: *"My dear Mistress Martha, I wish you well for the future, and trust that you will never come to any harm. Please convey my kindest regards to your dear children and your family and servants. I trust that some day we may meet again. Yours truly, Dominic Cunningham."*

I read the letter several times, and sat for a long time in my room, feeling as if my heart had been turned to stone. Then Bessie came in to make the bed and polish the furniture, and said immediately: "Why,

Mistress, what's wrong? Yesterday you were as chirpy as a sparrow all day long, and now just look at you!" Then she saw that I was holding the letter in my hand, and added: "From Master Dominic?"

I nodded, and passed it to her, inviting her to read it. She took it reluctantly, and quickly scanned its contents. "Bessie, I will never see him again," I whispered. "This is a farewell letter."

She came and put her arms around me as I fought to hold in my tears. "I think I would agree with you on that," she said. "Maybe this is for the best, Mistress. Why, there was nothing between you, apart from that silly kiss. And you and he are from different worlds. You know, and I know, that he is not gentry, whatever he might say. Maybe he has gone now, while the going is good, before a passing fancy and a little flirtation turns into something much more serious."

I sniffed and nodded, sensing that she was telling the truth. "Maybe, maybe, Bessie," I moaned. "Perhaps he does not want to hurt me, and is frightened of his own emotions. So he is off across the water, and lost without trace in the wilderness of Ireland........."

Bessie laughed. "You make this all sound very melodramatic!" she exclaimed. "I accept that you are upset, Mistress, but by tomorrow I guarantee that you will have regained your equilibrium and will look back on your little encounters with the Irishman with amusement rather than despair."

"Oh, I hope you are right, Bessie. But as things are I feel in some way unfulfilled. I have certain physical needs -- don't we all? And just at present I feel desperately that I need a strong man at my side, given my responsibilities for my estate and my family. There are things I need to share."

Bessie kissed me on the cheek. "I know all of that, Mistress, and understand it too. But is Dominic the right man to be a lover and a father? I doubt it. I suspect that he is a romantic rogue, playing a little game and then, like a small boy, running away when it starts to get out of hand. In my estimation, from what I have observed, and from what you have told me, he is scared to death of commitment and responsibility. An inveterate bachelor, perhaps slightly mad, and probably a coward too.........."

"He is certainly not that, Bessie!" I snapped. "Remember that he has just fought a duel and placed his life at risk!"

"My point exactly, Mistress. Only cowards fight duels. They are the ones who have not the sensibility or the diplomacy to resolve petty matters amicably, and who have not the moral strength to place responsibility above piffling self-esteem."

In the end, I had to agree with Bessie, and I breathed deeply and decided that I must put Dominic behind me. Now he is gone. But I have to admit that he has taken a little piece of my heart with him, and that there is now an empty space in it that might be hard to fill.

31st March 1809

Today I received a letter from Master Charles Hassall. This is what it said:

My Dear Mistress Morgan,
It was a pleasure to receive your letter, which encouraged me to recall -- with equal pleasure -- our brief conversation about surveyors some months back.

I am not a man for beating about the bush, so I will come straight to the point, without further ado. You ask about Reynard Foley. It is my misfortune to know him -- and I have to say that I have never met a more dissolute and lazy young fellow. I count myself as a good friend of the Foley family (and indeed of a number of other great families of the county) and know its branches and its estates well. In fact, I would go so far as to say that I know the Great Canaston estate better than any other living person, having made an accurate map of all its lands and farms for Mr Herbert Foley of Ridgeway shortly after he had acquired it. Reynard is his son, who was entrusted with the running of it around 1795. Under his supervision, or lack of it, over thirteen years or so, the estate has fallen into a ruinous condition, with good land allowed to become derelict, unpaid servants brought to the edge of despair, and mounting debts. He spends nearly all of his time in London but refuses to appoint an agent or steward to look after the estate in his absence. He still has a few servants in the mansion, who stay -- I suppose -- because the place does at least give them a roof over their heads and food for their bellies.

It is well known that young Foley has dissipated most of his fortune on riotous living in London, in the company of the Prince of Wales and others of the so-called "Carlton House Set". They turn vices into virtues (in their own minds, at least) and indulge in every form of sensual gratification they can imagine -- excessive eating and drinking, gambling at the races and the card table, fornication and the publication of obscene literature. While the other great houses of Pembrokeshire take delight in graceful and indeed gracious balls and other social events that would not be out of place in the London season, Foley has organized various events at Great Canaston which would not have been out of place in Babylon, Sodom or Gomorrah. At least three of his "celebrations" have so scandalized the local community that complaints have found their way into the pages of the Cambrian News. You might have seen these items yourself.

It might also be of interest to you to know that young Foley is addicted to laudanum, and spends much of his time at the extremes of the emotional spectrum. I have personally seen him in a state of wild and frenetic activity, writing pieces of nonsense poetry which he considers to be masterpieces; and then a few days later I have seen him again in a state of deepest melancholia, bewailing his inadequacies and quarreling with all his servants and friends.

Talking of his friends, he has several that I know of. They come to stay at Great Canaston every now and then, especially when a "celebration" is planned. They were here, so I am informed, in the middle of October and again at the end of that month. Young Foley's best friend is, I think, a fellow called Edwin Dashwood. Grandpa Isaac Morgan will know that surname, for in the middle of the last century Sir Francis Dashwood of West Wycombe was one of the most famous -- or infamous -- men in the country, who scandalized high society with his bizarre and lurid rituals and his libertarian philosophy. He of course founded the Hell-Fire Club, which used the caves on his estate for orgies and ceremonials. The Club is now defunct, much to the relief of the Wesleyans and the Baptists. I met Sir Francis once, shortly before he died, and was disgusted, since he has a handshake with less energy in it than a dead fish. At any rate, Edwin is the grandson of this fellow, and is apparently intent upon keeping up some of the ancient family traditions. Another friend is a strange fellow called Joshua

Palmer, from London. And yet another is a wild Scot who is one of the McCleod clan -- I fear that I do not know his first name.

Could those four be your four impostors posing as Government surveyors? Or would that be too hasty a conclusion to jump to? Whatever they are up to, it is probably not for the good of mankind, and I urge you to be careful.

Please do let me know if I can be of any further assistance. It is a part of my purpose in life to bring misdemeanours to the attention of the authorities, to call the guilty to account, and to ensure that good order prevails.

Your friend

Charles Hassall

Eastwood, Narberth.

Postscript: My Dear Mistress Martha, I was about to post this off with the next mail coach when I was in receipt of appalling news. I hear that Reynard Foley has been involved in a duel somewhere near Llawhaden or Canaston Bridge. Pistols, not swords. He is injured, with a ball in the thigh. His opponent, so I gather, came within an inch of losing his life, but is still alive so far as I know. He was apparently an Irishman with the name of Cunnington or some such thing.

Second Postscript: I have just had an inspiration about that Scot. I recalled seeing something in the paper about some fracas on the streets of Narberth in which he was involved, a couple of years ago. So I have gone through my collection of ancient newspapers and have discovered the relevant item from May 1807. Geordan McCleod is his name. He beat up some drunken fellow outside an inn, but got off with a caution. Once again I have cause to congratulate myself for my meticulous record keeping.

In view of the obvious importance of this letter I showed it immediately to Grandpa and Grandma. They remembered the press coverage of the outrages committed by the members of the Hell-Fire Club and the Mad Monks of St Francis, quite a few years ago and before I was born. They agreed that we now had the names of all four of the sinister surveyors, and further agreed that vigilance must be maintained. Grandpa then had to go down to town to talk to some of his cronies, as is his wont, and that left me alone with Grandma. She urged me to be more than a little wary of the advice and involvement of Master Hassall.. "That fellow," she reminded me, "has a reputation for stirring things up, for making accusations against those of whom he disapproves, and for interfering in other people's business. We all know about the vendetta which he conducts to this day against the Knox family, following his dismissal from the post of agent to the Llanstinan and Slebech estates of William Knox almost twenty years ago. He has a short fuse, a long memory, and a tendency to misjudge situations. Use his information if you like, my dear, but take it with a pinch of salt, and do not necessarily trust him....."

2nd April 1809

I should be happy, because the sun is still shining, and the children are well, and the spring work on the estate is proceeding as it should. Green shoots are appearing in the fields, and the dawn chorus is drowned out each morning by the rattles and bangs of the patent bird-scaring devices employed by three little boys from the *cwm* whom I have employed, dawn to dusk, to keep away the crows and the pigeons which would gorge themselves on our plump seeds and tender shoots, given half a chance. I prefer to feed my family and servants if possible, and think that the price of thruppence a day is worth paying for that privilege.

Joseph called today, and I shared with him the contents of Master Hassall's letter. I discovered that he already knew all of it, from Grandpa. That made me very disgruntled. I am beginning to piece together small indications that Joseph, Grandpa and the servants are in possession of certain information which is being hidden from me. There have been whispers in corners, notes passed back and forth, and nods and nudges. There is no frivolity in any of this -- and the faces of the men are always serious if not concerned. So they are not organizing a jolly party, or the gift of a new dress -- of that I am sure. I try not to feel threatened by this secrecy, for I would trust every one of them with my life, but I am a woman, after all, and I should have expected a little more consideration from these wretched fellows. I let them know now and then that I am less than pleased with their behaviour, but they just roll their eyes and tell me not to worry.

In my latest conversation with Joseph he was very guarded in everything he said, but I am certain that he knows far more than I about what is going on. I pressed him for information, and under interrogation he more or less admitted that he had been to see Dominic at Wiston Mill before he went off to Ireland. I also began to suspect further meetings in town with Skiff (who is now recovered) and with some of our spies and informers. Even Bessie seems to be somewhat secretive and evasive today. It is all very well for her and the others to encourage me to get on with my life and to concentrate on the children, but they do not seem to appreciate that ignorance of things that others know about is a heavy burden which reduces one's ability to concentrate on anything else.

3rd April 1809

Today it is Easter Day. At ten o'clock this morning Grandma and Grandpa, the older three children and I went along to Cilgwyn Church for the traditional Easter service, which I always try to attend so as to ensure that God does not forget about my existence. Dewi grumbled and said he had important things to do down in the woods, but I insisted that he came on the grounds that as a future master of the Plas Ingli estate he needed to get to know his neighbours better and to familiarise himself with the essential fixtures of local life, of which the church is one. In retrospect, that was very unsporting of me, since he is still only six years old. I had no such squabbles with the girls, since they both had new Easter bonnets and gowns which they wanted to show off to as many people as possible. We walked all the way to the church in the bright sunshine, greeting neighbours as we went. I must say I did feel immensely proud of my elegant family as we made our stately way along the Cilgwyn Road. Even Grandpa contrived to look like a stylish London gentleman, although I knew full well that he hated wearing his creaking and shining black shoes with the silver buckles and felt that his free spirit was insufferably constrained by his tight breeches, his starched shirt and his old-fashioned itchy wig.

4th April 1809

One day, comfort and joy, and the next day cold fear. This morning, on a grey and windy day, I walked down to town with Bessie, to do some shopping. We strode along arm in arm, carrying our baskets in our other arms, chatting busily and stopping now and then to talk to the residents of the cottages and farms along the Cilgwyn Road. We did our shopping, drank some tea in Hettie's lodging house, and set off for home again. We started to climb up Greystone Hill, and then I stopped in my tracks, and in the middle of a sentence, when I saw a very large funeral procession coming down the hill towards us, not in the shadowy gloom of eventide, but in broad daylight. I gripped Bessie's arm, and she said: "Good gracious, Mistress. What is the matter?"

"Coming towards us, Bessie! That funeral! Don't you see it?"

"You must be imagining it, Mistress. I see nothing at all......"

Instinctively, I moved aside, and pressed myself against the high stony hedge, expecting myself to be jostled by the press of people who filled the narrow roadway. In a few seconds I noticed that there were several coffins, some of which were small ones, carried on a gambo pulled by a black pony. And then I saw all of our neighbours and tenants and labourers, and some of the good people of the town. At the head of the procession walked Rector Devonald, dressed all in black, moving towards me, step by step, his face quite expressionless. Then, with my eyes wide with horror, I saw the person walking along behind the Rector. It was Mistress Martha Morgan of Plas Ingli............

At that point I must have collapsed with fear, and I have no further recollection of the episode until I became aware of Bessie slapping my cheeks in order to revive me, in the middle of the road. "Mistress!

Mistress! Come along now! Please! Please!" she urged, with obvious consternation in her voice.

"Oh Bessie, didn't you see it?" I gasped.

"See what, Mistress?"

"The funeral. Coming down the hill!"

"I swear that I saw nothing, Mistress. I thought you had come over all dizzy, for some reason."

"No no -- it was a funeral, and no doubt about it. A big one. There must have been a hundred people in the procession. You were in it, and so was I. And there were several coffins. Some were small......."

At last Bessie got me to my feet, and we managed to continue with our journey home. As we walked, she put her free arm around my shoulder and gripped me tight. Gradually I adjusted to the fact that I had witnessed a *toili* or phantom funeral which presaged some grim event in the community in the coming days. Whose were the coffins? I was petrified that they might have contained the bodies of my own children, and I articulated my concerns to Bessie. She had seen nothing at all, but to her credit she did not for a moment question my sanity, or the accuracy of my observations. She simply listened grim-faced, and said at last: "Well, Mistress, it has fallen to you to observe this strange thing. But you have no reason to think that this was a foreboding of some great personal tragedy involving the Plas. Some neighbouring family, maybe? One of the tenants? That is most likely, don't you think, if you were at the head of the procession behind the Rector?"

"Maybe, dear Bessie. But now I am truly frightened. Oh God, why does this knowledge have to be given to me, and nobody else?"

"It's your destiny, Mistress. You have your special powers -- you know that, and so do I, from things that have happened before. Should we keep this secret?"

"Oh, we must, Bessie,"I whispered. "Not a word to anybody. Joseph taught me long since that the workings of fate cannot be interfered with, and that nothing that is foreseen can be diverted or prevented. Something bad will happen -- of that we can be quite sure. The only consolation -- for you and for me -- is that we are forewarned and thus just a little better prepared for the consequences than others may be."

7th April 1809

Today it was the anniversary of the fire which destroyed the old Plas Ingli and consumed the bodies of five members of the Morgan family in the year 1794. So it was necessary for Grandpa, Grandma and me, and the children, to visit the churchyard in Cilgwyn so that we could leave flowers in the family enclosure where the victims -- or what was left of them -- were buried. We walked to the little church and picked spring flowers on the way, and when we had left our little posies we all stood there silently for a while with our memories and tears. My tears were not just for David's family, but for my beloved husband too, for this is where he was buried just four years ago following his death on Newport Sands. As we stood there, Sara and Brynach wandered about amongst the gravestones, not fully understanding what this was all about, but the older children showed a quite wonderful awareness of the emotions that reside in the breasts of all adults. Without a word, Betsi came and held my hand, and Dewi held Grandpa's hand, and Daisy cuddled against Grandma. As I write this, I have a tear in my eye............ not out of sadness for the past, but out of a love of life, and hope for the future.

On our walk home, our spirits were lifted, for this was, after all, St Brynach's Day, the day on which the cuckoo is supposed to arrive in Nevern Churchyard and the day on which little Brynach was born. The little fellow was as excited as a molly lamb presented with a bottle of milk, and he skipped about all over the road with such enthusiasm that I thought he would fall asleep as soon as we got home. That is exactly what happened, but it gave us a breathing space for the preparation of our picnic. I had determined that since it was a bright, fresh day, with the wind in the West, we should walk up to the rocks of Carn Edward, only about half a mile from the Plas, and enjoy a picnic feast in the lee of the great blue crags. Within an hour we had everything ready in our big picnic hamper, which we were planning to carry ourselves up to the rocks. But Billy and Shemi would not hear of us carrying all of that weight, and insisted that they should come with us. I did not object, and in retrospect they wanted to come, not in order to avoid a couple of hours of hard work in the fields, but to give us protection in such a wild and exposed place from threats about which maybe they knew more than I did.

We had a wonderful time. The clouds wafted away during the picnic, and we ate well, drank well, and played assorted silly games appropriate for a two-year old. Then Billy, Shemi and I lay back and dozed in the sun while Dewi and Brynach explored among the rocks. When we returned, the sun was sliding down and we saw the makings of a fine clear evening. We all agreed that this must become an annual tradition. St Brynach's Day would henceforth be Picnic Day.

Now I will sleep well, content that all is as well as it can be with our little world.

Oh my God. I was about to blow out my candle, when Billy rushed upstairs and banged on my door. "Mistress," he shouted. "Look out of your window! There is a fire in the *cwm*..........."

I must go.......

8th April 1809

Once again, euphoria has been displaced by horror. I have to relate the most terrible events. To start at the beginning. Having scribbled the words at the end of my last diary entry, I rushed to the window and opened the shutters. On a cloudy night faintly lit by a waning moon, I could see smoke and flames down in the woods near the river. I could not work out the precise location, but it was clear that a house was on fire. We all rushed into the kitchen, and Billy, Will and Shemi followed their instincts by dressing hurriedly, rushing into the yard and grabbing buckets and other containers that might come in handy for fighting the flames. I was in the process of putting on my boots and rushing out too, but Billy shouted at me: "Mistress, don't you dare! Just you stay here, in the house, where you are safe. Grandpa and Bessie, don't let her out of your sight!" Then the three men grabbed lanterns prepared by Mrs Owen. They rushed down the track to alert the neighbours, and we saw nothing of them for several hours. I was infuriated by the manner in which Billy had spoken to me, but as soon as some sort of calm had returned to the kitchen, Grandpa took me to one side and said: "You will not take offence with Billy, Martha. He is exactly right. This might be a decoy, to get the young men out of the house. If you go rushing out into the dark night you will be easy pickings for anybody well placed to grab you and stick a knife between your ribs. As long as you remain between these four walls, nobody can get at you." Then I noticed that Grandpa, that most peaceful of men, was carrying a pistol in his hand.

We all crowded around the upstairs windows that overlooked the *cwm*, and after a while we agreed that the fire must be at Brithdir or Gamallt, down by the river. It was past breakfast time when the three men returned from the fire, with the horror of the experience etched across their faces. They were so exhausted that they could hardly stand. "Where, Billy?"I asked.

"Gwynfor's cottage, Mistress."

"Oh, no! Did they get out? Are they all right?"

"No, Mistress. All gone. All five of them. They had no chance." And Billy, who never weeps, wept.

We were all in a state of shock, and when we had done what we could to console the three men who just had seen the most awful things, we got them cleaned up and forced them to eat some breakfast. The story emerged over the course of an hour or so, in bits and pieces. This is my understanding of what happened. The three men, and assorted others who had spotted the flames from a distance, traced the column of smoke and flames to Gwynfor's cottage. But in the darkness it was a nightmare to reach the place using feeble lanterns, and because of the quaking bog just outside the front door, and the difficulty of getting water from the river, it was almost impossible to fight the flames. When the men reached the hovel it was already too late. Gwynfor, his blind wife and the three children had already died in the fire. The roof had collapsed and the inferno was so intense that nobody could get close. But the men noticed immediately that a heavy log had been placed across the door, and that the single small window had been blocked by a branch which was still blazing.

"Bastards! Bastards!" said Will. "The door and the window were deliberately blocked. They were shut in, and then the fire was started. They had no chance, Mistress. No chance....."

We were still trying to come to terms with this cold-blooded murder when news came from town that attorney Will Probert's house in Newport had also gone up in flames during the night. We could see no sign of that from the Plas, since Newport is on the other side of the mountain, and in any case we had all been looking the other way. He and his family were lucky -- they all got out in time, and because of the proximity of one of the town's water pumps the neighbours were able to fight the flames. They put the fire out, but apparently the house is gutted in any case, and the contents were consumed in the inferno.

Now a day has passed, and the whole community is in a state of shock. This afternoon, when the smouldering remains of Gwynfor's hovel had cooled down sufficiently for some of the local men to venture inside, they found the charred remains of the five inhabitants. They were taken immediately to the mortuary on the Parrog, and there they will lie until they are examined by Doctor Havard and Joseph. The two experts will have to report to an inquest, and once the cause of death has been determined, and the jury has reached its verdict, the Coroner will release the bodies for burial. Rector Devonald has already agreed that they will have a Church funeral and a burial on hallowed land, but there has been much debate about a location for the *Gwylnos*. As Gwynfor's employer I offered the use of the Plas, but my tenant Jeb Phipps from Brithdir Mawr pleaded with me for it to be held there, on the grounds that he and his family were the nearest neighbours of the deceased family, and also close friends. I went along with that, and I will help with the food and other arrangements.

It is widely assumed, even among those who do not know the details, that these two fires were not accidents, and that there are arsonists at work in the community. But I knew, as soon as the fire alarm went up, that the men responsible were those four men who caused such mayhem last autumn.

9th April 1809

Joseph is on the case, and he called by this morning to discuss his findings with Grandpa and me. He says that no notes have been found this time, and that he cannot find any clues in spite of a thorough search and thorough questioning of scores of people who might have seen or heard something. He is very irritated by his lack of progress. According to Billy, Gwynfor was at work as usual on the day before the fire, but he was very morose and uncommunicative. Will, who had become a special friend of Gwynfor, asked him what was wrong, but he would not say. Later it emerged that he had been seen in animated conversation with a stranger on the Cilgwyn Road. I assumed at once that the stranger was one of the four villains -- probably the Scot called McCleod, since he seems to have been the one communicating with Gwynfor back in the autumn.

"We all know who the guilty men are," said Joseph. "We do not need to give a moment of extra thought to that matter. But what makes me very nervous is that they are now much more careful than they were..........."

"As you anticipated some time ago," I said.

"Precisely. They must have ridden into town on the very night of the two fires, knowing exactly what they were doing. Meticulous planning, and no clues. I have not even found any hoofprints or footprints -- but that is perhaps not surprising, since the street around Will Final Testament's house is hard gravel, and since so many men were milling around Gwynfor's hovel, and trying to fight the flames, that any traces of earlier visitors were entirely obliterated."

"And motives, Joseph?"asked Grandpa.

"Revenge or retribution, Isaac, in the case of Master Probert. Do not forget that his name was on their list. Will Probert knew that, because I warned him to be very vigilant, but still they caught him by surprise and extracted their price. Although we have watchful people all over town, and further afield, nobody can maintain a high level of vigilance for a period of almost six months. This fellow Palmer and his cronies knew that, and decided on a lightning strike. In and away in less than an hour. Very clever."

"But Joseph," I said, "in spite of our suspicions and our preparedness, I for one never thought for a moment that poor Gwynfor and his family would be slaughtered. Had you anticipated it?"

Joseph shook his head sadly. "No, I had not. I will never forgive myself. Now, with the benefit of this monstrous thing called hindsight, we assume that the four villains felt that Gwynfor had betrayed them. He had taken their silver shekels and gone on to work for the very woman -- Mistress Morgan of Plas Ingli -- who was and is their greatest enemy. They suspected, quite rightly, that Gwynfor had passed on information that might be useful in bringing the forces of law and order down on their heads. There can be no doubt that they have now murdered this poor family in cold blood because Gwynfor had broken a bond with them and had failed to feed them further information over the winter."

"And who will be next, Joseph?" I asked bleakly.

"My dear Martha," replied the Wizard, equally bleakly, "your guess is as good as mine."

13th April 1809

We have reminded all of our spies and informers to be especially watchful in the coming days, and we have told all of them through our network of contacts that the arrest warrants are still in place, and that the two rewards -- from Judge Wynn-Evans and Lewis Legal -- are still on offer. Grandpa also arranged yesterday for the warrants to be amended, with the proper names of the four villains -- Joshua Palmer, Reynard Foley, Geordan McCleod, and Edwin Dashwood -- added.

We fully expect that the final storm will break at any moment. What form the confrontation will take, we cannot know, and neither can we locate the site of the battlefield. I think the target will be the Plas, and all of us who dwell beneath its roof -- but would that be too obvious? So we are all waiting, waiting. And watching. There is tension in the air, and it is increasingly difficult for us to maintain the workings of the estate.

Speaking for myself, I have to admit to living on the edge of my nerves, and for the past few nights I have hardly slept at all. I admit to being short with the servants, and I have had to apologise several times for my outbursts and for cruel words used thoughtlessly. I also find it increasingly hard to cope with the children, for they have picked up on the tension in the household and have been behaving very badly.

But in spite of everything we have to maintain a semblance of normality. Three days ago we heard the first cuckoo of spring. The children were excited, and claimed that it was a special cuckoo this year, arriving in the neighbourhood just for Daisy's 8th birthday. Poor Daisy! I had promised her a little party for her friends, but because of the tragic event in the *cwm* I said that such frivolity was now out of the question, and that the party would be delayed for a month. Daisy then had a tantrum, weeping and screaming and throwing her dolls about, and I had to punish her by confining her to her room for two hours. That left my nerves in shreds, and created a cloud of gloom over the whole household.

On the very same day the inquest for the five members of the Rees family was held in Newport. Billy, Shemi and Will had to attend as witnesses, and they said afterwards that it was not an event for people with weak knees and sensitive stomachs. The Coroner, Daniel Thomas, had forced them, along with the members of the jury, to look at the corpses "so as to identify them and to better understand the evidence presented by the medical profession as to the cause of death." Since so little was left of the bodies, and since the remains were so horrendously charred, the sight and the smell of them was too much for some, and two members of the jury passed out, and two others were violently sick, before the coffins were closed up again. Joseph and Doctor Havard gave evidence that all five -- two adults and three children -- had died as a result of asphyxiation and incineration in a fire started deliberately by persons unknown. The Coroner pressed them on the use of the word "deliberately" and asked whether the fire might have been ignited accidentally, or might have resulted from a blanket or some such inflammable thing catching fire within the cottage. Billy and several other witnesses attested to the fact that the door and the window had been blocked when they arrived and first saw the conflagration, causing them to come to the view that the guilty party or parties had been determined to stop the residents from escaping from the blazing cottage and had thus committed premeditated murder. Joseph confirmed this, saying that although little was left of the log placed across the door, by his estimation it was originally of such length and weight that it would have been impossible for one man (for example Gwynfor Rees) to have moved it single-handed. At least two men, said Joseph, must have dragged the log from somewhere in the wood and placed it in position. The jury, or what was left of it, decided virtually without discussion that the members of the family were all "unlawfully killed by burning, in a premeditated fashion, by a person or persons unknown." That decision was about as unequivocal as it could be, and it means that if and when the guilty parties are brought to justice, a hanging verdict is inevitable, with no pardon from the King. Immediately after the inquest, Daniel Thomas, in his capacity as Coroner and Mayor of the Town, and Will Daniels, the clerk to the justices, issued a "Wanted for Murder" notice which will be printed and spread far and wide. One might think that would be enough to be going on with, but Will Final Testament has also now entered the fray, with a notice offering a reward of £25 for information leading to the arrest of the person or persons responsible for the burning of his house. He has no evidence to go on, but he is sure that the conflagration was the result of an arson attack.

After the inquest the bodies in their sealed coffins were released for burial and taken to Brithdir on a gambo. There the *Gwylnos* was held by friends and neighbours with the coffins in a line in the front room. They remained sealed, but in any case the smell of charred flesh pervaded the house, and I for one found it impossible to stay for very long, and to enjoy any of the food and drink on offer, before retreating back to the Plas with waves of nausea breaking over me. The *Gwylnos* before a funeral is often a convivial affair -- but not this time. There were no relatives present, and indeed nobody knew whether there were any close or distant relatives anywhere, either on Gwynfor's side or on the side of his poor blind wife. There will be notices in the paper, of course, but we will be surprised if there are any members of the Rees family left, anywhere in the world. They left no wills, and they had no property and no possessions. Their deaths will be recorded in the church and parish records, but otherwise these poor people will go unremembered by a cruel world that did them no favours. But I will remember them. I will pay for the funeral, I will pay for their grave in St Mary's Churchyard, and I will provide for them a simple headstone.

On the day after the inquest and the sombre *Gwylnos* at Brithdir, the funeral was held. The long procession walked all the way from Brithdir to the church, with Rector Devonald at its head and with me, in the absence of any family members and as Gwynfor's employer, a few steps behind. The coffins were carried on a gambo pulled by a black pony. All of my servants walked in the procession, as did many of the men who had taken part in the administration of rough justice by the *Ceffyl Pren* jury down on the estuary last October. To their eternal credit, those men who yelled and whistled at Gwynfor from the safety of a vindictive mob were now prepared to walk out of respect for this same man, in recognition of his efforts to improve his life and the lot of his family, and in united condemnation of the actions of a gang of brutal murderers. There is not much more to write about the funeral, except to say that in all its details the procession was exactly as I observed it ten days ago on Greystone Hill.

14th April 1809

In mid-morning, a trap clattered into the yard at high speed, with old Ellis Prosser of Frongoch cracking his whip on his pony's rump and risking life and limb in the jolting driving seat. He is one of Grandpa's cronies, and we know him well, but he does not habitually rush about, so when I saw him I was immediately concerned.. "I have the Wizard on board!" he shouted as he skidded to a halt. "Get him inside quickly!" We looked into the back of the trap, and there we found Joseph in a dishevelled heap, more dead than alive.

"Oh no!" I cried. "Joseph, have they caught you again?"

"Never fear, Martha," he moaned, giving a weak smile. "I assure you that I am quite well. My present condition is something which I have brought upon myself......"

A wave of relief swept over me, but there was no time for celebrations, since the poor man was as white as a sheet and was so weak that he could not stand. His teeth were chattering. We carried him into the house, wrapped him in blankets, and sat him in the settle next to the kitchen fire. Mrs Owen made a great fuss of him, and fed him several cups of hot tea. She reckoned he was suffering from starvation as well as shock, and eventually we managed to encourage him to eat some breakfast. At last he revived, and we relaxed.

"Another of your ten lives used up, Joseph?" I asked.

"Not at all, Martha. Self-inflicted injuries this time. I will tell you more in the privacy of your office, when I have enjoyed a little more pampering from the beautiful Mrs Owen."

"When last did you eat anything?"

"I can't remember. Yesterday? The day before?"

While the blushing and beautiful Mrs Owen ministered to the needs of the Wizard of Werndew, I took Master Prosser to one side, and asked him what this was all about. He replied that his servants had found Joseph early in the morning, unconscious on the floor of the barn. I was mystified, and said: "Are you sure he had not been attacked?"

"No, I doubt that, Martha," said the old squire. "Joseph uses the barn quite often, for magical purposes. He finds it to be remote and peaceful -- and also spacious. I don't mind -- we are old friends, and I keep an eye on him in case things get out of control."

After an hour or so, with Joseph somewhat recovered and able to stand again, I invited him into the privacy of my office. If we were going to talk about magic, I knew he would not want to have several eavesdroppers in the vicinity. He explained to me that he has been involved in an invocation of his spirits, in an attempt to find out more about the fires. This was a matter of last resort, since he had nothing else to go on. From the protection of his magic circle, he said he had summoned down a dog, a goat, a horse and a bull, and got nowhere with his requests for information. But at last, after consulting three demons whose form he would not describe, he got the information he needed.

Palmer and McCleod were responsible for the fire and the deaths of Gwynfor Rees and his family. Dashwood and Foley were responsible for the burning of Will Probert's house. The emotional struggle required to extract this information was almost too much for Joseph. "It was a close-run thing, Martha," he said, with perspiration on his brow.

"And if you had not prevailed?"

"I will not talk about the consequences. Too terrible to contemplate. No matter -- I succeeded, and here I am, almost hale and hearty."

"So they are here again," I sighed. "Did they ever go away, do you think?"

"Oh yes -- on their previous expedition they were too careless, and things got too hot for them. They had to get away, and quickly. I think they have learned their lesson. This time they are staying at Great Canaston............."

"You know that, Joseph?"

"I know it. The black bull never lies -- like my other spirits, he may be stupid and ferocious, and reluctant to divulge what he knows, but he cannot tell a lie. At any rate, I assume that on their visits to Newport -- however many they plan to make -- they will travel independently and will not stay in town. I doubt that they will even appear in any of the inns. They will leave no evidence behind them; they may use diversionary tactics; and they will be as brutal as they were with Gwynfor and his family with anybody who betrays them or who gets in their way."

"And I am still their prime target, do you think?"

"Yes, Martha. I am sorry to say you are. That means you must go nowhere from now on without an armed bodyguard, until this miserable business is resolved."

After our mid-day meal, Joseph was still not back to his usual self, so I packed him off to bed in the spare room at about two in the afternoon. Now it is ten in the evening. The house is quiet, and Joseph is still fast asleep. I will try to get some sleep myself, but that might well be difficult in the circumstances prevailing.

15th April 1809

Joseph slept like a baby for eighteen hours. After breakfast he sat with me in the orchard, on a bright still morning, with mist swirling in the *cwm*. Very few words passed between us as we both delighted in the peace and beauty of the moment. It is a strange thing, I thought, that there can be such tranquillity and such a delicate interplay of light and colour in the middle of a war. Then Joseph said: "Martha, I was thinking when I woke up this morning, and have decided that I must tell you why I think these men are so dangerous."

"More dangerous than any other men who are on a mission of revenge?"

"I believe so, my dear friend. What do you know about the effects of laudanum?"

"Not much, I have to admit. I have seen you use the tincture at various times, to deaden pain or to send a terribly injured person off to sleep."

"That is its proper purpose, Martha, and it is a great boon in the hands of a trained physician or wizard like myself. But I am now convinced that some, if not all, of the men who have caused us such distress are habitual users of Sydenham's tincture, and it sounds as if young Reynard Foley should be considered an addict. They will therefore all display characteristic changes of mood and behaviour -- and that is why their actions are proving almost impossible to predict."

"So what changes might we expect in their personalities?" I asked. "Wild swings of emotion, for example?"

"Yes, and a great deal more. The habitual laudanum user will be almost impossible to live with -- and I predict that not one of these four fellows will have a loving wife at home while they are out and about causing mayhem. Typically, the heavy user will have his body so adapted to the use of the substance that he will require at least a hundred drops of the tincture to reduce pain or induce drowsiness........."

"Compared to how many drops for you or me?"

"Ten is usually sufficient to affect a healthy adult. When I treated Will and Skiff, for example, back in the autumn, they were both fast asleep after the administration of fifteen drops, and they are both big and healthy fellows. But more to the point is the effect of the tincture on the mind. A state of deep melancholia is often induced, but on the other hand users say that they experience a relief from their worries and often a sense of euphoria. Imagination and creativity are enhanced (so they believe -- but I personally doubt it) and it is common for users to make wild linkages between unexpected and unrelated things and to have vivid dreams."

"Nightmares, Joseph?"

"Sometimes, yes, of such violence that they are almost scared out of their wits. Sometimes the dreams have extraordinary colours in them. Sometimes they are erotic. Addicts refer to their "visions" and their "enlightenment" and look down on those whose lives are mundane and who simply seek to stay alive, to do a good day's work, and to feed their families. And I have seen appalling side-effects -- hysteria, unbearable headaches, insomnia, a sense of guilt, and great mental confusion. Sometimes heavy users are stupefied and drowsy, and then later go into destructive phases of self-criticism, self-loathing and even paranoia. Once or twice I have seen fellows arguing and even quarreling with those whom they normally trust -- including friends and family. Have I said enough?"

"Indeed you have, Joseph," said I. "But from what you say, those who depend upon a regular supply of Sydenham's Tincture are probably more of a danger to themselves than to anybody else. So why should we worry?"

"Because, Martha, I cannot predict what they might do next -- and they cannot even be sure of that themselves. My biggest nightmare relates to a situation in which they are all in a state of high euphoria at the same time. Then, they will be convinced that they are uniquely in possession of the truth; that whatever they do is virtuous and that whoever stands against them is evil; that they are superior in intellect to all other members of the human race; that they can outwit others as easily as a cat can outwit a mouse; and that they are utterly invincible."

"But surely, Joseph, these fellows -- if indeed this is a pattern of behaviour we can expect of them -- will not be so stupid as to commit murder?"

"They have done it already, Martha. I suspect they killed the Rees family in cold blood, and not in a drug-induced frenzy. And they will do it again, for they will be convinced that because of their essential superiority they cannot be caught and that they will therefore never be brought to justice."

"Oh my God!" I whispered, hardly able to find my own voice. "Do you mean that the prospect of the gallows has no meaning for them, and acts as no deterrent to whatever they have in mind?"

"I mean precisely that, Martha. I have dealt with many villains in my time, and you and I together have succeeded in bringing a number of them to suffer from the full and terrible weight of the law. With most of those fellows, their behaviour was predictable, and I always felt that I could outwit them or, through meticulous sleuthing, track them down and get them -- in due course -- to face the stern gaze of an Assize Court judge. But with these four impostors, I do not know where I stand. To tell you the truth, my dear Martha, for the first time in my life I feel inadequate, and seriously afraid.........."

9. The Hunters and the Hunted

20th April 1809

Some days since I received an invitation from my friend Mary Jane Stokes to a *soiree* in Trecwn. And she wanted me to bring my harp. I was reluctant to accept, since we are all suffering from a siege mentality in our blessed house, but Grandma, Grandpa and the servants all said it would do me good, and that I needed a break. They, poor things, have to cope with my black moods, which afflict me these days with alarming frequency. But they are very understanding. Indeed, who would not feel exhausted, and on edge, in the circumstances? They all feel this way themselves, and struggle to remain cheerful. "Mistress, you must not allow this business of the surveyors to turn you into a hermit," said Bessie, wagging her finger at me. "That would be a victory for them. You have been short with the children, and your usual devotion to the affairs of the estate has been notable by its absence. Enjoy a convivial evening in the company of old friends, and forget about fires and funerals and villains for a little while!"

So here I am in the grand house at Trecwn, spending a night away from home, and enjoying it. It is past midnight, and I have the rare pleasure of writing in my little book while sitting at somebody else's dressing table. I have been given a well-appointed and cosy room at the west end of the mansion, and I feel thoroughly pampered. I have eaten well, and drunk too much wine, and I will undoubtedly -- for a change -- sleep well.

Dafydd Stokes even sent his carriage to collect me, with two burly fellows as armed guards. I appreciated that, and assumed that Mary Jane had told him of the precautions we are all having to take just now, in view of the threat that we face. Half a dozen old friends were in attendance, including Ellie Phillips and her husband, and my sister Catrin and her husband James Bowen. They have all gone home now, since they live not far from Trecwn, and I am the only guest staying for the night.

It is a pleasure to write of something quite unexceptional, for a change. We played cards for a while, and after that James sang some sad ballads in his fine baritone voice. I was prevailed upon to play some old Welsh airs on my harp, which were well received, although I felt ashamed of my sloppy fingering and my lapses of memory. Grandma, who is an exceptional musician, tells me that I do have a talent on the harp, and I do admit that I enjoy playing this most wonderful of instruments, but I do not practice enough. Ellie and Catrin played a charming piece for four hands on the pianoforte, and Mary Jane and her husband (who had obviously rehearsed meticulously) sang a moving duet. Then Walter recited a long and heroic poem which was, he assured us, a translation he had made himself from one of the Norse sagas. He was very pleased with himself, but to tell the truth I was thoroughly bored, and would prefer not to know about Viking heroes chopping each other to bits with bloodaxes.

As is inevitable on such occasions involving married couples, we women drifted towards one end of the room as the evening wore on, while the men drifted towards the other. I was able to bring my dear friends up to date with respect to the terrible events in and around Newport, and they listened wide-eyed to my narrative. They all seem to lead lives that are entirely uneventful, and I wondered why one disaster after another appears to afflict me and the Plas, while nothing at all happens on the other side of the mountain.

Ellie, in particular, urged me to take care, and I did notice that when I mentioned the names of the villains -- Palmer, Dashwood, Foley and McCleod -- her body stiffened and the colour went from her cheeks. I cannot imagine Ellie, with her Methodist background and her modest and abstemious lifestyle, having anything at all to do with these fellows. But her husband Walter is a different matter, for he is a surly and bad-tempered man who will, I suspect, bring nothing but grief into her life. I really know very little about his background, or who his friends might be. When I get the chance of talking to Ellie privately, I think I might ask her a few questions.

21st April 1809

I am back at the Plas, amazed and not a little entertained.

When I was helped down from the Stokes carriage on my return from Trecwn, I walked into the kitchen and found the whole house in celebratory mood. Apparently there had been a considerable expedition to Great Canaston, the home of Reynard Foley and the place currently being used, according to Joseph's friendly spirits, by the four sinister surveyors. My jaw dropped when I heard this, and I asked Billy: "Have you organized a posse armed with an arrest warrant, and gone thundering off over the mountain to arrest those fellows and claim your magnificent reward?"

"Not quite," laughed Billy. "We did have that in mind five or six days ago, when Joseph told us where they were hiding, but then a strange thing happened which made us change our plans. Isn't that right, boys?"

Will and Shemi nodded sagely. Then, with euphoria in the air, everybody started talking at once, and I had to sit down and try to work out what this was all about. As far as I understand it, this is what happened.

On the day after Joseph's invocation in the Frongoch barn, my friends Fancy and Nancy received a strange message. It contained an invitation to a "celebration" at Great Canaston on the night of 20th April -- not just for the two of them but for other "sisters"as well. *"Your friends are very welcome"* said the note, *"especially if they are young and fresh, if you get my meaning."* It was signed by John Hughes -- in other words Reynard Foley. The girls decided that the four impostors were clearly in residence at Great Canaston, and that they were in need of women. They were offered £5 each for a night's work (a huge amount of money in these hard times) on condition that absolute discretion should be observed. They were told that the house would be locked and carefully guarded, but they were instructed, on arrival, to give three knocks in quick succession, followed by a pause and then three more quick knocks.

The girls were apprehensive about this invitation, given what they now knew about the activities of these evil men in the neighbourhood, and so they immediately consulted with Patty and Joseph. Together they conceived a plan which would be much more effective, Joseph thought, than sending a posse which might meet armed resistance and lead to injuries and possibly deaths. On the grounds that incriminating evidence might be found in the house, a search warrant was signed by Ellis Prosser of Frongoch in his capacity as a magistrate. Somehow or other, Joseph managed to speak to Billy and the other servants, and they decided that the Plas would have to be the base for a raid on Great Canaston. They had to get me out of the house, and so they encouraged Mary Jane to arrange a soiree and to invite me along. Without too much difficulty, they convinced me to attend, and off I went in the Trecwn coach, in all innocence, leaving the house to the plotters.

A *Ceffyl Pren* jury was then assembled, involving fifteen men who would travel in conditions of great secrecy over the mountain, to meet up at Canaston Bridge not far from Foley's mansion. From what I can gather, the planning was meticulous, involving both Grandpa Isaac and Joseph. The plan was that Billy and Skiff, together with three others, would secure the grounds of the mansion, and that Shemi and Will, with eight comrades, would get into the house, carrying both the new search warrant and one of the old arrest warrants. They would carry ropes, axes and knives, truncheons and staves, but no firearms. They hoped that they might be able to identify Palmer and his three cronies, grab them and cart them back to Newport. The raiders went over the mountain in the afternoon, travelling in twos and threes, and with women's clothes stuffed into their bags. They met at the bridge as planned, and then hid in the bushes near the entrance to the driveway. They observed that there were two guards at the main gate. They saw maybe twenty other people arrive, both men and women. All of them had their faces covered, presumably because they were intent upon protecting their anonymity. A few arrived in rather grand coaches. At about midnight the "sisters" changed into their female costumes, put on their bonnets, blackened their faces, and girded their loins. They easily overpowered the two guards at the gate and trussed them up, as they did with three servants who were looking after the guests' horses in the stables behind the house. Then, on receipt of a signal that the outside of the house was secured, Will went up to the front door and gave the special knocks, as instructed by Fancy and Nancy.

"Who's there?" said a voice from the other side of the door. "Fancy and Nancy, and a few sisters," said Will in his best falsetto voice. When the door was opened the eight men stormed into the house, waving their warrants. They found a few servants in the hall and the kitchen, and "encouraged" them to get out of the house at high speed. Will said that they were more than happy to do that, and they were last seen trotting away down the drive as fast as their legs could carry them.

The foreman of the *Ceffyl Pren* and his jury burst into the parlour and found an orgy in full swing -- with unclothed and partly clothed men and women all over the place. They were so inebriated, presumably as a result of alcohol and laudanum consumption, that there was little resistance. But by all accounts there was a lot of screaming and shouting, with both men and women trying to hide behind tables and sofas, trying to grab their clothes, and attempting to escape. They must have been terrified out of their wits at the sight of a gang of muscular "sisters" with black faces, pretty bonnets on their heads, and big boots upon their feet. The "sisters" tried to identify Palmer and his three cronies, but nobody would admit to the names that were shouted out by Will, and nobody would point the finger either. So Will shouted out the pseudonyms as well, and was met with blank stares. He came to the conclusion that few of the guests knew each other's names, which I suppose might be common practice in orgies. He also thought that the four villains might have been in one of the other rooms upstairs, for various bedrooms were also in use, some of them with locked doors. They smashed down some of these doors and encountered more scenes of debauchery rudely interrupted, with men and women hiding under beds and under blankets, yelling and whimpering with fear. They searched the house, but Will says, in retrospect, that they should have done better research, for it was a veritable rabbit warren of passages and dusty rooms, with any number of cupboards and attics that could have been used as hiding places by Palmer and the others.

Angered by their failure to apprehend the men they were hunting for, Will and his friends remained in occupation for two hours. They burned many of the piles of clothes that had been discarded here, there and everywhere by assorted guests, by throwing them onto the fire in the parlour and the big open fire in the kitchen. That caused maximum confusion, which the "sisters" greatly enjoyed. Then they smashed the house up and beat up many of the men. "Maybe we shouldn't have done that, Mistress," said Shemi, "but we were very frustrated and angry that those four bastards were nowhere to be found, and anyway, the men who were there as guests deserved a bit of a lesson as regarding the rules of etiquette." I could not see what beating up a bunch of naked old men might have had to do with etiquette, but I let it pass. The "sisters" enjoyed the remains of the great feast laid out in the dining room. They stuck to a very strict "no alcohol" rule, although there were flagons and bottles of wine, beer and spirits everywhere. Eventually the "sisters" threw all of the guests out into the yard, in various states of undress, and chased them down the driveway. Then at last they left a note on the dining room table which said: "*Palmer, Dashwood, Foley and McCleod, you bastards, we will get you.*" Then the men left the house in a considerably worse state than it had been in to start with. But they were not empty-handed. With the justification of their search warrant they came away with some very good finds -- Palmer's fine saddle from the livery room, his long coat with the letters JRTP inside the collar, a bottle of ink from the library, several empty and half-empty bottles of Sydenham's Tincture, and a big red-covered book that was lying around in the parlour, with the title *The Myvyrian Archaiology of Wales: Volume Four: On the Rituals of the Ancient British Bards,* by my friend Iolo Morgannwg. It had a bookmark inserted at page 386, dealing with druidic rituals and initiations involving virgins.

"Very entertaining, it was, Mistress," says Shemi, reliving the events of the night with some relish. "I have led a very sheltered life, and have never before seen such things. When we burst into the parlour and the bedrooms there was indeed much hiding behind sheets and cushions and much covering up of private parts."

"That is a very interesting thing," said Grandpa. "When I was a foolish young fellow in Oxford there was a great scandal involving learned professors, lawyers and clerics who were discovered in the middle of their frolics in a house of ill repute. When some jolly students burst in upon the scene it was the instinct of almost all of the learned gentlemen present to cover up their private parts, upon which they were of course all recognized. But the brightest of all of them, whose name is not known to this day, instantly covered up his face instead, and thus escaped recognition. Now that man was truly a genius!"

Everybody roared with laughter. Shemi continued: "I have always, in the past, thought of the human body as a very wonderful thing, and the cause of much excitement, but now I declare that I have changed my mind, for I have never before seen so many rolls of fat, and sagging breasts, and bandy legs, and flabby buttocks, and distended stomachs. In truth, the human body is for the most part a sad and unlovely thing............"

"I am sorry to intrude on your philosophical musings," I intervened, "but can we return to the four impostors? Are you sure they were all present at the orgy?"

"We still cannot be certain who was there and who was not," said Will. "Only one or two of our number had ever seen their faces when they were in Newport, and to make matters worse they all had rings of flowers upon their heads. In truth, there were perhaps thirty fellows present, and I got the impression that most of them were too far gone to know their own names anyway, let alone the names of anybody else."

"And what about the evidence which you collected with or without the aid of the search warrant?"

"It is all deposited with Joseph," said Grandpa, "and he is subjecting certain items to scientific tests. He is quite sure that he now has all the evidence he needs to bring a full prosecution and to succeed to a conviction that will carry the death sentence. Assault is one thing -- the cold-blooded murder of an innocent family is quite another. Will and Skiff will tomorrow enter complaints relating to the murder of the family with Will Daniels -- he is going to attend here with a scrivenor to get everything down. He will then have to issue an arrest warrant for all four of those fellows in their proper names, on the basis that they have now committed murder. Lewis Legal and Will Final Testament, as aggrieved attorneys whose homes have gone up in smoke, have now increased their reward for the apprehension of the guilty men -- now also named -- up to £50. It is not a good idea to upset one attorney, let alone two. The "Wanted" notices will be printed in 500 copies and widely distributed.

Notices will be placed in *The Times* and in other national newspapers. The net will now close upon those fellows, and it will not help them if they flee from Wales and seek refuge in London or West Wycombe. Those who have been harmed by these bastards -- and there will be many such people -- will be jostling with one another in order to report them or arrest them. I predict that before seven days have passed, they will be quaking in their shoes, and that within a fortnight they will be behind bars."

"Oh my God," I said. "This has dragged on for quite long enough, and I for one am quite worn down by it. I pray, Grandpa, that your predictions will come true. And quickly."

The rest of the evening was given over to an extremely jolly party, to which Fancy and Nancy were invited, as honoured guests. They took an evening off, much to the disappointment of the crew of the *Mudlark* of Avonmouth, which has just come into the Parrog on the high tide with a general cargo.

25th April 1809

The new statements and complaints have been entered and a fresh arrest warrant has been issued. "Wanted" notices are now posted on church doors and public buildings all over West Wales. I think that if I was Joshua Palmer, or any of his cronies, I might be a trifle worried. The whole town has been buzzing with news of the Great Canaston raid by the beautiful sisters of the *Ceffyl Pren*, and I dare say the details have become more lurid and explicit with every telling of the tale. It will keep the inhabitants of both the low inns and the high mansions of north Pembrokeshire entertained for weeks if not months. Anyway, I am glad that I had no part in it, although it does occur to me that the four villains might assume that it was I who dreamed up and orchestrated the whole operation. I am now utterly confused by the welter of arrest warrants, search warrants, amended arrest warrants, "Wanted" notices and "Reward" notices that are in circulation, and Grandpa says he can never remember a hunt for a group of criminals on such a scale.

Today news came from our spies in the Narberth district that the four wanted men have fled from the mansion at Great Canaston and nobody knows where they are. The Narberth constables are searching for them, not very effectively, even though there is a substantial sum of money on offer for whoever manages to apprehend them. The *Cambrian News* has already carried a brief report of the orgy and riotous events at Great Canaston on the night of 20th/21st April. As one would expect from a newspaper that habitually wears its hypocrisy on its sleeve, it adopts a high moral tone, and thunders in a fashion that would do credit to *The Times* of London. It says the community is utterly scandalised by what happened, and various brief comments are carried from the local vicar and the mayor of Narberth. The editor of the newspaper is no fool, and he promises that the next edition (which will no doubt be printed in ten times as many copies as the current one) will carry a "full and exclusive expose of the shameful debauchery and lamentable events" that have shocked the nation. I would have thought that the paper should have given the murder of the Rees family far greater coverage, but it merits but a small mention on an inside page.

28th April 1809

I am still feeling edgy and vulnerable -- and I know that I will not be able to relax until the four murderers are behind bars. I do not know, at the moment, who are the hunters, and who are the hunted. I feel trapped, since nobody will let me out of the house without an armed guard. If this goes on for much longer, I fear that I shall go out of my mind.

Joseph called this afternoon on his donkey. He told Grandpa and myself that he has no clues as to the whereabouts of Palmer and his confederates. He thought they may have gone back to England, on the basis that the alternative is to live rough and to risk being discovered. He doubted that they were capable of living rough -- they were all too soft for that, he said, and probably could not survive without their .creature comforts. I disagreed with that, and said they were not as soft as all that, having spent days and weeks in the saddle, having set four houses on fire (including one in the middle of Fishguard and another in Newport) and having displayed a capacity for brutality and even sadism on a number of occasions. I told Joseph I was convinced that they were still in Pembrokeshire, and Grandpa agreed with me. Joseph was out-voted, and so we decided to tighten our security arrangements even more. We have now set a round-the clock watch, with one man always on duty with a shotgun at the ready. Rules about travel have been tightened up -- all journeys in future, even to town to do the shopping, must be done by three people travelling together., and somebody must have a pistol in case of armed attack. This will stretch our resources almost to breaking point, and it is my view that if the final confrontation has not come within three weeks or so we will all be asleep on our feet.

2nd May 1809

I feel as if I have been pushed through a chaff cutter and chopped into little pieces. Once and for all, if there was any doubt about it, I have shown that I am an incompetent and cruel mother, quite lacking in sensitivity and in a basic understanding of the world of small children. I fear that I will never again be able to restore the respect and the love of my children. This is what happened.

As is our tradition on Mayday, we had a little celebration, with a maypole put up and dressed in its finery in the field next to the house. Each of the older children had permission to invite four special friends. It was unseasonally hot, and even before the sun was at its zenith I was feeling tired and irritable. Shemi was discreetly on patrol with the shotgun, lurking behind one of the field walls above the house. The children, their friends, and Sian and I enjoyed a splendid picnic in the sun, and all the children were in high spirits after dancing round the maypole and getting themselves into a frightful tangle. Afterwards, I was snoozing in the garden alongside Grandpa and Grandma, when I was woken up by a great whooping and yelling from five little boys behind the wall. They came rushing into the garden waving spears and bows and arrows. They had taken their shirts off, and wore only their shoes and breeches. Their faces were covered with streaks and twirls of soot. "Yahooo! Hocus pocus," shouted Dewi. "I am Big Chief Black Bison, and me and my braves have come to scalp you and to sacrifice you to the Great God of the North Wind. Prepare to die!" I smiled indulgently and rubbed my eyes -- and was horrified to see that the five boys had black stripes across their chests -- three diagonal stripes, starting above one nipple and ending beneath the other. I fear that I reacted hysterically, feeling as if a cord had snapped inside me. I shouted at the boys, grabbed Dewi and frantically tried to rub the marks off his chest. I grabbed each of the others and did the same to them. Then Brynach came toddling along, having failed to keep up with the rest of the Indian war-party -- and I saw that he had the marks on his chest as well.

I recall shouting: "Dewi, how could you do this to me? How could you spoil such a happy day? You wicked, wicked boys! You should be ashamed of yourselves! How could you? How dare you?"

Soon all five of them were wailing, and the girls and their friends, who had been playing with their dolls in the shade of the barn, were also milling about, with concern and fear all over their faces. Grandpa and Grandma attempted to calm me down, but I fear that I was in a state of uncontrollable fury, and I sent Dewi to his room, still wailing. I told Sian to take the other boys home immediately, after washing off all of the soot. The whole party was destroyed, and afterwards I recall that I was shaking like a leaf. Then, to make matters even worse, I broke down and wept.

Bessie (who had been in the kitchen until she heard all the commotion outside) put her arm around me and led me, still sobbing, to my room. At last, when I had calmed down, Bessie said: "Mistress, that was not a very edifying spectacle, and seldom have I seen a jolly party destroyed at such high speed. Whatever got into you?"

"Those marks, Bessie," I moaned. "How dare they?"

"We saw them too," she said, "when the Red Indians raided the kitchen, and we also appreciated their significance. But the rest of us thought it best to restrain ourselves while the children were so happy, and to ask Dewi afterwards, in a measured way, where on earth the idea of the three parallel lines had come from............"

"That is all very well for you, Bessie, but you and the others have not suffered from this damnable affair as I have!"

Bessie gave me a withering look. "I think we have, Mistress."

"How dare you, Bessie? You have no idea of the torment I have felt, month after month, while the rest of you have simply been observers."

"Have you been beaten up and left for dead, like Will and Skiff? Or trampled beneath the hooves of stampeding cattle, like Joseph? Have you had a knife dragged across your chest, or been left covered with blood, or had notes pinned to your flesh? Have you had your home reduced to ashes, or lost any loved ones to these impostors?"

"Enough, enough, Bessie!" I sighed. "You are right -- I have to admit it. Others have suffered far more."

"And if I might make so bold, Mistress, you are, not for the first time, your own worst enemy, interfering when you might be wiser to stand back and stop running about on your amateur sleuthing when you might be wiser to leave things to Joseph........."

"Now that is unfair, Bessie. You must recall that when Joseph had his broken leg he was in no position to discover the truth, or to pursue those impostors. It was my duty -- to my servants and friends, and to this beloved house and family of mine -- to try to get to the bottom of things."

"At the beginning, I suppose your efforts were laudable and appropriate, but subsequently there have been many occasions when I have seen Joseph rolling his eyes, and heard him sigh, when confronted by the results of your latest investigations. You get in the way, Mistress, and put yourself in danger -- and those of us who love you are sometimes in despair as to how to deal with you........"

Now Bessie was also weeping because of the raw emotions brought to the surface in this encounter. The two us embraced, weeping together. At last I whispered through my tears: "But their list, Bessie -- I am on the top of it. Everybody knows that."

"And that is why we seek to protect you."

"That is why you wanted me out of the way when the *Ceffyl Pren* mob mounted that expedition to Great Canaston?"

"Correct, Mistress. And that is why there has been a great deal going on in this house and in town which you are unaware of."

"You have all been conspiring behind my back? That is outrageous, Bessie! I must know what has been going on."

"So you shall, Mistress. But not now. You have a terrified and very sad little boy to deal with first, and you must also make peace with your daughters. You are, after all, their mother........."

"And do you really think that I forget that sometimes, Bessie?" I whispered, fearing her answer.

"I'm afraid that you do, Mistress. Not often. But it does happen sometimes, and Sian then worries about the happiness of the children."

"Oh my God! I had not realized.......... and do you all see me as a bad and neglectful mother? I would never forgive myself if anything happened to the little ones."

Bessie laughed. "No no, Mistress. You are a wonderful and loving mother -- and it is a miracle that you manage to carry such responsibilities for the estate, the tenants and the servants, and discharge your duties with such care and competence, while giving so much love to the children. They suffer far less than many other gentry children I can think of, caught up in unhappy marriages or with tyrants for fathers."

"Oh Bessie, don't mention fathers to me! If only I had a man by my side right now, to give me wise counsel, to share my fears, to hold me in a warm embrace, to give me love............ David is gone. Owain is gone. And Dominic -- do I dare hope that he will return, Bessie?"

"You have plenty of time to think about Dominic, Mistress. Just now you must think of Dewi."

"So what shall I do, Bessie?" I sighed, feeling drained of energy.

"You must ask him, Mistress, where this fantasy about the parallel stripes came from................"

"Do you think he has overheard conversations, or seen things he should not have seen? We have all tried to protect the children from the injuries and chaos caused by those evil men, and Sian has been a saint in looking after them, and keeping them amused, at one end of the house while great dramas have been played out at the other."

"I have no more idea than you, Mistress. He and his friends have been having fun with their Secret Red Indian Tribe for months now, whispering in corners, having secret ceremonies, and chasing the girls away when they have been too inquisitive. Boys have very vivid imaginations, which we women sometimes fail to understand. They mimic the things they read in their books about heroes and great adventures, just as we girls mimic mothers and babies."

"So I will go and talk to Dewi, and ask him about the source of this fantasy about the stripes, and ask for his forgiveness."

"Just now, Mistress, Sian will be giving the children their supper, and getting them off to bed. Shemi has, I think, cleaned the other little boys up, cheered them up, and delivered them to their homes. He has probably explained your outburst to them as one of those things that happens with women, at a certain time every month!"

I managed a feeble smile. "Maybe. Maybe. Children these days know far too much -- in my day such things would never have been mentioned."

"Can I suggest, Mistress, that you wait for half an hour, tidy yourself up, calm yourself down, and then go and see the girls? Apologise to them first, tuck them up and kiss them goodnight, and then go and do the same with Dewi."

I agreed to do as Bessie suggested, and my beloved maid helped to tidy up my hair and apply some of my favourite scent and rouge, before putting out a fresh dress. So I went and made my peace with the girls, and they went to sleep happily enough. Then, as apprehensive as a small child seeking the forgiveness of a fierce father, I knocked on Dewi's door.

"Dewi -- can I come in? It's Mam."

"Go away!" he shouted.

"Please, *cariad*, I want to come in and say sorry for what happened in the garden. And I want to tell you that I love you."

There was a long silence. I was very tense, with my ear to the keyhole. At last he mumbled: "All right then. But make it quick."

I entered the room, to find that Dewi was hiding beneath the blankets. "Dewi, you can come out now," I said. "I want to talk to you, and see you at the same time."

"I am fast asleep."

"Oh no you're not. Please just pop your head up for a moment."

There was another long pause. At last Dewi popped his head up. His eyes were red, since he had been crying a great deal. I found it very hard to control my own emotions. But I had to try. "Have you had your supper?"

He shook his head. "Do you want some of that nice Mayday cake that Mrs Owen made?" He nodded. I went down to the kitchen by the back stairs and fetched him a big slice of cake, with a thick layer of marzipan on it, and a glass of milk. I watched the little fellow with a smile on my face as he wolfed it down. I put some more coal onto the bedroom fire, since the evening was chilly after the warmth of the day. Then I said: "I want to say I am very sorry, Dewi. My behaviour in the garden was unforgivable, and I am very ashamed of myself. Tomorrow I will go and visit your friends, and I will say sorry to them too. Mothers should not behave like that, and I will never, never let it happen again. Do you accept my apology?"

Dewi looked at me for a long time, and said: "Oh, all right then."

"Are we friends again?"

"Yes, Mam."

"Then get out from under that blanket, and come and give me a hug. I need it."

He climbed out from under the blankets and flung himself onto me as I sat on the side of the bed, with his arms around my neck. We cuddled for a long time, and much as I tried I could not prevent tears from trickling down my cheeks.

"Why are you crying, Mam?"

"Because I love you so much." I kissed his blonde head of tousled and curly hair and loved the close contact with this little boy who was growing up so quickly and who thought that hugs and kisses were just for "stupid girls."

"I love you too, Mam."

"Thank you, *cariad*. That means the world to me."

Then I settled onto the bed, with my back against his pillow, and with Dewi's head in my lap. As I ran my fingers through his hair, I asked: "Dewi, can I ask you a question or two?"

"If you like."

"Your Secret Red Indian Tribe. Where did you get the idea from?"

"It's a secret."

"Well, I promise I will not tell the girls. My lips are sealed."

"Oh, very well. From books and things -- and I met a real Red Indian Chief when we went to the fair last year. For a halfpenny he let me into all the secrets of his mighty tribe."

"That was very kind of him. And those marks on your chest, made with soot. Your friends had them too........"

"Until you came and rubbed them all off."

"Yes, I know. I know. That was silly of me, and very unkind. I am sorry for that, too. But where did that idea come from?

"That's a secret too."

"Remember that my lips are sealed, and that I will be taken by the Great God of the North Wind if I should ever betray you."

"Very well, Mam. You sound like a good Red Indian squaw. Master Dominic."

I froze with horror and disbelief, and could not say a word. Then I regained then power of speech, and said incredulously: "Master Dominic? But that's impossible, Dewi. Has he been here recently, without me being aware of it?"

"No, no, Mam," said Dewi, with the voice of a child whose patience is sorely tried by parental stupidity. "Our tribe has been around for years and years, almost. Do you remember that Master Dominic came at Christmas, and was all soaking wet when he arrived?"

"Yes, I remember that."

"Well, he had to change all his clothes and have a hot bath to warm himself up, since he was shivering and his teeth were chattering. He had a bath in the tin-tub in the scullery. Billy and the other men were busy with other things, and so I was the only other man able to help. Mrs Owen sent me in with five jugs of hot water for his bath........"

"And where is this leading, Dewi?"

"I thought you wanted to know, Mam?" he grumbled. "Anyway, I watched him having his bath, and saw that he had some scars on his chest -- three lines sloping down........"

"He had scars on his chest? Are you sure of it?"

"Oh yes, Mam. I asked him about them, and he said he got them in a secret ceremony when he was a scout out on the prairies, and got captured by the Indians, and tortured, and then so impressed them with his amazing strength and his way with horses that they made him into a special chieftain, with the name of Big Chief Mighty Stallion. He is sworn to secrecy with his Red Indian brothers, and he swore me to secrecy too. Later on, when Christmas was all over and done with, me and my friends had a secret meeting of our tribe, and Billy Watkins and me decided that it would be great to use those secret marks ourselves. We didn't think that Big Chief Mighty Stallion would mind............"

As he proceeded with this long explanation, Dewi's speech became slower and slower, and suddenly, in the middle of a sentence, he fell asleep, with his head still on my lap. I pulled some blankets over him to keep him warm. I continued to sit there on the bed, just where I was, and cried myself to sleep.

9th May 1809

I cannot find words strong enough to describe my desolation and indeed my fury at being betrayed by that charlatan Dominic Cunningham. Since my small son alerted me on Mayday to the scale of the Irishman's deception and duplicity, I have discussed things endlessly with Bessie, Grandpa and Grandma. I am now quite convinced that Dominic has been a member of Palmer's gang all along, and that it was his task to infiltrate the family with a view to feeding information back to the four evil impostors. In my mind, it all adds up, when I recall the various incidents in which he has been involved. I have no doubt that the meeting at Portfield Fair was not down to chance. It was carefully planned and cleverly executed. Bessie and Grandpa tend to agree with me on that, but Grandma is not so sure. She has, I think, developed a soft spot for Dominic, and cannot believe him capable of such a cunning betrayal. But I am adamant, and in a sense of deepening gloom I have sworn that I will get justice -- or revenge.

A couple of days ago I had to pay homage to my precious Owain, for it was the second anniversary of his disappearance. Or his death. He was a true gentleman -- a **gentle man** who taught me a great deal about loyalty and sensibility. He was not only brave and kind, but also, I think, incapable of deceit, and his face was an open book, at least in my limited experience. I still struggle with the fact that he is gone, and while my head says I must finally accept that he is dead, my heart (especially in the light of my latest exposure to masculine manipulation and cruelty) says that there can never be another man capable of replacing him in my affections. I have talked to Grandma about loss, since I have lost David through a cruel death, Owain through his disappearance at sea, and now, in a sense, Dominic as well, having been led by him on a merry dance before his flight back to Ireland. Grandma Jane knows more about loss than I will ever do, and remains wise and serene in spite of it. "Oh Grandma," I sighed, "I opened up my heart to that fake gentleman, and felt that he had opened up his heart to me too, at least as much as he dared!" Grandma did her best to console me, but all she could say to me, a woman betrayed, was: "Well my dear, he is gone, and good riddance to him. You are better off without him -- and remember that if he had really loved you or respected you, he would still be here." Platitudes, platitudes ..... and no consolation whatsoever.

The *Cambrian News* today contains a salacious report of the rudely interrupted orgy at Great Cansaston. It told me nothing that I did not know already, although the aftermath appears to have been interesting in that *"up to twenty well-known local personages from the ranks of the Pembrokeshire gentry, whose names are known to this newspaper, were found in various states of undress in the lanes and fields around Canaston Bridge early in the morning. Some appear to have returned to the house and to have recovered their horses after the disappearance of the mob, but most were assisted by kindly local people who have subsequently stressed to this newspaper that they were driven by human kindness and humanity, and that their actions should in no way be interpreted as condoning the debauchery at the mansion."*

I was minded to write to the newspaper's editor and enquire into the identities of these "local personages," but then thought that Joseph has probably done that already. I was also interested to read that the local constables and magistrates are not minded to search for or prosecute any members of the *Ceffyl Pren* mob, or indeed to enquire into the brutal punishment meted out to the guests at what was after all a private house party, since they have received no complaints from any of those that might have suffered. And one last matter of interest. Apparently, following the issue of the "Wanted Notice" for Foley and his cronies, the mansion at Great Canaston has now been abandoned. All the servants have left, and on the instructions of Foley's father the house has been stripped of furniture and the estate is on the market. Because it is in a run-down condition, and the house is in poor repair, it may be difficult to find a buyer. I suspect that the house may soon be in the possession of spiders, rats and jackdaws. But the land is potentially fertile and productive, as Master Hassall informed me some time since, and will certainly be incorporated into some other estate. The whereabouts of Reynard Foley and the others are, said the newspaper, not known.

14th May 1809

Two days ago we celebrated my 31st birthday. It is one of those birthdays best forgotten about, since I feel that the bloom of youth is slipping away, and that middle age is just around the corner. So I wanted to do nothing, and to have no reminders of it. But the children love parties, and they connived with Sian and Bessie and Mrs Owen to arrange a special feast, and we contrived to eat and drink well, and have a good time playing silly games. Joseph came, as he always does.

When the children had gone off to bed, I decided to return to a matter raised by Bessie a couple of weeks since but not explored -- that is, the conspiracy to hide certain things from me in case I might get upset. Grandpa, Grandma and the servants agreed at last that they might as well be honest with me, in view of recent happenings, and revealed that attempts had been made on the lives of Billy, Shemi, and Grandpa within the last three months. Billy was attacked in the woods near Gwynfor's hovel one day in February while the building work was in progress there, and escaped only because Shemi came along a minute later and helped to drive off the attackers. Then Shemi and Grandpa were shot at near Glandwr in March, when they were on their way to Cardigan Market. There was an attempt to send the Plas up in flames, also in March. According to the servants, this happened when I was away in Brawdy with the children, for the meeting with my father and Master Iolo Morgannwg. Apparently, very early in the morning, while it was still dark, somebody set fire to a pile of papers and boxes placed against the kitchen door. Luckily Mrs Owen was reading by candlelight in her bed at the time. She smelt smoke and raised the alarm, causing the arsonist to flee before he could also light another pile of inflammable materials piled against the front door. The fire was quickly extinguished, but the door was seriously damaged, and Gwynfor quickly had to manufacture a new kitchen door while everybody else worked desperately to remove all traces of the flames. I recall being impressed with the new kitchen door on my return from Brawdy, and being slightly bemused because I could not remember that there was anything much wrong with the old one.

An attempt was also made on Jake's life last month. He was on the quayside near one of the the Parrog warehouses at high tide one evening just as the sun was setting. He was all by himself, smoking his pipe and gazing out to sea, enjoying the last of the sun's rays, when he heard a sound behind him. He turned just in time to see three men with long coats and mufflers. He was hit on the head and although he fell to the ground he was then bundled over the edge of the quay into the murky water below. Incredibly, the cold sea revived him, and he had the presence of mind to swim under water for ten yards and to emerge on the seaward side of a fishing boat moored just offshore, out of sight of his attackers. They waited for a few minutes, and when they were convinced that he was drowned, they turned on their heels and strode away. He swam ashore, and was helped by a neighbour who gave him a stiff drink or two to revive him. Then he went home to Patty, soaking wet and with a thunderous headache, and pretended that he had imbibed a few too many in the Royal Oak and that he had slipped off the quay into the water on his way home. Patty was furious with him, but apparently believed his account of the proceedings.

I was shocked when I heard all of this, and even a little angry, although in truth I could not let that show since my beloved friends had all been seeking to protect me from things that would undoubtedly have caused me great distress had I known about them. So I simply asked: "Do you mean to say, all of you, that these fellows have not actually stayed away from this area over the early months of this year, as you have allowed me to assume?"

"I fear so, Martha," said Joseph. "We don't think they have been here all the time. But they have made visits, with murderous intent."

"So have you really allowed me to settle into a mood of complacency while all of this was going on?"

"You have not been noticeably complacent, Martha," said Grandpa. "On the contrary, I think I might describe your mood since Christmas as paranoid. You have not been alone in that -- we have all felt like hunted animals. You have had quite enough on your plate. Anyway, the rest of us have not been content simply to await developments."

"Will you explain, Grandpa?"

"Since Christmas, my dear, we have maintained a watch system in this house, with somebody awake all of the time......"

"Even during those weeks of snow and blizzards?"

"Quite so," nodded the old fellow. "We have all taken it in turns, including Jane and myself."

What could I say, other than to thank them all from the bottom of my heart? And I was able to laugh with them when I remarked that I had been a little concerned of late to see various individuals nodding off at strange times of the day, sometimes in the middle of mundane tasks. "In fact," I added with a grin, "I was just about to dismiss the whole lot of you and appoint as my servants some other people from the town who know what hard work is all about!"

15th May 1809

Yesterday, as I sat at my desk with quill in hand, I was able to make light of serious revelations. Tonight I have no such luxury. At dusk there was a knock on the front door. Mrs Owen thought that was strange, since everybody who visits the Plas regularly -- like Rector Devonald, Dai Darjeeling and the cobbler Billy Clog -- comes to the back door. Also, nobody was supposed to be able to approach the house, since Shemi was on duty with the shotgun at the entrance to the driveway. Somewhat bemused, she opened the door. She was confronted by a big man, tall and massively built. He stood on the doorstep, perfectly still. It was a cold and windy day, and his face was hidden behind a muffler. He had a wide-brimmed hat on his head. My dear housekeeper said afterwards that although she is a very formidable woman herself, wide enough to fill the doorway and well able to protect herself against all comers, she felt quite intimidated.

The stranger said, in a voice not much louder than a whisper: "I think this is yours, Madam" and handed over the shotgun. Mrs Owen took it, not knowing what else to do. Then he whispered that he had a message for Mistress Martha Morgan, to be delivered personally. He was invited in by Mrs Owen, but declined simply with a gesture of his hand. She came into the kitchen to fetch me, and returned to the door with me in case something unpleasant might happen. Without further thought, I introduced myself to the stranger as I might to any other visitor. He simply looked at me and handed me an envelope. Then he turned on his heel and strode off down the drive, leaving me shaking like a leaf. Mrs Owen slammed and locked the door, and gave me her arm until I was safely back in the kitchen.

"What about Shemi, Mistress?" she asked. "He was on watch......."

Sian, to whom Shemi is betrothed, almost collapsed at that point, and had to be helped to a chair. Will and Billy rushed down the drive towards the entrance gate, and there they found Shemi, who is a big and powerful man, trussed up with ropes, and with a gag stuffed into his mouth. He had a massive bump on his head. He was otherwise unharmed, but was furious that he had allowed himself to be struck on the head from behind and overpowered with relative ease. "I might have dozed off," he admitted. "Keeping watch after a good day's work is a hard thing, Mistress." But the poor dear man was distraught at having let his Mistress down, and having allowed the defences of Plas Ingli to be breached. I had to console him, and told him not to worry, since no real harm had been done.

I knew immediately that the stranger at the door was Joshua Palmer. This was the first time I had set eyes on any of the four impostors, and my fear must have been as obvious to him as it was to Mrs Owen and the others. While the other servants fussed around Shemi, and Sian gave tender attention to his bump, I sat down, and with trembling hands opened the envelope. There was a simple note inside, with the words *"Time for Ceridwen."* I knew what this meant, and I think I must then have collapsed, for my memory is hazy until the point at which I was revived with smelling salts by Bessie and Mrs Owen. At last, when I was feeling calmer, I called a council of war around the kitchen table. I knew from my studies of the old Welsh tales that Ceridwen was a beautiful witch and a goddess, mentioned by the bards in association with grain, the bursting of the seed, sacrifice and death, birth and transformation. "You know the old books, Grandma," I said. "This is another ancient name which, in the absence of Master Iolo Morgannwg, you will have to help me with. How does it relate to the other names that were used on the notes last autumn?"

"Well, *cariad,* it is similarly old. The name is certainly used in the stories in the Four Ancient Books of Wales, and I suppose in the Triads as well. But the other names you gave me are all male -- Ceridwen is the only female. We were taught as children that she was one of the main Celtic goddesses, associated with motherhood and fierce protection."

"So in their eyes I am Ceridwen?" I asked weakly.

"It would appear so, Martha."

"And due to be sacrificed?"

"That seems to be their intention........"

"But don't you worry, Mistress *bach,*" said Billy. "We will protect you, and we will get those bastards, never fear. How many men jumped you, Shemi?"

"There must have been at least two or three, I suppose. I didn't see anybody......."

"Well, that's not much help to us. That big fellow might have been all alone, or he might have his friends lurking in the hedge. Shall we go after him, Grandpa?"

"There is no point. That fellow is long gone -- he probably left his horse somewhere on the Dolrannog Road. And it is now dark. If you go charging after him he will have every advantage a military commander could wish for. You will be ambushed, that's for sure. Palmer -- for it must be him -- probably knows we will do nothing until morning."

"So what was the point of his visit, at great personal risk to himself? After all, Shemi might have shot him."

"No no," said Grandpa. "He probably calculated that Shemi, even if he had been alert at the end of a long day, would not shoot first and ask questions afterwards. He assumed -- quite rightly -- that the inhabitants of Plas Ingli are gentle people who are not used to using firearms."

"He is playing games with you, Martha," said Grandma. "He is trying to scare the wits out of you, in the hope of inducing some irrational behaviour which will give him and his colleagues an opening......"

"Well, he is succeeding," I moaned. "Tonight I shall not sleep a wink, and every cry of an owl, every bark of the dog fox on the mountain, and every rustle of the branches in the wind, will send me deeper into despair. And with my mind paralysed, I cannot decide what to do next. Tell me, dear friends, what must we now do to protect ourselves, in addition to what we are doing already?"

Grandpa took control. "For a start, we need two men on watch all night, with guns -- one watching the mountain side and the other watching the road and the fields towards the *cwm*........"

"How many firearms do we have?" I asked.

"Six all told. Two old shotguns which Billy and Will use for hunting rabbits and wildfowl. Two rifles won as trophies by David at the time of that absurd French Invasion before the turn of the century. And two pistols which may or may not work. We will keep lanterns lit in some of the windows. I doubt that they will attack, but if they are watching they may be deterred by our obvious alertness. Then in the morning we need reinforcements. Billy, you know the mountain like the back of your hand -- can you go up over the summit and down to town before dawn, to alert Skiff, Abby, Halfpint and various others to the crisis, and ask them to get out here as fast as they can, with whatever weapons they can muster?"

"I can do that, Master Isaac, even without a lantern," said Billy. "There is a faint moon, and that and the starlight will suffice. I will be back at six in the morning with a veritable army!!"

16th May 1809

As anticipated, I did not sleep a wink, and I was exhausted when I staggered down to breakfast. But by then there were men with firearms stationed at strategic points all around the Plas. There were even two men with rifles on the summit of the mountain. I was appalled, and saw that as sacrilege, but I held my tongue, knowing that the safety of the house and the family was paramount. The men came in for breakfast one by one. Billy acted as a sort of general, organizing their routine and telling them how to react in certain scenarios.

Nothing happened. The spies reported no strange men in town, and as reports came in from Dinas, Fishguard and further afield we had to accept that there was nothing untoward happening anywhere.

Will Daniels, the mayor and the two constables heard about the assembling of men and weapons to protect the Plas. They marched up to the Plas in the early afternoon, were allowed through our defences, and hammered on the front door. When they were let in, Master Daniels said: "You cannot have a private army at the Plas -- it is not allowed."

"Oh yes we can, William *bach,*" said Grandpa. "I and all the male servants of this house have been attacked while going about our lawful business. What have you done to protect us, apart from writing out arrest warrants and sticking up "wanted" notices? I will tell you -- nothing at all. When you show that you can look after us and enforce the law, we will remove the friends who have an instinct to stand guard on our behalf.

Until then, they will stay, and if you don't like the arrangement, kindly summon the dragoons from London and put their costs on the parish rate." And he showed them the door.

Day by day, bit by bit, over a period of more than six months, the noose has been tightened by these monsters who called themselves surveyors. There have been moments -- even weeks -- of respite when we have gone about our business as usual, and when we have even had fun, but now the tension in the house is inescapable. It is probably reflected in my demeanour and my behaviour, and I have noticed it in my servants also. I still come out in a cold sweat whenever I think of the episode involving little Dewi and his friends a fortnight ago. I should not be surprised, I suppose, that the children have now picked up on my fear, and on the sombre mood within the house, and have started to behave very badly. There have been petty squabbles over toys, tantrums, rudeness and disobedience, and Daisy and Dewi have been waking a lot in the middle of the night. Dewi has started to wet his bed. Sian is at her wit's end, and says she cannot understand what has brought about this change of behaviour -- but of course she knows full well what is going on, and can do nothing about it. All we can do is try and keep their lives as normal as possible, and protect them from encounters with armed guards or from the serious discussions going on in the kitchen. None of us can do anything about what is happening in their youthful minds, not even Grandma and Grandpa with all of their accumulated wisdom. I am spending as much time with the children as I can, and I reassure them that everything will soon be back to normal, but now that I am on a torture rack, I fear that I am not very clever and find it difficult to think straight.

I will admit in these pages of my little book that what I fear above all is a kidnap, and I have relived over and again, in the bright light of day and in the blackest hours of the night, the nightmares of losing Daisy (when she had wandered off one day, three years ago, and I thought she had been kidnapped) and of the abduction of little Sara by the monster John Fenton.

I have thought long and hard about this, but I now know that I fear the abduction of one, or all, of these little children far more than I fear for my own safety. So I have to do something about it. In the conviction that something bad is going to happen in the very near future, I have started to work on plans for moving the children to a safe place.

17th May 1809

With armed guards on all sides I felt safe enough to take a walk on the mountain at dusk. I wanted to climb to my cave, and creep inside, and stay there for ever in its warm seclusion, but with watchful armed guards on all sides, including those on the top of the mountain, I thought that my every movement would be followed closely, and that as a consequence my cave might be discovered by others. So I simply walked to Carn Edward, and up onto the summit, taking care not to stray outside the protective ring set up by Billy and his friends. I passed the time of day with Gwyn Williams from Gelli, Levi Abbs from Penrhiw Fach, and Will Ifans from Dolrannog Uchaf, who were stationed on top of assorted rocky outcrops, and thanked them for their kindness in looking after us. But although I tried to keep a smile on my face, my heart was heavy, for I knew that these good men were neglecting their own farms, holdings and vegetable gardens to be here, just as the frantic activity of the summer season was about to start.

Even at the Plas, I thought, it is difficult to maintain the working of the farm, even with the help of Hettie and Patty, who are both here almost every day to help with the milking. Piles of manure are accumulating outside the stables and the cowshed, because we have not sufficient manpower to clear them. The garden, which should be clean and bursting with new life in rows of beans, peas, carrots, potatoes and beetroots, is a mess of weeds. And with so many mouths to feed, our food supplies (which are precarious in any case in the month of May) are dangerously low. I noticed today that Mrs Owen is cleverly incorporating things like nettles and sorrel into our meals, in an attempt to put good food on the table for family, servants and armed guards. She is even using oats set aside for the horses to make oatmeal cakes and porridge for consumption inside the house. This makes me sorry for both the humans and the horses.

After my walk, I should have felt refreshed, but I returned to the Plas with a sense that things are now coming to a conclusion. I have an instinct that I am being drawn by fate into one final confrontation. After all, I am now the only one on the original list of "targets" who has not been attacked. One question which goes round and round in my head is this: Is it my fate to be sacrificed, in order to achieve the safety of the others? I should resist thoughts like that, but I fear that my will is almost broken, and that I feel like a bound prisoner standing a few feet away from the gallows, contemplating my fate. Then I think that maybe I **have** been attacked, not physically but in my mind? Maybe they are being fiendishly clever, these four men, and will not harm me physically at all, but will simply manipulate things from a distance and watch me slowly losing my mind? Whatever the truth of the matter, I seem to be settling into a state of mind which is resigned, and almost serene.................

18th May 1809

Today I received an urgent letter from Master Charles Hassall of Eastwood, by special delivery. A horseman came galloping up to the gate at the bottom of our driveway, where he was challenged by a man with a shotgun. He held up his hand in a gesture of peace, and threw a letter to the ground. He said: "Message for Mistress Morgan" and then turned and rode away.

In the letter (which was surprisingly brief, given his propensity for flowery language), Master Hassall has invited me to visit him at his residence tomorrow, on 19th May, at 2 pm. Pursuant to the arrest warrants and the "Wanted Notices" he says he has certain other information relating to the four criminals which will undoubtedly speed up their apprehension and conviction. He says he knows where they are, and how they may be captured. He says he is not interested in any rewards, but just wants to see justice done. He will pass this information to nobody other than me, face to face.

I have read the letter over and again, and I have to say that its tone is secretive and even conspiratorial. This, I know, is the way that Hassall works. This afternoon I showed the letter to Grandpa and Grandma, and Bessie, and asked them for their advice. Should I accept the invitation, or not? They all advised against it, on the grounds that if Master Hassall really meant well he would have alerted the constables and had the four murderous villains arrested already. But I said that Hassall knows full well that the local constables, in a remote place like Eastwood, would run many a mile in the opposite direction rather than confront the four evil surveyors, in the light of their track record of cunning and brutality. I considered it most likely that he wants me, once in possession of key information about the location of the hideaway, to organize a posse of brave men and to affect an arrest. "Charles Hassall is at heart a good man, and means well," I said. "I have thought long and hard about this, but I think that I can trust him. We cannot retreat into this place and pretend that the world outside does not exist. If we hide ourselves away and cut off social intercourse with those who assist us, that would be to admit defeat and to leave the field to those evil men. We must show them that we will not be cowed by their tactics of intimidation and secrecy..... and since I appear to be at the heart of their vendetta, and much harm has been done because of me, I feel a responsibility to see this matter through personally."

"Martha, this might be a trap," said Grandpa, sombrely.

"I agree that it might be," said I. "We have no way of knowing the truth of the matter. If it is not a trap, and I do not respond to the letter, an opportunity is missed. This miserable charade goes on and on, and nobody wins. If it is a trap, and I am destined to walk into it, I think I will have to trust fate, and my own preparations, so as to get out of it alive."

So I have decided that I will go to Eastwood tomorrow, even if there is a grave risk. I will take certain precautions, with the help of Billy and the others, in order to protect myself.

10. The Visit to Eastwood

19th June 1809

One month after that fateful day, I can report that I am still alive, but not yet kicking. I know that for the sake of my own sanity I have to write about it, and about what happened afterwards, but before I embark upon the task I have to admit that I may not be able to bring myself to describe everything that occurred. What I do write may be garbled nonsense, written with tears upon my cheeks and with a trembling hand. I will try. I **must** try. I cannot tell until I get to certain points in the narrative whether I will be able to put words onto paper, or whether I will simply leave a blank page with tears upon it. I have little recollection of certain things that happened, and of some conversations, but with the help of my servants and others who were involved, I think I now have a modest understanding of matters, and a reasonable grasp of the sequence of events. Grandma and Grandpa, Mrs Owen and Joseph know that I write a diary in my own secret language, and they say that I **must** record what happened at Eastwood. So does Bessie, who was there, and who is standing at my side, with her hand on my shoulder, as I write. So I will take their advice, and put it down.

But not now. Not now -- it is still too raw.

20th June 1809

I fear that I was too emotional to continue last night, and Bessie insisted on packing me off to bed. As she has done every night for the past month, she slept by my side, in the big bed once occupied by David and me, as she might with a sick child in need of reassurance and consolation.

I cannot wallow in my misery any longer, and so I will record this sequence of appalling events.

The Visit to Eastwood

Early in the morning of that fateful day, I sent the children off in the coach with Sian to Haverfordwest, for a holiday with their Uncle Morys and Aunt Nansi and their three cousins. Edward is now ten, Jane is seven, and Robert is four, and I thought they were just the right ages to give my five little ones all the fun they needed to bring them back to some sort of normality. I had arranged the holiday, with the blessed and spontaneous help of my dear brother and sister-in-law, partly to avoid the risk of an abduction which might lead to ransom demands and all sorts of mayhem, and partly because I anticipated some sort of tragedy which would make the Plas distinctly unsuitable for children for maybe weeks to come. I also still feared that the house might go up in flames, although that fear was perhaps irrational, given the level of protection that we now enjoyed. There was an emotional scene, at least on my part, as the coach prepared to leave. I wept as I hugged each of them in turn, and begged them to be good, and told them that I loved them, and sent them on their way. They were perfectly pragmatic about everything, and the younger ones shouted "Bye bye, Mam!" as they settled into their seats. Betsi was a different matter. She knew that something serious was going on, and that she might not see me for a very long time, and although she fought back her tears she gave me a long and intense embrace which almost took my breath away. She whispered "I love you so much, Mam. Take care! Take care!" and then climbed the step to join the others, leaving me a shivering wreck. Then they were off, with waves and cheers, with Will driving the coach, and Thomas Tucker of Penrhiw travelling shotgun. I stood in the yard and watched the rocking vehicle clattering away down towards the *cwm*, and listened until I could hear it no more against the background of singing birds.

At 10 o'clock I set off for Narberth with Bessie in attendance, and with Billy and Shemi as armed bodyguards. Billy drove the trap, and Shemi came on horseback, with the shotgun. There were enough other men guarding the Plas, and I wanted those two with me. As we crossed Mynydd Preseli the bleak moorland was swathed in low cloud, with a fierce blustery wind from the west. We did not talk much during our journey of about two hours. We were on high alert as we approached Eastwood, which is in a remote location in the country near Narberth.

Shemi went ahead of us on his horse, and returned to report that all seemed perfectly normal. The house was so quiet that it might have been deserted. But I was not surprised by that, since Master Hassall does not run a farm with activity focussed on a busy farmyard. Billy knocked on the door while I remained in the trap. After a while Charles Hassall opened it himself. "Ah, Billy," he said. "Good to see you. And Mistress Martha! Welcome!" In retrospect, there was not much warmth in his voice, and a sort of forced conviviality, but we had no time to analyse his mood. "Come in if you please," he continued. "Martha, your servants can take the horses and the trap round to the back, and my man will attend to them." He turned to Billy and said: "There's a warm kitchen in through the back door. It's open. Just you go on in, and you are welcome to a flagon of ale with my servants."

It was all done so smoothly. Bessie and I disembarked from the trap and went inside. To this day I do not know why Billy and his gun did not go in with us, because our plan had been that he would not leave our side, come hell or high water. But he and Shemi went round to the back of the house, and that was the last we saw of them. And again, with the benefit of hindsight, I do not know why we women were not immediately alerted by the fact that the door, which would normally have been opened by a servant, was opened by the master of the house.

We were led by our host to the parlour, the same well-appointed room on the ground floor in which I had met Master Hassall on my previous visit. It was semi-dark inside, with heavy curtains partly drawn across the French windows that opened onto the unkempt lawn and garden. As my eyes adjusted to the dim light, I realized that a tall man was standing in front of the curtains. It was Joshua Palmer, and he was holding a pistol. "Ah, Mistress Martha! We meet again" he whispered. "And you must be Bessie. I have heard about you, and of your special bond with your mistress." When I saw him, I almost fainted -- and I am sure that Bessie was equally terrified. I knew immediately that we had been betrayed by Charles Hassall, and that the betrayal had succeeded because of our own naivety. I looked at him, and if looks could kill he would immediately have been reduced to a small pile of ash. I saw that he was himself on the point of collapse, and now he was transformed into a snivelling wretch. "Mistress Martha, I can explain everything," he whined. "These men captured me and took over the house yesterday. They have taken my wife and daughter, and gave me no option but to help them..........."

"Shut up, Hassall!" whispered Palmer. "You have done your job, and I am tempted to dispose of you here and now, since I despise traitors. Or maybe I will wait and let you stew in your own juice, if I feel benign." He turned towards me and Bessie. "This wretched busybody has been nosing about into the affairs of my friend Cai for weeks, if not months. It came to our notice that he had enjoyed a visit from you, and that he was in correspondence with you. So he started to feature in our plans. After a while living rough and visiting friends we decided to keep an eye on the empty house at Great Canaston, and along came this clown, pretending to be a sleuth. It was the simplest thing in the world to grab him and encourage him to talk. We then decided to move in here so as to enjoy some creature comforts. It was so easy as to be disappointing. We have sent the three servants packing, with a warning that if they raise the alarm we will kill their master and his family. Mistress Hassall and the daughter are safely locked up in one of the bedrooms. I doubt that they will batter down their door, or that they will seek to escape by shinning down a drainpipe, since neither of them is cut out for heroics."

As he spoke, I was able to look at him properly, and this was the first time I had seen his face. His hair was cut so short as to be almost absent, and he had bulging eyes and a broad nose, and although his face was partly in shadow I could see that he was disfigured by a patch of purple skin and a rough scar on his chin and throat. I understood suddenly why nobody in Newport had seen his full face before, and why he always wore high collars and mufflers.

"Sir, this is an outrage!" I said, beginning to recover my composure and trying to disguise my own terror by keeping my voice level. "Do you mean to say that you are keeping these good people captive in their own house? And you know that Miss Oriana is seriously ill............"

"Ah, some of the famous Mistress Morgan spirit! I like it! Yes, I know that poor girl is ill -- but she will survive a day or two of inconvenience. She is used to inactivity."

"But she needs her medication!" spluttered Hassall.

"And she will get it, before the day is out, as soon as we have finished with our business here, and have left you to your own devices. We have given our word on that, and we always keep our word."

"And what is your business, sir?" asked Bessie.

"You will find out soon enough"" said Palmer. At this point three other men came into the room, carrying pistols and also the firearms which I recognized as having been carried by Billy and Shemi. I knew immediately that these were Palmer's three accomplices, none of whom I had ever seen before. One was a real dandy, dressed in elegant and expensive clothes which had become filthy over the time the men had been living rough. I guessed, correctly, that he was Edwin Dashwood. Reynard Foley (for it had to be him) was a pale-faced and rather effeminate fellow, who moved awkwardly. I thought that he was probably in pain from the injury sustained in the thigh, in the duel with Dominic. And finally Geordan McCleod was much as I imagined him to be -- a red-faced stocky man with a prominent chin, who looked more like a prize fighter than a member of the gentry. All three were quite a bit younger than Palmer. He also towered over them, and was clearly their leader.

"Those two servants are dealt with," said McCleod, speaking with a prominent Scottish accent.

"Billy and Shemi?" I gasped. "You haven't.......?"

"Good Lord, no," said Foley, in a voice that had a slight trace of a South Pembrokeshire accent in it. "To harm them now would make life far too complicated. They are trussed up and otherwise unharmed. They walked straight into our little trap, as innocent as new-born babes. Country bumpkins, both of them." He spat into the fireplace. "If they had had some military training like mine, they would have scouted out the land in advance, or made some show of protecting themselves. So now here we are, all as happy as can be. At long last. We have all been longing to meet you, Mistress Morgan, for a considerable time."

"Quite so," said Dashwood, in a voice that sounded slurred. Then he walked over and stood in front of me, and looked at me carefully for what seemed an age, before continuing. "And you are as beautiful as

Ceridwen should be. Isn't that right, my friends?"

"Agreed," said McCleod. "A very fitting conclusion to a business that has taken far too long. You have caused us more than a little bother, Mistress Morgan, and have forced us to rearrange our plans on a number of occasions. We are not used to such inconvenience. Gruddnei here likes things to go smoothly when there are rules to be enforced, and retribution to be obtained. Is that not right, my friend?"

Palmer nodded. "Enough talking," he whispered, in a manner that made me think of snakes and venom, and made me very frightened. "Get Hassall out of the way -- he has served his purpose and we have no further need of him. Lock him into that upstairs room with his wife and daughter." He turneed to Hassall. "I advise you to cooperate," he says. "If you do not, and you try to escape or raise the alarm, I will kill all three of you with my own hands. I have done that before, and am quite happy to do it again. Understood?"

Hassall nodded and gulped. Foley and McCleod grabbed him by the arms and marched him towards the door. Suddenly he struggled, turned towards me and blurted out: "The letter, Martha. It was written with a knife to my throat! I had no option........." He could say no more, since he was struck repeatedly by McCleod until he fell to the floor. He was then dragged across the floor and out through the door into the passage. I heard him moaning as he was pushed, pulled and carried upstairs and then presumably locked in with his wife and daughter. Then I heard the two conspirators clattering back down the stairs, and they came back into the parlour.

I was horrified by this brutality, but I suppose I should have expected it, given the past record of these monsters. I tried desperately to gather my thoughts so as to play for time or to gain some advantage. Thus far, Palmer had stood stock still, and he still had his pistol pointing towards us. Bessie and I stood with our arms around each other, in the middle of the room. "Sir," I said to him, "I have no idea what this is all about. Kindly explain yourself so that we can make our peace and go our separate ways."

"Hah! No idea? No idea!" whispered Palmer. "You have a perfectly sound idea what this is all about, madam. You have long since worked out that we act out of respect for various dear departed brothers -- Henben, Urien, Tinwaed and Rhiwallwn -- who suffered at your hands......"

"Who suffered at my hands? Sir, whoever these fellows were, I have certainly not harmed them, since I seek to act out the noble principle of harming no-one."

"There you are wrong, Mistress!" shouted Dashwood. "Women such as you, trained in the dark arts of temptation and seduction, harm people all the time! With a flicker of your eyelashes you make men mad, and drive them to do things which other men then count as crimes!"

"I beg your pardon, sir! Are you saying that these dear departed brothers of yours, whoever they are, have been turned into criminals because I, or some other lady of good breeding, have looked them in the eye, or worn a fashionable dress, or put a spot of rouge upon my cheeks?"

Bessie patted my arm, and clearly wanted me to desist. She was, I suppose, afraid that my belligerent attitude was going to get us into even deeper trouble. But I was playing for time, and in any case my fighting spirit had been aroused, and would not allow me to keep quiet.

"The point is proved!" chortled Foley. "Look at you now, Ceridwen! Blazing eyes and wagging fingers, and a hearty defence of the rights of womankind to tempt and manoeuvre and manipulate men whenever it suits them!"

Now Bessie intervened. "Sir, my mistress and I are not goods and chattels. We deserve respect just as you do, if it is earned. Now please will you let us go? You gain nothing by holding us here, or by holding the Hassalls captive upstairs............"

"On the contrary, Bessie," whispered Palmer. "We gain a great deal. We gain time, and we have earned the right, through meticulous planning, to administer justice in an appropriate fashion, for the crimes committed by your Mistress. And we are seriously angry with her, are we not, brothers?"

The others nodded, and Palmer continued, like a sinister judge in some mad court of law, reading out a list of indictments. "Your list of crimes is a long one, Martha Morgan. Not only have you personally reduced the ranks of our brotherhood and brought it to a parlous state within the past year or two, but you have delved into affairs that are none of your business and which must remain mysteries. You have interfered in our administration of justice. You have organized a hue and cry involving search warrants and arrest warrants, not to mention Wanted Notices and rewards. Then you assembled all those clowns dressed in women's costumes and sent them down to steal our property and disrupt our little celebration a month since. That was a private affair which did no harm to anybody."

"Sir, I had nothing whatsoever to do with that."

Palmer waved his hand dismissively, and said: "You are an intelligent woman, Ceridwen, and you should not be surprised that we seek retribution."

"Master Palmer, whatever you seek in the way of retribution will simply be added to your list of offences, which is already sufficient to lead each of you to the gallows."

"Precisely," said the big man, still hissing like a snake. "We are gravely inconvenienced by you and your little flock of guardian angels. But never fear. We thrive on inconvenience and spit in the faces of those who show hostility and prejudice. We always prevail. Always. Nobody can plan better than we do, and nobody can match the manner in which we execute our plans. We strike as avenging angels, and we move on. By this time tomorrow we four will be waving farewell to the little town of Milford, cursing the cliffs of West Wales, and looking forward to a new life across the Atlantic. It is all arranged."

"And what of the Irishman, Dominic Cunningham. Is he not a member of your little group?"

Palmer spat into the fire. "Hah! A deceitful bastard, that one. Not his real name, of course. He was one of us, and had a job to do, but turned out to be worse than useless. Never trust an Irishman. But we taught him a lesson, and he has gone scuttling back to Ireland with his tail between his legs. Neither you nor we will ever see him again."

I still tried to play for time. "Sir," I said,"you have still not told me what this is all about. You talk of your brotherhood, and crimes which I and others have supposedly committed against you, and justice, and retribution, without ever explaining yourself. What is your brotherhood, for a start?"

"You know full well that we cannot say," said Dashwood. "Others may break oaths with carefree abandon, but we four know about loyalty."

Then I asked, perhaps foolishly: "And what about laudanum? What part does that play in your brotherhood?"

"Hah!" said Palmer. "We use laudanum when necessary, in exactly the right quantity. Today, you will be pleased to know, we have used just the right amount to sharpen our intellect and to enhance our appetite for what is about to happen."

McCleod was restless, and I recall that he was prowling about, looking round the edge of the curtains into the garden and listening intently for any sound that might cause him concern. "Brother," he said at last to Palmer. "Enough talk. Time is passing, and there may be others watching this house or following in the wake of our friends from the north. Let us get this over and done with, and then we must be away."

"Too true, Afaon," nodded Palmer, turning towards me. "Are you ready for your sacrifice, Ceridwen?"

I knew what was coming, and at this point I almost collapsed. "And Bessie?" I asked, as if in a dream. "Promise that you will not touch her..............."

"We are not interested in Bessie," said Dashwood. "She is very pretty, that is for sure, and might have suited us on another occasion. But today you are the one who has to pay a small price for all the troubles heaped upon us. She will watch, and be entertained."

Now I fear that I am shaking so much that I cannot continue. Bessie has noticed my distress from her chair on the other side of the room, and she says that I must stop anyway. She says she is going to drag me outside, to join the midday picnic with the haymakers, and I have not enough strength to refuse. I will try to nibble something while the others gorge themselves, and smile when the others laugh. Tomorrow, I will try to force myself to continue my narrative, even if this is the most difficult thing I ever have to do.................

21st June 1809

Midsummer Day. Today I should be writing of the joys of summer, and celebrating everything that is good, and fresh, and clean. Instead I have to try to describe the blackest and most terrifying moments of my life -- a thousand times more terrible than my encounters with Moses Lloyd in my cave and with John Fenton in that little cottage that is no more.

I have decided that I will never, to my dying day, describe what happened next, either in the pages of this diary, or to those whom I love, or in a court of law. Neither will poor dear Bessie, who fought like a she-cat to save me, say anything about what happened. That is agreed between us. The events will go with me and Bessie to our graves. And may those four men, who were brought up to be gentlemen and who then turned into wild beasts and demons, be burned in the hottest fires of Hell without reprieve, from now unto eternity.........

I fought, until there was not an ounce of energy left in my body. When it was all over, I was left naked and almost unconscious on the thick carpet in the middle of the floor. I have virtually no coherent memories of the following minutes, and only small fragments of memory about the following hours. Bessie has helped me to piece together what happened. She says I remained on the floor, battered and bleeding, for what seemed like an age, whimpering, and curled up like a child in the womb. She says I was unable to speak. But she says that in my struggles I had drawn blood too, leaving my four assailants nursing bruises and wiping blood from scratches on their faces and bodies. Bessie must also have been terribly traumatized -- and she recalls that after screaming and fighting to protect me, she was subdued and held down by one or another of the men, and ended up cowering in the corner, shivering as if it was the coldest day of winter, and incapable of tears.

Then Dashwood buttoned up his breeches and said: "She is a warrior, that one. Boudicca, rather than Ceridwen. I am almost tempted to give her a degree of respect..............."

"Shut up, Edenawg!" snarled McCleod. "What is done is done. She had it coming to her, and finally we have delivered retribution on behalf of our brothers. Now it is time for us to slip away. The horses are saddled, and have been waiting tethered for far too long."

"Ladies, we bid you good-day," whispered Palmer, wiping blood from his mouth. "A worthy sacrifice, with a degree of difficulty about it. Honour has been satisfied, according to custom, by me first, and then the others, and then me again. You may, if you wish, tell the world what has happened, and it may be a warning to others of your kind who seek to interfere in the affairs of gentlemen that they should know their station, and stand aside. But I think you will not say a word to anyone, for that is the way of the world following occasions such as this."

Just then there was a furious hammering at the front door, which was of course locked. The four men instinctively turned towards the doorway leading to the passage and looked for their weapons. Almost simultaneously there was a great crash, and the French windows that led into the garden were smashed in by booted feet. Bits of glass and splinters of shattered wood flew everywhere. Dominic Cunningham jumped into the room, followed closely by Skiff, Abby and Halfpint. All four of them were armed with pistols. Before the four rapists could grab their own pistols four shots rang out and all four of them fell to the ground, moaning and screaming. Not one of them managed to return fire. Dashwood, grovelling on the floor, tried to reach out to where he had placed his pistol, but Halfpint ran over to him and hit him over the head with a club which he carried as a reserve weapon. Bessie says that McCleod was killed immediately, but that the other three were still alive following the initial assault.

Dominic saw me on the floor and then looked at Bessie cowering in the corner. He moaned. "Oh, Mother of God!" he said in a voice heavy with emotion. "We are too late. If only......if only........."

He ran across the room and helped to cover me up. He kneeled at my side. I think I remember seeing his face close to mine, with his eyes filled with tears. "Oh, Mistress Martha!" he whispered. "I am so, so sorry. This was my nightmare, and I moved heaven and earth to prevent it.........and still it has happened. So this is what evil men are capable of -- miserable cowards and barbarians, every one of them. And to think that I once trusted them......" His voice faded away, as he was struck by the full implications of the scene that now confronted him.

He rose to his feet, thought for a moment and then turned to his companions. Bessie says that at this point his demeanour changed, and grief was replaced with a red-hot rage that verged on insanity. Perhaps, in retrospect, it was madness that overwhelmed him. He seemed to become another person, quite unlike the Dominic Cunningham we had known up to that point. He stood erect, and in total command of the room, in spite of his own modest stature. "Skiff," he said in cold, measured tones, "will you take care of Mistress Martha and Bessie? Abby and Halfpint, I want you to help me to deal with these bastards. Abby, you can have Foley. He's that one, with the blood all over his left shoulder. Halfpint, you take Dashwood, the one with a lump of lead in his stomach. And I will take great pleasure in dealing with this demon who is spitting blood, whom I used to call my friend."

"You would not dare, Tristfardd," whispered Palmer, who was kneeling close to the fireplace, coughing up blood. He was just about able to speak. "You have sworn the oath of blood brothers -- one for all and all for one. You cannot harm any one of us............."

Suddenly Dominic was overcome with rage. He strode across the room and kicked Palmer full in the face, sending him sprawling. His nose was probably broken, and he was now bleeding even more profusely than before. "Have you not harmed me?" shouted Dominic. "I can, and will, harm all three of you, and am disappointed that the bastard Scot appears to be dead already. Skiff, your aim is too good. Now, you miserable swine, give me the knife." Bessie says that Palmer had a wild fear in his eyes, and tried to crawl away. But Dominic kicked him again. "Give me the knife!" he demanded.

"I cannot give it up," moaned Palmer in a voice so quiet that he could hardly be heard. "You know it is mine to protect, in keeping with our bond."

"No longer. The bond is broken, and these are the final moments of the brotherhood. Give it to me!"

Palmer still resisted, and moaned: "It is a sacred object, never to be defiled..........."

Dominic kicked him again, repeatedly, and then when he was all but unconscious on the floor, he searched him. Finally he held up an elaborate curved knife in a sheath. It was about eight inches long, with a gleaming blade and a splendid carved ivory handle. "Right," he said. "This knife has one more job to do -- or four jobs, to be precise -- before it is finally disposed of in the murky waters of Milford Haven."

At this point three other figures appeared against the light in the smashed French windows -- Joseph, Billy and Shemi. It appeared later that Joseph had found them and released them while Dominic and the others hunted around the outside of the house for the room in which Bessie and I were being subjected to our ordeal. They had been guided to the room, as we now know, by Charles Hassall making desperate signals and gestures from the upstairs window where he and his wife and daughter were held captive.

Joseph, with horror writ large on his face, immediately rushed in to help Skiff who was already seeking to console Bessie and me. Then Shemi and Billy, who could hardly believe what had happened, and who seemed to be almost paralysed with shock, were pressed into helping Dominic and the others to drag the body of McCleod and the three survivors along the passage and out into the yard. When they left the parlour, that was the last time I saw Dominic.

Much later, I discovered what happened to the four members of the brotherhood, and I am now in a cold sweat as I write about it. They were taken to an empty stable. Then Dominic quite deliberately and calmly took the ceremonial knife and castrated the dead Scot first, in full view of his confederates, and then he did the same to Dashwood, Foley and Palmer while they were still alive. They were conscious, but too badly injured to resist. I recall with surprising clarity the screams that echoed round the house and the yard. Billy has said to me since, in recollection of the event: "Oh my God, Mistress. Their eyes! Their eyes! I will never forget the looks in their eyes! There will be nightmares, indeed, for the rest of my life -- I know it." Dominic then executed each of the condemned men in turn, without further ado, by slitting their throats. Perfectly calmly, he then said to his horrified helpers: "So that's done. Now they know what bullocks have to put up with." He threw the bloody testicles into the nearby pigsty, where they were immediately consumed by the hungry pigs which had not been fed that day. Now, looking back, I realize that there was a grotesque and planned symbolism in this act, since Ceridwen is associated with swine and is sometimes known as the "sow goddess" -- or a goddess who is, like a great white sow, fiercely protective and even deadly when looking after her young.

I have no recollection of the passage of time after this, but I recall that Bessie helped to dress me, and that we two were then wrapped up in drapes and tapestries and taken to the kitchen, still in a deep state of shock. Joseph gave us steaming mugs of tea. I was shaking so much that I could hardly hold my mug, and I had to be helped by Joseph.

Upstairs Hassall was hammering on the bedroom door, demanding to be let out. Nobody paid much attention to him, or to his wife and daughter, who were both wailing and weeping, having picked up from the sounds below more or less what had been going on.

There were now four bloody corpses to be disposed of. They were left where they were, and covered with straw. Billy, who was with Dominic, said that the Irishman was as cold as blue ice. He had got everything worked out, down to the smallest detail. "In ten minutes this stable will go up in flames," he said, "with the bodies inside it. It will be a nice little funeral pyre. But first, everything else covered in blood must be in here too."

The Newport men then returned to the parlour and cleared up the mess as best they could. They swept up broken glass and fragments of the French windows from the floor. There was blood on the carpet, on the curtains, on some of the chairs, and on various loose chair covers and tapestries. They gathered all of these items up, and dragged them to the funeral pyre. They fetched brushes, cloths and soapy water from the kitchen, and washed away blood from the floorboards, from the paving stones outside the window, and from the gory trail left when they dragged the dead and injured to the stable. Then Dominic went up to the bedroom where the captives were held, unlocked the door and let Hassall out of the bedroom. He checked that the two women were unharmed, and then told them to stay where they were, even though they were hysterical at the time. He pushed Hassall roughly down to the parlour, which was now in an appalling mess, having been stripped of many of its contents. I did not see him, but Shemi says he was a broken man whose shoulders drooped and whose face appeared to have aged decades in the course of an hour. He knew full well what had happened to me, and he felt that his interference, and his cowardice, had led to utter mayhem and to the commission of terrible crimes.

According to the others who were in the parlour, Dominic now told Hassall what his story had to be. He was instructed to say -- if asked by the coroner or anybody else -- that the conspirators captured him when he was out walking, and then moved into the house. They sent the servants away with threats to keep quiet, and with a promise that their master, and his wife and daughter, would be killed if the constables or anybody else turns up at the house. They were on the run, and wanted money and provisions prior to escaping by sea, from Milford. (That was all correct, and could be verified by the servants if need be.) Hassall was then instructed to say that he and his wife and daughter were held captive, locked in an upstairs room, for a night and most of the next day, while the 4 men helped themselves to wine from the cellar and food from the kitchen. Every now and then, they checked on the hostages upstairs and gave them some food. (That was mostly true, too.) They ransacked the parlour and the office, looking for money, but found none. There was much noise, and Hassall will say that he thought the men were quarreling and drinking a great deal. In the afternoon, he heard a great crash and a tinkling of broken glass, and he realized that one of the men must have fallen against the French windows in a struggle, and ended up on the paving stones outside. As a result, he cut himself quite badly on the glass, and left a trail of blood in the room, which the others tried to clear up. Hassall heard much swearing and shouting. Then it went quiet, and after a few minutes he smelt smoke. Realizing that the four men were now intent upon setting fire to the outbuildings and maybe the house, he had to take desperate action. He escaped by using some knotted sheets, and saw the men piling up straw in the stable as they tried to feed the fire. He ran back into the house, loaded his pistols which were still in their hiding place in the office, and crept across the yard. There he confronted the four men in the stable. He stood in the stable doorway. A number of shots were fired in a gun battle in which all four of the villains were injured. They were too drunk to shoot straight, but Hassall (as befits the hero of the hour) was calm and deadly. They tried to chase after him before he could reload, but he slammed both parts of the door and pulled the locking bars into place. They were now trapped in a burning stable, but Hassall feared for his life should they manage to escape. So he retreated in horror as the fire took hold. The men were burned to death in the conflagration.

At that point, according to Dominic's fabricated sequence of events, Mistress Martha and Bessie, with Billy and Shemi, turned up on a social visit, in response to an invitation from him some days earlier. They tried to help with fighting the fire, and stopped it from spreading, but the women were so upset by the news that there were four men inside the burning stable that they almost collapsed, and they pleaded with their servants to take them home. A group of men from Newport then turned up, quite independently, having travelled to the Narberth area on a man-hunt, with a view to obtaining the reward money for apprehending the villains. They saw the smoke and flames, and found their way to Eastwood. They bravely tried to fight the flames, but there was nothing they could do to save the stable or the men within it. This story would, said Dominic, enable Hassall to claim the reward for dealing with the four wanted men, and would make him something of a local hero. That would suit him very well, as a fellow obsessed with status and reputation. In view of the previous record of the four deceased men as arsonists, nobody would doubt the truth of this story.

"Now then, Master Hassall, you yellow bastard, are you happy with all of that, and sure you can remember it?" asked Dominic.

"No sir, I am not! I am not accustomed to lying. We must tell the truth," said Hassall.

"Enough righteous indignation from you, you pathetic creature," snarled Dominic, grabbing him by the throat and threatening to choke him. "You are a conniving bastard who has knowingly led an innocent woman into a fiendish trap, and who did nothing to save her until it was already too late. You are a miserable, vindictive weasel who cannot keep his nose out of other people's business -- everybody between St David's and Carmarthen knows that. And you are stupid, to boot! If you tell the truth, you will be shown in your true colours, and you will be prosecuted

-- Joseph Harries will see to it -- as an accessory to the most heinous of crimes. So far as I am concerned, I'll be happy to see the locals string you up from the nearest tree. Even if you are not, you will be left with no reputation, and no status, to crawl in the gutter with drunkards and vagrants." Dominic tightened his grip on Hassall's throat, and repeated: "Are you happy with all of that?"

"Yes, yes, very well," moaned Hassall at last, slumping to a kneeling position on the floor. "I see that I have very little alternative."

Dominic kicked him and sent his sprawling. "Very little alternative?! You have **no** alternative, you bastard! Now get up off the floor and talk to the wizard."

Joseph was then called to the parlour, and after some discussion he agreed with Hassall that he would provide "scientific" evidence to demonstrate the previous crimes of the dead men and -- depending on how much was left of the bodies -- to verify the fabricated version of events. He also assured Hassall that the inevitable inquest would not delve too deeply into the precise details of the scenario, since when criminals or wanted men are killed, there is a presumption of "justice being done" and an assumption that somebody or other has acted in self-defence. Hassall's wife and daughter then came downstairs, looking like ghosts, and agreed that they would hold to this story. They agreed that they would do everything possible to cover up all evidence that Bessie and I had ever been inside the house.

When we were over the worst of our initial shock, Billy and Joseph led us gently to the covered trap and with my faithful servant at the reins we set off on our journey over the mountain and back to the Plas. Luckily we passed nobody on the way who might have recognized us or who might, at some later stage, have questioned the cock and bull sequence of events that would now be put about by Charles Hassall.

Now I am exhausted again, and relieved to some degree that I have been able to put down, in abbreviated form, what happened at Eastwood. Tomorrow, perhaps in a calmer frame of mind, I will continue with this miserable history.

22nd June 1809

Once we had left Eastwood, the men who had stayed behind worked feverishly with Charles Hassall and Dominic Cunningham. First, Dominic went through the pockets of the dead men and found the papers confirming their paid passages to America from Milford, on the very next day. He took various other possessions as well. The men lit the fire in the stable. After a suitable time, when it had really taken hold and was impossible to control, they miraculously "turned up" and started to fight the flames. Then Dominic disappeared, with no farewells or grand gestures. He must have quietly slipped away, when nobody was looking. Hassall then raised the alarm, and after a while various neighbours turned up and helped in fighting the flames. One or two other buildings around the yard were slightly damaged, but the house itself was unaffected. The horses belonging to the four dead men were unharmed, since they were tethered in the yard in readiness for a rapid exit from Eastwood in the direction of Milford. Each of them had saddlebags which had been packed up in readiness for the anticipated voyage to America. They contained personal possessions which were later used as evidence of the identities of the four men.

When the fire had been brought under control, the Newport contingent travelled home, apparently with all of them in a shocked and sombre mood as they contemplated what had happened to me. They also had to try to come to terms with the full horror of the justice meted out by Dominic. Shemi, poor man, was utterly dejected, and for days and weeks afterwards he and Billy felt that it was all their fault, and that they were naive and irresponsible to have allowed themselves to be captured and trussed up when they should have been protecting their Mistress.

At the time of our return to the Plas, those who knew what had happened at Eastwood were Bessie and me, and seven men who were involved in the *fracas* -- Dominic the executioner, Joseph the wizard, my servants Shemi and Billy, and Skiff, Abby and Halfpint from town. Will was away delivering the children to Haverfordwest, and was thus far away from the scene of the tragedy. Then there was Charles Hassall and his wife and daughter who also knew almost everything, and who would have to be trusted to keep quiet.

On the journey home, the only words I could utter were these: "Nobody must ever know! Promise me -- nobody must ever know................" Joseph, Bessie and Billy all made that promise, and while I remained in a state of deep shock, and slept for part of the journey home, the three of them decided that they would go with the story which Dominic had given to Hassall. They agreed to say that when they arrived it was all over -- Hassall had shot the four villains and had trapped them inside a burning stable, where they had then all died in the flames. They found the fire raging, and helped to fight it in the vain hope of rescuing the four men inside the stable.

When we arrived home the neighbours and townspeople who had been guarding the Plas were told this news, and a great wave of euphoria swept over the house and all the way to Newport. Not surprisingly, they all felt that at last they could get back to normal life. They all wanted to celebrate. But Joseph held up his hand and explained that Bessie and I (still invisible and inside the covered trap) were very upset as a result of the terrible scene that confronted us when we arrived, with four men screaming in a burning stable and then being burned to death. "Celebrations would not be appropriate just now," said Joseph. "Maybe, when the inquests are over and done with, and when Mistress Martha and Bessie are recovered, we can then celebrate in style." The men who had been on watch were very tired anyway, and after being thanked profusely by Grandpa for their unstinting support, they all went home to catch up on a great deal of lost sleep. That was an anticlimax, maybe, but I thank God that Joseph and Grandpa insisted on it.

Then Bessie and I were helped into the Plas by Billy and Joseph. Grandma and Grandpa, and Mrs Owen, were appalled when they saw the state I was in -- they say I was shivering uncontrollably and that I was still in deep shock. Bessie was only a little better, and Mrs Owen, with concern and compassion writ large on her ruddy face, fed us hot tea laced with rum. Then we were carried upstairs in turn by Billy, who was as gentle as a father with a newborn babe in his arms. As he carried me, I looked up at him and noticed that there were tears running down his cheeks. "There now, Mistress *bach*," he whispered. "We will look after you, never fear. And you will be all right. You will be all right......." Bessie would not leave me -- she spent the night by my side, and at last we two women, after the worst day of our short lives, managed to sleep.

Downstairs, Joseph told Grandma, Grandpa and Mrs Owen what had actually happened. They were horrified, and for a long time there was a stunned silence . Then the other men arrived on horseback, and all of them sat round the kitchen table far into the night, discussing what to do. They all agreed that they would abide by my wishes -- and they shared an oath that none of them would ever divulge, even to their nearest and dearest, what had happened.

On the following day, I gather that Bessie and I simply wanted to sleep, with Grandma and Mrs Owen looking after us. I woke for a short time around midday, and Mrs Owen examined me gently, attended to my wounds, and gave me some medication prescribed by Joseph. My dear friend the wizard stayed at the Plas for the time being, in case my condition deteriorated -- but he and Grandpa stayed away from my room, on the basis that the time was not yet right for any male involvement in the healing process. In the late afternoon, Will returned to the Plas with the empty coach, having settled Sian and the children in with Morys and his family, and having spent the night in Haverfordwest. When he was told the truth, he flew into a rage and stamped around the kitchen shouting "Bastards! Bastards. If I had been there I would have personally carved them up into little pieces, indeed, while they were still alive! Bastards! Bastards!" Joseph had to calm him down by telling him that rage was not appropriate just now, and that what was needed was calm reflection and very careful planning.

By all accounts, news of the fire and the death of the four sinister surveyors was all around town within twenty-four hours, and indeed all around the county. In the evening Patty called at the Plas, having heard the doctored news of our visit to Eastwood and of the fire. She had an intuition that the version of the story given out for public consumption was not necessarily the truth. She was told by Mrs Owen that Bessie and I were awake, and immediately came upstairs to see us. I was sitting on my chair by the window. She was shocked when she saw our faces and our demeanour. So Bessie told her what had really happened, and my dear friend opened her arms and invited both me and Bessie into a long embrace. We stood there by the window, as three friends who have each suffered from the most terrible cruelties, holding each other tight. I clung to Bessie and Patty, and at last the tears came. For the first time since the visit to Eastwood, in the company of my two dearest friends, I obeyed the instinct to weep -- and the tears flowed for a very long time. I suppose that they wept too, but I was in no fit state for observations.

News came in the evening, while we were all eating a sombre supper, that in the Narberth district Charles Hassall was being hailed as a hero. He was apparently basking in the limelight. Billy said: "Humph! That cowardly bastard is the one who made all of this happen -- he should be dealt with by the *Ceffyl Pren*, not cheered from the rooftops."

"You are quite wrong, Billy," said Joseph quietly. "This is exactly what we want to happen. Let him take the praise. The more he elaborates on his heroics the less will be the attention paid to the role of Newport people in the whole episode. With a bit of luck, the press and the local gossip network will entirely forget that any of us ever did visit Eastwood." Everybody nodded, and Billy had to agree that on balance the elevation of Hassall's status and his own self-esteem was a price well worth paying, to keep the truth away from the public.

On the following morning, Grandma handed me a sealed letter. "This came for you, *cariad*, by special delivery, about half an hour after you left for Eastwood. The sender was your friend Ellie Phillips of Ambleston. You were in no fit state for reading letters yesterday, but maybe today her birthday greeting will help to remind you that you are greatly loved.......?"

On the front of the envelope were my name and address, and the words "Birthday Greeting -- Post Haste." This is what the letter said:

Ambleston Hall
18th May 1809

My Dearest Martha
I pray that I can get this letter to you before it is too late. I send it on the pretext that it is a belated and cheery birthday greeting for you, but in truth it is much

more serious than that. I just hope that I can get it into the hands of our young servant Eifion today, with a request that he should gallop with it all the way to the Plas, but as you will know my husband Walter keeps a very tight control over the activities of our servants, and I will have to wait until he is away from the house. When he discovers that I have sent Eifion off with a message, he will be furious with me -- but I will just have to deal with his fury as best I can.

If you receive an invitation to visit Eastwood House near Narberth, I urge you not to accept it, for it will be a carefully laid trap. I know this because a week ago we had visitors at Ambleston. You will know their names -- Joshua Palmer, Geordan McCleod, Edwin Dashwood and Reynard Foley. We talked of them briefly, as you will recall, when we last met at Mary Jane's soiree at Trecwn. I had met them briefly before, on one or two occasions, and still remember those encounters without affection. They turned up without warning, looking very dirty and tired, and riding horses that were exhausted. Walter was not exactly pleased to see them, but he insisted that we should give them hospitality. He actually appeared to be frightened of them. I have never seen Walter frightened before, and I think they have some hold over him. I pressed him on that in the privacy of our own bed, but he got angry with me and refused to talk about it. There is something in his past, I fear, that he wishes to keep under wraps.

Those four were despicable guests -- arrogant and abusive towards the servants, and apparently incapable of sensibility when in the company of Walter and myself. They drank their way through a good proportion of our wine cellar, and I am sure that they used laudanum as well when they were in their own rooms. They stayed for three days, and we only got rid of them when I told them that I was with child, and that I felt very unwell. (That, as it happens, is true, dearest Martha.) Both Walter and I tried to spend as little time as possible in their company, but on a number of occasions I overheard them talking about you and the Plas. They did not, I think, know that there was any link between us, let alone that we are the best of friends. One night, well after midnight, when I thought everybody was in bed, I had reason to go downstairs on a visit to the pantry, and passed the library on the way. The door was ajar. Our four guests were in there, well lubricated by drink, and I overheard some of their conversation. They were furious that they could not get at you, because there were armed guards everywhere around the Plas. And they were furious about something that happened at Great Canaston last month which led to great coverage in the newspapers. Walter will not allow newspapers in the house, so I can only guess at what happened, but I assume that there was a raid of some sort, from which they only just escaped. Am I right? So they decided that they would have to get you out of the Plas, by tempting you to somewhere else. I heard the name Hassall in their conversation, and his house of Eastwood was mentioned. Their voices were indistinct, and I dared not lurk behind the door any longer for fear of being discovered -- but dearest Martha, BEWARE!!

I urge you not to trust anything relating to Charles Hassall or his house, to take all necessary precautions, and to stay well clear of Narberth. I hope this letter reaches you in time to prevent anything untoward from happening, and if I find out more I will let you know just as soon as I can.

Your loving friend
Ellie

When I had finished reading the letter, I moaned and buried my head in my hands. "Oh my dear Ellie," I thought. "As kind and loving as ever. But too late..... too late......."

Regarding the next few days, my memories are confused, for my emotions were in tatters and my moods swung wildly from despair to anger, from self-loathing to self-pity. Sometimes I raged against myself, and sometimes against anybody else to whom I could apportion some blame. I think that I was rude and aggressive with Bessie and the others in the house, but to their eternal credit they treated me with saintly gentleness, patience and forbearance. They did not once take me to task. Why me? Why me? This single thought was stuck inside my brain, and no matter how I tried, I could not drive it away. Was some sort of healing was under way? I think not.

And I was unclean, a leper and an untouchable, contaminated and defiled, and likely to spread the filth within my own body by the slightest of contacts with others. In a frenzy I insisted that every single item of clothing worn by me and Bessie when we were in the parlour at Eastwood was burned on the red coals of the kitchen fire, and I even had the carriage scrubbed down with carbolic soap. Over and again I bathed myself in water as hot as I could bear, and lathered myself with soap suds. Somehow, I thought, I must rid myself of every minute trace of what had happened. It must be washed away, scrubbed away, scraped away........ And Bessie only just managed to stop me one day when I seized a pair of scissors and said that I was about to cut off all my hair.

A couple of days after my fateful visit to Eastwood, Joseph travelled there again to make "investigations" so that he could give evidence to the inquests into the deaths of the four men. He met Hassall and his wife and daughter, and spent a long time talking to them. Then, on 24th May, Joseph and the other men from Newport, including my servants Billy and Shemi, travelled to Narberth for the inquests conducted by the local Coroner before a chosen jury. Joseph has told me all about it. The key witness was Charles Hassall. He gave his story, exactly as dictated by Dominic and exactly as he had rehearsed it in Joseph's presence on the day before. Then Joseph gave his evidence, carefully manufactured to corroborate what Hassall had already said, and no doubt full of learned asides and titbits of evidence designed to lend scientific credibility. The Narberth constables, who arrived on the scene late in the day, described what they saw. Skiff told his story as typical of what the Newport men saw, and the Coroner decided he did not need identical accounts from three or four others. The Coroner then said he wanted Mistress Martha Morgan and Mrs Bessie Walter to appear as witnesses, but Joseph took it upon himself to explain that both of us had been so deeply affected by the horror of the scene at Eastwood that we were still in no state to talk about it. The Coroner nodded gravely, and said he quite accepted that.

There were a few inconsistencies in the various accounts of the witnesses, said Joseph, but that was quite typical of all inquests which follow distressing and violent events, since recollections are often scrambled by panic and desperation. The Coroner clearly wanted things over and done with quickly, and the jury seemed satisfied and even relieved that the four men wanted for murder and mayhem were now out of the way. In each case the verdict was "Accidental death during the commission of a crime." Joseph says that Hassall was very much on edge during the proceedings, in case of any suggestion that he might be guilty of manslaughter, or that he might in some way be held responsible for the deaths, but he need not have worried. At the end of the inquest he was commended by the Coroner for his quick thinking and his bravery, and the "men from Newport" were also commended for their courage in trying to rescue the victims and trying to put out the fire. Everybody, said Joseph, was satisfied.

At the end of the inquest Lewis Legal and Will Final Testament, who had been in attendance but who had said nothing, honoured their promise of a reward. They presented £50 in gold sovereigns to Master Hassall in recognition of his bravery, but in a magnanimous gesture, and with fine words and much back-slapping, he gave it to the men of Newport who (according to this version of the truth) came upon the scene and so bravely fought the flames at grave risk to themselves. Joseph grinned when recounting this, and said that it would no doubt enhance the fellow's local stature even more. The Newport men were of course delighted, and when Shemi turned up back in town with £50 in his pocket, surrounded by the other heroes of the hour, a great celebration was organized in the Black Lion. It is not easy to spend £50 during a single evening, but I gather that all those involved in the Eastwood episode (and many more besides) managed to get rid of every penny by getting gloriously drunk.

After healing and herbal treatment by Joseph, I recovered very slowly. Nobody in the house wanted to talk to me directly about what had happened at Eastwood, which is perhaps not surprising , given my violent swings of mood and my obsession with cleansing myself. So as I got better, we talked about everything else instead. One day I said that I longed to see the children again, and Grandma asked: "Shall we send a message to Morys and send Will to fetch them?"

"Oh Grandma," I moaned. "How I would love that! But please -- not yet. They are enjoying themselves, and they have after all only been away for a week. The novelty of life in the big town will not yet have worn off. I fear that they will be harmed by the dismal atmosphere of this place, and by my unpredictable moods. Things are still too raw, and I feel too fragile to cope with a reunion just yet..........."

With each day that passed, I felt that the Plas was gradually returning to normal. After the siege mentality, the closed shutters, the armed guards and the whispered and conspiratorial conferences around the kitchen table, fresh air wafted through the house. My family and servants were exhausted by lack of sleep and by living off their reserves of nervous energy, but they pulled themselves together. Billy and Shemi were, I fear, still very morose, and still blamed themselves for what happened. But I told them, more than once, that they must not punish themselves, since the responsibility for walking into the trap was mine alone, with a decision made in the face of abundant advice from everybody else that I should desist. While the world was still rocking wildly in the wake of what happened, dear Mrs Owen was a pillar of strength, taking every decision off my shoulders and organizing the meals, the house and the servants as if nothing had happened. And without a word, Grandma and Grandpa simply took on the management of the estate and all the dealings with tenants and labourers. I dare say that this dear place has never before been run so smoothly, without the interference of Mistress Martha Morgan.

One day, in beautiful early summer weather, I felt that I had recovered sufficient of my strength to go for a walk on the mountain. Bessie was pleased, and although she has stuck to me like a limpet since we came back from Eastwood, she sensed that this was an important step on my road to recovery, and she did not offer to accompany me. She simply told me to be careful on those slippery blue rocks, and watched me as I climbed unsteadily towards Ffynnon Brynach. Without thinking, I anointed myself with a sprinkling of the holy water, just as I always do, and suddenly I became very emotional as I realized that the anointment was a cleansing ritual, used by generations of men and women, down through the years, who feel themselves to be defiled by sin, and in need of renewal. I had made this little gesture a thousand times before, as a means of reassurance, or as a mark of respect towards the mountain, and old Saint Brynach, and the angels. On all of my previous visits to this bubbling spring I had not actually felt defiled, or unclean. But now I did, and I was overwhelmed with a sense of guilt. I stood there, feeling unsteady on my feet, and looked back down towards the Plas. Bessie was standing there, watching me. I waved to her, and she waved back. I had to press on and reach the sanctuary of my cave. So I turned and carried on climbing, with my head spinning and with no real idea where I was going. By instinct, and by some miracle, I got there without falling and without even scratching a finger or bruising a leg. Then, with relief flooding over me and perspiration dripping from my brow, I slumped onto my sheepskin at the back of the cave, and stayed there for a very long time.

The events of the first week of June are still blurred in my mind, since I have failed, until these last few days, to put anything in my diary, and since my ability to keep track of things and organize the lives of others has been somewhat reduced. I remember the sheep dipping, down in the ford by Cilgwyn Mill. That was on one of my bad days, and I could not bring myself to go down with the men and the flock; but I listened to the cacophony of confused ewes and lambs from the open window of my bedroom. On the same day, I think, I received letters from the older children and drawings from the younger ones. They had clearly been told by Morys and Nansi that I was not well, and the older ones asked when I planned to get better, and said that they longed for me. I fear that when I saw their shaky handwriting and their innocent little drawings of me and the Plas, I broke down and wept, and had to remind myself afterwards that I was still in an emotional state that was far too fragile for reunions.

Then there was the sheep shearing. As ever, some of the neighbours came to help. For some reason I love the pandemonium of shearing time. There is noise everywhere, with sheep rushing here, there and everywhere until they are penned, and shouting men and barking dogs, and wise old ewes trying to escape the shears, and lambs trying to find their mothers, and the smells of human sweat, and lanolin, and sheep droppings. I forced myself to become involved in what was going on, and got myself thoroughly filthy tying fleeces alongside Bessie and Liza Griffiths from Dolrannog Isaf, while Billy, Will and Shemi did the shearing. I was pleased with myself afterwards, for fighting my tendency to withdraw and spend time by myself in my room. The other women were very attentive and caring, and Billy was so concerned for my wellbeing that I had to warn him to look at the sheep between his knees rather than at me, if he had a mind to keep all of his fingers and other spare parts. At that, he gave me a wink and a grin, in recognition that I still had a little spark left in me, in site of everything...........

The Visit to Eastwood

One day I received a note from Master Charles Hassall. He wrote that he wanted to pay me a visit so that he could explain his actions and make his peace with me. I am afraid that I wrote back briefly and declined that offer, stating that everything was still too raw, and that I was not ready to relive what happened at Eastwood. What I did not say was that I hated the very idea of that self-righteous and pompous fellow sitting in my parlour and seeking to justify his treachery, on the basis of a very feeble understanding of what I had been through. What can any man know of the terrible injury inflicted on the mind and the body of a woman who has been subjected to such barbarism? Maybe he thinks I should be happy to be alive, and that it could have been worse? The stupid, arrogant ass. What does he know? Let him fester, and maybe, some time in the future, when I have regained some sort of composure, I will feel able to meet him face to face, and handle the encounter with good grace.

On another day I received another letter from Ellie, who had heard the fabricated story of the happenings at Eastwood from various of her friends in the county town. She clearly had no idea as to the truth of the matter. She wrote that she was sad to hear of the traumatic scene which Bessie and I had encountered on our arrival at Eastwood, and quite understood that we had been, in the circumstances, too shocked to attend the inquest into the deaths of the four villains. She wrote that she was glad that all had worked out for the best, and that we had avoided any actual bodily harm. I could not bring myself to reply to her letter, let alone to tell my dear friend what had really occurred. What good would it have done if I had reminded her that she might have saved me, but had failed to do it?

On the tenth day of June the children returned to the Plas. As might be expected, there was a very emotional reunion, since they had longed for me as I had longed for them. They had only been away for three weeks or so, but it had felt like an eternity. All five of them chattered away at once, at the tops of their little voices, telling me all about the big town, and Morys and Nansi's house, and their cousins, and their bedrooms, and where they had visited, and what they been doing. Suddenly I realized how quiet the house had been, with no singing, or dancing, or music, or even laughter, since the day of the fateful visit to Eastwood. I discovered that I had even missed the squabbles and the childish tantrums, and the wails that followed -- in the normal course of events -- childish bumps and bruises. I fear that it was all too much for me. I broke down and wept, and continued in a very emotional mood, with frequent tears, for the rest of the evening. At bedtime I insisted on tucking them up in their familiar beds, one by one, and kissing them goodnight, with tears still dribbling down my cheeks. "Mam, why are you weeping all the time," asked Daisy, "when you say you are happy to see us?" All I could do was explain to them that I loved them so much and had missed them so much that my tears were tears of happiness, like the tears of laughter we all shed together when we were on the jolly journey to Portfield Fair, long, long ago. I know not whether they were content with that explanation, but they went to sleep happy, and I could not resist creeping into their rooms several times as the evening wore on, just so that I could sit with them, and smooth their hair, and listen to their gentle breathing.

8th July 1809

I thought, a couple of weeks since, that I was regaining my equilibrium and coming to terms with what happened at Eastwood. I thought that in the last paragraphs of my last diary entry I had described the aftermath. But now I know that I am still trapped in Hell, because I have now missed two successive bleeding times.

11. Aftermath

11th July 1809

For the last three days, since I came to the realization that I am pregnant again, I have been incapable of making the simplest of decisions. I do not feel well, and I have an ache in my breasts that refuses to go away. I cannot decide what to do about the child in my womb, and I cannot decide whom I can trust to give me sound advice.

It is not easy, but I must seek to bring some order to my thoughts, and to remind myself that my world is not as black as it might be. I cannot deny that I have known great happiness. I have had four children of my own, in a loving and wonderful marriage, and they have given me all the blessings of motherhood and taught me some of the mysteries of maternal love. I even had the bonus, two years since, of finding little Brynach on the doorstep of the Plas, and adopting him as one of my own. Five children, and I love every one of them with a ferocity that sometimes frightens me. I know -- in spite of the events at Eastwood -- that I am surrounded by love.

But the situation that I face today brings back painful memories of my first pregnancy, when I was unmarried and miserable, and when I wanted desperately to lose the baby. I even contemplated taking my own life. Then on my first meeting with the Wizard of Werndew, he was furious with me, and persuaded me that to **want** to lose a baby was a mortal sin, especially since the father was the man I loved. So I decided that I **did** want the baby, and settled into a serene expectation of motherhood, only to do something stupid and lose the little mite anyway, when I was all alone one day in the house. That led me into a dark vortex of despair, from which I only just escaped. God only knows that I do not want to go through all of that again. I fear that if I were to lose this child, through some deliberate act or through the intervention of fate, it would destroy me. A new life, or another death? Do I really have to make that choice, at a time when I cannot even decide whether to get up in the morning, or to stay in bed?

My mind is spinning, for this poor child was conceived with no tenderness, no love, no choirs of angels. In fact, the circumstances were so filled with hate and terror and brutality that I still shake when I have to recall them. I do not even know the name of the father. It could be any one of those four monsters, each one of whom was probably insane. Do I really want a child that might inherit just a fraction of the evil that resided in the breasts of those men? And do I really want a child who will remind me, at every moment of contact and closeness, of what happened at the time of conception?

And yet -- and yet -- what is there in the world more innocent, more pure, more helpless, more free of sin, than a newborn baby? A child in the womb should be the greatest of blessings, a new life, a new person who will bring magic and joy into the lives of others, and who cannot, in spite of what the miserable theologians may say, carry forward the evil deeds of the parents. I will **never** accept the nonsense about original sin which I have heard thundered from the pulpit, because if I was to be called to account for the sins of my father, and he was to be called to account for the sins of his father, there would be no justice in the world, and no beauty either. What is more, there would be no foundation for the law of the land. There would be no escape from a vicious circle of sin and misery, and every man and woman walking this earth would be weighed down by guilt. In spite of the nightmare in which I may currently be trapped, I know that outside, on this very day, there is a world of beauty, with the breeze rustling in the furze and the heather on the mountain, and skylarks tumbling in the sky, and bright sunshine warming the old blue rocks. Somehow, some day, I must contrive to rediscover my serene and sensual love affair with the little world that has Carningli and Plas Ingli at its heart. And if that is what I cherish when I have it, and long for it when I am in another place, in body or mind, how honest would it be to seek to deny the opportunity for a similar love affair to the little mite in my womb? He -- for I think it is a boy -- is growing day by day, and maybe, in spite of everything, fate will decree that he is not a monster like his father.

I fear that I am rambling on, and talking nonsense. Maybe I am simply procrastinating, and seeking to avoid a terrible decision. Do I want this child, or not? I fear that in the midst of my fury and my despair I have lost my capacity for rational thought, and in such circumstances it is probably inevitable that whatever I decide to do will be wrong, and will lead me into yet another vortex of self-loathing and melancholia. Why me? Oh God, why me?

12th July 1809

A new day. Bessie tells me that the weather is beautiful outside, but I cannot face the sunlight. Furthermore, I feel that if I were to wander about in the fresh air, and meet some cheerful soul who might smile at me and say: "Good day, Mistress Martha! A wonderful day, is it not?", I would end up raging against him or her, and making a fool of myself. For it is **not** a wonderful day at all, but yet another day of unremitting gloom, during which I am destined to relive nightmares and blame myself and everyone around me for the circumstances in which I am trapped. For fear of making everybody else miserable, I prefer to stay in my room. The boy child is still in my womb, and I still do not know whether to hate him or love him. I have no particular urge to eat, and Bessie gets angry with me when she brings up meals that she says are tasty and nutritious, and when she has to take everything away again except for a few titbits which I might have forced down my throat. I know that the other women in the house, including Grandma, feel a sense of despair about my behaviour, but I see no great reason to flit here and there like a busy sparrow, or join them in their jolly meals, just to please them. What do they know? Nothing! How can they? This is my problem, and mine alone, and I will deal with it..................

Now it is far into the evening. Today Joseph called at the Plas, I dare say at the instigation of the others, and wanted to see me, but I refused to meet him, since I know that he will simply try to cheer me up and tell me to think of others -- and especially the children -- instead of wallowing in my own misery. Well, I will wallow if I like -- that is my privilege, after what I have been through. And in any case, what would a mere man know of my situation? I want nothing to do with any man just now -- not Grandpa, not Joseph, not Billy or any of the other servants. They surely cannot blame me if I hate and mistrust every man on the planet, after what has happened. Even those who hide beneath a veneer of civility are probably, in the depths of their beings, no better than wild animals.

So as far as I am concerned, that stupid fellow Joseph can stay in the kitchen instead, and talk to the others to his heart's content. They will talk about me and worry about me, but that is as it should be. They will never understand me, for they know nothing about what it means to be violated, and soiled, and isolated and abandoned within the invisible prison walls that press in upon me.

Words, and more words! Here I am, scribbling away like a woman possessed, with tears rolling down my cheeks, pretending that a few rows of scratches and symbols and dots on a piece of paper, made with a goose-feather and dipped into some liquid filled with black pigment, can communicate to others what is going on in my soul. What do these little strings of marks that we call "letters" and "words" actually achieve in passing on to others what I mean -- what I feel -- when I refer to anger, or betrayal, or humiliation, or violation, or pain, or self-loathing, or uncleanliness? Nothing! Real communication is utterly impossible, and anybody who thinks otherwise is a deluded idiot. Whoever might read these words of mine in years to come will probably think "What pretty words!" or "Poor Martha! What a pity!" before going off to make a cup of tea or take the dog for a walk. Will they hear the screams that are inside me as I put quill to paper? No, they will not. They will hear nothing, feel nothing, know nothing...........

Oh, thank God for a moment of peace. While I was writing all of that, in a frenzy of ink and tears, Bessie came into the room, without me noticing, and put her hand on my shoulder. "Mistress," she said, "enough is enough. It's time for bed." So I will stop, and try to get some sleep.

13th July 1809

Another day has passed, and I have remained in my prison in spite of Bessie's attempts to drag me out of it. I have been reliving the nightmare at Eastwood, having previously forced myself not to think of it in any depth, apart from recounting the narrative, as sparsely as I could, in the pages of my diary. That brought me some comfort, I suppose, and forced me to admit, rather than deny, what had happened, and to confront some of my demons. But other demons remain. And there is a rage within me, and a despair that extends into the depths of my soul, and a pain that just will not go away. If anything, it intensifies day by day..............

It is not easy, but I must try to ease the pain by bringing some focus to my thoughts. When evil is visited upon somebody -- man or woman -- one has to wonder as to the cause of it, and I have been pondering throughout the day on the apparent obsession of those four men with justice and retribution for my sins. **My** sins! They seemed to think of themselves as men with a sacred mission to right some perceived wrong. That wrong, they said, had been done by me to their friends or brothers, causing them to be led to the gallows or to suffer violent deaths at the hands of others. I have always held to the belief that I have played some small role in visiting justice upon the heads of those who are guilty of evil deeds. But what if those evil deeds were committed in the heat of the moment, or in the honest pursuit of some ideal of family loyalty, or out of a warped sense of what constitutes virtuous behaviour? Should I have sought to understand those men instead of condemning them and pursuing them with whatever weapons that I, as a feeble woman, was able to muster? The monsters called Moses Lloyd and John Fenton, in terrifying encounters from which I escaped but they did not, seemed to think of me as a powerful threat! A threat! They thought that I used my femininity to force them into subservience or submission. So they thought that they needed to dominate me and possess me, just to restore their own pathetic self-esteem. Are men who strut and posture and seek to control things really so weak that they all think in this way? I begin to suspect it...............

What do these creatures **want** of me and the others of my sex? To be pretty coloured ornaments, or trophies, or playthings with the minds of butterflies? I will never accept that, until my dying day. When I look in the mirror and confront my own image, what am I supposed to see? A desirable piece of property who should be for sale in the market-place? Never! But maybe, if I am honest, I do see a woman who has, in the past, taken too much pleasure from the humiliation of certain pompous gentlemen, and who has strayed too far across the delicate line that separates justice from revenge. Maybe. Maybe. And I can freely admit in the secret pages of my little book that I have experienced something akin to euphoria when threats to me and my family have been removed, and when guilty men have died violent deaths, or have gone to the gallows. Are those the reactions of a good woman, or an evil one? Have my own reactions been acceptable in a civilized human being, arising out of release or relief, or have they demonstrated some basic flaw in my own character? Should I have accepted injustices, as many women do, as somehow inevitable or predestined, or as part of the "natural order of things"? Should I have demonstrated a greater capacity for humility, and compassion, and even subservience? Should I have tried, much harder, to understand the ways of men, to flatter them and to do their bidding? May God forgive me. I have mulled over these questions for hour after hour, and I really do not know the answers. I have prayed, and received no answers. Still I rage against the darkness, and scream for help, but even Bessie does not hear me.

Those men who ensnared me and then used me in the mansion at Eastwood were mad, all four of them, but that does not mean that everything they said was nonsensical. Perhaps they were right to some degree, and perhaps it was appropriate, at this time in my life, for me to have to suffer retribution for my weaknesses and my failings? Perhaps, in some grotesque way, these men were used as the agents of Cruel Fate, or of a vengeful God, sent to teach me a lesson? In my desperate search for explanations, I am more and more inclined to this view, and in my calmer moments I think that I must accept at least some responsibility onto my own shoulders for what has happened.

Will I gain absolution and find peace if I make my admissions of guilt? Let me try. My life has been anything but perfect, and I suppose that had I been a Catholic I would have been forced to confront my sins regularly in the confessional. I have confronted them in the privacy of my cave on the mountain, but those confrontations were those of a coward, kneeling before an altar of my own making.

So today I have tried to recall just some of the occasions on which I have been guilty of loose morals. I made love with David before we were married, and I fear that I was the one who led him to it. Within my own marriage I admit that my appetite for sex was insatiable, leading David to complain sometimes that he had no energy left for running the estate. I had a number of amorous encounters with dear Owain, and lustful thoughts about him when I spied on him when he bathed in the pool at Pandy. On many occasions I have used my good looks and even my body to get the better of men for whom I have had no respect. I still shiver when I think of the many occasions in my short life in which I have worn revealing dresses just to be provocative, or in which I have taken too much delight in adding rouge to my cheeks or putting up my hair so as to appear as beautiful as may be. God only knows how many hours I have spent in front of a mirror. I have now recalled, with shame, the moments when I was a teenage girl, thinking lewd thoughts about boys and imagining what it would be like to feel a man's body next to mine. Like a courtesan I have luxuriated in hot soapy baths and enjoyed my own body, perhaps in a fashion which more modest and virtuous young women would never have done. When I was a girl, I remember running my hands over my tight little breasts and feeling surges of pleasure as they grew day by day and week by week........and there have been many times, as a young woman and even in recent months, when I have enjoyed sensuous pleasures that have been self-induced. Are these things a normal part of a woman's life, or am I obsessed, to an unhealthy or sinful extent, with my own body and my own carnal desires? And if the latter is true, should I therefore not expect, and accept, punishment or retribution in some form, as a means of cleansing?

As the long day has run its course, the more I have become convinced that I have been a woman of questionable morals who is responsible for her own downfall. I have gone through phases of thinking that I am no better than a whore -- and indeed far worse than a whore, because a whore is at least not hiding behind a veil of respectability and is acknowledging and flaunting her own sensuality and sexuality. This afternoon I thought it incumbent upon me to exonerate and even forgive my assailants, on the basis that they were acting out God's punishment or retribution for my multiple misdemeanours. I knew that they were now dead because of me, and because of my insistence on bringing their blood brothers (whom I thought to be evil) to justice in the past. I wondered whether I had been petty and intrusive in seeking to understand things that were really none of my business. More and more I have felt unclean and even filthy, not because of what happened, but because of my own loose morals and because of other blatant imperfections in my character.

And then, deep within my soul, I have screamed: No! No! This cannot be! Whatever my imperfections may be, nothing in Heaven or on earth can excuse what those men did! The evil was theirs, and not mine! And I will never, ever, accept the twisted logic which apportions to me some of the blame and some of the guilt.

So the pain, and the desolation, continue. But there has been a change in my mood. My screams of rage and desperation have faded and turned into the low moans of utter despair. This evening, at the end of a day spent all alone, at my own insistence, I fear that I became so obsessed with my own misery that I thought it would be better for my family and my servants if they could simply get on with their lives without me. So I called Bessie to my room and asked her if she could get me some laudanum to help me to sleep. Quite a lot of it, I said. Bessie refused point blank, and I had a furious confrontation with her that left both of us in tears. Now I will have to sleep without assistance, or maybe not sleep at all. And tomorrow, if my mind is clearer, I will give further thought as to the best way to end the suffering which presses me inexorably towards oblivion.

Aftermath

14th July 1809

When I blew out my candle and collapsed onto my bed last night, I fancied that I had a grim set to my jaw, and that I was set upon a certain course of action from which nothing would deflect me. I stared at the ceiling in the warm darkness, and thought of knives and high cliffs and bottles of poison. But then I realized that there were tears in my eyes, and before long I was weeping as I have never wept before. I wept with a rage and a passion that I cannot explain, nor will I ever be able to, no matter how long I might live. Images rushed through my brain, and I think that I must have plunged into the blackest sort of desolation -- blacker and deeper than anything I experienced with the loss of my first baby, or on learning that my husband David was dead. I think that my wailing must have woken the house and echoed round the dark mountain, for suddenly Bessie was at my side, and I was in her arms, still weeping for my own sins and the sins of others. I must have cried myself to sleep, like a small baby. When I woke, sunlight was creeping through the cracks in the shutters, and I was still in Bessie's arms. She did not remonstrate with me, and she looked at me with the eyes of a saint. She kissed my forehead and smoothed my hair, and said to me what she says every morning: "Good morning, Mistress! Have you slept well?"

I think I managed a smile. "I think I must have, Bessie," I said, "when I got round to it."

Bessie had certainly had very little sleep herself. But she climbed off the bed, puffed up the pillows, settled me down, and pulled the blankets up over my chin. "Now then," she said," I can't sit here all day with your head on my bosom. There are things to do. First, you need some daylight." She strode across the room as if she was wading into battle, and flung open the shutters, allowing the golden rays of the early morning sun to come flooding into the room. The light was so bright that I had to close my eyes momentarily. Then I blinked like an idiot, for my eyes were still red with tears and heavy with sleep.

"Then," she continued, "I am going to make you a hot frothy bath and force you to lie in it while I scrub your back and wash your hair, for at least half an hour. Then I will give you a good going over with that favourite soft towel of yours, get you dressed in your blue cotton frock, and spend another half hour doing your hair up........."

"Bessie!" I scolded. "Who is the mistress here? I am perfectly capable of deciding what I will and will not do, and it is I who give the orders in this house!"

"Not today, Mistress. There is a revolution, and the workers have taken over the world. Until the old order is restored, which I suppose it will be in due course, I shall enjoy myself by bossing you about!"

And she whistled a happy tune, and flounced out of the room to fetch hot water for my bath. I tried my best to be angry, but in the end I decided that being angry was not worth the bother, and I had to smile. Besides, I did not have enough energy to resist any of Bessie's plans, and so I luxuriated in all of them with hardly a whimper of protest. I did manage to say, when I was standing naked in the middle of the floor and she was drying me with that fluffy towel: "Oh Bessie! Thank you for all of this pampering -- it is quite wonderful. Am I not involved here in some terrible sin, for which I will have to beg forgiveness?"

Bessie slapped my bare bottom with her hand. "Stuff and nonsense, Mistress! What you need is more pampering, not less!"

Then she stood back and looked at me for what seemed like an age. At last she said: "Mistress *bach*, you are truly very beautiful, and don't you ever forget it!"

I think I blushed, and spluttered: "But Bessie, I hate myself! I have decided that I will never again look at myself in a mirror."

"Well, you'd better think again about that. You probably think that if you look, you will see a black monster with red fangs and yellow horns. In fact you will see a very lovely woman in her prime........"

"Oh, Bessie, do you think that any kind gentleman will ever want to look at me again? After what has happened? I fear -- I fear deep within my soul -- that I will be like a leper, and that they will cross the street when they see me coming..........."

"Wild imaginings, Mistress!" she laughed. "You have spent far too much time in your own miserable company lately. You are not a jot less beautiful today than you were three months ago, and I will hear no more of it. Now then, I have special permission from the Good Lord to make you presentable, and then to drag you down to breakfast with all the others who have missed you of late."

"But Bessie........."

"No buts if you please, Mistress. You will do exactly what I say, now that I am in charge."

I had no option but to follow instructions, such was the ferocity of my captor. First, I had to go to the children's rooms and wake each of them with a kiss and a cuddle. They were warm and sleepy, and they smelt as only small sleepy children can smell. Betsi, wise beyond her years, did not remonstrate with me for my recent idiotic behaviour and for my absence from their lives for the past few days. She must have heard me crying in the night. But she simply said: "Good morning, Mam! Oh, you do look pretty today in that blue dress, and I love you so much........" before giving me a kiss and a hug. That almost brought the tears back, but thank God I managed to maintain my composure.

Then I obediently went down to breakfast, with such greetings and compliments from around the table that I might have been Christ, newly emerged from that black old tomb. In the warm embrace of the kitchen, with steaming water in the kettle over the fire, and the smells of freshly baked bread on the table and sizzling rashers of bacon in the pan, my appetite suddenly returned. "About time too," beamed Grandpa. "Eat up, my dear girl, for you are as thin as a rake, and we hardly recognize you."

"My sentiments exactly," said another voice. "We must all do what we can to fatten her up, for she is no use to anybody as she is."

Suddenly I realized that Joseph was sitting there, with his back to me. He turned round and grinned. "Oh, Joseph," I squealed. "How wonderful to see you!" And I could not resist running across to him and giving him a kiss on his cheek. He blushed like a shy five-year-old who had just been kissed by an ancient aunt, and everybody else thumped the table, and clapped and laughed. They knew, and I suddenly realized, that this was the first time I had been anywhere near a man since the day of that fateful visit to Eastwood.

Breakfast turned out to be a somewhat extended and very jovial affair, and when we had all finished, and the platters and cups and dishes had all been cleared away, I asked Joseph if I might take a little walk on the mountain with him.

"Of course, Martha. It will be my pleasure. That is why I am here."

"You mean you knew that I would want to talk to you today, and came over the mountain for just that reason?"

"You could say that. And purely by chance, I arrived just as breakfast was put onto the table by that saintly Mrs Owen of yours."

Twenty minutes later we were sitting on a big rock in the sun, on the south side of the mountain, out of the wind. We were in good spirits, but then I suddenly remembered that I wanted to talk of serious things. "Joseph," I said. "You may or may not be surprised to know that I am with child. I have missed two bleeding times.........."

"Yes, my dear Martha, I knew it already."

"Did one of the servants tell you?"

"No. Shall we just say that I knew it? Sometimes people tell me things with words, and sometimes with their faces or with their bodies. No matter. I came here because I feared that you might try to do something stupid, and thought that you might press Bessie or one of the other servants to help you in the execution of some idiocy. Am I right?"

"Well, I did ask Bessie if she could obtain some laudanum to help me to sleep," said I, shamefacedly.

"I am not surprised. Women who have been through what you have been through often try to take their own lives."

"That is not what I said, Joseph."

He brushed that comment aside, and continued: "I have an excellent herbal potion for you. It will help you to sleep, and it will not harm either you or the baby. It is in a little bottle in my bag, down at the house."

"Joseph, do you not trust me?" I asked, feeling like a naughty child left in charge of a pile of ripe strawberries.

"My dearest Martha," said he, putting his hand on my arm, "you know full well that I would trust you with my life. But I do not trust you always to do the right thing, especially when you have been through Hell and are not yet back to your usual self."

He then reminded me of our first meeting, when I asked for

something to help me to lose my baby or to end my own life -- and he asked me directly whether the scenario was the same now as it was then.

"Yes -- I mean, no," I whispered. "Dear Joseph, I just do not know what to do for the best. I spent much of yesterday thinking that the children, and the rest of you, would be better off without me............"

Joseph kept his counsel, and there was a long silence. At last, tears started to roll down my cheeks, and I felt that I was about to be possessed yet again by that demon called Desolation. So I whispered: "Hold me, Joseph.. Hold me. Please!" He moved across and held me tight while I wept for a long time. I think we both knew that this was the start of a long and painful healing process.

When I had regained my composure, Joseph gently encouraged me to talk. With very little prompting from him, I talked about my guilt and about my own sense of uncleanliness, and of my growing conviction that I must understand or exonerate the four rapists and carry the blame for bringing everything down on my own head. Those are the things I have already recorded in the pages of my diary.

"Oh Joseph," I sighed, "have I really done anything to deserve what those monsters did to me?"

"Nothing, Martha!' he exploded, getting red in the face. "**Nothing** exonerates them. This was their evil manifested, and their crime. You must not -- will not -- accept even an ounce of the blame! Don't you dare ever to think it again!"

I had to smile, and placed my hand on his arm. He calmed down, returned my smile, and continued. "My dear Martha, you are not the first, or the last, to have expressed those sentiments to me. Common reactions to an all too common tragedy."

"You mean that you have come across others who have suffered as I have?"

"I have, Martha. The victims, who all too often do not have the support that you have, endure years of suffering afterwards, and all too often they refuse to enter complaints against the guilty men. So summonses and convictions are rare. I know of certain men in our own community who still walk the streets in the knowledge that they have committed appalling crimes against innocent women. Spare a thought, if you will, for those of your sex who frequently meet, in their daily lives, men who have defiled them and destroyed their lives, and who smile at them, and doff their hats, and hide barbarism behind the gestures of gentlemen........"

"Please forgive me, Joseph, but it is difficult just now for me to allocate sympathy to those who are worse off than I."

"Do you wish that those men had survived?" he asked.

"Yes ...... I mean no! Truly I do not know, Joseph. But I think there has been a sort of fury and frustration within me because I have not been able to rage at them, and hate them, and gain some small pleasure from seeing them hunted down, and left to hang on the gallows."

"Quite so. Very inconsiderate of them to have gone off to burn in the fires of hell so promptly after the event that condemned them. What would you have done, Martha, if they had survived and been arrested for their other crimes? Would you have entered a complaint against them? And would you have testified against them in a court of law for what they did to you?"

"I have asked those questions of myself a thousand times, Joseph. In truth, I doubt that I would have found the strength to do either thing. I would probably have done what I am doing now -- namely to try and hide what happened, and to convince the world that everything is just as it was."

"So it is a blessing that they are dead?"

"Yes, yes. Of course, now that I come to think about it. If they had still been alive, life would have been infinitely more complex and miserable."

"You are right. Those men deserved to die for what they did to you and to others. I am not sure that I approve of the manner in which they were despatched by Dominic -- that was unnecessarily gruesome and brutal. But I am not sure it would have been any less brutal if they had been condemned to hang by a judge, and then left to die by choking on the end of a rope, with hundreds of gawping townspeople looking on and enjoying their day's entertainment. Brutality in private or brutality institutionalised? A difficult dilemma indeed."

"But I remember you telling me once, Joseph, that these men were in some way to be pitied as sad and inadequate people, starved of affection maybe as children, or dominated by brutal fathers, and incapable of real love............."

"Martha, I was seeking to explain or understand evil, not to justify it or to exonerate the men who have committed appalling crimes. They were entirely responsible for their own actions, and your feelings of guilt or uncleanliness do nothing to change that. You dishonour yourself by seeking to take responsibility for the wickedness of others. Let us get one thing straight. I will say this again --you have never, in the past or in recent days, done anything to deserve what they did to you. Your life has been that of a wonderful wife and mother, full of love for your own family and compassion for others. You have had the normal desires of a woman, and the normal instinct for looking as beautiful as nature intended you to be. You ARE beautiful, too beautiful maybe for some people to cope with. Your fate maybe is to deal with envy and pettiness -- but it is not, and never was, your fate to be used and defiled by those monsters! They were worse than animals, all four of them!"

Joseph was shaking with emotion as he spoke, with fire burning in his eyes. I managed to smile again. "Thank you, dear Joseph," I said. "You are truly my most wonderful friend. What on earth would I do without you?"

"Oh, you would probably survive. You are a survivor, Martha, although your fighting qualities seem occasionally to lie dormant."

"So I will stay and fight, Joseph, instead of fleeing. And you have not yet told me what to do."

"I take it therefore that you have, once and for all, abandoned the wicked idea of taking an overdose of laudanum and going to an early grave?"

"Yes. On balance, that would be to flee from my current situation in a fashion that would do no good for my family and might even harm my health."

"I am pleased to hear it. I say that because yours will be a long life well lived. You have ten lives, and when you go to your grave that will be the end of the ninth of them."

"Joseph, you are talking in riddles again. That's the trouble with you wizards. What on earth do you mean?"

He shrugged his shoulders and gazed at me over his spectacles. "I have no idea myself," he grinned. "That was my message, and for your edification I have passed it on. And I also gather, from my contacts, that you have much work to do. You will do something important with a lady called Rebecca, in years to come. Then you have to save this mountain, and do various other things that I had better not describe to you in your present state. With such a busy schedule ahead of you, you might as well stay alive."

My instinct was to explore these prophecies or revelations further, but Joseph suddenly changed tack. "And the baby?" he asked. "Do you want to keep it or kill it?"

That knocked me backwards, and I said: "That is a very heavily loaded question, Joseph."

"Of course it is, Martha. The question contains the advice of a mere man who has studied ethical matters. What might be the response of a woman and a loving mother?"

"Another loaded question. You play with words too much, Master Harries." I looked across the sunlit *cwm*, and thought for a while. Then I said: "My head tells me that I do not want this child, following the events connected with his conception. I will never know -- cannot know -- who the father was.........."

"And neither did the Virgin Mary."

I could not resist laughing. "Blasphemy, Joseph. You will get into trouble with the Rector. I was about to say that my heart tells me that I do want the baby, and that he must be born. There now. That is obviously what you wanted to hear."

"You are right, Martha. You understand me as I understand you. From your standpoint, you must follow your maternal instincts -- to do otherwise would be to deny what it means to be a woman. From my standpoint, you need to forgive yourself and you need to forgive mankind, and rediscover the fact that not all men are monsters. Most of all, you need to rediscover love. And what better way to do that than through the delivery and nurturing of a new baby? I do believe in miracles, Martha, since I have seen many in my life, and have, I think, been responsible for a few. Your miracle will wipe away the trauma of Eastwood and replace it with love. I know it."

"You know it, Joseph? Or do you simply hope?"

"I know it, Martha."

So I cuddled up to this dear, eccentric, intelligent man as we sat there on the rock, and we said nothing more to one another. We simply sat there and watched the sun go down. And strange to relate, I experienced the same warm sensation of wellbeing that I had felt previously, more than once, from close physical contact with Joseph. He knows all about demons, and by some miracle those which had inhabited my mind were somehow now banished into outer darkness.

12. Redemption

15th July 1809

Joseph was very tired last night (as he often is after healing work) and I saw as soon as we got back to the Plas that he was incapable of walking home over the mountain. He would probably have staggered into a bog in the darkness, never to be seen or heard of again. So I offered him a bed for the night. In the morning, after breakfast, we had a Big Meeting. While the children went out to play in the sunlit garden, all of the adult residents of the house met around the kitchen table. I told them that I was pregnant, which was not news for any of them. They have probably known it for at least a week, and have assumed (quite rightly) that my recent bleak mood has had more than a little to do with it. Without going into detail I explained that I had decided to keep the baby and to put up with whatever consequence might follow. Nothing was said about it, but they all knew that I had lost a baby once before, and had been almost destroyed by the experience; and they also knew that the process of inducing the loss of an unformed baby carried such risks that my own survival would have been seriously in doubt. So they smiled, and immediately promised me their love and their support.

I then said that I had decided to keep this pregnancy and birth from the children and the rest of the community. I explained -- and they all understood -- that a child born out of wedlock to the Mistress of Plas Ingli would scandalise the neighbourhood, harm the estate, and make life unbearable for the children. There would be endless speculation as to the name of the father. The status and reputation of the Morgan family of Plas Ingli -- nurtured over many years -- would also suffer, and I and my children would all henceforth be ostracised from the "respectable" social circle of North Pembrokeshire. Some people, I thought aloud, would certainly work out from the date of the child's birth that conception had occurred around the time of the Eastwood episode. That would open up old sores, and I said that I doubted that I could cope with the pain. Again, the others agreed with that, since they had probably already had quite enough melodrama from me already. The last thing they wanted, I was sure, was to see me descending into another episode of deep melancholia. "So, dear friends,"I concluded, "what should I do?"

The discussion went round and round for an age, but at last we all agreed upon a course of action. First, I should continue my recovery at the Plas for maybe a couple of months more, and wait until I begin to look pregnant. "As we all know," I said, "I hide my babies well, up to the fifth month. And during my last two pregnancies I have not suffered too much from the morning sickness. I have to hope that this might be the case with this pregnancy as well. One can only get so far with disguising morning sickness bouts as chills and indigestion............."

Then, it was agreed, when the time is right, I must go away for maybe five months, have the baby in some friendly and safe environment, and return to the Plas with the pretence that I have adopted another child, just as I adopted Brynach two years ago. My departure (which will be noticed within a very short time) will be explained by the others as being down to exhaustion, and to the after-effects of the campaign against me and the men of Plas Ingli by the four sinister surveyors. That distress, they will say, was compounded by the terrible scenes I witnessed at Eastwood, which I had been unable to get out of my mind.

Then Grandpa developed the theme. He addressed the others. "It is quite well known," he said, "that Martha tends to suffer from occasional bouts of melancholia, and so her departure can well be explained by a sickness of the mind rather than the body. We can put it about that Dr Joseph Harries, who knows the patient well, has prescribed rest for several months, and a change of scene, as being essential for her recovery. I am sure Joseph will play along with that?" He turned to Joseph, who nodded. "Good, good. The community, and people like Martha's dear parents, will be inclined to accept all of this as perfectly reasonable and commonplace." I squirmed, but the others murmured their assent, and so it was all agreed.

My greatest concern, as this plan was developed, was that the children would be very upset, and I said as much. But we thought that all we could do was to explain to them in detail and in advance that Mam had to go away for a complete rest, and that she would come home feeling much better. For them, not a lot would change, since Sian looks after the little ones for most of the time anyway. I consoled myself with the thought that if the cheerful and unflappable Sian was to go away for an extended period, they would probably miss her far more than they might miss me.

Where should I go? That was the next question that we addressed. I did not want to go too far away, although I had relatives in various parts of England who might take me in with complete discretion and keep an eye on me during my advancing pregnancy. On the other hand, anywhere in West Wales would be a problem, since somebody would be bound to recognize me and ask awkward questions. Suddenly Billy had an inspiration. "Now then, I have a cunning plan," he said, sounding like a general about to go into battle. "I have a cousin called Morton Hitchings, who has just taken a lease on the island of Skomar, indeed. A very kind fellow. He has just recently moved across to the island and refurbished the old farmhouse, and he and his wife Janet have taken on the big task of making the farm into a going concern. A nightmare, if I may say so, since the island is a place of hellish winds and mighty waves in the winter, although he says it is paradise in the summer. He told me about it once, he did. Shall I go on? Do you see where I am leading?"

I was immediately excited, since Skomar is a place that has featured in my dreams since I was a child. From the cliffs near Brawdy and Solva, where I wandered about with my brother Morys and my sisters Elen and Catrin when we were little, we could see Skomar on the horizon, across the wide waters of St Bride's Bay. It seemed distant, and very mysterious, and I wondered often what birds nested there, and what wild flowers cascaded over its cliffs, and what caves there might be to explore. At that time it was deserted, we knew, with a ruined farmhouse built by some ancient farmers and long since abandoned. Nobody ever went there, except for pirates and smugglers and shipwrecked mariners..........

"I see where you are leading, Billy,"said I. "Pray continue."

"Well, they are not wealthy people, Morton and Janet, but they know all about hard work. Never seen a tougher woman, I haven't, and Morton is therefore a lucky fellow. They are also good Christian people, I would say, honest and thrifty, and full of good cheer. If you like, Mistress,

I could write to Morton and ask him if you might stay there for a few months, out of the way, as it were, until the little one is born. I will have to tell Morton the truth about what happened at Eastwood, but from what I know about my cousin, there never was a more discreet fellow. Take it from me, his lips will be sealed. There is a risk, maybe, that they will want nothing to do with a pregnant woman, let alone the birth of a child, while they are trying to carve out a living for themselves in the wilderness, but then again, Janet might just enjoy some female company. I think you might get along like long-lost sisters. And Morton might gain something from your knowledge, Mistress, of farming methods and managing a big estate. Worth a try?"

This was, we all agreed, a radical solution to our problem. Grandma Jane, who has always struck me as an adventurous soul stuck in a mundane lifestyle, said: "If you want a quiet life of knitting little socks and jackets, Martha, go somewhere else. But if you want adventure, with a very high level of risk, then Skomar might be the place to find it. You have my support, if that is what you want to do."

But Bessie was horrified. "Mistress," she said, "we agreed that for the sake of you and the baby you should go to a friendly and safe environment. This is anything but that. It is both hostile and dangerous. If Morton and Janet will have you, and if you do go across to the island, you will have no medical attention if anything goes wrong. Remember that the baby will be born in the middle of winter, when you will only have Janet to help with the birth. You will be stuck on the island for weeks at a time once the winter gales start. And I can only suppose that the old farm, even with a new roof and some new windows, will be small and damp and draughty -- a veritable nightmare after the space and the comforts that you enjoy at the Plas. And what if you do not get on with those two good people whom Billy thinks of as the salt of the earth? You will be closeted with them, for days on end, with no privacy and no escape!"

"Wonderful!" I exclaimed. "All of that sounds just perfect. I think I could cope with modest discomfort, and it will be a good penance for the predicament in which I find myself. And a wild island lashed by winter gales sounds like the sort of place that might get me out of myself and force me to think of cooperation and survival..........."

"Even if it means placing the baby at risk?"

"Yes, even that. Babies are always at risk, and we all know of women who have lost their babies even when Doctor Havard has been in attendance. I am prepared to take the chance, in the firm belief that all will be well."

And so Billy has now written to Morton and Janet. He has asked if I might come to Skomar for up to six months, and if I might bring Bessie with me. Once the decision had been made, my beloved handmaiden insisted that she would not allow me to go alone, and that she would follow wherever I led. I did not object, for that was exactly what I had hoped for. Bessie will cope, and indeed thrive, on Skomar. After all, she comes originally from Eglwyswrw, and if you come from there, you can cope with anything.

30th July 1809

For the last fortnight we have been waiting for a reply from Skomar Island. I have expressed my irritation with the postal service, saying it was certainly not as slow as this in the old days, but the others have reminded me that letters to and from islands need minor miracles to be transported safely across the stormy seas, and that patience is required. While we have been waiting, my recovery has been erratic. On some days I have felt better and stronger, and at other times I have been very emotional and distressed. That makes me angry, since I thought that the traumas of Eastwood were all behind me and that I was now concentrating entirely on the future. But I suppose that there is one benefit flowing from these erratic moods. In the circumstances, it is not at all difficult to convince the children, and others in the community, that I am not well, either mentally or physically. Joseph has called several times, with due ostentation, so everybody knows that my ailments -- whatever they are -- are being attended to.

Today Billy did get his reply from Morton. He and his wife will be delighted to help me! He says that he and his wife Janet have prayed together, and received guidance that it is their Christian duty to take me in and to offer me a room in the farmhouse in exchange for whatever assistance I can give on the farm. Bessie can come too, but she will have to share my room, which just has space for two beds. So we two women have started making plans for the visit. Today I wrote to Morton and Janet and thanked them from the bottom of my heart for their generosity of spirit, and suddenly the mood of the Plas is changed now that we all have something to focus on.

1st October 1809

Two months have flown by, and although I have occasionally been wracked by bouts of insecurity and misery, I have received wise counsel from Bessie, Grandma and Joseph, who between them seem to understand all of the strange and convoluted things that go on in my mind. And on the whole I have contrived to remain cheerful while feeling physically strong. I have had the appetite of a horse, and have been caught several times by the fierce and lovely Mrs Owen in the act of stealing things from the larder. I have spent much time with the children, and now that I have made my peace with Dewi and his friends I have even been accepted as a squaw into their Secret Red Indian Tribe. I am sworn to secrecy as to our activities.

In August, once my future plans had been settled, I resumed my normal role in the management of the estate, quite spontaneously, as Grandpa and Billy increasingly passed the daily decisions back to me. I hardly realized what was happening at the time, but suddenly it came to me that I was deciding which days Hettie should come and help with the milking, which labourers should be asked to help with the corn harvest, and how much should be spent on groceries and new harnesses for the horses. I am sure that this involvement has kept me out of my bedroom, stopped me from slipping into introspection, and generally helped me in the healing process. I suppose I am a contrary creature and not an easy Mistress, but my angels always seem to know what to do with me.

Thank God that the harvest was a good one this year. In the spring and early summer, with vigilantes prowling about and with armed guards stationed inside and outside the house, we suffered not just from raw fear, and a lack of privacy, but from being almost eaten out of house and home. Those wonderful fellows from town and from the labourers' cottages had prodigious appetites. It will take an age for us to build up our food reserves again, but at least Mrs Owen is able to plan for two less mouths to feed over the winter months. And we got a great surprise in the first week of August when Master Skyrme, the miller from Wiston, turned up at the Plas with his horse and cart, with five bags of wheat flour for us. They were a gift for us, he said, already paid for by a certain gentleman who prefers to remain anonymous. He would not be drawn on the identity of the benefactor, and after sharing a pint of cider with the men in the kitchen, he went on his way. We think that the gift came from Dominic or Charles Hassall, but maybe we will never know the truth of it. That flour was manna from heaven, and within the hour Mrs Owen was hard at work making dough for her wondrous crusty white bread.

We started with the harvest in Parc Haidd this year. It is a sandy field, in which the soil warms up quickly, and while it also dries out too quickly for comfort, if we judge things correctly it produces excellent wheat. As ever, Shemi told us what the weather was going to do, and I called in the harvesters for 12th August. In the past we have had more than thirty harvesters at work at the peak of the barley harvest, but this year I limited the number to twenty-four since they all have to be fed, and since Shemi predicted a longish dry spell which would enable us to use fewer harvesters over a longer period. The Irish harvesters who always come to the Plas in August were very disappointed that I only wanted three of them this year, but they did not suffer too badly since my tenants at Brithdir and Dolrannog have planted more wheat and barley than usual, and they needed labour at the same time as I. So half a dozen members of the O'Connell family worked on the neighbouring farms, within shouting distance of the Plas, and they all got paid and fed.

Billy said we would have a record harvest, and so we did. He was Lord of the Harvest, and he decided to use more sickles than hooks this year since the wheat we have planted has short stalks (so as to stand up to the wind and the rain on this exposed mountainside) and has a tendency to drop the ripe grain if it is cut too violently. So that gave more work to the women with sickles, with a lower rate of loss and less grain left on the ground. (That, of course, was a sad thing from the point of view of the gleaners who followed after harvest home, but I cannot afford to think of charity above the welfare of the estate.) Bessie, Sian and the tenants' and labourers' wives did much of the sickle work and acted as partners responsible for gathering up the swathes and making them up into sheaves. I helped as much as I dared, but not with the cutting. The men gathered up the sheaves and made them into stooks, which were left out for four nights this year because there were heavy dews each night. The August heat was pleasant but not unbearable, and the harvesters were able to work at a steady pace which enabled them to finish Parc Haidd in two days, and my second wheat field on the third day. Then the men cut one big field of oats and went straight into the reaping of my two barley fields. Barley is traditionally cut with scythes, and when the barley harvest is under way, exhaustion begins to set in after five or six ten-hour days -- but we all know that the end is in sight. As always, I loved the barley harvest, for there can be few sights more wonderful in the farming year than ten fit young men in a row, each one stripped to the waist and gleaming with sweat, working their way through the golden crop step by step, with their lethal scythe blades flashing in the sun, in wonderful harmony. The children and I worked with six of the women in raking the swathes into rows which were then left on the stubble for two days and nights. Then the barley harvest was pitched onto wagons and carted to the barn, where it will stay until it is threshed in the coming winter.

I left all the details of the harvest to Billy, since he is a genius at working out exactly how to cut each field, how long to leave the cut harvest out in the sun, and how many people to use for reaping, raking and gathering, stook building and carting. He seems to be a simple fellow, but he has a wonderful facility for sniffing the wind, assessing moisture levels, and calculating yield and human effort. He works a full ten-hour day with the scythe himself, but still contrives to move people about, from one field to another, like a general manipulating his forces in a battle. He always leaves the rick building to the Jenkins brothers, since they can build them faster and safer than anybody else within ten miles of the Plas, and leave them looking magnificent. It is all a matter of professional pride, and it is through the provision of this service that they pay the bulk of their rent. What is more, they thatch and ventilate their ricks properly, and we hardly ever lose any wheat or oats to rats or the weather. This year, when the harvest was all over on the fifth day of September, we had a full barn, and there were three wheat ricks and two oat ricks in the rickyard alongside the hayricks. Then there was the usual horseplay surrounding the cutting of one little tuft of barley, in the middle of the last field to be cut. This was the *wrach* (in English the witch or hag) that had to be cut by a flying harvesting hook flung by one of the harvesters. This year Will was the man who managed it, and with great delight he was pursued around the field by all the women (married and unmarried) who screamed and giggled like a crowd of twelve-year-old girls. He made very little effort to escape, and at last the eager females caught him, flung him down onto the stubble and claimed however many kisses he was prepared to give them. I resisted the temptation to become involved, thinking it more appropriate for the mistress of a grand estate to watch from a distance, with an expression of amused tolerance on my face. Then Will gave the *wrach* to Brynach, the littlest person involved in this year's harvest, and he carried it proudly back to the Plas, where it was brought into the kitchen with due ceremony and hung up on the beam closest to the fire as a symbol of fecundity and harvest home.

Then the kitchen was given over to festivities. Mrs Owen had prepared a splendid harvest supper, and all the helpers were invited to an evening of eating, drinking, dancing and singing which went on noisily until it was past midnight. I pride myself on the fact that I remained fully involved in the jollification until I was suddenly struck by the symbolism and the significance of the situation. I thought of the joy of the harvest, and then my own harvest of fear, and of fertility and the plumping of the grain, and the small child in my womb, and of Ceridwen, the goddess of fecundity, sacrificed at Eastwood in a weird ceremony that did not have procreation at its heart, but domination and humiliation............ My head was spinning, and I must have looked as white as a sheet. I would have fallen over, I think, had Grandpa not spotted my distress and put his arm around my waist. Then Bessie stopped dishing out potatoes and came to my aid, and I managed to give my thanks to all and sundry, and say goodnight before being helped up to my room. I must have been exhausted, for I slept for ten hours. Next day I felt much better, and I was able to complete the last of my harvest duties -- the ringing of the Plas Ingli bell at mid-day which summoned the gleaners from the seven labourer's cottages dotted about on the estate to come and collect whatever ears of corn and pieces of straw which they might value. No men are allowed on the gleaning, for this is strictly work for women and children. They work laboriously, with bent backs and grubby knees, picking up basketfuls of grain which will, I suppose, give them a few loaves of bread in the months to come, and also collecting armfuls of straw which will be used for making chaff for their animals. They worked for two days, and then they were gone, and everybody on the estate started to think of vegetables and fruit instead of grain.

During August and September many messages flew back and forth between the Plas and the island of Skomar. In our correspondence Morton pointed out that it was not that easy for two strange women to appear on a remote island out of nowhere, without anybody else knowing about it. For a start, he said, there were boatmen and farmers on the mainland who maintained intermittent contact with the isolated residents and who kept an eye open for smoke signals which might indicate that help was needed. Then there were the villagers from Marloes who came out to hunt rabbits and paid for the privilege. They would certainly see two strange women and wonder what they were doing there. And as the pregnancy advanced, they would certainly be fully aware that there was a child on the way. So between us we had to fabricate yet another story. I would be a cousin of Janet who was in mourning for the recent loss of her husband, and who had been evicted from a rented home in the little town of Cardiff by an unscrupulous and insensitive landlord in spite of the fact that I was pregnant. So I had been cast out onto the street, together with my maid and my unborn child, with virtually no possessions. Morton had offered us a roof over our heads out of family loyalty and Christian charity, and we had accepted in spite of the harsh life which was all he could promise. The telling of that story, maybe over and again, would involve a pack of lies, and Morton and Janet had to go down on their knees and ask the Good Lord for permission to tell them, which they duly obtained. We just hope that we can all maintain the pretence and get away with it, and that I can be off the island, with my new baby safe and sound, before too many people start to get suspicious and ask awkward questions about the best place to buy ostrich feathers in Cardiff.

Then we had to make plans for the doubling of the island's population -- and for a new baby. Extra beds, blankets and fabrics had to be got over to the island in September, and a considerable quantity of extra food. That was all easier to organize, and Billy made three trips to Martin's Haven (the little beach used by the Skomar boats) with the cart loaded with supplies. Although the round trip was about sixty miles each time, Billy enjoyed that, as relaxation after the rigours of the harvest. Also it involved no pretence at all on his part, since he was simply helping his cousin to cater for the coming winter. In fact he met hardly anybody else on his expeditions, and was met on each occasion by Morton with his own sturdy rowing boat. He helped to load and row the boat, and even spent a little time on the island, and came back each time with glowing reports and a windswept complexion. "Mistress *bach*," he said following his last visit, "when you send me packing from the Plas, I think that in my old age I might become an ancient mariner, and have a little rowing boat, and live on fish and cockles."

10th October 1809

At the beginning of this month I looked at myself in the mirror and decided that it was time to go. I had prepared the children for my departure by saying that my moods were very up and down, and that I was not at all well. I said that we must send letters to each other, and they promised that they would write to me often. "But where will you be, Mam?" asked Daisy, perfectly reasonably. "If we don't know where you are, how can we send letters to you?"

"Don't you worry about that, *cariad*," said I. "I will keep Grandpa informed as to my whereabouts, and he has promised to send the letters on to me. Never fear -- they will reach me all right."

Joseph helped to prepare the little ones by taking them to one side one day and explaining to them that sometimes people are sick in their bodies and sometimes in their minds, and telling them that their dear mother was exhausted as a result of various things that had happened to her, and that she needed a complete rest and a change of scenery. I would be away for some months, he said, but I would then return restored and revived, and able to give them all the love that a mother should give to her precious children. They knew all about my good days and my bad days, and thought that this sounded like quite a good deal. And Joseph sealed the deal by saying that while I was away they would certainly be thoroughly spoiled by their great-grandparents, by being allowed to stay up extra late in the evenings and by getting special treats now and then. And even better, they might get some special presents from their Mam when she returned.

Shemi told us on the previous evening that there would be a gentle breeze from the south throughout the day. That was perfect for a voyage to Skomer, which cannot be reached when the wind is in any of the northern quadrants because both the leaving beach at Martin's Haven and the landing beach on the island face north. So the decision was made. We would go, and Morton would be expecting us. When Bessie and I climbed onto the coach at seven in the morning, with a mountain of luggage threatening its stability, we said our affectionate farewells to the children, the old folks and the servants. There were many tears, and Betsi said: "Now you look after yourself, Mam, and try not to weep too much, and come back safe and sound, and full of fun!" But the younger ones simply hugged and kissed me, and said goodbye, and asked what presents they would get in the fullness of time............

Then Billy cracked the whip, and we were off. Fifteen minutes later, as we clattered up the hill past Cilgwyn Mawr I looked back and saw the Plas gleaming white against the autumn colours of the mountain, and I became very emotional. I remained in a fragile state until we were over the highest point on the road to Haverfordwest, since on the north side of Mynydd Preseli the landscape is dominated by wild moorland and blue rocks, and Carningli is always in view. My heart is trapped in that landscape, and will never escape from it, so when we reached the summit and started our descent towards Tafarn Newydd and the county town, I felt, as ever, that a part of me had been left behind. Bessie knew my mood exactly, and placed her hand on my arm. I breathed deeply, and looked towards the distant horizon, and saw the hazy outline of Skomar Island, set in a glittering sea. I decided that I had to leave behind misery and introspection and look forward to a great adventure in a strange and romantic place. So for the rest of the long journey we chatted like excited children on a mystery tour. We imagined things, and speculated about the island scenery, and anticipated how wild the winter storms might be and how high the waves were as they rolled in from the open Atlantic, and what it would feel like to be totally isolated from friends and neighbours for weeks at a time.

When we reached Martin's Haven Billy climbed up onto the clifftop and lit a fire which was more smoke than heat, and sent some mysterious smoke signals to the island. An hour passed. Then a small rowing boat came into view round the headland on the west side of the haven, rowed by two people. Soon it was on the beach, and we met Morton and Janet, who would be our hosts and our friends for the months to come. They greeted us warmly, and I liked them immediately. He proved to be a short, stocky man with a weatherbeaten face, blue eyes and a mop of curls on his head. I reckoned that he was probably forty-five years old. He had a distinct family likeness to Billy, and the two cousins were obviously very fond of one another. Janet was taller than Morton and, I suspect, just as strong. She was not particularly pretty, but she was certainly attractive in that her eyes sparkled and because she always seemed to have a smile on her face, even when she was serious. She wore a long woollen skirt and a flannel blouse with long sleeves that were rolled up to expose muscular brown arms. She wore no bonnet, and her dark hair was cropped quite short, no doubt to keep it out of the way while she was milking cows or carrying hay. Hard-working people, I thought, with no pretensions and a love of freedom and independence. Nobody would dare to tell either of them what to do, since between them they could probably do anything and everything. Out on their island, they would be in charge of every aspect of their daily lives, with no rules or routines to follow, and with the nature of the working day determined by the weather.

Soon everything was loaded onto the boat, and we each embraced Billy and said our farewells. He stood on the beach and waved to us as Morton and Janet pulled on the oars and moved us clear of the seaweed-covered boulders in the shallows, and away into deeper water. Then we lost sight of Billy and the beach as we rounded the headland, and we looked instead to the west, to the island that was to be our home over the winter. The breeze was a gentle one, still in the south, and the sea looked calm, but as soon as our little craft reached Jack Sound, the treacherous strait between Skomar and the mainland, Morton shouted: "Hold on tight! This is where it gets exciting!" and soon we were bobbing about like a little cork in the middle of a great ocean, with man and wife pulling hard and unceasingly on the oars for more than twenty minutes while the current tried to pull us southwards towards jagged black rocks. This was the closest I had ever been to a *maelstrom,* with breaking waves appearing out of nowhere and no clear pattern to the streams and currents on the water surface. There were even whirlpools where the water threatened to spin us round and drag us down into the depths. There was flying spray everywhere, and we all got soaked, and while Morton and Janet shouted and laughed with exhilaration, Bessie and I were quite scared. Then, as suddenly as we had entered the tide race, we were out of it, and into water so placid that it might have been the Plas Ingli duckpond. "Ha!" shouted Morton with a grin. "That was fun, wasn't it? You looked a bit frightened, the pair of you, if I may say so. But that was Jack Sound on a calm day. You should see it when there is a gale blowing, and a falling spring tide!"

In another half hour we were approaching the landing beach, overlooked by steep rocky cliffs in some places, and elsewhere by gentler slopes covered with bracken and late-flowering gorse. Twenty or thirty grey seals, accompanied by their plump white pups, had to get out of the way before we could land, and Morton shooed them off as I might have done with a herd of young bullocks that were blocking a gateway. "Wretched creatures!" he grumbled. "This island has been uninhabited by humans for so long that they have taken possession, and think it is theirs. But I mustn't complain. They are easy to catch. I will kill three of them for the winter, and that will keep us going for meat and blubber. And the skins are pretty useful too. Tell me, Mistress Martha, how do you like your seal liver -- medium or rare?"

I looked at Bessie and grinned. She rolled her eyes and shrugged her shoulders, and then we both burst into laughter. We knew that we had entered another world.

29th October 1809

I am now more than five months gone, and I am happy to report that I feel as strong as a shire horse and as happy as a little foal let loose among the buttercups. There are no buttercups here, at least not at the moment, but there is beauty on all sides, and this is a world so different from that of Carningli and the Plas that I can hardly credit it as being in the same county. We can see the mainland from the higher parts of the island, and when it is bright and clear we can even see Foelcwmcerwyn, the summit of Mynydd Preseli. That summit is also visible from the Plas, and I sometimes wonder whether any of the children are gazing at it too, making a little link between us in spite of the difficulties and the dangers of moving between this place and that. I have my little waves of *hiraeth* for my home and my mountain, but truly I am very happy here, and I have hardly had any time for mulling over the happenings at Eastwood or for reminding myself that I should be miserable. Misery is well nigh impossible in the company of Morton and Janet, and both Bessie and I have grown to love them dearly, in the space of just four weeks or so. They are thoroughly jovial people blessed with a simple and deep faith that the world is beautiful, that the Lord will protect them, and that their reward for good cheer and hard work will come when they stand before the Pearly Gates. They are up at the crack of dawn and off to bed shortly after darkness falls, and because the farmhouse is so small we are forced to fit into their routine. Mealtimes are different here from those of the Plas, and indeed almost everything else is different too. There are no proper washing facilities, so one has to go around feeling grubby for most of the time, in clothes smelling of sweat and cow dung, but that is something one gets used to. There is no pantry or scullery, and all of the food is stored in a little stone shed next to the garden. The farmer and his wife are not worried about rats, since there are none. There are no adders either, so one can wade through the bracken happily, even in warm weather, without bothering too much about where to place one's feet. Every morning we have to make up our beds promptly when we get up, for they are then used as sofas, wardrobes and even tables. Every word of conversation is heard by every person in the house, for the two internal walls are just flimsy partitions. One room serves as kitchen, scullery, washroom, dining room, office and parlour.

The one feature which makes the Skomar farmhouse feel like home from home is the large open fireplace and the coal fire which never goes out. So it is warm and cosy all the time, even when there is a gale screaming in from the West. Shortly after we arrived I asked Morton where he got the coal from. He grinned, and said: "Come with me, and I will show you my coal mine!" We dressed up warmly and he led us from the centre of the island (which is where the farmhouse stands, nestled behind a big rock) to a place called The Wick. There, at the bottom of the cliffs, was a wrecked sailing ship called *Eliza Griffin*, stranded high on the rocks. The masts, sails and rigging were all gone, having been collected and dragged to the farmhouse by Morton and Janet and their two horses, but the happy fellow told us that the hold was full of coal, and that whenever he needed some he simply had to clamber down and fetch it.

Talking of ships, there are vessels around the island all the time -- local fishing smacks, ketches and schooners taking out wool, coal, salted herrings and flour from the Pembrokeshire ports and bringing in salt. sugar, fruits, clothes and luxury goods of all descriptions from Bristol, the ports of Devon and Cornwall, and even as far afield as London. We may see thirty or forty ships going past in the course of a single day. Many of the trading ships are not visiting the Pembrokeshire ports at all, but are on their way North and South rounding this western tip of Wales in the middle of some voyage lasting maybe a week or two. Some of the bigger ships are not hugging the coast at all, but sail past with steadfast intent, heading west and into the great Atlantic Ocean. Some of them are set for southern Ireland, but the main destination is America.

In addition to the two horses on the island, there are ten cows, one bull, twenty sheep, three pigs and assorted chickens, ducks and geese. Morton has one border collie of which he is inordinately fond; it is more like a family pet than a working dog, but it is well trained and knows how to work the animals. There are no barns, cowsheds or stables, and the only shelters to which the animals can retreat in bad weather are primitive constructions with rickety roofs supported by old ships' timbers, and with no walls. On the other hand, the plateau which makes up the central part of the island has a number of craggy rocks standing up above the wider land surface, and the animals seem to know how to get away from the wind and the driving rain. There are five big fields and three small paddocks, each one bounded by a substantial stone wall. These walls, says Morton, are inherited from the past, and have been built, stone by stone, by many generations of island farmers, going back to the time before written history began. They too provide shelter for the animals. Janet milks the cows in the open. Morton has manufactured little wooden shelters for the poultry, but they are not shut in at night, since there are no foxes. The hay from the summer season just past is contained within three low ricks which are covered with pieces of sail canvas taken from the *Eliza Griffin* and held down with sturdy ropes. Janet told me shortly after my arrival that anything projecting above the surface is likely to be blown away if it is not well built or soundly anchored. She also said that the last farmers to try and make a go of farming in this windswept environment were forced to leave when all of their winter fodder, held in two ricks, was blown into the sea and when all six of their cattle were washed away by a giant wave during the same storm.

Wind is indeed the feature of the weather that dominates all else. It is blowing almost all the time, mostly from the West and South-West, but swinging to other points of the compass now and then. It whispers, murmurs, moans, growls and screams according to its mood, and because it is so incessant and so powerful there are no trees on the island. There are just a few scrubby bushes, struggling to survive in the small valleys that provide just a little shelter. When you go to sleep at night, and when you wake in the morning, the wind is buffeting the house, and for most of the time you cannot even hear the waves -- which are less than half a mile away -- because there is an incessant low roaring sound made by air streaming across an open landscape and flowing round and over whichever obstacles might stand in its way. Some people, said Morton, are sent mad by the wind, but he loves it, and so do I. And when it stops, you are reminded that this place truly is paradise. In the middle of the month we had four days of breathless, bright weather which felt like midsummer. There were insects buzzing about everywhere, and although there were few birds present because October is a quiet month, they sang as if it was March, and we could hear the sounds of the mother seals and their pups in distant coves and caves at all points of the compass. Some sounds even reached us from the mainland. Then we could also hear the sea, whispering all around the island, at the foot of the beetling cliffs.

And what has happened? Truly a great deal. We have had two gales since our arrival -- one from the North and the other from the South-West. The former involved no rain at all, but it lasted for three days, and the wind was so strong that we could hardly stand up outside the house. In going about our business of milking and feeding the animals we had to walk, bent double, in the lee of the high stone walls, and once or twice I had to drop to my knees to avoid being blown over. I thought, wryly, that this particular gale would probably not even be noticed at the Plas, since it is entirely sheltered from the North by the bulk of Carningli. Five ships came and sheltered in South Haven while the gale blew itself out. Some sailors came ashore from one of them, and we spent a pleasant hour or two in their company. They gave us five bottles of wine and a smoked ham, simply out of goodwill, because of the bond that exists between islanders and mariners. The other gale was less ferocious and less prolonged, but it was accompanied by a veritable flood of rain. God only knows where all that water came from. It was travelling horizontally, and was therefore unlikely to have come from the pitch black sky. As it battered against the windows of the farmhouse and threatened to break the glass, Morton rubbed his hands in glee and explained that the biggest problem on the island, apart from the wind, was the lack of water, since most of the rain that falls in Pembrokeshire passes over the islands and affects the mainland instead. Now, he said, the ponds would be full for a while, and the water level in his well would make him slightly less apprehensive about the future. One day when there was no wind and a glassy sea, Morton allowed me to go fishing with him in the rowing boat about a mile offshore. He would not allow me to help with the rowing, but I was as delighted as a ten-year-old when I hauled up ten splendid cod from the depths. On another day a sheep got stuck half-way down one of the tall cliffs near the Garland Stone. We had to fix ropes on the clifftop, and we three women had to let Morton down before hauling the stupid sheep up first, and then the farmer afterwards. That operation occupied most of the day, and we were all exhausted afterwards. On the tenth day of the month Morton shot three female seals and three pups in North Haven, and we three women spent the next three days cleaning out entrails, skinning the animals, carving off blubber, and butchering the rest of the carcasses. As I slaved away alongside Bessie and Janet, with my arms plunged into entrails and with blood all over my dress and apron, I wondered what the cream of the Pembrokeshire gentry at the Glynynmel Autumn Ball would have thought of the Mistress of Plas Ingli, had they seen her now...........

3rd November 1809

Today Billy came over to the island, having negotiated a lift from one of the Marloes fishermen who was heading out to his fishing grounds between Skomar and Grassholm, far out on the horizon. He was picked up again in the evening and returned to the mainland. We were of course delighted to see him, and he commented immediately he saw me on my good health. "Why, Mistress,"he beamed. "I have never seen you looking better! Your eyes are bright again, and the colour in your cheeks is indeed a pleasure to behold. You are a very good advertisement for life on an island, indeed. Maybe we should all come out here and join you!"

"Quite impossible!" said I. "Morton will not have you. He will only have hard and grizzled people who know how to clean a cod and skin a seal, and you landlubbers are all too soft to survive out here anyway."

Dear Billy shared a simple meal of boiled cod and mashed potatoes with us, and brought news of the Plas and the neighbourhood, some letters from the children, and a bulky envelope from America that had travelled here, there and everywhere before finally reaching me. I knew at once that it contained a very long letter from Dominic, for the envelope was not addressed to me in the handwriting of my sister Elen. When Billy had gone, I settled down on my bed and read the children's charming letters first, and with a tear in my eye I proudly showed the others the drawings that Brynach and Sara had done for me. Then I read the letter from Dominic. This is what it said:

St Louis, Louisiana, United States
16th day of July 1809

My Dear Martha,
May I address you thus? Please forgive my presumption of intimacy, but since I think of you with more than a little affection, I dare to hope for your forgiveness. Besides, I have to crave your forgiveness for allowing the terrible events at Eastwood to take place, and for all that happened to you and your dear friend Bessie. I do that now from the depths of my being. I cannot begin to imagine how those events might have affected you, and I can only trust that your reserves of inner strength, and the love of your wonderful family and friends, will enable you to return to some sort of normality in due course. Joseph told me, before I left Eastwood to travel to America, that you have an amazing resilience and such a love of life that you will pull through. And he says that you have many great things ahead of you, and many worthy tasks to perform, before you finally leave this world a better place than you found it. Dear Martha, I know that all that is

true, and I pray that by the time you receive this letter the healing of your soul will be well under way.

When I had read thus far into the letter, I realized that I was shaking with emotion. The writer sounded so erudite and sensitive that I could hardly credit it. Was this man really Dominic Cunningham, who had behaved as a maniac and a murderer in the parlour at Eastwood? Was this the man who had kicked his erstwhile brother full in the face, over and again, who had taken a ceremonial knife and castrated three men in cold blood, while they were still conscious, and who had then slit their throats and lit the fire that had consumed their bodies? Suddenly the recollection of all of those appalling events came flooding back into my mind, and I thought that it might all be too much for me. But to my own surprise, I was able to breathe deeply, restore my equilibrium, and hold back my tears. Perhaps, as Dominic and all of my angels hoped, my inner strength really was being restored, and my soul really was being healed? So I was able to read on.

I have two days in which to write this letter. You need to understand everything that happened before your fateful visit to Eastwood, although I think you know some of it already. Let me start at the beginning, and let me tell you about myself. As you might have guessed, I come not from a gentry family but from a background much more modest. My father, who died some years since, was a merchant in Limerick who could not find the means to support five sons and three daughters, so when I was eighteen years old I was pushed out to make my own way in the world. I did various jobs in Cork, Dublin and Wexford, and then I made my way to London, thinking that the streets were paved with gold. While I was there I invented a new personality for myself, and since I was blessed with reasonably good looks and a way with words I was very successful. I managed to buy some good clothes, and had some visiting cards printed, and lived a rather pleasant life for several years by insinuating myself into house parties, attending weddings, and even staying as a house guest in assorted grand mansions for weeks on end. It suited me very well, being the younger son of the Squire of Limerick. The trick was to find out which of the gentry were away in Brighton, or Paris, or wherever, and to discover when they might return. Then I would send my card and call at their mansions, and stay for as long as it suited me. My manners were impeccable, and I never caused any trouble. But I was always given a beautiful room to sleep in, and I was always well fed. The English code of hospitality in the higher echelons of society is indeed a wonderful thing. The only price I had to pay was to spend a great deal of my time in the presence of other house guests, most of whom were dull and very old, and to sing various Irish folk songs as my contribution to evening entertainments. I took to playing cards with the other gentlemen at these house parties, and found that by using certain tricks I had learnt in Ireland as a boy, I could come out at the end of each evening a hundred pounds or so better off than I had been at supper time. I was also befriended by an ancient dowager, whom I kept on meeting on this strange social circuit, and she at last started to look on me as the son that she never had. Then she suddenly died, and I discovered that I had been left two thousand pounds in her will. Luckily, the attorney who disbursed her assets was an incompetent fool who did no checks on the credentials of the beneficiaries, and I emerged from his office in Kensington one bright day with a pile of crisp banknotes in my hand.

Thus far my life had been that of a petty confidence trickster and card sharper, and I do not suppose that I really did anybody any harm. But then, with money in my pocket and a growing reputation among the young dandies of London, I met Edwin Dashwood and Reynard Foley. For a year or so we met often, and I slid into a life of wild excesses and indulgence. I will not describe my activities, but when I look back on them I am truly ashamed, not just because of my own hedonism and irresponsibility, but because of the harm I did to others. I took to using laudanum, which made me feel wonderful, but I fear that it did strange things to my brain, and my moods are now so variable that I sometimes think I am not one person any longer, but two. I do not blame those fellows for leading me astray -- I was a willing confederate. My wealth increased, simply because I discovered that if I stayed sober at the card tables while others were sliding into inebriation, I could win even without cheating. Then I was introduced into the Carlton House Set, and became quite friendly with the Prince of Wales. I won a lot of money off him at the card tables and in other wagers. He was an irresponsible idiot on a grand scale, and God only knows what his excesses will have done to the national economy.

About four years ago I was invited by Dashwood to become a member of The Mysteries of Ceridwen. It was (I write "was" because it is no more) a secret society for gentlemen, created to honour the memory of the Hell-Fire Club which Dashwood's grandfather created back in the last century and which scandalised society at the time. The West Wycombe estate in Oxfordshire was the centre of activities for Dashwood and his Mad Monks, but they were involved in any number of outrageous happenings in London as well. Sexual indulgence, driven by alcohol and opium, was at the heart of their activities. When all the fellows involved in the Hell-Fire Club had died from their excesses, or had become old and respectable, various of their grandsons thought it would be fun to return to the bad old days, but in a much more secretive fashion. The new society called The Mysteries of Ceridwen stayed clear of politics, published no seditious books or pamphlets, and managed -- for the most part -- to avoid newspaper publicity. The founders, probably on one of those evenings when they had all taken too much laudanum, decided that their organization would be thoroughly intellectual, based upon ancient Celtic wisdom. Some of them had a vague understanding of it, and some of the Welsh members knew about the old Welsh legends, and about Taliesin, and about the Triads. They talked endlessly about the Welsh and the Irish heroes, and eventually came up with a garbled set of rules, rituals and core beliefs which all members were supposed to subscribe to. I dare say it was all terribly exciting, the more so because it was a society that nobody else was supposed to know about. Looking back on it, it was all nonsense, and the key members of the original society should probably have been shut away in lunatic asylums -- but I was young, and I was drawn into it willingly, and I have to take responsibility for that.

Everything was in threes. The society was built around the Triads, and there were supposed to be thirty-three members or brothers. Somebody who supposed himself to be a learned fellow said there were 33 Triads. (There are actually many more than that, but that inconvenience was simply brushed to one side.) There were to be eleven categories of membership, with three members in each. So there should be three heroes, three princes, three warriors, three poets and so forth. If one or more members died, the membership was to be brought up to the magic number again by new recruitment. Every member was given a name plucked from the Welsh Triads. We were not supposed to know each other's proper names, but of course we did. In our ceremonials and our conversations we were always supposed to refer to each other by our brotherhood names. I was given the name Tristfardd, because I was deemed to be a bard, and because one of the Three Bloody-speared Bards of the Island of Prydain had recently died. The members I knew about were Alban Watkins, whose name was Rhiwallwn; John Howell, whose name was Urien; Joseph Rice, whose name was Tinwaed; Reynard Foley, whose name was Cai; John Fenton, whose name was Henben; Edwin Dashwood, whose name was Edenawg; Joshua Palmer, whose name was Gruddnei; and Geordan McCleod, whose name was Afaon. All of those names were supposed to represent the special talents of the brothers concerned -- so Gruddnei was one of the three heroes of Britain, because of his military record, and Cai was one of the battle leaders of Britain because of his ability to invent stirring speeches out of thin air; and Rhiwallwn was one of the three fettered ones, because of his unfortunate tendency to be incarcerated at His Majesty's Pleasure.

Another one who almost became a member, but shied away at the last minute, was Walter Phillips of Ambleston Hall, who married your friend Ellie not so long ago. He was a dark and gloomy fellow, and as hedonistic as the rest of us, but maybe he was saved at the last minute by the love of a good woman. Then there was the mad bard called Iolo Morgannwg. Palmer was very keen on his researches and writings, and indeed adopted his third volume of "The Myvyrian Archaiology of Wales" as a sort of bible for the society. He carried it everywhere with him, and insisted on reading long passages of it out loud (or rather, quietly, since he had no voice) to his companions, in the hope that they might some day reach his level of enlightenment. But Iolo took fright at the last minute, and accused Palmer of shallowness and opportunism, and of a total lack of understanding of Wales and the Welsh. For God's sake, the man could not even speak Welsh!! And there were insurmountable differences between Iolo and Palmer on things like the rights of man, religion and slavery. So he went off one day in high dudgeon, intent upon setting the world to rights, and we never saw him again. The last I heard of him was that he was trying to set up his own mysterious Order of Druids, and was busily inventing ancient ceremonials and myths. I suspect he was inventing ancient texts as well. But I liked him, and thought him quite mad, but relatively harmless.

That obsession with the old tales of Wales was all jolly fun, and I was greatly taken by it. In retrospect, I should have shied away from involvement in The Mysteries of Ceridwen as soon as those fellows in charge started talking about beliefs, oaths and such things, for that was the point at which a silly little social club transposed itself into a cult or a religion and became sinister and potentially evil. When I had already accepted the invitation to join, I realized that this was a blood brotherhood, sealed by a mingling of blood, and that I had to swear an oath that if any brother should die through violence, there should be a sacred duty to avenge the death through the spilling of the blood of the person responsible. That was not all. The vengeance should also extend to "all those who caused our brother pain." There was a weird belief that when a death had been avenged, the dead brother would be brought to a place of peace and light, somewhere in the Celtic Otherworld. A key text in their system of belief was Triad 33, which concerned the Three Oppressions of the Island of Prydain; the third of these (and therefore the most important) was the oppression of the Saxons. So a vague sense of some great past injustice pervaded everything they believed and said, as did the sense that revenge or retribution was a necessity if the world was to be put to rights. Then we come to Ceridwen. She is of course, in the old Welsh stories, the mystic goddess and the mother of all, and although I think there is nothing about this in the Welsh tradition, these fellows concocted the belief that Ceridwen must be sacrificed and reborn as part of the process of cleansing the world, and as a means of redeeming the souls of dead brothers. I suppose there have been Ceridwens before, and thank God there will be no more in the future. It was your misfortune, my dear Martha, to be the last.

When I was initiated into The Mysteries of Ceridwen, probably considerably under the influence of laudanum, I had to have three stripes cut on my chest with the ceremonial knife without making a sound. My silence was taken as a sign of my courage and my stoicism. Then my blood was mingled with the blood of my brothers, so making us blood brothers. I also had to swear the oaths of The Mysteries of Ceridwen, most of which I do not remember. They were all mumbo-jumbo anyway.

There was a special bond of brotherhood between the men initiated at the same ceremony. Fenton, Dashwood and Palmer were initiated together, so the latter two had a special allegiance which committed them to revenge the death of the former. Some years before that, Howell, Rice and McCleod were initiated together. Watkins was, at the time of his death, the oldest brother in the society, which was already greatly reduced in numbers since there were no more people left in the world who were idiotic enough to subscribe to its beliefs or to submit to its bloody and grotesque initiation ceremony.

When John Fenton was on the run from the forces of law and order, some two years ago, he wrote a letter to his two closest brothers who were at that time in London. I have that letter in my possession, having taken it from Palmer's pocket before he went up in flames. It was written on 12th December 1806. It is not a nice letter, being full of bile and rage, so I will not reproduce it here. But in essence that despicable fellow wrote that one person above all others was responsible for the deaths of Urien (Howell), Tinwaed (Rice) and Rhiwallwn (Watkins). Her name was Mistress Martha Morgan of Plas Ingli. My dear Martha, I think that Fenton was obsessed with you, and that he wanted both to possess you and destroy you. He wrote that he would seek vengeance in his own way, and that he had high hopes of success in "sacrificing the Goddess Ceridwen on the sacred altar." He wrote that he would report on the success of his sacred mission within the month. If no further message was received from him, it was to be assumed that he was dead. In that case, he wrote, there was a sacred duty placed upon his brothers to extract vengeance "as appropriate" upon Mistress Morgan in particular and upon assorted others who were also held responsible for the deaths of assorted brothers and the decimation of the brotherhood. He named these people on a list, which he included with the letter.

The names on the list were Martha Morgan of Plas Ingli, Joseph Harries of Werndew, Isaac Morgan of Plas Ingli, Skiff Abraham of Newport, Billy Ifans, Will Owen and Shemi Jenkins of Plas Ingli, George Lewis (Attorney) of Fishguard, William Probert (Attorney) of Newport, Judge Wynford Wynn-Evans of Llandeilo, and Jake Nicholas of Parrog. In total, that made ten men and one woman.

Once Palmer and Dashwood were in possession of this letter and the list of people on whom retribution should be visited, it became an obsession with them to carry out the last wishes of the dear departed brother. By this time there were only five members of the brotherhood left. I think you know all about me, and about Foley and Dashwood, but Palmer and McCleod were not gentry at all, but impostors and confidence tricksters like myself. Palmer was the son of a wealthy London merchant, and the apple of his father's eye. If we were in France, he would be called one of the nouveaux riches. He had more money than sense, and he was very close to the Prince of Wales. He was given a good commission in the army (by the Prince himself, so I believe) and distinguished himself as a soldier. Apparently he was brave to the point of foolhardiness, and I suppose he deserves admiration on that score. But from my conversations with him I think he developed a liking for killing French soldiers, and French civilians too, and turned into a man obsessed with blood lust. He was almost court-martialled for disobeying orders and for breaking the military code of behaviour, but he managed to buy some influence in the senior ranks of his regiment, and he was let off with a warning. Then he was hit by a sniper's bullet which entered his throat and smashed his jawbone, and that was the end of his war. The army surgeons did what they could for him, but he was left disfigured, and with no voice. He became very bitter as a result of his disability, and I think he directed this bitterness into the campaign of retribution against the people on Fenton's list. As for McCleod, he was just a brute. He was a member of a noble Scottish clan, and I never did find out how he ended up in London. Palmer had some sort of hold over him, but I never could get to the bottom of it. He seemed to have an abundance of money, and he had great contacts in the London underworld. I think he was involved in "protecting" people in exchange for cash. He also did a great deal of dirty business for Palmer, who was too smart to go around killing people himself, at least when he was in London. So McCleod, like me, pretended to be from a gentry family, and for the most part got away with it.

So much for the background, my dear Martha. I now come to the events that led to that terrible afternoon at Eastwood.

We began planning our campaign of retribution in the summer of 1807, as I recall. At first it was all very vague and disorganized, but over the course of twelve months or so, while the rest of us carried on with our dissipated life style in London, Palmer did more research into the demise of our late brothers by reading old newspapers, letters and court reports, and by talking to some confederates of two fellows called Thomas Elias and Julius Smyllie, who had somehow been caught up with Alban Watkins in the search for some mythical treasure on Plas Ingli land. As you will know, they were shipped off to the colonies for their pains, while Watkins was executed by somebody or other on the shore of the estuary in Newport. But the more that he read, and discovered from talking to his low contacts, the more he became obsessed with tales of your famous beauty and intelligence. He accepted the accusation, in Fenton's letter, that you were responsible for the deaths of four members of the brotherhood in rapid succession, and got it into his head that you knew too much, and that you were conducting a vendetta against the Mysteries of Ceridwen, with a view to wiping all traces of it from the face of the Earth. He conceived the notion that you were the latest incarnation of the Goddess Ceridwen, and that you had to be sacrificed. For months before he came with the others to Newport, he was obsessed with two ideas. First, that he must meet you face to face, and look you in the eye, and assess your beauty, so as to decide on whether you were worthy to be sacrificed; and then to subject you to a ritual humiliation which would leave you still alive but destroyed in mind, body and spirit. That was a better punishment, he thought, that slitting your throat or putting a pistol ball through your head.

Because we were all using laudanum heavily at the time, we failed to realize that these were the obsessions of a madman, and we all applauded our "oldest brother" and gaped in admiration at the brilliance of his planning. We did have our sensible moments when we should have realized that a plan that might result in eleven violent deaths in a short space of time might create some suspicion; but we were swept along by the conviction that we were infallible and invincible, and we convinced ourselves that we could make most, if not all, of the deaths look as if they were accidental. While all this was going on, our comfortable and hedonistic lives in London were beginning to unravel. I was caught cheating at cards, and the Duke of Cumberland quietly informed me that he would see to it that I would be dead before the end of the year. McCleod failed to pay one of his henchmen for services rendered, and ended up in hiding, pursued by five very angry Italians who were sworn to chop him up into little pieces. Dashwood lost his entire fortune of £6,000 in a day of gambling at Newmarket races. And Foley made the Duke of Gloucester very angry indeed by making his younger daughter pregnant and refusing to marry her. We decided that it might be prudent to get out of this country and make new lives for ourselves in America, and once that decision was made, caution was effectively thrown to the winds. Palmer conceived the idea that all of our victims (except you) should have little notes pinned to their chests, and that they should be carved with the three-striped symbol of the brotherhood. The notes should be written with the blood of the victims if possible. He also thought that little notes should be left in the vicinity of the houses to be set on fire -- the judge's house, the two houses belonging to the attorneys, and Plas Ingli. When we heard all of that, we were all lost in a laudanum haze, and we chortled with glee and slapped our knees, just as small boys might celebrate a wizard wheeze of knocking on an old lady's front door and running away.

Looking back, we had all lost touch with reality, and had no sense at all that our insane activities would cause mayhem, and untold suffering in your little community. I also think that we had lost all sense of what was right and what was wrong. We simply thought that whatever our dear departed brothers had done was somehow pure and noble, and that whatever might have been done by those who stood against them was, by definition, evil. We thought of ourselves as crusaders riding into battle so as to save the world from the forces of darkness...........

So the plans were laid. We all fled from London at the same time, and moved about, spending some of our time at West Wycombe, some at Great Canaston, and some in the mansions of assorted London cronies. Because I was the youngest of the group, I was given the task of scouting out the land, discovering the whereabouts of everybody on Fenton's list, and finding out what the daily and weekly movements of the intended victims might be. I set myself up in Wiston, just far enough from Newport to be well out of the way, and I made a free and easy arrangement with Master Skyrme which allowed me to work for him whenever it suited me. I visited Newport on a number of occasions and managed to ask a few questions on the pretence that I was an Irish ploughman looking for work on the autumn ploughing. I don't think that I aroused any suspicion at all. I also chatted to people in Fishguard and elsewhere, and discovered that there was to be a wedding at Treffgarne Hall on 11th October , and that among the guests expected to attend were Judge Wynford Wynn-Evans and his family from Llandeilo. I passed that information to my confederates, and they decided they would travel to Llandeilo, fire his mansion while he was away, and then continue westwards to Pembrokeshire. Then I heard from a farmer in the Black Lion inn that Mistress Martha and the children from the Plas were planning to visit Portfield Fair. This was the opening that I had been waiting for. I had made an agreement with my brothers that I should ingratiate myself with you, and seduce you if I could. I was rather good at that particular activity, and looked on it as a sport. I knew that you would come into town via Prendergast, and I simply stationed myself there early in the morning and watched the traps coming into town. At last your trap came rolling past, with you and the children giggling and laughing like mad things. It could only have been you, for I had never before seen anybody so beautiful. My heart missed several beats, but I composed myself and followed at a safe distance as you went to your brother's manse and then up to the Fair with a gaggle of small children in tow. The rest you know.

That kiss was my downfall. From the moment that our lips touched, my resolve as a brother of The Mysteries of Ceridwen started to weaken. During the weeks that followed, my mind was in turmoil, since I did sense that there might be some mutual attraction between us. For some of the time I thought that I must be loyal to the blood oath that I had made to look after my brothers; and for the rest of the time I dithered and wondered how I might get out of this mad enterprise and indeed prevent it. While I dithered, I wrote to Palmer at West Wycombe and suggested a delay or a change in our plans, but he would have none of it, and refused to put back the date of the arrival of "the four surveyors" in Newport. Without any further involvement from me, they rode to Llandeilo and set the judge's house on fire as planned. Then they arrived in Newport and embarked upon the task of extracting their revenge on Joseph Harries, the attorneys and the servants from the Plas. They recruited Gwynfor Rees as a spy, and McCleod met him a few times to receive reports, and to pay him for his information. They tried to kill Joseph, I think, but they decided to stop short of killing Will and Skiff, and to leave them terribly injured as a warning to others. I think they failed to appreciate at the outset what a little place Newport is, and just how much interest there might be in their activities. People started digging into their affairs, knocking on the door of the lodging house, and asking questions. At last they realized that fingers were being pointed at them as the likely perpetrators of various crimes, and as the community closed ranks, and as the net began to tighten, they decided that they had better get out of town. So they left in a considerable haste, leaving poor Gwynfor Rees to the tender mercies of the Ceffyl Pren.

Having got this far into their campaign, my four confederates appeared actually to be enjoying it, and they decided to see it through. Besides, they still had Mistress Morgan to deal with, and she was proving elusive. I was taken to task for not making more rapid progress by getting into your house and in getting you into my bed. When arrest warrants, Wanted notices and Reward notices began to appear, they retreated to West Wycombe, where they felt safe. They stayed there for most of the winter and waited for the hue and cry to die down, as indeed it did. Anyway, there was a lot of snow, and movement became impossible until the thaw came. Then, my dear Martha, you came to Wiston Mill to ask about me, and even engineered that little visit to Haverfordwest Market. It was clear to me that you were more than a little attracted to me, and that made my heart leap. Our encounter at the flour stall was a disaster, and I was in a foul mood, since I had just exchanged letters with Dashwood and Palmer in which I had tried to convince them to abandon their campaign and they had accused me of lack of resolve and even treachery. In any case, I was frightened of my emotions, and I tried to drive you away before those dark eyes of yours inflicted further damage. I think I was already in love with you.

Some time in December I decided to follow my heart and visit the Plas at Christmas. That was a triumph for you and your family and a disaster for the brotherhood, and you know what happened. I had never before come across such spontaneous and generous hospitality, such good cheer and such an atmosphere of caring and friendship. In short, I had forgotten that there could be such love within a house and a family, and in a community such as that which exists on the Plas Ingli estate. I knew that that was in no small measure down to you, Martha. Was it really possible that such a group of innocent and lovely people could be motivated by evil, and could actually be my enemies? Was it really possible that my colleagues and I were seeking to reduce your House of Angels to a pile of ashes and to destroy all of this warm beauty by picking off a group of good men one by one, and by sacrificing or humiliating the Mistress of Plas Ingli herself, whose love and compassion permeates everything? Suddenly the emptiness of my grotesque and hedonistic life came into sharp relief, and I realized just how far I had strayed from the values and the sensibility that my dear old father had tried to implant in me as a child. So, as you will recall, dear Martha, I wept for myself and for those insane men whom I had chosen to call my friends.

After that, I did what I could to subvert the activities of Palmer and the others, and to save you and your friends. It was not easy, for they now mistrusted me and did not tell me what they were up to. As you may or may not know, they came to Great Canaston at least two or three times in the spring, and made raids on Newport, with a view to harming Grandpa Isaac, Billy and Shemi. They tried to set the Plas on fire, and later on succeeded in burning down William Probert's house. They went after Jake Nicholas too. But they had not expected such tight defences, and they became aware that people were not only looking out for them but were actually seeking to track them down. It became a game of cat and mouse, in which I tried to intervene without fully knowing the tactics of the cat or the mouse. So my efforts were not very successful. I came to see you in February, as you may recall, in the hope of telling you everything, but then acted like a coward, in the hope that our tentative relationship might turn into something more substantial. For better or for worse, I decided that if I told you the truth about my past, and about my involvement in The Mysteries of Ceridwen, I would lose any respect that you might have had for me. So I placed my self-esteem and my hopes for the future above the immediate safety of you and your family. I thought that I might win your respect, and maybe your love, by doing something heroic and bringing Palmer and his cronies to justice single-handed. That was the worst decision I have ever made, and if I had not been so selfish the disaster at Eastwood would not, I think, have happened.

On the matter of Gwynfor Rees, I was horrified when I came to the Plas at Christmas and discovered that he was there with his family, and that you had given him employment. That meant that he had changed sides, and I was desperately concerned about his safety. I managed to have a word with him in the midst of the celebrations and warned him that he might have been safe after his suffering at the hands of the Ceffyl Pren, if he had then told McCleod that he wanted nothing more to do with him and his cronies. But to then go and work for the enemy! That would certainly be taken by Palmer and the others as treachery, and I warned Gwynfor that they might well come after him and ask for "inside information" about you and the Plas. He thanked me for my concern, and said he half expected trouble, but that he could look after himself. They did come after him, of course, and he had several confrontations with McCleod in the month of March. But he refused to betray his new Mistress, and McCleod said he would have to pay a heavy price for his treachery. And Holy Mother of God, what a price he did pay -- with him and his poor little family incinerated. When that happened, and I found out about it, I was so mortified that I actually felt sick, and I swore to myself that if I should ever get the chance, the four men who did that would also go up in smoke until there was nothing left of them. That was the point, I suppose, where my own vague ideas about bringing these men to justice turned into something much darker. In a rage the like of which I had never known before, I also swore that if I ever got the chance, I would kill those demons with my own hands.

You know something about my duel with Reynard Foley. I will tell you how that came about. I was trying to follow Palmer and the others in the hope that I might be able to ambush them, but their horses were better than the pony which I was able to borrow from Master Skyrme, and I have to say that Palmer, with his military training, was very clever at laying false trails and covering both his advances and his retreats. He had learnt his lessons from the fortnight spent in Newport in October of last year, and now he and the others left hardly any traces of their movements. I think Joseph Harries, who was also on their trail, was similarly frustrated. I knew they would come back to Great Canaston, which they did after they tried to set the Plas on fire. They were not best pleased by their lack of success, and they were in a black mood when I confronted them. My relations with them were not at that time too bad, for they were not aware of my efforts to track them. They still thought that I was a worthy brother, even if they also thought I was ineffectual and more of a hindrance than a help. I made one last attempt to convince them to abandon their mad campaign of vengeance, and told them it would lead all of us to our graves since there were now too many people involved in hunting us down. I also told them that the "enemies" who were on John Fenton's list were not such bad people after all, and that they had already suffered enough. Palmer was furious, and so was McCleod, and they accused me of betraying the brotherhood and going back on all my solemn oaths that had been sworn and sealed in blood. I said that in urging common sense I was betraying nobody and that I was still true to my oaths. But Palmer took that as a challenge to his leadership, and we ended up in a shouting match that would very soon, I thought, lead to violence. In that case, with four against one, I would certainly have had my throat cut.

I could only see one way of saving myself, so I shouted out: "My brothers, if you think me a coward and a traitor, let us test courage in an appropriate manner, with pistols at dawn. My courage has been questioned, and my family name dishonoured. In the memory of our blood brothers now departed, and in the name of the brotherhood itself, I demand recompense. I will face each one of you in turn, beneath the walls of Llawhaden Castle, as is the custom in these parts. Are you men enough to face me?" They could not very well refuse, since they were obsessed with this stupid thing called the Code of Honour. So it was arranged. I said I would shoot to kill each time, and they said the same. They drew lots for the privilege of facing me first, and Reynard Foley pulled the short straw. So after a couple of days spent in finding "neutral weapons" and seconds, we met as planned under the walls of Llawhaden Castle. Twelve paces, turn, fire!

I had duelled before, and I knew that I should wait a fraction of a second and let my opponent shoot first, while he was unbalanced. I assumed that he would miss, but Foley used the same tactic as me. He waited too, and we then fired simultaneously. I felt a searing pain in my shoulder and as I fell to the ground everything went black. I did not realize it at the time, but Foley was also hit, and had the ball from my pistol in his thigh. The seconds then intervened, and I gathered later that they assumed I would die from my wound. On the basis that honour was satisfied, Foley was carted off by his friends and I was carted back to Wiston Mill by my second, young Henry Barlow of Slebech Hall. Somehow or other I survived, and I have a vague memory of your visit and of the real concern which I read in your face. I will hold that as a very precious recollection for as long as I live, as a small sign that might have pointed the way to something better. Ah, if only..........

I knew that once Palmer and the others found out that I was still alive, they would come looking for me and would kill me without further ado. So I decided to disappear. I still hoped to do something heroic so as to impress you with my courage, but I was badly injured, and let it be known as widely as possible that I was returning immediately to Ireland to recuperate. So I wrote to you to inform you of that, assuming that others might also read my letter. I had an intuition that that would be the last contact ever between us. In fact I took to living rough, and it took me about a fortnight to recover my strength while I walked, mostly at night, towards Newport. On the 17th day of April I knocked on the door of Werndew, the cottage belonging to Joseph Harries. He treated my wound, which was still troubling me, and allowed me to stay there until I was better. I told him everything, and from that point on we worked together to try to bring the brotherhood to justice. I heard all about the raid on the orgy at Great Canaston, and indeed helped to plan it by telling Joseph all I knew about the layout of the house and the grounds. But I was mortified when I learnt that Palmer and his friends had somehow managed to escape from the net. I had a premonition that there was now going to be a final confrontation, but I did not know whether it might be at the Plas or somewhere else. In the hours when Joseph was out and about doing his sleuthing, I was alone in the cottage, and as my strength returned, so did my resolve that I would execute those four bastards with my own hands, if I should ever get the opportunity.

What I did not anticipate was the involvement of that idiot Charles

Hassall. On the morning of the nineteenth day of May -- a date that is imprinted on my memory for ever -- we got a message from the Plas to the effect that you had received an invitation from Hassall on the previous day and that you had already left with Bessie, Billy and Shemi to meet him at the appointed time. "Oh my God!" moaned Joseph. "It is a trap! She is like a beautiful moth, drawn towards the flame of a candle lantern!" Like mad things we got onto Joseph's pony and clattered off down to Newport, causing the poor pony to almost die from his exertions with two people on his back. We managed to find Skiff, Halfpint and Abby, grabbed four pistols with balls and powder, and borrowed five good horses. That all took time. Then we galloped all the way to Eastwood, hoping against hope that we would make up time on you and your companions in the trap. We were quite frantic, and feared that we would kill the horses.

As you, poor dear Martha, know to your cost, we were too late. As we five men galloped over the mountain and southwards towards Narberth and Eastwood, I had the image fixed in my head that we were five avenging angels, on a mission to save an innocent woman and to bring retribution down on the heads of those four madmen. I think that during the journey I almost became mad myself, and when we burst into the parlour with our pistols at the ready, and fired at those men who had just done the most appalling things to you, I think I was tipped over the edge. Red rage turned into black despair when I saw you on the floor, and then I was possessed of something I cannot explain to this day. I turned into a man devoid of emotion and incapable of compassion, with one objective -- the execution of those four bastards, involving as much suffering as it was possible to inflict. I do not think I had planned anything of what followed, but I knew what to do and what to say, with crystal clarity. I did what I had to do. I fed their testicles to the pigs, as was appropriate, in revenge for the despoiling and humiliation of Ceridwen, the goddess of motherhood and the fierce protector of her piglets. I executed them with the ceremonial knife, signifying the end of The Mysteries of Ceridwen. Then, finally, I sent them up in flames, as I had vowed to do in revenge for the burning of Gwynfor Rees and his family. Blood was spilt, and flesh was consumed, and justice was done.

There is not much more to tell. I knew that I could not face you ever again, having brought this terror down on your innocent head when I might have prevented it. I knew that you would be well looked after by Joseph and the others, and I knew that they were also smart enough to ensure that my fabricated version of events would go into the official records. So with the tickets for the passage to America in my pocket and with some of Palmer's possessions in my saddle bag, I slipped away and made my way to Milford. I gave three of the tickets away to other travellers, and used one myself. Luckily there were no careful checks at the port into credentials and identities. A fortnight later I landed in New York, determined to make a new life for myself.

By the time you read this, dearest Martha, I will be dead. I am in the condemned cell of the St Louis town jail, having been found guilty (two days since) of cheating at cards in the Moulin Rouge Saloon and of shooting to death one Billy Simms, who had the nerve to denounce me in the presence of twenty or thirty other gamblers. I did cheat, and I did kill Billy Simms. So when they string me up tomorrow morning at dawn, justice will be done. To tell you the truth, I am tired of life. I have myself committed untold crimes, only some of which you know about. My wild swings of mood make me a danger to myself, and to others. I have caused many, many people to suffer, and with the prison chaplain I have asked for forgiveness. And in my dissipated life I have wasted whatever talents God gave me in the pursuit of gratification and oblivion in the company of charlatans and madmen. My mind is filled with nightmares, and I have had enough of them.

So when I stand on the gallows in the morning, in the moments before the drop, I will not resist. I will think of the few moments of real beauty in my life. Spring flowers on the Burren. The Christmas at the Plas with you and your beloved family and friends. Our short walk upon the mountain which you love so much. Your eyes, on your visit after my duel. And the kiss at Portfield Fair. Especially the kiss at Portfield Fair.

Farewell, dearest Martha. I will love you always.
Your friend
Dominic

13. Morfran

4th November 1809

I suppose that letter must have taken Dominic the best part of two days to write. It took me several hours to read it, for the handwriting was not good, and there were parts which I had to read over and again as I recalled how I had reacted at the time to the events described. There were parts that I found so callous that I felt sick in the pit of my stomach, and other parts so tender that they could have been written by the most sensitive of gentlemen. And many other parts brought back memories so raw that I had to stop and compose myself before reading on. But everything was now explained. Or almost everything. There were still many questions in my mind, not least about Dominic himself. I still did not know his real name, and I never will, for I will make no further researches into his background. He is gone to his grave in some dusty hole in distant America, taking just a little piece of my heart with him.

Was he as mad as those other fellows who were his friends, and who became his implacable enemies, and who did unspeakable things to me in the name of "brotherhood" and "honour"? He certainly did not appear mad during our brief encounters, and while he was certainly capable of quite breathtaking brutality and ice-cold resolution, there was a side to him, which I will try to associate for ever with his name, that was charming and even child-like. Perhaps his over-indulgence in laudanum did something strange to his brain, and split his personality in two, making him into a sensitive gentleman one minute, and a brutal sadist the next? Or perhaps there is a sort of madness that resides in all men, even those who appear placid and stoical, that manifests itself in extreme violence when circumstances dictate. Perhaps men have violence built into them in a way that women do not, and perhaps there is a tension within their souls that increases inexorably as they become angry or frustrated -- or even when they are in love -- to the point where something snaps, and they lose control of their minds and their actions? I have seen the same thing in Moses Lloyd and John Fenton. Were they mad, all three, or were they normal men, tipped over the edge...........?

And I mulled over the strange business of The Mysteries of Ceridwen. What is it that drives men to make secret societies, and join silly little clubs which others are excluded from? Are they in essence so insecure and lacking in self-esteem that they have to seek the approval of their peers, and demonstrate their loyalty to each other in ways that are childish and even grotesque? Do men who are quite sane swear oaths of secrecy and loyalty, carve stripes on each others' chests, and mingle their blood so as to become blood brothers? The absurd notion of "honour" that drives men to feel "dishonoured" if somebody who has had too many glasses of wine makes the smallest of criticisms of them, and to throw down the gauntlet, and to end up firing pistols at dawn, is to me quite incomprehensible. And yet it appears to be so deeply embedded in the male psyche that even small boys cannot resist it. This much is obvious to me, as I recall the excitement which was generated in the breasts of four or five small boys, including little Dewi, when they invented their Secret Red Indian Tribe. Even the most gentle of men, like my husband David, seemed to derive great pleasure from his membership of the great club of a thousand tough fellows from far and wide who struggle for the honour of Newport in the annual *Cnapan* contest on Newport Sands, and he was as proud as a peacock when he achieved some great sporting feat which caused him to be carried from the field of play shoulder-high, and slapped on the back, and forced to accept endless flagons of ale from those who admired him. Even Grandpa Isaac has his little club of old cronies who meet regularly in the upstairs room of the Llwyngwair Arms to discuss the state of the world, sink a few pints, and make cunning little plots to reduce the status of those whom they do not respect. Harmless enough, one might think, but I will never forget that it was the obsession with the *Cnapan* game that led my dear husband to his death, leaving me a widow and my children without a father.

Should I feel guilt for the terrible train of events that led to the parlour of Eastwood House? As Dominic's letter reminded me, more than once, it was some sort of obsession with me, or my looks, or my status, that led Watkins, Howell, Fenton and the others to pursue me with such passion and violence that they lost their own lives in the process. And it was the same obsession with me, Martha Morgan of Plas Ingli, that led Palmer and the others to seek retribution by sacrificing me and defiling me. They too are dead and gone. And finally Dominic, who said that he loved me, was driven by that obsession to do unspeakable things to those whom he called his enemies. He too has gone to his grave. Somehow or other, I have survived. Am I somehow to blame for all of these deaths? Should I feel guilt because of the madness that resides in men's breasts? Bessie, and Grandma Jane, and even the men whom I love (like Grandpa, and Joseph, and Billy) insist that I must not, and argue that if there is free will, each one of us must take responsibility for our own actions, and make peace with God. And they are right. If I felt guilt once, it is gone.

If I had read this letter a year ago, I suppose that I would have been reduced to a quaking wreck, weeping for an hour or a day for the sins of the world or indeed out of my own misery. But so much has happened to me that I must have increased the strength of my own defences, for not a single tear ran down my cheeks yesterday when I read Dominic's long and rambling explanation of everything that happened. That gave me a sort of satisfaction, and did more than a little to increase my confidence that all would be well.

"My goodness, Mistress," said Bessie, "you are very thoughtful today. That letter from Dominic has had the effect of keeping you quiet for several hours, which must be some sort of record."

I had not noticed that my dear friend and handmaiden was sitting opposite me, on her bed, in our little room in the Skomar farmhouse, while the wind buffeted the window and rattled the heavy slates on the roof. She was reading a cheap novel with one eye, while keeping the other one on me in case I might become distressed. "Yes, Bessie," I replied. "I have not thought so much for a long time. Maybe that is just as well. Everything is explained........."

"And you have not shed a single tear, I think."

"Correct, Bessie. Nor will I. It is over and done with. A time of madness, that did no credit to anybody involved in it. Here, read it for yourself."

I passed the letter to Bessie, and she read it carefully while I went outside and let the wind blow away the last traces of my pain. I walked right around the island, and stopped often on the clifftops to watch the Atlantic rollers far below and to feel the salt spray on my lips as waves crashed onto the rocks and sent white spume swirling two hundred feet into the air. When I returned Bessie was in a sombre mood, and she said: "What a sad tale, Mistress, from a sad man who has gone to his maker. But who, out of all those in the middle of the action and on the fringes, was dishonoured and disgraced?"

I thought for a long time, and then said: "Not me, Bessie. Not me."

20th January 1810

Now I am eight months gone, and, as ever in my pregnancies, I am full of energy and looking forward to the birth of my little one. More than three months have passed since I last wrote anything in my book, and I put that down to the fact that in this place I seem to be much busier than I ever was at the Plas. Maybe I am being a little disingenuous there -- and I should admit that I do sleep a great deal just now, and that there is very little privacy in the farmhouse, so that it is not easy to settle down and concentrate on putting words onto paper. Just now there is a mighty gale blasting across the island, accompanied by drenching rain, and we have thanked God, and the builder of this place, that he chose shelter from the South-West as the building priority. Even in the lee of the little rocky knoll which we call Carnllys the house, which is solidly made of stone and which has walls three feet thick, is shuddering with every fresh assault from the assembled forces of nature. No matter. We are used to this sort of weather now. The fire is burning merrily in the big open fireplace. Bessie is reading her latest Gothic horror tale, although I tell her that it is all tame and timid nonsense compared with what she and I have gone through together. Morton is snoozing in his settle, and Janet is working on a pretty piece of embroidery. Soon they will have to go out and feed the animals and milk the cows, and I am grateful to be under strict instructions to stay put and keep warm.

This winter, which is by no means over yet, we have had considerable adventures on the island. In November a big three-masted naval vessel hit the rocks in Jack Sound. It was travelling from Liverpool to Milford in a hurry, and the captain (who is probably scrubbing decks now, instead of striding the bridge) decided that he would take a short cut through the sound with a following wind and a falling tide. Morton saw what was coming, and shouted to us three women: "Come and watch! A mad naval commander is trying to go through the sound!" So we hurried up to the highest point on the island, and got there just in time to see the captain lose control of the vessel in the beginnings of the tide race. Then we lost sight of the ship behind the bulk of Midland Isle. We watched for a long time to see if it would emerge at the southern end of the sound, but it did not, and we all knew that a tragedy had happened. Then we saw a rocket arching into the sky, and we knew that they needed help. Morton and Janet took the rowing boat and managed to get the little sail up, and off they went into the tide race. That was no danger to them, since Morton knows where all the fast streams and eddies are, and he always goes through the sound by moving gently from one area of placid water to another. They found the vessel intact, but stranded high and dry on one of the hidden rocks. It was not very long until low tide, and Morton knew that the vessel would not tip over. So as soon as he got within hailing distance he advised the captain to stay put rather than launching the boats, and since the vessel was not apparently holed, the shamefaced fellow took that advice. Then two fishing boats from Martin's Haven turned up as well, and the three little boats stood by until the tide turned and the ship was lifted off the rocks again. By then the wind had turned as well, and since the captain of the ship could not tack southwards in such a confined space, he had to let the current take him northwards (from whence he had come in the first place) back into St Bride's Bay. Then he had to limp round the western end of the island and head for Milford through the gap between Skomar and the neighbouring island of Skokholm. The captain probably arrived at his destination twelve hours later than he should have done, having provided us all with considerable entertainment. Happily, the ship did not appear too badly damaged, and no lives were lost.

On another day in November we saw about a dozen great sea monsters close inshore, going south. They were truly enormous, and they must have been a hundred feet long. Each one broke the surface occasionally, and then swam beneath the surface for a while before coming up again. As they swam they sent up spouts of steam and spray that went up maybe thirty feet into the air, far higher than the peaks of the waves. We were perched on Skomer Head as we watched them, and we could hear the noises that they made as they sent up their spouts of water. Morton told us that in the spring these whales follow the same route going north, with their babies in attendance, no doubt heading for their summer feeding grounds off the coast of Scotland or maybe even further towards the Arctic sea ice. Our knowledgeable farmer also said that one of the Marloes fishermen saw the whales going past once, and put his ear into the water to find out what noises they might make, and was amazed to be almost deafened by a veritable symphony of sounds made as the creatures communicated with each other. Shortly after Christmas another whale, this time very much smaller, beached itself on the stones of South Haven. Morton was not sure what to do, for it was thirty feet long and weighed many tons. It was very much alive when we found it, but it appeared to be weak or ill. It did not seem able, or have the will, to turn its nose back down towards the water, and no matter how much we cajoled and prodded, it seemed determined to die. The tides were falling off the peak of a spring tide at the time, so there was no chance of it being lifted clear of the pebbly beach by the sea. In the end, Morton shot it to put it out of its misery, and for a good part of January we were engaged in the bloody business of cutting out the entrails, the stomach and the internal organs, and taking many cartloads of whalemeat and blubber back to the farm. I must say that I am very partial to whalemeat, which is best fried in its own fat, but I can do without the blubber. Morton says it is very good for you, and that the Eskimoes eat virtually nothing else, but he doesn't even like it himself, and so most of it will be rendered down in a great iron pot left here years ago by some whalers or sealers, and turned into oil.

We have had several visits from passing seafarers, including fishermen, merchant vessels and a number of ships with no names which were involved either in piracy or smuggling. We had several convivial evenings, eating and drinking until the early hours, with fellows who were anchored up in either South Haven or North Haven while they waited for a change in the wind. Sometimes we invited them up to the farm, and sometimes they asked us on board, where we were treated to all manner of good things, including bread, pastries and puddings which were rare luxuries on the island. They brought us news of the wide world, and of the state of the war in Spain and Portugal. Some of our gentle hosts were battered seamen with grizzled chins and more eyes than teeth, and truly I would not like to have encountered them in the darkest corner of the Black Lion on a Saturday night. But they were respectful and generous to a fault, and when they saw that I was in the last stages of my pregnancy they offered me their arms, and asked after my health, and generally behaved as if they were proud expectant fathers themselves. Ah, I thought, what miracles are wrought in the souls of even the roughest seafarers by a small child, or even by the presence of an expectant mother. When they discovered that I was from Cardiff (at least, that was my story, and I could not deviate from it) the members of one crew wanted to talk about that port, and the quality of its brothels, and I was pleased to divert the conversation onto ships and shipbuilding instead.

Our closest brush with disaster came when a customs cutter came into North Haven. Bessie and I were on the point of rushing out to welcome it, when we heard Morton say: "Ah, that will be Griff Hickey and friends, come to check that the house is not filled with smuggled rum and wine. Put the kettle on, Janet, and we'll give them a cup of tea."

"Oh my God," said Bessie, "Griff Hickey! He knows both of us from assorted episodes in Newport! If he sets eyes on either of us, our whole story will collapse............"

"Right. Out of the house with the pair of you,"said Morton. "Go and hide behind the big rock in West Park. I'll tell him we have two ladies from Cardiff staying, and that they are out for a walk on the island. We'll give him and the other three fellows some tea and buns, and they'll go away again very happy."

We rushed off as instructed, and hid behind the rock, greatly concerned that Hickey might come looking for us. But we need not have worried. Morton and Janet kept them very happy, and they went on their way at last, satisfied that the island was not being used as a base by every smuggler west of Bristol. That taught us a lesson, and we realized that we must not let down our guard for a moment, no matter how safe we might feel in this far western outpost of civilization.

Christmas was a blissfully peaceful occasion on Skomar. On the day before, one of the fishermen from Marloes came out with a basket of good things including sweetmeats, pastries, dried fruits, pots of blackcurrant jam, smoked hams, currant cake, and cheeses that could only have come from the Plas. There were some letters and drawings from the children and even letters from Grandma and Grandpa and the servants. Those latter items were all in a big sealed and unmarked package. "This hamper is from a fellow called Billy," he announced when he delivered it. "He says he is Morton's cousin, and wanted to give him a little surprise." "Indeed he is," replied Morton. "My favourite cousin, he is, and generous to boot." We enjoyed a few glasses of wine with the fisherman, and then he set sail back to Martin's Haven before the short hours of winter daylight came to an end, leaving the others to sample some of the good things and me to settle into a reading of my mail.

On Christmas Eve, on the stroke of midnight, Morton and Janet led us in prayers and Bible readings from the Gospels, and we sang a couple of Christmas carols. Bessie and I taught our hosts two of the old carols used at the Plygain service in Newport Church every Christmas morning, and they were delighted to have these additions to their repertoire. For our Christmas dinner we enjoyed pickled herrings, roast goose with abundant vegetables, grey seal liver pate, plum pudding and as many of the good things from the Plas as we could cope with. We were bored with whalemeat, and left it off the menu. We enjoyed a few bottles of red wine that came from the cache that Morton keeps in a cave near The Wick. He showed it to us a month ago, and it would put many of the wine cellars of the finest Pembrokeshire mansions to shame, for he has red and white wines for every occasion, Madeira and port, rum and gin, and Scotch whisky so strong that I dare not touch it so close to my delivery time. What is more, the temperature in the cave is perfect for keeping bottles of everything, for in the salty darkness down close to the level of the sea it is never too warm or too cold.

Then we celebrated New Year in appropriate fashion, with a little party just for the four of us, and on *Hen Galan* Bessie and I introduced them to the delights of the traditions of Cwm Gwaun. They did not complain, for if one enjoys celebrating New Year one might as well enjoy it more than once.

When I was anticipating my stay on the island, and trying to imagine what it would be like, I feared that I would be desperately nostalgic, and that I might not be able to cope with my absence from the children and from the mad noise and bustle of the Plas. I was afraid that I might be reduced to tears. But to my surprise I coped perfectly well. I cannot deny that I longed for the children desperately, and worried that they might miss me so much as to be thoroughly miserable, but I was reassured by their letters, and the calm and uneventful Christmas in the farmhouse on Skomar was exactly what I needed. Even the weather was cooperative, and Christmas Day was completely without wind, with a cloudless sky. The four of us sat for an age on the high cliffs near the Garland Stone, watching the seals doing nothing in particular on the seaweed covered rocks far below.

Today I have been sitting on the rocks near High Cliff, out of the wind, chatting with Bessie. We have been greatly blessed by our time in this remote place, and we speculated on what might be the source of our contentment. The place itself, we agreed, was as close to paradise as it was possible to get, in spite of the gales, and the rain, and the mighty waves crashing incessantly onto the coast. Even when the island is swathed in sea mist or sprinkled with snow, the colours of the rocky cliffs and the little plants that live on them have to be seen to be believed. We wondered what it must be like in the summer, with the bluebells and red campions crowding in on the cultivated fields and with thrift and sea campion saturating the clifftops with colour washes. Then the birds would all be here as well, with puffins, razorbills and guillemots in their millions, and shearwaters in their burrows providing countless omelettes for the human residents of the island. Quite possibly, that would all be too much of an assault on the senses for simple souls such as us...........

Then we thought that Morton and Janet, the kindest and loveliest people on God's earth, must be responsible for the joyful optimism that pervades the place. They are childless, and have said to us many times that they long for a child or two, but nonetheless they have a capacity for accepting whatever life may bring, and for seeing something positive in every situation.

Bessie and I came to the conclusion that what makes this place so special is that life here is lived, quite literally, right on the limit of what human beings can cope with. We have no excesses here, and no luxuries. We wear the simplest of clothes, and we eat the simplest of food. You have to be a special sort of person to enjoy whalemeat steak and potatoes for fourteen days in succession. We know nothing about what is happening in the world. We look at the sky far more than we look at the land, for the clouds and the wind tell us what the next few hours and days will bring, and what we can and cannot do. We are utterly dependent upon each other, and we are all forced to accept each others foibles and bad habits without comment and with good grace. We accept and even admire Morton's and Janet's simple faith, and they accept without question that we have our doubts about some of the things they accept as God-given truth. We talk endlessly and read quietly for hours on end, without anybody speaking a word. We cooperate instinctively in the tasks that have to be done around the farm. And we accept danger as a fact of life. One day Morton was far out in St Bride's Bay fishing for herring when the wind changed and he was quite unable to tack back to Skomar. We watched with our hearts in our mouths through the powerful spyglass that is essential for island life, as he struggled to avoid the fierce rocks called the Bishops and Clerks at the far end of the bay before he managed to get into the lee of Ramsey Island, ten miles away. We hoped he might be safe, but Janet was distraught, and thought he might have gone onto the rocks after slipping out of sight. The brave fellow stayed there all night, and at dawn we trained the spyglass on the distant island again, and cheered when we spotted a small white sail emerge from Ramsey Sound and set course across the bay for Skomar. When he got home Janet was furious with him, as wives always are when their husbands have had close shaves, and the poor man was exhausted and starving. What is more, he had lost his nets and had not a single fish to show for his heroics. On another occasion Bessie slipped on the wet grass on a clifftop, and slid over the edge, only to have her fall stopped by a grassy ledge just a few feet below. She would have plunged two hundred feet onto the rocks below, had not fate intervened. We got her back to the farmhouse and packed her off to bed, but she was shaking uncontrollably with shock for several hours after the incident.

Dear Billy, we thought, the servant who purports to be just a simple fellow with no understanding of human nature! He was the one who thought that Skomar could be the place in which I could recover some of my self-esteem, breathe the salt air, and live a life stripped of everything except the bare essentials. He thought that this would be the place where my baby could be born quietly and calmly, with friends in attendance, and with love and beauty on all sides. Wise fellow indeed! And thinking of my baby, he is kicking a great deal at the moment. He is clearly getting impatient.

9th April 1810

Morfran, my littlest angel, was born on the 21st day of February, in the middle of a day on which the island was swathed in dense fog. My labour was long and hard, but Bessie and Janet were the most gentle and patient of midwives, and they knew exactly what to do, as did I. The birth was quite straightforward. When my little boy came into the world, he cried for a few minutes as he was being cleaned by the others, but when I took him in my arms he stopped crying, and he never cried again.

As soon as we saw him we knew that there was something wrong, and when we examined him properly we saw that he had a twisted back and a head that was too large. One arm was also deformed, and because he had no colour in his eyes we knew that he was blind. I wept as I held him, and Bessie and Janet had tears rolling down their cheeks as they stood by my side. Poor Morton, when he came in to join us, wept uncontrollably and had to leave the room for fear of making us even more upset.

I called him Morfran, for that was the name of Ceridwen's son in the ancient Welsh story in the writings of Taliesin. He had black hair when he was born, and they say that he looked like me, but that was probably a fantasy on their part, since newborn babies are red and wrinkled, and are renowned for ugliness rather than beauty. But I thought him beautiful, and as the days passed I thought that his beauty increased with every day. He looked old, and unutterably wise. When I gave him the breast he sucked with perfect contentment, and he responded to my love in a way that I will never, never forget, whatever else may happen in my life. He smiled at me, although he could not see me, and he made the little noises that all babies make when I nursed him and held him close. When, after a few days, I was strong enough to go for walks on the island, carrying him in my arms, he smiled when he felt the sun and the wind on his face. He was the calmest and easiest of all my babies, and caused me not a moment's irritation or exasperation. The little mite deserved -- and got -- every second of my undivided attention, and all the mother's love that welled up within me. While he lived, I thought of nothing and nobody but Morfran.

On the day after he was born, Morton rowed to the mainland in a panic and sent an urgent message to Joseph Harries. My dear friend travelled to Skomar immediately, and arrived on the island three days later with his big bag of medical instruments and potions. He rushed up to the farmhouse from the landing place, and after the most cursory of greetings he examined Morfran in great detail. I saw from his face as soon as he listened to the little one's heart that there was nothing to be done. He had some internal deformities, said Joseph, and his heart was very weak. What is more, he was so disabled that it would be a miracle if he could be saved, either through operating or the use of herbal remedies. He tried his own healing by laying his hands on the little one for two hours without a break, but that did not help either. He slumped into a chair, exhausted and dejected. Then he said: "Oh Martha, I am so sorry.........." and buried his head in his hands, and wept.

A week after he was born, Morfran died in my arms. Joseph was still on the island, and I suspect that he knew, from the moment he examined the little one, that his life would be mercifully short. We buried him in the shallow sandy soil near Skomar Head, at the far western end of the island, with a simple Christian ceremony devised by Morton and Janet. We marked the grave with a wooden cross made from driftwood, inscribed with the words: *Morfran. I will always love you.* The five of us embraced and stood there for a long time, without any tears. Then the others returned to the farmhouse, and left me there with my thoughts.

Morfran, the sacrificial lamb, I thought. Gentle, innocent, undefiled. He came into the world, suffered without complaint, and smiled, and went on his way, carrying with him my sins, and the sins of so many others. What reason had I for self-pity, when I was in the full bloom of womanhood and when I had a house full of angels waiting for my return?

I sat on the warm lichen-covered rocks on the highest point of the headland, gazing out to sea and watching the foam-crested waves rolling in from the Atlantic, inexorable and uncountable. My eyes drifted to the little island of Grassholm, one of the most special places in the old Welsh stories, inhabited by gods and heroes and reputed to be one of the entrances to the Otherworld. The island was also home to a thousand gannets. As I looked, twenty or thirty of these huge and beautiful birds swooped close inshore, closer to the cliffs than I had ever seen them before. They glided effortlessly on their great white wings among the sunlit sparkling waves, brushing the foam, hunting for their prey. Then, one after another, they wheeled high into the air, turned, folded their wings and went plummeting down into the water like arrows. Then up they came again, one after another, bobbing on the surface for a moment before lifting off for another glide, another ascent and another dive. I had never seen anything more beautiful. That is the way it has been, I thought, from the beginning of time. And so it will be until the end of time.

Then I turned, and said goodbye to Morfran, and took the first steps of the long journey home.

POSTSCRIPT

15th September 1812

Having given the matter a great deal of thought, I have decided that for the sake of my family I will take out the foregoing section of my diary relating to Dominic and The Mysteries of Ceridwen. I will put it to one side, and at some later date I will come to a view as to what I should do with it. I also vow to make no mention of Dominic or the four monsters who harmed me, or of Eastwood Mansion, or of little ~Morfran, anywhere else in my later diaries, whatever else might happen in my life.

Martha Morgan

For you, my beloved Morfran. I will always love you.

Acknowledgements

This book has been written in response to many requests from readers of the Angel Mountain Saga for another story about Mistress Martha Morgan and her family and friends. As may be imagined, given the subject matter, it was not an easy book to write, but as ever my wife Inger gave me unstinting and loving support at every stage of the writing and production processes, and offered detailed advice on some very difficult material. She has also acted as proof reader and editor, and it is a pleasure to thank her above all others for the book as it appears. Then I must thank my readers' panel of Ian Richardson, Helen Redfearn, Irene Payne, Charleen Agostini, and Robert Anthony for their diligence and timely advice, and for deciding on my behalf that the novel was worth printing! Irene has also given invaluable help with marketing and book-keeping while I have been preoccupied with writing. I thank my son Martin and his wife Alison for designing the fantastic book cover -- the fourth which they have now designed from their home on the other side of the world. The cover images are copyright JM Paget and Brian John. I am indebted to the Welsh Books Council, whose support in the fields of marketing and distribution is invaluable to many small publishers in Wales, and to Academi which tirelessly promotes Welsh literature in both the English and Welsh languages.

In my research for this book I have used books by Francis Jones, Daniel Poole, T Gwynn Jones, Richard Rose, Trefor M Owen, Catrin Stevens, John Vince, EH Stuart-Jones, and William Donaldson. I record my debt to them, and indeed to that wonderful thing called the internet, which, with the help of something called Google, allows instant access from almost anywhere to information about almost anything. Finally I thank the readers who have sent me letters and Emails and who have rung me up to express their appreciation of the other volumes of the Angel Mountain series. If it were not for their tears and their laughter, I might by now have given up writing and taken up stamp collecting.

The Angel Mountain Saga

On Angel Mountain, Greencroft Books 2001. ISBN 0905559800. A5 paperback, 328 pp, £6.99. (Corgi edition 2006)
House of Angels, Greencroft Books 2002. ISBN 0905559819. A5 paperback, 432 pp, £7.99. (Corgi edition 2006)
Dark Angel, Greencroft Books 2003. ISBN 0905559827. A5 paperback, 432 pp, £8.50. (Corgi edition 2007)
Rebecca and the Angels, Greencroft Books 2004. ISBN 0905559835. A5 paperback, 432 pp, £8.50.
Flying with Angels, Greencroft Books, 2005, ISBN 0905559843. A5 paperback, 400 pp, £7.99.
Guardian Angel, Greencroft Books, 2008, ISBN 0905559865. A5 paperback, 256 pp, £6.99.
See also:
Martha Morgan's Little World, Greencroft Books 2007. ISBN 0905559851. A5 hardback, 252 pp, £12.00. The companion to the novels of the saga.

From the published reviews of previous books in the Saga

This is a splendidly-imagined and well-told tale of good triumphing over evil. The local colour is brilliantly imagined and the incidental historical detail, unobtrusively woven into the fabric of the narrative, is fascinating. Here is an adventure story in which the narrative never flags. The delineation of the main characters, especially the headstrong and irresistible Mistress Martha, by turns spiritual and earthy, is vivid and true. **Western Telegraph**

Successive books have turned Martha into Pembrokeshire's best-loved fictional character. The books have also turned Carningli (the key location in the saga) into a place of pilgrimage, climbed by many readers who generally stay well clear of mountains. **Western Mail**

Unusual and beautifully written...there are shades of Thomas Hardy's Wessex. **Nottingham Evening Post**

The writing is vibrant and alive. The author lives in one of the most beautiful parts of Britain, and he has used that landscape and scenery to fuel his imagination. **Writer's Forum**

We are swept along in a gripping tale that often leaves you breathless. **Western Telegraph**

Beautifully written, this book takes you on a journey which you will never forget....... **One Wales Magazine**

It's got the lot -- love, nature, mystery, mysticism and charm -- a bit Wilkie Collins. The period detail is so authentic you forget it's recently written. **Welsh Living**

This novel has all the feisty and awe-inspiring ingredients to be found in John's preceding books relating to Martha........ The author, as always, has a magical feeling of place and his narrative is full of dynamism and perception. **Welsh Books Council**

The author's obvious appreciation of the Welsh countryside comes across to the reader in some excellent descriptive prose; indeed, like its heroine, this is a book of many parts. **Gwales.com**

One of the country's most successful series of historical fiction. The author's interest in local history has allowed him to use his knowledge to best effect in a fictional format. **Pembrokeshire Times**

A colourful tale full of tension and authentic period detail and with a large supporting cast of characters both imaginary and drawn from history. But the author's greatest creation is Martha Morgan herself, a flawed heroine who recognizes her own mistakes but is powerless to stop making them. **Western Telegraph**

There's a lot of colourful period detail woven into the story.... The author shows life as it was for the poor tenants as well as the rich landowners, with no attempt to romanticize the past...... It's a well-paced and well-plotted tale with a gripping finale and a strong sense of place. **Pembrokeshire Life**

The magic of Martha Morgan and the mystical mountain of Carningli continues to weave its spell. Here author Brian John's storytelling reaches a rich maturity. **Western Telegraph**

About the Author

Brian John was born in Carmarthen in 1940 and brought up in Pembrokeshire. He is married and has two grown up sons and two grandsons. He studied at Haverfordwest Grammar School and at Jesus College Oxford, where he read Geography and obtained his D Phil degree for a pioneering study of the Ice Age in Pembrokeshire. He then worked as a field scientist in Antarctica and spent eleven years as a Geography Lecturer in Durham University. He has travelled widely in the Arctic, Antarctic and Scandinavia. Since 1977 he has made his living as a writer and publisher. He is also actively involved in environmental and community organizations. He has published hundreds of articles and around 70 books, and among his publishers are Collins, Pan, Orbis, Aurum Press/HMSO, Longman, David and Charles, Corgi, Wiley and Edward Arnold. His published output includes university texts, walking guides, coffee table glossies, and books of popular science. Many of his titles have been published by Greencroft Books. In recent years he has completed a series of novels under the umbrella title of *The Angel Mountain Saga*, and these have gone through many printings under the Corgi and Greencroft Books imprints. Some of the titles have also been published as audiobooks and in large print editions. In 2008 he wrote and published a radical reassessment of the bluestones of Stonehenge, under the title *The Bluestone Enigma*.